WARLO

Also by Chris Ryan

CHRIS RYAN

WARLORD

CORONET

First published in Great Britain in 2017 by Coronet
An imprint of Hodder & Stoughton
An Hachette UK company

1

Copyright © Chris Ryan 2017

A CIP catalogue record for this title is available from the British Library

Hardback ISBN: 978 1 444 78342 1
Trade Paperback ISBN: 978 1 444 78340 7
Ebook ISBN: 978 1 444 78339 1

Typeset in Bembo Std by Hewer Text UK Ltd, Edinburgh
Printed and bound by Clays Ltd, St Ives plc

Hodder & Stoughton policy is to use papers that are natural, renewable
and recyclable products and made from wood grown in sustainable forests.
The logging and manufacturing processes are expected to conform
to the environmental regulations of the country of origin.

Hodder & Stoughton Ltd
Carmelite House
50 Victoria Embankment
London EC4Y 0DZ

www.hodder.co.uk

PROLOGUE

Sierra Madre Oriental. Mexico. 2011.
When Mikey saw the roadblock up ahead, he knew there was going to be trouble.

Mikey looked like your average stoner kid, fresh of out college. Shoulder-length hair. Wispy beard. Surf shorts and a Motorpsycho T-shirt. Sandals.

But appearances can be deceptive. Mikey had never smoked a joint or snorted a line. He'd drunk a single bottle of Coors Light on his sixteenth birthday and not touched the stuff since. After this road trip through Mexico, he'd be returning home to take up his place at Virginia Theological Seminary. The first step on his path to the priesthood.

Mikey's friends had told him to avoid this part of Mexico. His father too. It was cartel country. Lawless. Violent. Stick to Mexico City, they said. Guanajuato. Playa del Carmen. The safe places. Mikey listened carefully to their warnings, before deciding that he would trust in his faith. In the goodness of his fellow man.

He had, however, agreed not to travel these roads after dark. *Everyone* agreed that would be foolish. Even Mikey.

Now he was beginning to wish he'd listened to what they said about daytime travel too.

As the bus slowed down, Michael craned his neck to see through the bus windscreen. The roadblock came into clearer view. An articulated lorry, bodywork corroded and tyres burned out, lay across the road at right angles. Big white letters were graffitied across its side. Mikey could make out the word

1

muertos and a huge letter *Z*. And he could see armed men sitting atop the lorry. For a moment, he wondered if they were army personnel.

Then he looked around at his fellow travellers.

They were all male, and all Mexican – Mikey was the only American on the bus. They were clearly poor. Their jeans were torn and their T-shirts grimy and saturated with sweat. Work clothes. One of them, sitting two seats ahead of Mikey, was making the sign of the cross. Another, several seats behind, was muttering to himself and looking at the floor.

The bus came to a halt, but the engine continued to tick over. A passenger in the rear seat called something out in Spanish to the driver. Mikey, who could speak a little of the language, understood what he had said. 'Go back, *cabrón*! Don't stop! *Can't you see who it is?*'

Too late. Two gunmen were hammering on the entrance door with the butts of their rifles. Mikey felt his bowels go weak. The driver stumbled out of his seat and wrenched the door open. If he thought he would gain some goodwill by being compliant, he was wrong. As the two men barged their way in, one of them struck the butt of his rifle against the driver's jaw. He collapsed, bleeding from the mouth.

'Okay, *pendejos*!' one of the men barked in Spanish. 'Get out the bus.'

Nobody moved. Mikey assumed the others were, like him, paralysed by reluctance and terror.

The men gave it five seconds. Then, without another warning, one of them turned his back on the passengers and pulled the driver up from the dirty floor of the bus. He slammed him face forward against the windscreen. Mikey saw the driver's head pressed sideways against the glass, his hands palm outwards on either side. The gunman raised his weapon. The barrel was no more than a foot from the driver's head. He fired. The shocking, deafening report penetrated Mikey to the core. The driver collapsed. His brain matter, like jelly, left a thick goo on the blood-spattered windscreen. The glass had splintered at the point where the round penetrated his head and cracked into the glass. Mikey felt himself retch, and had to cover his hand with his mouth.

'Get out the bus!' the other gunman repeated.

This time there was no hesitation. The passengers snapped to their feet and pressed their way out of the bus. Mikey included. Sandwiched between the other passengers, he got a whiff of urine. Someone had wet themselves with fear and Mikey had to try hard to stop himself doing the same. He averted his eyes as he passed the butchered body of the driver and stumbled down the steps of the bus on to the hard-baked ground outside.

The midday sun was dazzling. The dry heat caught the back of his throat. A heat haze rose from the metal bulk of the graffitied lorry. Beyond it, he saw the mountains of the Sierra Madre, grey and rocky against the piercing blue sky. A few metres from where the bus was parked was a roadside shrine, one of many that Mikey had seen on his journey. This one was in the form of the Virgin Mary, gaudy and brightly coloured, a metre high and housed in a wooden casing with a pitched roof. From the corner of his eye he saw some of his fellow passengers making the sign of the cross. He hurriedly did the same to stop himself standing out. The gunmen lined them up against the side of the bus, shouting several at a time. Mikey couldn't work out what they were saying. His ears were still ringing from the noise of the gunshot. But through his half-closed eyes he could see one of the men was hanging back maybe ten metres.

He had the features of a man in early middle age: close-cropped black hair, a pencil-thin moustache and eyebrows that pointed up at the sides, as though he was constantly asking a question. While everyone else's lips were dried and cracked, his were moist. His eyes were black, and there was a deadness to them that chilled Mikey far more than even the sight of the driver had done. He wore jeans, leather boots and a white vest that showed impressive upper arm muscles. The arms themselves were covered with tattoos. He stepped toward the line of terrified passengers, his own rifle hanging loosely from a strap around his neck. It was obvious, from the way the other gunmen got out of his way, that he was the main guy.

The man stood two metres in front of the centre of the line. There was a moment's silence. Mikey was able to make out the tattoos more clearly. On one arm he saw a grotesque angel of death wearing a red military beret and pointing a gun. Beneath it, in an ornate Gothic font, the text: *Z1*.

The man spoke in quiet – almost whispered – Spanish.

'We're going to play a game,' he said.

He turned to the nearest gunman. 'Choose two of them,' he said.

'Yes, Z1,' the gunman replied. He stepped toward the line of passengers, grabbed the two nearest and dragged them so they were standing in front of the roadside shrine. One of them was an older man, perhaps in his sixties, with dark leathery skin and a lean, lined face. The other was much younger – twenty, perhaps, certainly no older than Mikey himself – but not in nearly such good shape as the older man. He had a noticeable double chin, and those parts of his upper arm that were visible below his T-shirt were flabby and without definition.

'The game is called, "Who will be the next hitman?"' the man called Z1 announced. He looked around on the ground and found two flinty stones, each about the size of a grapefruit. He gave one to the older man, one to the younger. 'The rules are very simple,' he said. 'You fight in pairs. The one who survives will join us. The one who doesn't . . . won't.'

He looked to the two passengers holding the stones and nodded.

At first, neither man moved. They stood, three metres apart, and stared at the stones in their hands.

'Fight, *pendejos*!' one of the gunmen shouted. Mikey recognised his voice as belonging to the man who had ordered them off the bus, but he couldn't take his eyes off the two reluctant gladiators. The younger man was trembling, licking his lips and glancing left and right, as if trying to decide whether to run. The older man was still staring at the stone in his hands. He was as still and craggy as the mountains in the distance.

4

'Come on, man,' he muttered. 'I have a family. Children.'

Z1 gave a harsh bark of laughter. 'Good!' he said. 'So if you don't put up a proper fight, we can hang them from the nearest bridge with their guts spilling out.'

The other gunmen laughed.

Mikey could see there were tears brimming in the older man's eyes now. He took a tentative step forward and held up the stone so it was level with his shoulder. The younger man stepped backwards. 'Don't do it, *señor*,' he breathed. 'We don't have to fight.'

'Of course we have to fight,' the older man said. 'Don't you understand who these people are?'

'But . . .'

'I'm sorry. My family . . .'

The older man raised the stone a little higher. With a speed that belied his age, he moved on the younger man and cracked the stone down hard on the side of his head. His victim sank to his knees, and there was an involuntary moan from the rest of the passengers. Z1 watched the proceedings with the same dead look in his eyes. The old man looked over his shoulder at him.

'To the death,' said Z1.

Mikey averted his eyes after the second blow to the younger man's head. But he couldn't close his ears. He heard each of the following three cracks of stone against skull, followed by a horrible silence that could only mean one thing.

Ten seconds passed. Mikey dared to look up again. He wished he hadn't. The younger man was sprawled on the ground. His head was a pulp. The ground was stained a dark brown. There were spatters of blood on the statue of the Virgin. The older man was looking in disbelief at the rock in his bloodied hands. Tears were now streaming down his grizzled face.

Z1 nodded at one of his men, who stepped over to the older man and ushered him at gunpoint toward the roadblock.

'Okay, *pendejos*,' Z1 said. 'Who's next?'

All of the passengers, Mikey included, bowed their heads. Z1 walked slowly along the line, looking each man up and down.

Bile hit the back of Mikey's throat. He prayed hard. He tried not to catch Z1's eye as he inspected each of the travellers. But he found it impossible. He felt giddy when he saw a small smile cross Z1's lips.

'What have we got here?' Z1 said. 'A *yanqui?*'

Mikey backed away, but there was only half a metre between him and the bus. Z1 gave an instruction to his men. One of them approached, holding the bloodied stone that the older man had used to kill his victim.

'Hold out your hand, *yanqui,*' he said.

Mikey swallowed hard. Then he shook his head. 'No,' he said, in hoarse, stuttering Spanish.

Z1's expression did not change. There was a silence.

'You want to go, *yanqui?*' he said.

Mikey drew a deep, steadying breath. He nodded.

'Then go,' Z1 said. He pointed back along the road down which the bus had travelled. 'Go back to *yanqui* country, where you belong.'

Mikey edged away from him. He glanced back toward the terrified passengers and their tormentors. From the corner of his vision he noticed that already there was a fly buzzing around the head of the dead man. Nobody spoke.

'Them too,' Mikey said. 'Let them get back on the bus. Let them leave.'

Z1 turned to the passengers. 'Does anybody else want to leave?' he said. His voice was very quiet, but there was no doubt that everybody heard it.

None of the passengers responded. They all looked at the ground. It was as if nobody had spoken.

'Only you, *yanqui,*' Z1 said. 'So you should go.'

Mikey swallowed again. His fervent, silent prayer was being answered. Maybe, if he was fast enough, he could find a member of the *Federales.* The Federal Police. He'd heard that members of the regular police force were routinely in the pockets of the cartels. The *Federales* were a breed apart: highly armed, highly trained and desperate to stamp out the cartels.

Maybe, if he could alert them, he could stop this awful thing from happening.

He turned his back on them. The road stretched northwards into the distance, the horizon shaky in the heat haze. He took several hesitant steps away from the others. There was a tingling sensation at the back of his neck. It urged him to start running.

He had run maybe fifteen metres when he heard the report of the gun. At the same time, a thump at the back of his right knee, as though someone had kicked him there. He fell hard to the ground.

Seconds later, the pain hit.

Mikey had never known agony like it. Sharp, jagged pain that pierced his whole leg. He looked toward his knee and was horrified to see blood trying to pool around him, and being sucked up by the dry ground. Everything started to spin. He was aware of movement from where the others were standing. Vaguely, he could make out one of the passengers moving toward him, with Z1 following a couple of metres behind.

Only when the passenger – a teenage boy – was standing above him did Mikey see that he was holding the bloodied stone. The statue of the Virgin wavered in the heat haze several metres beyond him.

Mikey tried to say the word 'please', but instead he vomited from pain and fear. The kid with the stone swore under his breath, clearly disgusted. But then he looked toward Z1, who was standing grimly at the scene, his hands loosely holding his weapon.

Mikey knew what was coming. He tried to scramble away, but it was useless: his leg was a heavy weight and the pain was shrieking through him. He tried to speak, to *beg* the guy not to do it.

But the kid had no choice.

He knelt down by Mikey's side and lifted the stone.

The first blow cracked against Mikey's cheekbone. Mikey inhaled sharply, breathing in a lungful of dry dust through his mouth just as a burst of blood and mucus exploded from his nose. The young man muttered a word of apology under his breath. In that pain-racked instant, Mikey thought he understood why he

7

was saying sorry. He had intended to hit Mikey further up the side of his face, at the level of his temple, because then it would be over more quickly.

Now he rested the stone carefully against Mikey's temple, before raising it about fifty centimetres and preparing to strike.

Over the young man's shoulder, Mikey saw Z1 looking down at him.

'*Adiós, yanqui,*' he said.

They were the last words Mikey ever heard. The young man slammed the stone down against his skull. Somewhere, among the sickening, spinning pain, he felt the bone splinter.

Then everything went dark. Mikey's troubles were over as quickly as they had begun.

Mikey's humiliation did not end with his death.

The man who called himself Z1 stood above the young man's corpse. He turned to one of his men. 'Bring the bag,' he said. Thirty seconds later, a heavy bag fell at his feet. His guy opened it up. It contained knives. Twenty, maybe more. Long blades, short blades, broad blades and narrow. Plastic handles and wooden. He selected one at random. It was an old kitchen knife. He held the blade in a hammer fist, then stabbed it hard into the young man's torso. There was a slight resistance from the gristle and bone, but he had stabbed hard and the blade sank into the body up to the hilt. Blood oozed from the wound, but only a little.

Z1 turned to his guy. 'Everyone does it,' he said.

His men organised their prisoners into a line. They forced each one at gunpoint to take a knife and stab it into the corpse. Most of them looked away as they did it. Some cried. But nobody dared to disobey. Within five minutes, all twenty knives were sticking out of Mikey's body at different angles.

The prisoners lined up against the wall again. One of Z1's men took photographs of the desecrated body. Z1 turned to the prisoners, raised his hands and shouted, '*El puerco espín!*'

The porcupine.

'Who else wants to join the porcupine?' he demanded.

Nobody replied. Everybody gazed at their shoes.

'*Muy bien!*' Z1 said. 'The ones who survive will bury the ones who die, here behind the roadside shrine. Let us continue with our little game, shall we?'

WEDNESDAY

ONE

For an SAS man, situational awareness is as instinctive as breathing. After seven years in the Regiment, it was second nature for Danny Black to absorb and process every last detail of his surroundings. He did it almost without thinking.

So as he stood at the base of a thirty-storey tower block, which was as grey and unwelcoming as the sky, he was aware of everything. The graffiti that was concentrated on the north-west side of the building, telling him that was where gang members would likely hang out at night. The net curtain that twitched on the second floor. The workmen, barely visible on the roof. The grime music that filled the air. Some of it was pumping from the windows of the lower floors. Some came from the direction of the car park that surrounded the tower block.

In his peripheral vision Danny was acutely conscious of the three stocky guys in their early twenties sitting on the bonnet of the BMW. The music – 50 Cent – came from their car. They were eyeing Danny, threats in their gaze. Fine. They could look at him all they wanted. He'd only need to deal with them if they made the mistake of forcing his hand.

A helicopter passed overhead. A single glance told Danny it was a Bell Longranger, almost definitely civilian. Nothing like the military heliplanes in which he'd been on manoeuvres over the capital weeks before – part of the SAS's show of force in the wake of certain terror threats. He dragged his attention back down to

13

earth. A white Transit van pulled out of its parking space 25 metres to Danny's left. Written on the side were the words *TJ Painting and Decorating – one call will sort it all.*

Danny recorded every feature of his environment automatically. Situational awareness. The most important part of his job. Because a Regiment man doesn't like surprises.

Not that he was here on military business. Today's job was personal.

He entered the ground floor of the tower block. It was several degrees colder here. The concrete walls and floor made his footsteps echo. He trod more quietly, tuning his ears into the potential sound of an echo that would indicate the presence of another person. There was none. The door to the lift was jammed half open, the lift itself stuck a couple of feet from the ground. A strip light flickered overhead. There was an inevitable scent of stale urine.

He headed to the staircase at the corner of the building and climbed to the fifth floor, stopping at each landing to check up and down the stairwell. No sign of anyone. Good.

On the fifth-floor landing he moved through the creaking swing doors to find two corridors heading off at right angles. An old plaque indicated that apartments 500–515 were situated to the right, 516–530 straight ahead. He went straight ahead. His tip-off had told him he needed apartment 525.

The noise in the corridor was a mixture of blaring TVs and more music. Danny blocked it out. As he passed apartment 519, the door opened. A thin girl, probably no more than 16, with prominent black rings under her eyes, looked out. She wore ripped trousers and nothing but a filthy bra on top. Danny felt conscious that he must appear different to most guys she saw – healthy-looking, chiselled, with his dark hair and black leather jacket. She slammed the door shut again almost immediately. Danny continued walking.

There was no noise from 525. Danny put his ear to the door to check. Complete silence. Slowly and quietly he tried the door handle. It was locked, but that didn't matter. The lock was cheap and old. He pulled out his wallet and removed the credit–card–sized lock-picking set he carried everywhere with him. He inserted the tiny tension wrench and applied slight pressure to it. Then he inserted the L rake and gently scraped the top of the lock. He had the first four pins manipulated in a couple of seconds. The fifth pin was trickier and took him ten seconds to locate. The lock clicked quietly open.

Danny nudged the bottom of the door with his foot. It swung ajar. A disgusting smell hit his nose. Musty. Rotten. The air inside this flat was fetid and humid. Although there were no lights on, and there was still no sound, he caught a whiff of human sweat that told him the place was occupied. He stepped inside.

There was a bathroom straight ahead of him. No seat on the toilet. A mildewed shower curtain hanging from a broken rail over the bath. To the right, a kitchen. To the left, a closed door.

He scoped out the kitchen first. It was humming with fruit flies attracted by the dirty plates piled in the sink. Somebody was sitting at a small, square table. Their head was resting, forehead down, on the table. Danny couldn't tell if it was a man or woman. Short, greasy hair. Dirty blue sweatshirt. Next to him or her was a burned-down tea-light candle, a teaspoon, some tin foil and a used hypodermic syringe. The usual paraphernalia of a smack addict.

Danny could tell this wasn't the person he was looking for. So he left the kitchen and headed back toward the closed door.

The door was stiff, because it was ill-fitting against the carpet. It opened on to a room that contained a single old sofa, and three people. Like the guy or girl in the kitchen, they were comatose. One – a young woman – was splayed on the sofa. She wore a purple jumper, and nothing on the lower half of her body. Her legs were a mess of bruises, split veins and needle marks. On the floor, leaning against the sofa at her feet, was a naked man, his skin dotted with tattoos and similar needle marks on his arms.

In the centre of the room, lying on the floor, fully clothed at least, was Danny's brother.

Danny hadn't seen Kyle for two years. He'd have been happy not to see him for another two. But their father had begged Danny to find out where the idiot was, or if he was even still alive. As a Regiment man, Danny had enough police contacts to track down a helpless junkie with a history of petty crime to feed his habit. Twenty-four hours after making his first enquiry he knew exactly what counts the police wanted to speak to him about, and where they would look for him if they had the time and resources for such low-level stuff.

So here he was.

The floor was strewn with needles, cigarette lighters and condoms. Danny stepped over them, bent down, grabbed the top of Kyle's arm with one hand and pulled him to his feet. At first he was just a dead weight. After a couple of seconds his eyes flickered open. He didn't seem to recognise Danny, and instinctively tried to swipe him away. Danny simply pushed him so he stumbled toward the open door. He glanced at the semi-naked couple on the sofa. They hadn't even stirred.

He pushed Kyle out into the corridor. Standing by the open door was a figure. Danny immediately recognised the dirty blue sweatshirt of the comatose person in the kitchen. Narrow nose, crazy eyes. He was holding the hypodermic syringe in his right hand like a weapon. Aggressively.

'Choo fuckin' doin'? . . .' he growled. He could barely get his words out straight.

It was hardly a fight. But if you're going to start a fight, you'd better finish it. Danny strode up to the wild-eyed junkie, knocked the syringe hand away with one arm and kneed him in the groin. When he bent over in agony, Danny raised his knee and cracked it against the underside of his chin. It knocked the junkie out cold. Danny had struck him harder than he intended, but finding his brother in this shit hole made him angry. The junkie got the sharp end of that anger.

He turned back, grabbed Kyle and yanked him out of the flat.

In the outside corridor, Danny pushed his brother roughly toward the staircase. Kyle stumbled several metres. When Danny caught up, he pushed him again. At the top of the stairs he forced his brother against the wall. 'Try to run away from me, Kyle, I'll break your arm. Got it?'

Kyle looked hungrily back toward the flat. Danny sensed he was weighing up his hunger for another hit with his fear of his brother – Kyle had seen what Danny could do to a man. He nodded and started to stagger down the stairs.

'Best decision you've made all year,' Danny muttered.

A minute later they were back outside the tower block. Nothing had changed. The music was still blaring. The BMW guys were still there. They were staring aggressively at Danny, who felt Kyle try to wriggle out of his grasp, like a dog straining for his owner. 'Guys!' Kyle shouted. '*Guys!*'

The men were staring aggressively at Danny, shoulders back, chin jutting out. One of them stepped forward. 'What you doing with our best customer?' he growled.

Danny sensed the fight was coming, which meant he had to attack first. It was hard-wired in him. He stopped a metre away from the guy who'd shouted out, let go of Kyle, grabbed the man's little finger and snapped it hard to the side. The guy's eyes widened in sudden pain and he doubled over. He pushed the guy back toward his mates with a sharp jab from the heel of his hand. '*You* scumbags ever sell another wrap of H to *this* scumbag,' he said, 'our next conversation won't be so polite.'

Silence. The guy with the broken finger was doubled over, gasping, but Danny could tell the others were judging whether to fight back. 'If anything I just said isn't clear, now's the time to tell me,' he said.

The threat hung in the air. Could go either way, Danny knew. They'd either attack or retreat. Either was fine with him.

One of the guys raised his palms in an 'I'm backing away' gesture. Danny nodded curtly, stepped backward a few paces, grabbed Kyle again, who was staring dumbly at the unfolding scene, and only turned his back on the trio when he was well out of their reach. As he strode away, still pulling Kyle, he used the side mirrors of some parked cars to watch the guys. They were getting into their BMW. They wouldn't be giving him any more trouble.

Danny's own vehicle – also a BMW, but older – was parked 50 metres beyond the tower block. He forced Kyle into the back seat, then took the wheel. Kyle tried to open the door, but it wouldn't work.

'Child lock, Kyle,' Danny said. 'For children.' He knocked the car into first and drove off.

'Where we going?' Kyle said. His voice was reedy and cracked.

Danny didn't answer. He manoeuvred the car off the estate and on to the main road alongside it. Five minutes after that, he was pulling up alongside Walthamstow police station. He climbed out of the car, its hazard lights flashing, and walked round to the passenger side, before dragging Kyle out on to the pavement and hoisting him up into the police station.

'Kyle Black,' Danny announced before the duty sergeant even had time to speak. 'He's wanted on three counts of aggravated burglary, one GBH. Frisk him and you'll probably find he's carrying something he shouldn't.'

Kyle muttered a curse, but one look from Danny silenced him. He was scared of Danny, and with good reason. More than once, Kyle had called on Danny to dig him out of a hole. But you don't call on an SAS man and expect the nonviolent approach. Kyle knew what his brother was. So he shrank against the wall as the duty sergeant approached him.

Danny didn't want to see any more. He turned his back on his brother and left the police station.

Back in his car he took several deep breaths to calm himself. Then he picked up his phone and dialled a number. A frail voice answered.

'Did you find him?'

'Yeah, I found him.'

'Where was he?'

'You don't want to know, Dad.'

'I don't need protecting, Danny.'

But that wasn't true. Elderly, lonely and wheelchair-bound, with nothing but his memories of his army days to keep him company, Danny's father *did* need protecting . . . from the reality of Kyle's tawdry existence.

'Where is he now?' the old man asked.

'Having a chat with the Old Bill.'

A pause.

'He'll be safe in custody?'

Danny didn't answer immediately. The truth was that Kyle might find himself serving a short stretch, where he'd find it easier to get hold of the junk that had messed up his life than he would do on the street.

'Yeah, Dad. They'll get him clean.'

The old man let the lie pass without comment.

'When can I see you?' he asked. 'What about that granddaughter of mine?'

Danny suppressed a wave of emotion. *He* couldn't even see his daughter, so there was no way his dad could. Perhaps ever.

'It'll be a while. I have to go away.'

'On a job?'

Danny didn't reply.

'Where are you going?'

'You know I can't tell you, Dad.'

Danny immediately heard the heat in his father's voice. 'Of course you can tell me, I'm your—'

'Dad,' Danny interrupted. 'You know the rules. It's for your benefit as well as mine.'

Another pause. Then:

'Stay safe, son.'

Danny allowed himself a wry smile. Stay safe? He'd settle for staying alive. Safe was too much to ask for.

'Sure Dad,' he said. 'Course I will.'

He hung up, checked his watch and then pulled out into the north London traffic. He had an appointment to keep, and he was late.

TWO

San Antonio, Texas. 120 miles from the Mexican Border.
1200 hours North American central time.
Jesús loved his wheels.

Like, *loved* them.

He'd driven the Range Rover Sport new out of the dealership in his home town of Nuevo Laredo a week ago and almost non-stop ever since. He drove it even when he had nowhere to go. He especially enjoyed crossing the US/Mexican border in it. The *yanqui* border guards gave him the usual trouble as he tried to enter the US. Normally he had to make do with waving his green card at them – Jesús's mother was American. Now he could rub their noses in the fact he was driving a vehicle that they could only dream of owning on their pathetic salaries. 'You want to get into another business, *cabrón*,' he told one of them just before he was waved through the border at the Rio Grande river crossing at Nuevo Laredo and on to American soil. The border guard knew what he meant, of course, but as the vehicle was clean and so was Jesús, there was nothing he could do about it.

He enjoyed driving the Range Rover through the dusty streets of the run-down border towns where he'd collected money from his employers' network of small-time dealers. It made him feel important. He enjoyed showing it off in front of the cartel workers, slightly higher up the food chain from the dealers, who gave him packages of heroin and meth to distribute back to the streets. It made them realise he wasn't to be messed with.

And now he was enjoying driving along this well-heeled, suburban street, music pumping from the car stereo, taking in the manicured lawns, large houses and cars of similar value parked up in the driveways. He felt like one of the beautiful people.

Jesús was *not* beautiful. A childhood of running drugs for the cartels had left its marks. A broken nose, a lip split more times than he could count and a scar on his right shoulder where a bullet had grazed him. The motherfucker who fired it was the first man Jesús had killed. He used a knife, and dumped his victim's dead body naked on the doorstep of his family, a *Z* etched on his abdomen with the knife tip. That was five years ago, when Jesús was fourteen.

He was proud of his scars, though, just like he was proud of the tattoo on his chest: a skeletal face with a beret and an Uzi. It marked him out as a member of the most feared cartel in Mexico.

It marked him out as a Zeta.

He arrived at a particularly fine house on the left-hand side of the road. Palm trees in the yard. Lawn so neat, with perfect stripes, it looked like a freakin' tennis court. Columns either side of the door. All that posh shit, like he'd seen on TV. If you looked to the side, you could just catch a glimpse of the swimming pool out back. A white Range Rover – the mirror image of the one Jesús was driving, and his inspiration for it – was sitting at the front. Jesús parked up behind it and killed the engine. The music died with it. He clicked open the glove compartment and pulled out a Glock 43 9mm semi-automatic and a brown envelope. He looked inside to make sure the three small ziplock plastic bags, each containing a little white powder, were still there. They were.

One hit per day. When the dope ran out in three days' time, he'd be back with more. For a price, of course.

Jesús wasn't an idiot. He knew not to skim a single dollar off the money he collected for the cartel. Money was the only thing they cared about. If so much as a nickel went missing, they'd be all over it. It was harder for them to keep a precise inventory of the merchandise itself. Jesús felt safe enough stealing a little.

Not that he took this shit himself. He'd seen too many people throw their lives down the can to follow that path. But he also knew that to a junkie, the guy who supplied the junk was God. They'd do anything for him.

Like, anything.

He tucked the Glock into the back of his jeans and let himself out of the car, locked it with the fob and trampled across the lawn to the front door, clutching the brown envelope. He knew he looked out of place with his tattoos and baseball shirt. He wasn't surprised to see the middle-aged woman on the opposite side of the road, standing just next to the white van parked opposite the house, giving him an unfriendly stare. This was a 'good' neighbourhood. Soccer moms with perfect kids and husbands whose boring jobs brought in a couple hundred k a year, plus benefits. Truth was, guys like Jesús didn't fit in, no matter what cars they drove.

Whatever. Jesús wasn't here to be adored.

He knocked on the door. It opened immediately, like it always did. A woman stood there. Talk about a MILF, Jesús thought. Great rack, pert little ass. Plenty of make-up, just the way he liked it. A bit thin round the cheeks, maybe. Hardly surprising, given her appetites.

She stepped aside to let him in, then closed the door quickly.

'Did you bring it?' she said.

Jesús held up the brown envelope. The woman made to snatch it, but Jesús pulled it away. He sauntered into the house, making a big show of admiring the gleaming marble floor, the sweeping staircase and the soft-focus photographs, massively enlarged, of her beautiful family on the wall.

Jesús pointed at the picture of her husband. 'Where is he?' His English was perfect, but he had a slight Mexican accent.

'Away on business,' she said. 'Vancouver.'

Jesús didn't know where Vancouver was, but gave a shrug to hide his ignorance.

'Couldn't I just get a hit now?' the woman said. 'I'll make it, you know, worth your while.'

'Bullshit,' Jesús said. 'You'll be out of it. Don't want my bitches sleeping on the job, you feel me?'

'I won't . . . I'll . . .'

Jesús clicked his fingers and made a 'get here' gesture. The woman walked toward him. She was clearly trying to make eye contact, but couldn't help glancing at the brown envelope in Jesús's fist.

When she was standing in front of him, he made a 'kneel down' gesture. She sank to the floor and, with trembling hands, started to undo his zipper.

'Slowly, bitch,' Jesús said. 'You make me think you're not that into me, there's plenty others want my little present.'

He closed his eyes and let her get to work.

'*Where is he?*'

'*Away on business. Vancouver.*'

'Vancouver my ass. Twenty bucks says he's nuts deep in his PA right now.' Rav Patel – that was the name he used in this time and place, and he was sticking to it – took a swig of his Starbucks iced coffee, then put his finger to his earpiece and carried on listening.

Rav wasn't the only guy inside the white van opposite the house with two Range Rovers in the drive. His longtime colleague, a Hispanic comms and surveillance specialist whose work name was Michael, had his eye to the covert camera that was right now watching the front of the house. Their boss, Ethan Kleinman, was sitting in the back of the van, face intent, one finger also on his earpiece.

To look at Ethan Kleinman, you'd never chalk him up as a CIA man. With his full beard, the colour of wet sand now turning grey, little round spectacles, corduroy jacket and small, watery eyes, he looked more like a minor-league university professor than an intelligence agent. He'd been with the Company for thirty-five years, and was surely approaching the time when he ought to be thinking about retirement, or at least a comfortable desk job to see out the rest of his working life. But Kleinman still operated in the field. Nobody knew why, and anybody who asked was patiently deflected to an alternative topic of conversation. Kleinman walked with a slight limp – a souvenir of fieldwork south of the border more than ten years ago, though exactly what was a mystery to everyone.

'*Couldn't I get a hit now? I'll make it, you know, worth your while?*'

Kleinman removed his earpiece. 'I don't think I need to hear any more,' he said quietly.

'You joking?' Rav said. 'Who needs YouPorn when you got this?' He sighed when Kleinman gave him a disapproving look. 'We're recording anyway,' he said. 'We can always read the transcripts.' Which was true. It had taken them just under twenty minutes that morning to fit microphones behind the light switches in each of the rooms, while the lady of the house was dropping the kids off at school. He took another slurp of coffee, then tapped one of his two daisy-chained computer monitors. 'Shouldn't she be baking cookies or some-thing? What happens when the kids get home and she's away with the fairies?'

'High-functioning heroin addict,' Kleinman said.

'Sure,' Rav said. 'High-functioning till she ODs before the school run and we find her sprawled over the dashboard of her SUV.'

'Welcome to America,' Kleinman said.

Something on the screen caught Rav's attention. 'Okay, passen-gers,' he said, 'we got a match.'

Rav's left-hand screen had four still images, taken minutes previously, of the young man climbing out of his Range Rover and heading across the front yard to the door. The surveillance team had lucked out when the young man had looked almost directly at their vehicle. It gave them a full-frontal shot to run through the NSA's facial recognition database. When Rav first came to work for the Company five years ago, a search like this would take 48 hours. Now it was a five-minute job.

His right-hand screen showed the full CIA file for the target. Rav read the salient details out loud. 'Jesús Sanchez, dual American and Mexican citizenship. No address on file. Affiliated with the Los Zetas cartel. Piece of work, huh?'

'Just read the file, Rav.'

'We got him implicated in twelve homicides.' Rav clicked a link. 'Oh *man* . . .' he breathed.

The link had taken him to a blog post by an anonymous journalist covering the atrocities of the Mexican cartels. Anonymous, because any journalist who put their name to an unfavourable article about their criminal activities could expect to be made an example of. The cartels didn't just own the police south of the border. They owned the newspapers as well.

The blog post detailed a drug-related killing that had occurred twelve months previously in the Mexican border town of Nuevo Laredo. Three members of a rival cartel were found, butchered, against the railings of a children's playground. The corpses were naked. The heads and genitals had been removed. The genitals were resting where the heads should be, and vice versa. The arms and legs were spreadeagled. A cardboard placard lay on the chest of the middle corpse. It was scrawled with the message, in Spanish: 'A present from the *sicarios* of Los Zetas.'

'*Sicarios*,' Kleinman said in an excellent Spanish accent. 'Hitmen. You know where that word comes from?'

Rav shook his head. He hated it when Kleinman went into teacher mode.

'Latin. It means murderer. I think I prefer that definition, no?'

Rav shrugged. Hitman. Murderer. What the hell difference did it make?

'Any doubt our boy was involved?' Kleinman asked.

Rav minimised the window and returned to the CIA file. 'No,' he said. 'It was him. We got witnesses, all of them too scared to go on the record. Usual story.' Rav turned back to Kleinman. 'We could bust him now,' he said. 'He's got the junk on him. Got to be worth two to three years. Stick him in San Quentin, hope the Aryan Brotherhood do us all a favour.'

Kleinman shook his head. 'No,' he said. 'The cartel will get him the best lawyers in town, make sure he's tried in Mexico. Even if the judge isn't crooked, those two years will be the most comfort-able he ever spends. The cartel will sort his family out financially. He'll be home and dry.'

'So why the hell do we bother tracking him?' Rav said.

Kleinman removed his glasses and started to clean them on the sleeve of his jacket. 'There are reasons,' he said.

'Care to share them?'

Kleinman didn't answer.

'I'd love to nail this son of a bitch,' Rav said.

'Not your job, Rav.'

'Then whose?'

Kleinman acted as if he hadn't heard. There was a moment of silence in the van. Then Michael spoke.

'The target's leaving,' he said.

Jesús was no longer carrying the brown envelope as he left the house and sauntered back to his vehicle. Inside the Range Rover he returned his handgun to the glove compartment, started the engine and knocked it into reverse. He felt good. His posh *yanqui* MILF had done her thing. His tyres screeched as he straightened up in the road.

He hit the brakes. The white van on the other side of the street was still there. It crossed Jesús's mind that it was out of place in this posh, leafy area.

Fuck it, he thought. Probably just workmen. And what did it matter anyway? No one could harm him. He was a member of Los Zetas. The most feared cartel in the world. He was respected by the bosses. He was untouchable.

He hit the gas and sped off down the street, his tyres screeching again and Shakira blaring from his open windows.

THREE

Emirates stadium, London.
1900 hours GMT.

Danny Black had his phone pressed to his ear. Crowds of football supporters swarmed round him outside the stadium. Night had fallen, and the Emirates Stadium was glowing like a beacon. For a moment, Danny was reminded of the way Camp Bastion glowed in the desert night out in Helmand. The similarities stopped there. Out in the Stan, the air was filled with the distant sound of mortars and the dry stench of cordite. Here, it was all klaxons and fried onions.

'You're late,' said a voice at the other end of the phone. 'It's serious drinking time you're wasting, buddy. I could've necked . . .'

Danny killed the phone and stopped behind a squat, broad-shouldered man. He tapped him on the shoulder. The man turned round. Spud Glover was Danny's best mate in the Regiment. The situations they'd shared, it was impossible not to be close. Right now, though, Spud – short, squat, balding and unmistakably similar in looks to Phil Collins – was looking at Danny as if he'd just shagged his girlfriend.

'Fuck's sake, mucker, you were supposed to be here half an hour ago. They'll have necked all the booze by now. Where've you been anyway?'

'Family reunion,' Danny said.

Spud sniffed. 'Right,' he said. 'Bad as that, huh?' He knew Danny's family life was a class A fuck-up. He turned and indicated two men who were standing just by him.

Danny nodded a greeting. 'Tyson,' he said. 'Spike.'

Jack 'Tyson' Fletcher took his nickname from his startling resemblance to the boxer Tyson Fury, down to the shaved head and crooked nose. He was taller even than Danny. He wore a black beanie over his shaved head – Danny couldn't remember a time when Tyson hadn't worn that beanie – and his slightly reluctant, over-firm handshake was more a challenge than a greeting. Tyson had served with the Regiment a few years longer than Danny, but weirdly they'd never found themselves on ops together. Danny detected a moment of friction. Their eye contact lasted just a little too long. Danny refused to break it. A couple of seconds later, Tyson released his hand and momentarily looked away, before grinning. 'Black,' he said. His voice was deep. Pure east London. 'I was beginning to think you'd got a better offer.'

'Not possible,' Danny said. He offered his hand to Spike, who took it much more eagerly. Spike was younger than the rest of them. He had just turned twenty-two, but barely looked older than sixteen – right down to the acne that still plagued his cheeks and the slightly wispy stubble on his face. Not that it mattered. Danny knew the guys in the training wing rated Spike very highly. Acne or no acne, he was a demolitions ninja, and the word was that he'd never been bested in hand-to-hand combat on the training ground. Despite being much slighter than Spud – more lean and agile-looking – there was something very similar about their faces. Which figured, because Spud and Spike were cousins. Maybe a couple of times removed, Danny couldn't remember.

'I was a bit worried,' Tyson said, 'that it might be past Snowflake's bedtime.'

'Call me that again . . .' Spike said.

Tyson shrugged. 'Chillax, kid. Come on, this way. East stand, hospitality. Hope you brought your drinking trousers, Black.'

He pushed through the crowd. Spike was flushing from the neck up, clearly embarrassed by the way Tyson had spoken to him. He followed without saying anything. Spud, walking shoulder to shoulder with Danny, looked a bit apologetic.

'Spike's a good lad,' Danny said. They'd spent the past week in briefings for the upcoming op, and Danny had grown to like the kid.

'Not going to lie, mucker,' Spud said. 'He nearly messed himself when he heard he was on the team, especially with the famous Danny Black. I had to tell him you're a bit of a disappointment in real life.'

'Friends like you . . .' Danny grinned at him.

'Spike's been on standby squadron for the last six months. Chomping at the bit to get out on a real op. Dumped his bird, just so's he can keep his mind on the job.'

'Really?'

'Between you and me, not such a big loss,' Spud said. 'Bit of a bobfok.' And when Danny gave him a confused look, he explained: 'Body of Barbie, face of Ken.'

Danny laughed. Spud was his best mate, and always good value. When Danny needed someone to put his head in a better place, Spud was first call. His fondness for his cousin was evident. Spud had told Danny all about Spike. Real name Simon Ramsay, but nobody remembered that. How, when he was a teenager, all he'd wanted was to follow his big cousin into the Regiment. How he'd spent three years visiting Hereford whenever he could. How he'd aced selection. Truth to tell, Danny would have preferred someone with a bit more experience on a job like the one they had coming up. But it was obvious Spud had a soft spot for the kid, and it wasn't as if Spike couldn't handle himself. He'd done his training, like the rest of them.

'What's the craic?' Danny asked, pointing at the football stadium. Even through the hubbub, he automatically picked out a plainclothes security guy standing by the gate they were approaching. The security guy turned his back to Danny and put one hand in his pocket. Danny immediately clocked an ASP retractable baton under his coat. Illegal, but that didn't stop some of the plainclothes guys carrying them, given that they couldn't carry firearms. 'When was the last time you gave a flying fuck about Arsenal versus . . . who are they playing?'

30

'Spurs, mate. Game of the season, apparently. Anyway, mate of Tyson's has a private box. Beats chucking empty pint glasses around the terraces with the plebs.'

'You reckon?' Danny said. He wasn't a private box kind of guy, and he wasn't here for the free booze. A pre-deployment social was an important part of prepping for an operation. A chance for members of the team to get to know each other away from the intense environment of HQ, but he'd have been just as happy doing it over a few pints in a Hereford pub.

At the gate, Tyson handed out some VIP passes and they gained entrance to the stadium. Tyson led them away from the crowds and up a concrete stairwell into the gods. It was clear he knew his way, he'd done this before. 'So who is this mate of yours, Tyson?' Spud asked. 'Got a few bob, has he?'

'Just a geezer I know,' Tyson said curtly. 'Friend of a friend, that kind of thing.'

Spud caught Danny's eye and mouthed the word: 'Touchy!' Danny grinned again.

They were walking along a wide corridor at the top of the stadium now. There were people milling around, though it was nothing like as busy as the lower levels. Tyson stopped outside a door where a good-looking blonde woman in her thirties stood with a clipboard. She wore a diamante collar around her neck, and the smell of her perfume was musky and expensive. 'Tyson party,' he said. The woman checked her list, ticked off a name then stood aside. 'Good evening, Mr Tyson,' she said. 'Welcome to the stadium.' Danny felt her eyes lingering on him as they filed into the private box.

There was quite a party buzzing inside. Danny estimated forty people, including them. A couple of smartly dressed waiters were carrying trays of champagne. Dolled-up women were making small talk to smart-suited middle-aged and elderly men. An overwhelming smell of aftershave. If anyone was interested in the Arsenal and Spurs teams lining up on the pitch, visible through the windows at the far side of the room, and on screens either end with the sound turned down, they didn't show it.

31

The four SAS men loitered slightly awkwardly by the entrance. Danny felt as out of place at a cocktail party as most of this lot would feel on the firing range. He was aware of people in the crowd glancing toward them: the men with a hint of bolshie arrogance, the women with a hint of something else. Danny hoped Tyson hadn't been shooting his mouth off about who they were and what they did for a living.

After thirty seconds, a very well-tanned man in his sixties approached from the centre of the throng. He wore a well-fitting black suit with an open-neck white shirt – Danny caught a glimpse of a gold chain around his neck. The smell of aftershave grew a bit stronger. Danny heard Spud hiss slightly under his breath, but the guy was in earshot before Danny could ask why.

'Thanks, darling,' medallion man said to the girl at the door. 'We'll look after ourselves now. Lock the door, there's a good girl.' He turned to Tyson. 'Tyson!' he roared. 'Long fucking time no see! These your boys?'

Tyson shook hands with the man. 'Danny Black, Spud Glover, Simon Ramsay, this is . . .'

'Aiden Bailey,' Spud interrupted. 'Yeah, I know.'

Danny frowned. He knew the name Aiden Bailey, of course. One of the London underworld's most notorious figures. Finger in every pie. Extortion rackets. Drug running. Arms deals. If there was a few illicit quid to be made, Aiden Bailey was making it. And if you asked any member of the CID who they'd most like to nick, Aiden Bailey's name was likely top of their list.

Bailey seemed oblivious to the note of distaste in Spud's voice. He made a little gun shape with two fingers and a thumb, then mimed taking a little pop at each of the Regiment guys in turn. The he laughed uproariously at what he clearly thought was their little in-joke. 'Come on in, fellas,' he said. 'Get yourself a drink. Don't suppose you get much of the decent stuff in darkest Hereford.'

One of the waiters approached with his tray of champagne.

'You got a beer, pal?' Spud asked. He sounded much more subdued than he had outside.

Danny turned to Tyson. 'This cunt knows who we are,' he said. A statement. Not a question.

'Relax, Black,' Tyson said. 'I've known Aiden for years. It's a party. We're all off duty. Including him.'

Yeah, Danny thought. Except a guy like Aiden Bailey was never off duty. He looked around the private room, scoping for CCTV. Four Regiment guys were hanging around with a crime boss like Aiden Bailey? Easy for people to come to the wrong conclusion. Danny felt uncomfortable being here.

The guys accepted bottles of ice-cold Stella from the waiter. Danny turned to the others. There was tension. Tyson was taking an exaggerated pull of his beer, clearly trying to appear to be at ease. Spike was peeling the corner of the label on his bottle with his right thumb, looking at the other guys like a kid trying to work out if his big brothers were about to fight. Danny was star- ing flintily at Tyson. It was bad form to be indiscreet about anyone else's membership of the Regiment. More than bad form – Danny knew better than most how dangerous it could be, both for him and his family, if the nature of his job became common know- ledge with the wrong people.

But he and Spud also knew better than most that bad blood between the members of an SF unit could be more dangerous than the enemy itself. Danny took a swig of his beer, just for show.

'So . . .' Spud said, clearly trying to break the tension. He was a good mate of Tyson's, as well as of Danny. 'When was the last time you were out there?' he said.

'Mexico?' Tyson asked.

Mexico. Where, a week from now, this SAS unit would be operating *way* under the radar.

'Three or four years ago,' Tyson said. 'Before that, maybe a decade. When I was helping train up their counter-terrorist boys, you know . . .'

Danny did know. Providing training to the special forces of friendly nations was part of the Regiment's bread and butter.

Danny had done similar work himself. Spud too. But the case of the Mexican special forces was slightly more complicated. In fact, so far as Danny could tell, *everything* about Mexico was slightly more complicated . . .

Over the past week, Danny and the team had been briefed thoroughly about the situation on the ground along the US/Mexican border. And the situation was messy. Violent. The drug cartels had practically taken over. Six different cartels carved up the whole of Mexico into different zones. Within each zone the cartels completely controlled the production, sale and movement of all illegal drugs. Heroin, cocaine, marijuana, crystal meth – ninety per cent of the street drugs consumed in the US were produced and smuggled over the border by the different Mexican cartels.

The cartels ran their business with a ruthlessness and a brutality that sickened even Danny. It wasn't enough for rival cartel members to kill each other. Examples had to be made of them. Their butchered corpses were routinely displayed out in the open. Their family members were targeted, tortured and killed with a breathtaking callousness. It astonished Danny that news of the Mexican drug turf wars wasn't more widely known. In the past ten years, there had been nearly 200,000 drug-related killings in Mexico. Double the death count in Iraq and Afghanistan combined.

Alongside the killings was the corruption. Police. Army. Public officials. Journalists. The cartels had such wealth they could buy anybody with any influence. And they had such a disregard for human life, they could kill anyone who refused to take their bribes.

No wonder that, back in the day, the Mexican government wanted help training up their special forces. In a country where the bad guys own the establishment, the good guys would have to fight them on their own terms.

Except that wasn't quite how it had turned out.

In the late 1990s, one of the major cartels – the Gulf cartel – spotted an opportunity. The Mexican government had spent a

34

load of money training up these special forces teams. The cartel could offer a much better wage to fight *for* rather than *against* them. So they encouraged these highly trained commando teams to break ranks and join the cartel. The Gulf cartel found itself with an enforcement wing that would be the envy of most small countries.

They called themselves Los Zetas.

The Zetas were the terror of Mexico. Like all special forces, these men were trained in extreme levels of violence. They had the stomach for more bloodshed than the ordinary man or woman, or the ordinary soldier. As the years passed, their violence was applied without mercy or restraint to rival cartel members and innocent members of the public alike.

With muscle like that, the Gulf cartel thrived.

But they failed to take something into account. Like all employees, these trained commandos had their sights set on higher things.

In 2010, the Zetas turned against their Gulf cartel employers, forming their own organisation. The Zetas soon became the largest cartel in Mexico. Their core business of drug trafficking was supplemented by protection rackets, kidnappings and extortion. Where other cartels preferred to use bribery as the first step to achieve their ends, the Zetas defaulted to immediate violence. Their rivals were beheaded, tortured, even hanged and quartered. Women were raped. Mass killings had become commonplace. The Zetas weren't just the most violent, feared and dangerous cartel in Mexico. They were one of the most vicious crime syndicates in the world.

'Put it this way,' the unit's ops officer had put it to them during their briefing. 'If B Squadron decided to jump the fence and set up a criminal gang in the UK, how hard would it be for the police or the army to shut you down? You're better trained than any of them. You're the best in the world at close-quarter combat and urban warfare techniques. As you recruited more people, you could instruct them in advanced military procedures. That's what's happened with the Zetas. The original members – those still alive

– are at the top of the tree, but there's a trickle-down effect to their subordinates. The Zetas are every government's worst nightmare: special forces gone bad.'

If the Zetas had kept their activities south of the Mexican border, all this would have been academic to Danny and his unit. But things had gone further than that. This brutal cartel now had such a firm grip on the eastern territories of Mexico that, rather than concentrate on maintaining their war of attrition with their rival cartels, they could now devote themselves entirely to business. To profits. That meant shifting more product over the border into the United States. They had done this with massive success. The quantities of heroin, marijuana, coke and meth heading north over the border had reached unprecedented levels.

Where drugs go, violence soon follows. The Zetas brought their cut-throat tactics over the border along with their product. Several DEA men had turned up with their heads separated from their bodies. A couple of cops had gone missing. People in Washington started to pay attention.

While the Zetas had kept their activities south of the border, it remained a Mexican problem. Now, however, the Yanks were taking an interest. Their war on drugs wasn't just failing. It was *obviously* failing. The Mexican government had formed a separate, highly militarised police force, the *Federales*. They were a good unit, and remained reasonably free of the corruption that plagued the regular Mexican police. But although they were well trained and well armed, and had a hunger to stamp out the plague of the cartels, they weren't up to the same level of expertise as special forces fighters.

So if the Americans were going to hit the Zetas, and hit them hard, they needed to look elsewhere.

Which was a problem.

The Yanks were constitutionally barred from using their own military on American soil. Any hard arrest would be thrown out of court on a technicality. Not to mention the diplomatic cluster-fuck that would ensue if it became known that American military personnel were assassinating Mexican citizens across the border, no matter what the justification.

No. American special forces were barred from doing a job like this. Delta units and Seal teams were out of play.

Which was where Danny and the boys came in.

Please lads, take a trip over the pond to kill some Zetas for us. We'd sure be grateful.

Special relationship? The average man in the street didn't know just how special it was.

Danny took another pull of his beer and looked around the room. Half the guys still had their eyes on the SAS unit. 'Look at these twats,' he muttered.

Spud grinned. 'Not exactly Zeta material, huh? Maybe we should take a few of these Ron and Reg wannabes out to Mexico with us. We could do with some cannon fodder.'

'Mexico?'

Danny turned quickly to find Aiden Bailey standing right behind him. He cursed silently, not knowing how much of their conversation the crime boss had heard. Their deployment was top secret and totally deniable. If they were caught on American or Mexican soil, neither the US nor the British would acknowledge their presence. Danny and the team knew that, and accepted the risk. It went with the job.

Before he could confirm or deny anything, Bailey had slapped one hand on his shoulder like they were old mates. 'So you must be Danny Black,' Bailey said. 'Tyson tells me you're the head honcho in this little outfit. Am I right or am I right?'

Danny didn't answer. He just looked meaningfully at where Bailey's hand was still on his shoulder.

Bailey didn't seem to take the hint. He carried on talking. 'Friend of Jack's,' he said, 'is a friend of mine. Anything I can do for you, son, you just say the word. And I mean, anything.'

'You can start by moving your hand.'

Aiden Bailey grinned. He let his hand fall but wasn't put off. 'Man in my position always needs a few good men, Danny. You ever need a bit of extra work, you just shout. Plenty of opportunity for a man of your talents, if you take my meaning. Proper pay and all.'

'A man of my talents,' Danny said darkly, 'isn't interested in the kind of work you've got to offer.' Aiden Bailey's reputation preceded him. Drug trafficking, extortion – Bailey's involvement in the seedy underbelly of the UK crime world was well known, as was the authorities' inability to make anything stick to him.

Bailey gave him a thin smile. 'Well,' he said. 'The offer stands.' He sniffed and addressed the others. 'Anything you need, lads, you just ask.' He looked over at a couple of attractive women in low-cut dresses who were standing nearby. 'Need,' he said, 'or want, you get my drift?'

He wandered back over into the crowd.

Danny turned to Tyson. 'I don't care who you spend your time with, Tyson,' he said. 'But don't ever mention my name to a scumbag like that again, okay?'

Tyson shrugged and took a pull on his beer. 'Whatever,' he said. 'Don't tell me it's the first dodgy job offer you've ever received. You're in the SAS, Black. You're not a bleeding Sunday School teacher.'

Tyson was right, of course. It was almost impossible to do this job without attracting the attention of the criminal fraternity. There were even guys inside the Regiment who he knew walked both sides of the law. He wondered if Tyson was one of them.

Tyson seemed to know what he was thinking. 'You've got it wrong,' he said. 'I already told you – Aiden and I go way back. I keep my nose out of his business, he keeps his nose out of mine.' He turned to Spud and Spike. 'I suggest we enjoy the party,' he said. 'Twenty quid says the Gunners take it two-nil. What do you say, Snowflake?'

Spike scowled as Tyson followed Bailey into the crowd. Thirty seconds later, Tyson was chatting to a woman whose little black dress revealed a whole lot more than it hid.

'Remind me why we need Tyson on the team again,' Danny muttered.

But he didn't need reminding. Tyson was a core component of the operation. Back in the day when the Zetas were bona fide members of the Mexican military, Tyson had been on the SAS training team that spent three months helping them hone their counter-terrorist skills. He'd lived and worked alongside them. He knew their ways and, in several instances, their faces. He'd taught them, if not everything they knew, then a good chunk of it. And he spoke fluent Spanish.

So yeah. They needed Tyson on the team.

Spike walked over to the window on the far side of the room and watched the match. He looked very slight from this distance. 'I know he's your cousin, mucker,' Danny said, 'but I can't cut him any slack if he doesn't pull his weight. You get that, right?'

'Just because Tyson's wound you up, don't take it out on Spike. He'll be fine.' Spud smiled. 'Regular little pyromaniac, that one. Blew up his dad's lawnmower with a nine-volt battery when he was thirteen. Put twenty years on the old fella. Better at close-quarter combat than you and me put together, and all.' He pulled on his beer. 'Heard from the missus?' he asked, obviously wanting to change the subject.

Danny looked away. The truth was, the last time Danny saw his girlfriend Clara and their baby girl Rose was when he and Spud forcibly extracted them from a house on the outskirts of Birmingham. They were abducted as leverage against Danny. Not for the first time, Clara had to witness the brutal realities of Danny's work as he and Spud dealt with their kidnappers the only way they knew how. Once the Regiment knew the full story, they cleared up the scene, hushed everything up. Clara, however, was still in counselling, and Danny's chance of seeing his daughter any time soon were smaller than Spurs' chances of a win tonight. Truth to tell, he was looking forward to starting the mission and getting in-country. It would take his mind off the grim reality of his life back home.

'Nothing,' he told Spud. He shrugged. 'Better that way.'

Before Spud could reply, one of the waitresses walked up to them with a dazzling smile. She carried a handheld wicker basket containing twenty or thirty small brown envelopes, a couple of inches square. 'Present from Mr Bailey, gentlemen,' she said.

Spud took one of the envelopes. Danny declined, but positioned himself so he was blocking the CCTV camera's line of sight of Spud. Spud opened his envelope up. It contained a small ziplock bag with a thimbleful of white powder. He licked his little finger, dabbed it into the powder, then smeared a little against his gums. 'Coke,' he said. 'Natch.'

Danny felt an irrational anger swell up inside him. After the time he'd spent with his brother that day, this was the last thing he wanted to see. Not to mention that it was far too easy for someone to see one of his unit with a wrap of marching powder and come to the wrong conclusion. 'Get Spike,' he said. 'I don't want him making the wrong decision.'

Spud nodded and headed straight over to grab his cousin. Danny scanned the room for Tyson. Their eyes met. Danny jerked his thumb toward the door to indicate they were getting out of there. Tyson shook his head and went back to chatting to the woman with half a dress.

Spud and Spike approached. 'I don't get it,' Spike said. 'Why are we . . .? This is pretty . . .' Spike had a habit, Danny noticed, of not finishing his sentences.

'Trust me,' Danny said.

'What about Tyson? How come *he* gets to . . .?'

'Tyson's a big boy,' Danny said. 'He can make his own mistakes.'

He turned toward the door where the girl with the diamante collar and the clipboard was still standing. 'We're leaving,' Danny told her.

She looked him up and down again. 'Shame,' she said. But she unlocked the door to let them out.

Danny looked over his shoulder as he left the room. He caught sight of Aiden Bailey watching them leave, an unknowable expression on his face.

Danny turned his back on him. He didn't need men like Aiden Bailey taking an interest in him. Life was complicated enough as it was.

THURSDAY

FOUR

Willesden, London.
1430 hours GMT.
He was an old man. His knees were gone. His spine was beginning to arch. His eyesight was cloudy and he couldn't hear well.

But none of these was the worst thing about being old.

The worst thing about being old was catching sight of yourself in the mirror. Seeing the lined face, the grey hair, the thin body.

So he turned his back on the mirror that hung above the old electric fire in the bungalow where he lived alone, wincing slightly at the knee pain that shot up his thigh and into his hip. The living room presented itself to him. It was shabby. A three-piece suite that had seen better days. An occasional table stained with coffee rings, yesterday's dirty dinner plate still sitting on it. An old TV in the corner. The curtains were shut, as they always were. He preferred not to have passers-by looking in. On the mantelpiece below the mirror was a photograph of his boy and his late wife in an old silver frame, but that was the only ornament in the room.

He walked over to the TV and switched it on. The volume was almost up full, because that was the only way he could hear it. It was *Countdown*. He turned his back on the TV and started walking toward the sofa.

He cocked his head. Had he heard somebody at the door? He wasn't sure, over the noise of the television. He squinted at his watch. Half past two. He wasn't expecting anyone today.

His first thought was that it was kids, playing him up. He even muttered the word. 'Kids.'

He headed across the room and out into the hallway. He peered through the frosted glass of the front door. He could see the outline of two people, one in front of the other. Too big for kids. Maybe a delivery. But he wasn't expecting one. And anyway, delivery men usually worked alone.

He had a security chain fastened across the door, as always. And the door was double locked. He stepped closer. 'Who's there?' he said.

'Read your meter, mate,' a muffled voice replied.

The old man cocked his head again. 'Someone read my meter last week,' he said.

'Probably gas, mate. This is electricity.'

The old man nodded and raised his hand to unlock the chain. Then he stopped. 'I don't have gas,' he said.

There was a pause. A little movement behind the glass. 'I can show you my ID, mate.'

The old man closed his eyes. *Had* they read his meter last week? It was so difficult to keep track, and he got so confused these days. Only yesterday, he looked in his kitchen cupboard for a tin of dog food, only to remember his dog died years ago.

Or was it months?

He fumbled with the Chubb lock halfway down the door, then unlocked the latch. This left only the security chain, which he kept in place. He opened the door the two inches that the chain allowed. The man he had been talking to was holding up a small laminated card, about the same size as a credit card. The old man couldn't quite read it. He stretched out his hand to take it, passing his fingers through the gap in the door.

It all happened so fast. The door slammed. The old man's fingers were caught between the door and the doorframe, and the impact was so violent that he felt his brittle bones crack. He gasped in pain, but as he did so the door burst open. The security chain was ripped from its fittings and the wooden frame of the door itself cracked hard against the old man's stooped head. He fell as the two men bundled into his house. By the time he hit the floor, they were inside and the door was closed again.

46

He tried to shout, but his voice was frail and the fall had winded him. His broken fingers were agonising. He waved his arms feebly, a pathetic attempt to stop the men bending down to grab him and pull him to his feet. 'Shut your pie hole, grandad,' one of them said as they yanked him up from the ground.

'You can't do this,' the old man gasped. 'My boy will be here any minute, he'll . . .'

The man swiped him hard across the jaw. His neck cricked with the impact. He tasted blood on his lip. He would have fallen again, if the men hadn't each been holding one of his arms. They dragged him roughly back into the main room. *Countdown* was still on.

The two men threw him on to the sofa. He hit his head again, this time on the wooden bar that formed part of the sofa's frame. Again he tried to talk, to tell them his wallet was on his bedside table, and his pension money in a tin by the kettle in the kitchen. All that came out was a frightened jumble of words. And he realised, even as he tried to speak, that these two men weren't here to rob him. One of them had a rucksack, which he removed from over his shoulder. He rummaged around inside it, and pulled out two black woollen balaclavas. They pulled them over their heads so that all the old man could see was their eyes and their mouths.

He fell silent. The two men looked down on him. Up until this moment, he hadn't had time to feel fear. Now, as the two masked men looked over him, he felt nothing else.

The man with the rucksack pulled something else out of his bag. The old man squinted to see what it was. A roll of black duct tape. The man walked round the back of the sofa. There was a sound of the duct tape being unrolled. From behind, the man slammed a strip of the thick adhesive tape over the old man's mouth, before wrapping it several times around his head and mouth again. From the corner of his eye, he saw a knife blade cut the tape from the roll. The man threw the roll to his companion, who was still standing in front of the sofa. The companion pulled out another strip of duct tape and used it to bind the old man's wrists in front of him.

'Kill the TV,' the rucksack guy said. His mate did just that. With the curtains shut, it was now very dark in the room. The rucksack guy turned the lights on. 'Jesus,' he said. 'What a fucking dump.' He walked round to the front of the sofa again. 'Alright,' he said. 'Let's do it.'

The rucksack guy kneeled on the sofa next to him and grabbed his thin hair with one hand. He put his knife up against the old man's throat.

The old man felt the blade against the loose skin of his neck.

The rucksack guy held the blade there for several seconds. The old man caught sight of the picture on the mantelpiece. His wife and son. The last thing he would see before he died.

He closed his eyes and waited for the rucksack guy to slice.

But he didn't.

The old man opened his eyes again. The blade was still pressed against his throat, but the other guy was holding a phone up. For a moment the old man didn't understand what he was doing. Then he understood.

He was videoing them.

Nobody spoke. The old man stared wildly at the phone. Then the guy lowered it.

'Done,' he said.

The rucksack guy removed the knife from his throat. Then he leaned in and spoke very clearly into the man's ear. 'This isn't over, granddad. Not nearly. Now why don't you be a good old geezer, sit there quietly and try not to piss yourself?' He turned to his companion. 'We need to move him somewhere else,' he said. 'Can't stay here. Some meals-on-wheels do-gooders might come round.' He stood up. 'Get on the blower. Ask if there's a safe house we can use.'

His mate nodded. 'Stick the kettle on while we wait,' he said.

FIVE

Nuevo Laredo, Mexico.
Night had fallen.

As a result, Ana Rodriguez had bolted all three deadlocks on her front door, double-checked every window, and switched on the floodlights that lit up every dark corner of her small front yard. She didn't own a dog, but had read somewhere that leaving a dog bowl out on the porch was a good way of preventing opportunistic crime. A small precaution, but in a town like this you needed all the help you could get.

The lights inside her tiny one-bedroomed house were dim. This served two purposes. Firstly, it meant she could see out more easily than other people could see in. Secondly, it meant her little boy Miguel had a better chance of sleeping. He was too frightened to sleep by himself in the small bedroom they shared off the main room of the house, so Ana had taken to making up a bed for him on the sofa, with a small stool for him to rest his comic book. She would carry him to the bedroom when it was time for her to go to sleep.

Ana had grown used to the fact that night was no longer a quiet, peaceful time in Nuevo Laredo. Distant gunshots regularly punctuated the air. The sound of tyres screeching in the nearby streets was so common she barely registered it any more. Maybe once or twice a night there would be the noise of a police siren, but that particular sound was becoming less frequent. Police corruption was endemic. It was increasingly worth their while to keep those sirens switched off.

Ana was exhausted. As a paediatric doctor at the local hospital, she hardly had a minute's rest from treating the children of the town and comforting their anxious parents. Mostly, the kids who passed through her care were suffering from the usual childhood ailments. Occasionally, they presented with an unexplained wound. Ana had learned not to ask any questions. Her first duty was to her patients and their health, not to the truth.

Away from the hospital, she maintained the same strategy. She was known throughout the area for her willingness to treat anyone, adult or child, from whatever side of the battles that raged across Nuevo Laredo and beyond. Law enforcement. Cartel members. Ordinary citizens caught in the crossfire. Ana Rodriguez provided medical care to everyone, no questions asked. She saw it as her duty.

She sat at her small kitchen table, eating beans with a wooden spoon straight from the saucepan. Her face glowed in the light from her clunky old laptop, which was tethered to her mobile phone to get an internet connection. She was reading a blog written by an anonymous journalist, entitled 'Narcoterror'.

The blog's mission statement was to detail every single atrocity carried out by the cartels. Such atrocities were seldom reported in the newspapers these days – partly because they were so common-place they were barely news, partly because the cartel had taken to targeting journalists who spoke out against their activities. Whoever was the writer of this blog, he or she was a brave man or woman. At some point, their identity *would* be revealed. When that happened, the cartel would surely make an example of them. For now, however, Narcoterror was the most popular news source in this part of Mexico.

It was also the most gruesome.

In Ana's line of work, there was no place for squeamishness. You didn't have to treat too many gun wounds, or pull the sheet over the face of too many corpses, to become hardened to the sight of them. But even she had to force herself to read some of these reports. Her eyes scanned over photographs of bodies with their heads and genitals removed. Of corpses swinging from bridges. Of naked torsos with obscene messages carved into the skin. The home page of Narcoterror always carried the same picture: a young man with twenty or thirty knives stuck into his torso. He was known as *El puerco espín* – the porcupine. He had been murdered as part of a gruesome mass killing by the Zetas. Nobody knew where he or his fellow victims were buried, but his picture had become emblematic of the horror of the cartels' violence.

Ana put the saucepan containing her frugal supper back on the table and pushed it away, just as a gunshot echoed somewhere in the distance. Her little boy stirred. Ana scraped back her chair and walked over to where he was lying. She stood for a moment, gazing down at his perfect little face. At his chest, rising and falling.

Then her phone rang.

She answered it quickly, not wanting the noise to disturb her son.

She knew immediately, from the chaotic sounds at the other end, that it was a call for help. The heavy breathing. The distraught noise of someone crying. A distinct moan of pain.

A panicked voice. Female. '*Help us!*'

'What's your name?' Ana said, suddenly brisk and efficient. No point asking how this woman had her number. There wasn't time for that.

'Rosa.'

'Tell me what happened, Rosa,' Ana said.

'We were driving into the city. They stopped us in the middle of the road, demanded our money. My husband tried to say no, so they shot him.'

Ana knew it was a lie. If things had been so simple, they'd have called the hospital. Or the *Federales*. It didn't matter to Ana. A patient was a patient.

'Where is the wound?'

'In his leg . . . they shot him in his leg . . .'

'I need you to tear away the clothes and look at the blood. Is it bright red or dark red?'

'I don't understand. Why does that . . .'

'*Rosa, what colour is the blood?*'

51

A pause.

'Bright red. I think it's bright red.'

Bad news. Bright red blood indicated that the bleeding was arterial rather than venous. She knew how the cartel worked. They didn't mess around. If they shot someone, it was to kill them, and they knew how to kill people. It sounded to her like they'd aimed for the artery at the top of the leg. Fatal if it wasn't treated immediately, but a slow and nasty way to go.

'You need to keep pressure on the wound. Hard pressure. Ignore the blood. Can you do that?'

'I . . . I think so . . .'

'And you need to tell me *exactly* where you are.'

'State highway 1. Maybe four kilometres from the centre of town.'

Ana cursed under her breath. Did people never *listen*? It was well known that these highways were one of the most dangerous places to be after dark. Tourists to the area had to be transported en masse and chaperoned by the police. And everyone knew not to drive at night. 'Keep the line open,' Ana said. 'I'll be there as quickly as I can.'

She grabbed her phone and car keys from the table. She hurried over to the wooden sideboard where she kept her cutlery and crockery. She removed the cutlery drawer and unfastened the handgun she had duct-taped to the back of it. She put it back, thought for a millisecond, and then took a small black and white photograph from under a pot on the sideboard. She put it in her back pocket. Then she ran over to where Miguel was lying. He was clutching his favourite toy – an old Buzz Lightyear whose left arm was missing. She knelt down by the side of the sofa and put one hand on his cheek. Miguel stirred. 'Mummy has to go out,' she whispered.

Miguel sat up immediately and tried to hug her while still clutching Buzz Lightyear. She unwrapped his arms from around her body and placed the handgun next to the comic book on the stool that doubled as a bedside table. 'Lock the doors,' she said. 'Don't open them for anybody except me. You understand?'

She knew he did. They went through the same routine every time she was called out at night. It didn't make it any easier, though. She kissed his forehead, then led him to the front door where she let herself out. She waited on the porch to hear the locks close inside and the small voice saying, 'Goodbye, Mama.' Then she hurried toward her cars.

Ana owned two vehicles. One was an old van, which sometimes acted as a makeshift ambulance, sometimes as a utility vehicle for fetching DIY materials for the house, or shifting her and Miguel's stuff. It smelled of disinfectant and paint. The second car was a dented old saloon with a smoking exhaust and a cracked wing mirror. She kept this vehicle for when she had to go out at night. The cartels were in the habit of stealing larger vehicles to move their personnel around. Why they needed to do that when they had so much money, Ana couldn't understand. But they did, so at night she drove a car that nobody could possibly want to steal. She kept a stash of medical equipment in the trunk, neatly packed in an old rucksack: clean bandages, packs of saline solution, swabs, tourniquets, steristrips, antibiotic shots . . .

She started up the engine, then put her phone on speaker and rested it on the dashboard. 'Rosa, are you still there?'

'The bleeding is very bad . . .'

'Keep the pressure on. Is he conscious?'

'Maybe . . . I think so . . .'

Ana cursed again. She knocked the car into gear and screeched out of her front yard. Her house was in a residential area in the southern suburbs of Nuevo Laredo. During the daytime, she could drive up to the top of the hill on which her house was situated and look across the US border, two kilometres away, into Texas. When crazy politicians talked of building 20-foot walls, this was the area they were talking about. Tonight, however, she headed south on the 85. It was the long way round, but it meant avoiding the centre of Nuevo Laredo, and the roads would be clear – for reasons Rosa had discovered. Of course, it meant Ana would be running the same risk as her patient, but that couldn't be helped. Response time was key.

As she expected, the highway heading south was empty. After three kilometres, she came to a crossroads where she turned to the northwest, heading up toward Highway 1. The parched low brush of the surrounding area zoomed past in a blur. Every minute or so, she shouted into the phone, 'Rosa, how are you doing?'

But Rosa's responses were increasingly muffled and confused. It was hard for Ana to tell what the status of her patient was. She instinctively put her foot on the gas, but she was already flooring it. The car was tipping ninety.

Which was why, when all four tyres suddenly blew, she lost complete control of the vehicle.

The car spun 720 degrees. Ana instinctively hit the brake and immediately sensed the hot stench of burning rubber. The car slid toward the side of the road, grating harshly against the tarmac. When it came to a halt, it was facing back the way she had come. Her headlamps illuminated the cause of the crash: a length of something resembling razor wire, stretched out across the width of the road. It was clearly meant to halt the next vehicle that came along. Which meant only one thing. Ana was being carjacked.

While the vehicle had been spinning, her body had been flooded with adrenaline. Now the fear kicked in – a tight knot in her stomach. She winced. Three sets of headlamps appeared at the side of the road, shining directly at her. She held out one palm to block the light, then fumbled with her other hand to find the cell phone that had fallen to the floor.

'Rosa!' she shouted. 'Can you hear me?'

'I think I'm losing him . . .'

'Is he breathing?' Silhouettes appeared in front of the head-lamps. Ana counted them. Seven.

'I . . . I think so . . .'

'Keep the pressure on the wound.' Ana was doing her best to sound calm. 'I'll be there very soon.'

The seven figures were standing five metres in front of the car, spread in a semi-circle, each of them a metre apart. Ana could make out their clothes and faces now. There was nothing unusual about the way they were dressed. They all wore jeans, and either black T-shirts or white T-shirts. They all wore chunky gold chains around their necks, and their arms were covered in tattoos. Three had goatee beards, the rest were unshaven. One of them – he stood in the centre of the semicircle – had a medallion. By the light of the headlamps, Ana saw it was embossed with an ornate letter *Z*.

Z for Zeta. Ana's mouth went dry.

They were all armed, of course. Assault rifles slung round their necks, or pistols with absurdly large handles shoved into the waist of their jeans.

The man with the medallion shouted, 'Out of the car, *pendejo!*' They clearly hadn't yet seen that the driver was a woman.

Ana glanced at the phone that was now resting in the passenger seat. Wishing now that she had not left her gun at home with Miguel, she drew a deep breath.

Then she opened the driver's door and stepped outside.

The reaction was immediate. One of the men wolf-whistled. Another couple of them chuckled. The guy with the Zeta medallion – Ana had him down as the leader of this little troop – took a few steps forward. He stopped a couple of metres in front of Ana, then slowly closed his eyes. He had fake eyes tattooed on his eyelids. They made Ana feel sick.

He opened his eyes again. '*Buenas noches, puta,*' he said. Good evening, whore. He looked over his shoulder at his companions. 'We've struck lucky,' he said.

Ana didn't reply. Shielded by the open door, she clenched her fists involuntarily into a hammer shape. Not that it would do much good against the handgun tucked in the man's jeans.

No. Ana couldn't fight these men. She would have to use other means of defence.

'Bad things can happen,' said the man, 'to whores who drive this road at night.'

He made an unpleasant clicking sound at the back of his throat.

'You're probably right,' Ana said, in as clear a voice as she could muster. 'But that's not going to happen tonight.'

The man grinned. 'No?'

'No.' She pointed to the three vehicles on the side of the road. 'Since you damaged my car, you're going to give me one of those cars, and you're going to let me go on my way.'

Laughter from the other men. The guy with the medallion stepped forward once more. Now all that separated them was the open car door. He leaned forward so his lips brushed Ana's earlobes. He stank of tobacco. 'No,' he whispered. 'I'm going to have you here on the roadside. Then I'm going to give you to my friends. If you're a good little girl, and you do what we want, maybe we won't kill you at the end of it.'

He closed his eyes again to reveal the eyelid tattoos.

'If you're a good little *boy* and let me have one of those cars, maybe – *maybe* – you'll still be alive when the sun comes up.'

The man opened his eyes again. He clearly didn't like being spoken to like this, but Ana could tell he was momentarily unsettled.

'And why would I do that, *puta*?'

She swallowed hard. 'Because my name is Ana Rodriguez,' she said. 'Perhaps you've heard of me.'

The man inclined his head. Narrowed his eyes, like he was trying to work out if she was telling the truth. 'I don't believe you,' he said.

'That's your problem,' Ana said.

They stared at each other.

'I'm going to take something out of my pocket,' Ana said, knowing how dangerous it would be to make an unexpected move. She slowly put her hand in her back pocket and pulled out the photograph. She held it up between trembling fingers.

The man stared at it. He said nothing. But Ana could tell the dynamic had suddenly changed.

He took a step back. But his companions were becoming impatient. One of them staggered forward. Ana could tell from his gait that he was high. 'Hey!' he shouted. 'What are we waiting for? Why is the *puta* still standing up?'

The man with the medallion turned. In a single, swift motion he removed the handgun from his waist and held it hard up against his companion's cheek.

'Do you want his head, Señora?' he asked.

'No,' Ana said weakly. 'I just . . .' She ducked into her car and grabbed her phone from the passenger seat. Then she hurried round to the trunk, opened it up and grabbed her medical ruck-sack. She looked toward the cars on the side of the road. 'Which one?' she asked.

The guy with the medallion moved his gun from his compan-ion's face – the companion staggered back, clearly shocked. He pointed to the vehicle on the left. 'Do you need an escort, Señora?'

Ana shook her head. 'If you have any friends on the road,' she said, 'call them now, tell them not to interfere with me.'

The man nodded. Ana hurried past the others. They were star-ing aggressively at her, but clearly knew better than to mess with their boss.

'Señora!' the man called when she was by the vehicle. 'Are you going to tell him?'

She tried to sound steely. 'Only if one of your people stops me again.' She climbed behind the wheel of the vehicle the guy with the medallion had indicated. The engine was still turning over. She slammed the door shut and hit the gas. 'Rosa!' she shouted as she screeched back on to the main road, scattering the Zeta gang and only giving her beaten-up old car the briefest glance in the rear-view mirror. 'Rosa, talk to me!'

'I can't wake him up!' came the terrified voice at the other end of the phone. 'There's so much blood . . . You have to hurry!'

The Zeta vehicle was faster and more powerful than Ana's old saloon. It could break a hundred without even grumbling. Ana's hands were clammy against the leather steering wheel. She kept her eyes on the road ahead, overtaking only two vehicles in the next five minutes. They both sounded their horns in protest at her exces-sive speed. When she came to the junction with Highway 1, she almost lost control of the vehicle as she hung a left, running the red lights. Two minutes later, she saw a vehicle parked a hundred metres further on by the side of the road, its hazard lights flashing. That had to be them. She waited until she was much closer, then slammed on the brakes and came to a sudden, noisy halt. She grabbed her medical rucksack and jumped out of the car.

Her patient was lying on the ground in front of his own vehicle, floodlit now on both sides by the headlamps of both his car and Ana's. He was on his back. Rosa – Ana assumed this was her – was startlingly young, maybe seventeen. She was obviously normally very pretty, with lustrous black hair and full lips. Tonight she was a horror show. Her face was smeared in blood. Her matted hair curtained a deathly pale face. Ana ran up to the patient and took in the situation with a single glance. He was the same age as Rosa, and had lost catastrophic quantities of blood. It had pooled, dark and sticky, all around him. He was unconscious. She took his pulse at the wrist. It was there, but only just. There was no sign of breathing.

She worked quickly. Everything in her medical pack had a place, so she managed to locate a tourniquet in seconds. She wrapped it round the top of her patient's leg, just above the wound, and pulled it as tight as she could in an attempt to stem the bleeding. She shuffled up so that she was kneeling by his chest – her jeans were sticky now with blood – and placed the heel of her left hand on his breastbone, resting her other hand on top. She started pumping the rib cage vigorously. It sank at least an inch with each pump. On the tenth compression, she felt a bone crack in the chest. That didn't matter. If she couldn't get him breathing again, the bones were insignificant.

After thirty compressions she gave two rescue breaths. But the skin on his face was extremely cold. She knew, from years of experience, that he wasn't going to make it.

Another thirty compressions. Another two rescue breaths.

She checked his pulse.

Nothing.

Ana bowed her head. Then she turned to Rosa. She looked as corpse-like as her boyfriend. 'I'm sorry,' she said. 'It's too late. He's gone.'

Rosa stared at her. She shook her head. Then she suddenly started beating her fists against Ana's shoulders. 'Make him live!' she cried. '*Make . . . him . . . live!*'

But Ana couldn't.

She let the girl's fury run its course. Then she wrapped her arms around her weeping, shivering body. 'We can't stay here,' she whispered. 'We have to leave him where he is. Come with me. I'll take you somewhere safe.'

And then, Ana thought to herself, she would hurry back home, where her little boy was waiting for her.

FRIDAY

SIX

Hereford.
1100 hours GMT.
The vehicle that was to transport Danny and his unit to RAF Northolt bore no indication that it was carrying a special forces team. The black Land Rover Discovery could just as easily have been a young mum on the school run. There was enough room for Danny, Spud, Tyson and Spike. Their driver up front, their gear in the back. Each man had a shoulder bag containing three sets of civvies. Nothing more. Their hardware was to be supplied in-country. They carried no ID, nor anything that would identify them in any way.

Under the radar.

Journey time from Hereford HQ to Northolt, two hours thirty minutes. It passed quickly. Danny hadn't forgotten Tyson's lack of operational security two nights previously but the team had moved on, having spent the remaining 48 hours in the briefing rooms of RAF Credenhill. Here, they received general, non-specific intel about cartel activity on the Mexico–Texas border where they were headed. They studied the mapping very carefully. They knew they were heading toward semi-arid terrain. That the border between the two countries was demarcated by the Rio Grande, a 2,000-mile-long river that flowed from Colorado out into the Gulf of Mexico. That the main official border crossing between the US and Mexico crossed the Rio Grande at the Mexican town of Nuevo Laredo – the epicentre of the Zetas' drug trafficking activities. They would, however, receive more detailed operational instructions once they landed on US soil. If everything went according to plan, that would be approximately 1700 United States Central Time.

Once they were inside the confines of Northolt, however, anyone with any military know-how would have realised that the Discovery did not contain regular personnel. The RAF base, used principally for executive flights for the royal family, government ministers and military commanders, was typically sleepy. They shouldered their bags and made their way into the terminal itself. Danny, who'd lost count of how many times he was deployed from Northolt, automatically led the way to a small reception desk at the north end of the terminal. 'Johnson package,' he said, giving the false name supplied by the ops officer back at HQ. The slight security guard behind the desk nodded perfunctorily, picked up his desk phone and made a quick call. Thirty seconds later the door behind the desk opened and another guy – mid-fifties, weather-beaten face that told of an army career spent in hot temperatures – appeared. There were no introductions. 'This way, gentlemen,' he said.

He led them down a bare corridor, into a sparse holding room that overlooked the airfield. There was no small talk. A soldier with that many years experience clearly knew not to ask a Regiment unit anything about their activities, or even their names. 'Your flight isn't here yet, guys,' he said. 'We're expecting wheels down in about five minutes, then probably a 45-minute turnaround. Make yourself comfortable, if you can.' He looked wryly at the hard plastic seats along one wall. 'Coffee over there.' He left the room, closing the door carefully behind them.

'Word of advice from an old lag,' Tyson said to Spike, who'd walked straight up to the coffee machine. 'Never touch the coffee at a British air base. Get you into Me-*hee*-co, *then* we'll find you some decent coffee.'

'Wonder what aircraft we'll be on,' Spud said, ignoring Tyson's comment rather pointedly and fetching a coffee for both him and his cousin.

Danny looked across the airfield. He could see a collection of private jets on the far side, and an Agusta Westland with its rotors powering down. He could also just make out, emerging from the grey clouds and slightly obscured through the haze, an aircraft coming in to land. 'That one,' he said.

Spud joined him at the window. 'Only the best when you're working for the Yanks, right?'

Spud was right. As the aircraft neared the runway, Danny identified it as a Gulfstream IV C-20 series. He could tell from the turbulent listing of the wings that there were high winds in the area, but the Gulfstream made an exemplary landing. SF flight, SF flight team. Two minutes after hitting the tarmac, it taxied off the runway and came to a halt no more than seventy-five metres from their waiting room. There were no military markings on the aircraft, just a registration number on the side of one of the jet engines. Danny would bet anything the plane was registered to an impossible-to-locate offshore company. A refuelling vehicle immediately sped toward it, but Danny's attention was on the personnel alighting from the aircraft.

It was immediately clear to him that the four tall, broad-shouldered men were also special forces personnel. They were wearing khaki trousers or jeans, with T-shirts that highlighted their impressive physiques. Three of them had white skin, but tanned. The guy at the front was black. Each carried a duffel bag, not unlike the bags Danny and his team had packed. They had short-cropped hair and moved with a slow swagger that wasn't exactly arrogant, but certainly oozed confidence.

'Seal team?' Spud suggested.

'Or Delta,' said Danny.

'Got it in one, Danny Black,' Tyson said. He had joined them at the window. Spike was loitering just behind him. 'Snake eaters.'

Spike looked confused.

'It's what they call Delta over the pond. I recognise the black geezer at the front. Good man. Got to know him in Iraq when I was out there under McChrystal. Crossed paths in the Stan, too.'

'What's a Delta Force team doing coming into Northolt?' Spike said.

Danny turned away from the window. 'Tit for tat would be my guess,' he said.

'What do you ...?' Spike said.

It was Spud who answered, but not before double checking the door was still closed. 'Big fucking favour the Firm's doing the CIA, sending a bunch of bruisers like us out to do their dirty work on the cartels. Bet they've asked for something in return – like a Delta unit to get their hands dirty on UK soil where the headshed doesn't want British soldiers involved.'

'Like what?' Spike asked.

Spud turned to Danny and Tyson. 'Always like this as a kid,' he said with a grin. 'Answer one question, ten more follow. His old man thought it meant he was clever, deluded old bastard. Spike, old buddy, if you don't like the spooks keeping secrets from you, you're in the wrong game.'

He ruffled his cousin's hair.

Spike flushed slightly. Danny felt a moment of sympathy for the kid. 'You've got my permission to kick him in the bollocks next time he does that,' he told Spike.

Spud squatted slightly, as if inviting Spike to do just that. 'Balls of steel, mucker,' he said with a grin. 'Balls of steel.'

The door opened. A guy entered. He wore a nondescript Nomex flight suit with empty Velcro patches on the arms and chest from which his badges had been removed. 'Flight Lieutenant Gray,' he introduced himself in a Midwest American accent, before shaking hands briefly with each member of the team. 'We've got an air traffic control window for wheels up at 1400 hours. That gives us 35 minutes to do the turnaround, but if you're ready, let's board now.'

The team turned instinctively to Danny, who simply nodded. They followed the flight lieutenant out of the room, then turned left down a deserted staircase that led to the tarmac. An MoD police officer was standing security at the bottom of the steps. He stood aside to let them through. Danny's team came face to face with the Delta unit.

Tyson hustled himself to the front of the team and offered his hand to the black guy. The Yank grinned. 'Tyson,' he said in a slow drawl. 'Long fucking way from Mosul, huh?'

'Almost didn't recognise you without the face fungus, Tam.' Tam gave him a confused look. Tyson stroked his chin to indicate he was talking about beards – an essential accessory for any SF personnel operating in the Middle East. Now, however, both units were clean shaven. 'How's it going, anyway?'

'Ah, you know, full of busy.' He looked meaningfully around the grey, utilitarian airforce base. 'Not going to lie, we'd prefer to be other places.'

'What brings you into the UK?' Tyson asked.

Asking the question was like flicking a switch. The expressions on Tam's unit mates' faces became immediately frosty. With good reason. Such questions were off-limits, especially with US units, who tended to be over-the-top with operational security. But as Danny had already seen, opsec wasn't Tyson's strong point. Tam slapped him on the arm. 'Good to see you, brother,' he said, pointedly ignoring the question. 'Next time, maybe we'll get the chance to grab ourselves a beer.' He turned to the rest of his Delta mates, nodded and led them into the terminal.

'Cagey fuckers,' Tyson said. He sniffed. 'Hate us because they ain't us, right? Still, I'd like to know what they're doing in the UK.'

'Yeah,' Danny said. 'Just like *they'd* like to know what *we're* doing in the US. Come on, let's board.'

There was a big difference, Danny knew, between a military private jet and a civilian one. The main cabin of the Gulfstream was decked out with ten extendable seats – a decent size and comfortable enough, but canvas lined and well worn. A thin, charcoal-grey carpet on the floor and a faint smell of fuel and sweat. Against the partition wall with the cockpit was a fixed catering unit with a selection of pre-packed sandwiches and bottled water. No booze, of course. Flight Lieutenant Gray was waiting for them. He pointed toward a door at the rear of the aircraft. 'You can dump your stuff in there,' he said. 'Wheels up in twenty, so make yourselves comfortable.'

Danny carried his bag to the door the Flight Lieutenant had indicated. On a regular private jet, this would be the bedroom. No such luxuries on a US army Gulfstream. Danny opened the doors to see a small, sparse cabin. The shutters were fixed down on the windows, the plastic moulded to the interior of the aircraft so they couldn't be raised. There was no carpet in here. Attached to the metal floor were six shackle points – hinged rings for clipping on handcuffs or leg-cuffs. 'I wonder how many people have been fastened to that floor,' Spud said quietly from just behind Danny.

Danny grunted. It was impossible to do this job without coming face to face with evidence of the darker side of military operations. Those shackles told him that the Gulfstream that was to ferry them across the Atlantic had carried any number of rendition targets as well, to whichever black camps were politically convenient.

He dumped his gear at the back at the room. As he walked back to the main cabin, he passed Spike. Spike was staring at the shackle points and looked a bit uncomfortable. For a moment, Danny was reminded of himself as a young trooper. It wouldn't take long, he told himself, for Spike to become hardened to sights like that.

The doors in the main cabin were closed now. Danny grabbed a couple of sandwiches and got them down him. Many operations had taught him to grab whatever rest he could, when he could. He intended to sleep his way across the Atlantic.

The captain's voice came across the PA system. 'Good afternoon, gentlemen. If I can ask you to get yourselves comfortable, we're going to start taxiing in approximately 5 minutes. We're hoping to get you down on the ground in southern Texas in approximately ten hours. That'll be about 1700 local time. I'll come back to you once we're at cruising altitude.'

Danny selected a seat up front. To his slight surprise, Tyson took the seat next to him. 'Black,' he said quietly. 'About that business back at the Emirates. I should have kept my fucking mouth shut.'

'It happened,' Danny said.

'So, are we good?'

'Sure,' Danny said. 'We're good, so long as you lay off Spike. He doesn't need you talking to him like he's a fucking three-year-old.'

Tyson glanced out the window. The tarmac slid past as they taxied toward the runway. 'We're operating a long way from home, anyway,' he said.

'Yeah,' Danny replied. 'Long way.' He reclined his seat and closed his eyes. Ten minutes later they were airborne.

SEVEN

Lackland Airforce Base, Texas.
1700 hours United States Central Time.

The Gulfstream's wheels hit the runway bang on schedule. As soon as it came to a halt, the guys grabbed their gear from the back cabin and made their way to the exit. The sun was deep red and low in the sky. Danny removed his aviator shades from the top pocket of his shirt and put them on. He took several lungfuls of the hot, dry air. Within seconds he was sweating.

This American Air Force base was not busy. There were a couple of vehicles driving around the edge of the airfield, and a few men in uniform milling around. At the edge of the tarmac was a selection of low, sand-coloured buildings. Beyond them, a high perimeter fence topped with rolls of razor wire. At the foot of the airstair leading off the private jet was a black Chrysler SUV. All the doors were open, and a soldier in American army combat uniform stood by it. He saluted as the unit alighted, then moved round to open up the trunk. The guys dumped their gear inside and took their seats in the SUV. Nobody asked them for ID, or even checked their names.

They drove in silence across the the tarmac toward a security gate. More crisp salutes from the two guys on guard, and the unit passed through into a square compound surrounded on three sides by low barracks. There was another SUV parked here – a black Tahoe. Unlike the Chrysler it looked as if it had seen better days. Scratches, small dents and a patch on the left-hand side where it might have been swiped by another car. Danny wasn't fooled. As the setting sun reflected off the vehicle's windscreen he caught a green tint from the refracted light. It told him this was toughened glass. If the windscreen was armoured, chances were the rest of the vehicle was too.

He didn't get a chance to examine the vehicle further. A man had appeared in one of the doorways just beyond. Early sixties, maybe older. Medium height, a full, sandy-coloured beard turning grey, corduroy jacket that was definitely the wrong choice of clothing here in this heat. He looked slightly out of place. Unfit, compared to the soldiers in the vicinity. His watery eyes had dark bags under them. He made no real effort to hide the holster strapped to his body beneath the jacket. He squinted at them as he walked in their direction. He had quite a pronounced limp. Yet another salute from the unit's driver as he approached.

'These guys should just glue their fingertips to their heads,' Spud muttered.

The bearded man spoke quietly to the driver. He nodded abruptly, removed the unit's bags from the trunk and laid them on the dusty ground, then got back behind the wheel and left the compound. The man waited until the sound of the engine had completely faded before speaking.

'Welcome to Texas, gentlemen,' he said. He looked at them each in turn. 'Danny Black,' he said, his eyes falling on Danny. 'Spud Glover . . . Tyson Fletcher . . . Spike Ramsay . . .' He identified each of them by their correct nicknames, though none of the guys confirmed their identities. 'I'm Ethan Kleinman, your CIA liaison. We'll be working hand in glove, so I'm happy to make your acquaintance.' He went round each member of the unit and shook their hands. Danny noticed he didn't seem keen to look them straight in the eye. 'This is just a meet-and-greet,' Kleinman said. 'We'll have an in-depth briefing when we get to our next location.' He tapped the beaten-up Tahoe. 'Unless you have any questions, I suggest we get moving.'

'No questions,' Danny said. 'Let's go.'

The guys picked up their bags and put them in the back of the Tahoe. Kleinman caught Spike looking rather dubiously at the vehicle. 'Don't worry about it, son,' he said. 'We spend a lot of

71

money making them look like a heap of shit. It's actually a brand-new vehicle. Tuned-up engine. We send them to a bodyshop to make them look like this.'

Spike flushed slightly. He clearly disliked being made to look as if he didn't know these little details. He stepped back and gently kicked one of the wheels with his right foot. 'Bog-standard pimp-mobile,' he said. 'I'm guessing if you've Kevlar-plated it, you'll have needed to upgrade the suspension. Fancy suspension is normally red or yellow, so I hope you've sprayed it to keep it camouflaged. And if you've put in a more powerful engine, you'll have upgraded the braking system as well. Extra weight, extra speed, normal brakes won't be up to the job.' He sniffed. 'Want to tell me anything else I already ...?' His sentence trailed away.

'Kids today, huh?' Tyson said. 'Amazing what they pick up.'

Kleinman inclined his head. 'Point taken, boy,' he said mildly. 'Glad to see you know your stuff. Shall we get out of here? Military bases always give me a headache.' He limped up to the car and got behind the wheel. Danny sat in the passenger seat. The rest of the guys took their places in the back.

Whenever Danny sat in a vehicle, he made a point of checking the hand position of the driver. You could tell a lot by the way they handled the steering wheel. Kleinman handled his like a pro: hands at nine o'clock and three o'clock, thumbs over the steering wheel, not under it where they could easily be broken in the event of an impact. Kleinman had the air of a bumbling old academic, but Danny suspected it was carefully cultivated. As their CIA liaison officer reversed carefully out of the compound, Danny made a mental note not to underestimate him.

They left the military base to a further series of salutes and no questions asked. Within ten minutes they were driving at a steady 55 mph along a clear, straight road. The sinking sun was half below the horizon now, and the flat desert scenery on either side was bathed in a dark, dusky pink. The terrain was level and hard-baked. It seemed to go on for ever. They drove in silence as the day turned to night. There was a definite tension between the unit and the CIA guy. Without any operational matters to discuss, both sides were obviously resistant to small talk. As darkness fell, the desert terrain flew by in a cinematic blur. They passed the occasional freight truck trundling in the opposite direction. Most of them, Danny noticed, bore Mexican number plates.

'Almost none, boy,' Kleinman said quietly.

'What?' Danny said.

'You're wondering how many of those Mexican trucks are involved in the drug trade.'

'You're quite the mind reader.'

'Answer is: almost none. One in five of those babies gets stopped and searched at the border crossings. Tyres get slashed to check they're not stuffed with product or cash. Seat stuffing gets examined. Random products of whatever goods they're transporting get opened up. A few of the small-time producers might think it's worth their while using a truck to smuggle their gear into the US. They might secrete a bit of product in the gas tank. But the big boys?' He shook his head. 'Too cute for that.'

'So how do they do it?' Danny said.

'How *don't* they do it, boy? I've seen it all. Female drug mules replacing their breast implants with bags of coke. Tunnels under the border. Light aircraft. They use special drug catapults to hurl mostly marijuana over the Rio Grande. Crude, homemade submarines to smuggle stuff in and out by sea. Past year or two we've had packages of crystal meth coming over mostly by cheap drones you can buy on the internet.' He scratched his beard. 'Yeah,' he said. 'They'll always find a way. Soon as we plug a hole in the dam, they find another one.'

The car fell into silence again. Danny couldn't help remembering the shitty little flat where he'd found his brother, comatose among the drug paraphernalia. There was something in Kleinman's blasé tone of voice that irritated him. Like he was leading them in to fight a lost cause.

They'd been travelling south for another hour when Kleinman indicated right and pulled off the freeway on to a narrower road that headed due west. Their surroundings gradually became somewhat more urban. An out-of-town gas station. A 24-hour convenience store. A couple of warehouses. Danny noticed that many of the signs were written in Spanish as well as English. The traffic grew busier and within 15 minutes they were in the suburbs of a small town. 'San Angelo,' Kleinman announced. 'Five miles north of the Mexican border, fifteen miles east of the border town of Laredo. I'll level with you, guys . . .' He indicated left into a large car parking area. 'It ain't Disneyland.'

At the far end of the car parking area was a single-storey motel. At one end, on a tall pole, was an unlit neon sign bearing the words *Desert Oasis Motel*. Kleinman pulled up in front. 'Welcome home,' he said.

The unit didn't get out of the car immediately. Like Danny, the others took a moment to orientate themselves. Everything about this motel made it look as if it was shut down. It comprised a single storey of seven units. Each unit had one door and one window. There didn't appear to be any lights on. At one end was a corner unit with a sign saying *Office* and a placard in the window saying *No Vacancies*. Again, no lights to indicate it was occupied. The masonry had once been whitewashed but was now stained and tatty, its render falling away. There were only two vehicles parked outside. Both of them were black Tahoes, just like the vehicle in which they were travelling, right down to the artful dents. The only difference was that these two had Mexican plates. On the other side of the road, perhaps a hundred metres away, was another – bigger – hotel. A cheap, pre-fab construction, but several storeys high and with a burger joint and a pizza place on the ground floor. If you were a traveller wanting a room for the night, that's where you'd go. You'd certainly pass by the Desert Oasis Motel, which made it as good as invisible.

Danny looked in the rear-view mirror. He saw the others were watching him. He nodded. As one, they opened the doors of the Tahoe and alighted. They reclaimed their bags from the trunk and followed Kleinman as he limped toward the motel. He led them to the door two along from the deserted office. There was no sign of it being occupied, but on closer examination Danny saw the window was covered on the inside with a piece of cardboard. It had the effect of making the motel seem even more run-down. Danny had seen enough covert ops rooms, however, to realise this was a deliberate piece of camouflage.

Kleinman knocked three times on the door. There was a pause. Then a muffled voice. 'Can't you read the frickin' sign? No vacancies. There's a hotel across the main drag.'

'It's Ethan,' Kleinman said.

Another pause. Then a scratching sound on the other side of the door as the person unlocked from inside. The door opened and a dim light flooded out.

'Inside, please,' Kleinman said. 'Quickly.'

They filed in, Danny leading the way. The room he found himself in stank of cigarettes and body odour. The built-in wardrobes on one wall told him it had once been a motel bedroom. Now it contained no regular motel furniture. Instead there were a couple of army cots along the far wall with rough, khaki-coloured blankets. The walls themselves were covered in maps of the surrounding area, as well as satellite imaging print-outs. Danny was right about the windows. There were two, one in the front, one in the back. Both had sheets of cardboard roughly stuck over them with thick strips of duct tape. There was a metal framed table in the middle of the room, with a couple of laptops, a stack of comms gear and wires snaking all the way across the floor to an entry point in the left-hand wall. Sitting at the table were two men. One of them looked like a Sikh – he had a black turban and wispy facial hair. The other had a Hispanic appearance – dark skin, black hair, slightly dishevelled.

'This is Rav Patel and Michael Hernandez,' Kleinman said. He took a Zippo lighter from his pocket and was flicking it open, sparking it, then flicking it shut again, though there was no sign of a cigarette. 'As you've probably guessed, that's not their real names, but don't ask them because they ain't telling.'

Rav raised a Starbucks cup in greeting, then looked inside. Seeing it was empty, he sighed and chucked it into one corner, where it joined another five or six empty cups. Michael made no sign of greeting. He just turned back to monitoring his laptop. Next to his computer was a plate of food. Tyson pointed at it. 'The four dicks of death,' he said. Danny knew that was the Yanks' nickname for a particularly disgusting MRE of beef and beans. 'Food of champions.'

'Rav and Michael are our intel guys,' Kleinman said, ignoring the interruption. 'Rav will be doing satellite, Michael will be on comms and operating a drone if we need it. They'll have all the information you need on targets, which I'll be giving you as the operation unfolds.'

None of the SAS guys made any response. It was clear Kleinman had a load to say. They let him get on and say it.

'Hereford have sent through details of your clothes sizes. You've a room each here, and you'll find packages of work clothes from Duluth Trading. Hard-wearing, khaki and sand colour, but not uniform, obviously. There's body armour for each of you. I strongly recommend you wear it. I've taken the liberty of order-ing in Salomon Quest boots for each of you. Any problems with that?'

No problems.

'Good. If the operation changes in any way and we find ourselves operating more on the streets, we'll just buy whatever clothes you need there and then.' Kleinman looked around the room and his eyes fell on a leather briefcase. He walked over, opened it up and drew out four brown envelopes. He gave one to each of the unit. Danny looked inside and saw a sheaf of used American dollars. 'A thousand bucks each petty cash,' he said. 'You need more, just say.'

'You want a receipt for this?' Spike asked. It was a reasonable question – on ordinary Regiment ops, every last pound needed to be signed for.

Kleinman seemed to find this very funny. 'Why?' he said. 'Don't you think we can afford it, boy?' He shook his head. 'I don't *like* receipts, and I don't want you guys keeping any. You're not offi-cially here, remember? Last thing we want is a paper trail that says you are.'

'Don't worry about Snowflake,' Tyson cut in. He had already greedily folded his notes and put them in his back pocket. 'He'll learn.'

Rav grinned. Danny had to grab Spike's arm to stop him kicking off. The moment passed, however, and the guys removed the dollars from their envelopes and shoved them into their back pockets. 'What about hardware?' Spud said.

'Follow me,' Kleinman said, sparking his Zippo again.

On the right-hand wall was an adjoining door to the next room. It had two mortice locks and a sturdy security chain. Kleinman unlocked them all, then led them through the door. The guys filed in. Tyson let out a low whistle.

The contents of this room were not quite as extensive as the armoury back at Hereford, but it wasn't far off. Along one wall was a rack of assault rifles – M4s and M16s. Another wall was given over to handguns. 'You can take your pick from 9 millimetres, 45s or 40s,' Kleinman said. He picked up a Sig 9mm. 'It was one of these bad boys that gave me this.' He indicated his bad leg.

'Where did that happen?' Danny asked.

'South of the border, boy,' Kleinman said evasively. He walked over to a corner of the room where several black crates were stacked. 'We've ordered in Kevlar helmets, cut away. Night sights. And ammunition, of course. We have C4 plastic explosives, remote detonators, yada yada yada. Anything you don't see, let me know and we'll have it ordered up.'

The guys were quiet. Danny knew why. Everything about this operation spoke of no expense spared. Tyson was greedily eying up the handguns, a kid in a sweetie shop.

'Shall we get going with the briefing?' Danny said.

'One more thing,' Kleinman told him. He led them back into the operations room. 'You have personal cell phones? Please hand them over to Rav.'

Rav stood up from his seat and handed round a plastic tub. The guys dropped their Regiment-issued phones into it. Rav took them to one corner of the room where there was a small safe. He deposited them inside before handing round a new set of Iridium sat phone handsets. 'CIA issue,' Kleinman said. 'Fully encrypted. Our ops room number is programmed to speed dial one.' He watched as each member of the team switched on their phones and memorised the number, because if they lost their phones for any reason, they still to make contact with base. 'Now take a seat please,' Kleinman said when they were done.

He indicated some plastic chairs stowed under the table. The guys sat down. Rav and Michael stretched back on their own chairs. Kleinman stared at one of the maps on the wall for a moment. Then he turned to look at them. 'You know, in general terms,' he said, 'our problem with the Zeta cartel?'

Kleinman barely waited for a response before continuing.

'The Zetas were originally Mexican special forces. Trained up by the British SAS in the first place.' He glanced at Tyson with scarcely disguised disapproval.

'Hey, granddad, how about we have a chinwag about how the CIA trained up the Muj in Afghanistan in the seventies?' Tyson said.

'How about we don't, boy. What's done is done. The original Zetas were a cadre of about forty special forces soldiers who switched sides and started working for the Gulf cartel. Eventually they turned against their employers and started a cartel of their own. They're now the most successful and most violent cartel in Mexico, and their principal area of operations is . . .' He pointed in a direction that Danny knew to be south. 'Just over the Rio Grande from here. Clearly they've massively expanded in personnel since the original forty Zetas. Many of the originals have been killed, but the remainder have instilled a culture of extreme brutality and violence. The current-day Zetas are better trained and more ruthless than any cartel members we've yet come across. Their success across the border means they're able to ship unprecedented quantities of product into the US. We've got middle-class Americans comatose over the dashboards of their SUVs because they're high on heroin. We've got DEA officers being mown down in broad daylight. It's got to stop, and the only way we can do it is by destabilising the Zetas. And that means getting to the top guys.'

Kleinman picked up a sheaf of A4 photographs from the table. He held one of them up. It was a picture of a Mexican man. Middle-aged. Short black hair. Pencil moustache. 'The Zetas refer to themselves numerically,' Kleinman said. 'The head of the cartel is Z1. His lieutenants are Z2, Z3 and Z4. And so on. This is Z1. Real name . . .'

'Augusto Chavez,' Tyson interrupted. 'I'd know that fucker anywhere. He used to find dead animals and pin them to the targets on the range. Said it helped him get his eye in if he had something real to shoot.' Tyson shook his head at the memory. 'He was a fucking psycho. I flagged it up to the head shed at the time. Told them to watch him – a regular little warlord in the making. They chose not to listen to me.'

Danny was only half listening to Tyson. His attention was on Kleinman. As soon as he'd held up that picture, his hand had started, almost imperceptibly, to tremble. He appeared relieved to put the photograph back down in favour of two more, which he held up to the unit. 'Z2 and Z3,' he said. 'But really, the identity of these individuals is, for the moment, academic. We don't know where they are. The Zeta leadership has a network of safe houses throughout Mexico. They no longer need to trouble themselves with the day-to-day brutality of their cartel – they have a whole army of underlings to do their dirty work for them.'

'And if I know Chavez,' Tyson said, 'he won't give a flying fuck if we whack a few of the little guys.' He said it with a dismissive sneer in his voice, as if Kleinman was being unusually stupid.

'You're quite right,' Kleinman said. 'Targeting the regular Zeta foot soldiers will have precisely zero effect on the situation. The *Federales* have been doing that for some time, but they're not suitable for the kind of work we have in mind. We want to eliminate Z1. But if we're going to draw out the Zeta leadership – including Z1 himself – we need to target the thing that matters far more to them than human life.' He removed his round glasses, cleaned them on the material of his corduroy jacket and put them back on his face. 'We need to target their money.'

Tyson, it seemed, had no argument with that.

'Money is the only thing these people care about,' Kleinman elaborated. 'If that comes under threat, we predict the Zeta leadership will have no alternative but to take command of the situation and put themselves on the front line. And when they do *that* . . .'

He left the sentence hanging.

'So how do we hit the money?' Danny asked.

'That,' Kleinman said, 'is a very good question.' He held up yet another photograph, this time of a light aircraft, taken from a considerable distance by a telephoto lens at night. 'And this is the answer,' he said.

EIGHT

'We've known for a few months now,' Kleinman continued, 'that the Zeta cartel are using this very aircraft to shift their drug dollars back into Mexico under the radar – literally.'

'Where does that intel . . .?' Spike asked. His face was very intent. He was clearly listening hard.

'Classified information, and you're not on the list. It doesn't matter *how* we know. We just *do* know the aircraft flies regularly from a private airstrip about fifteen miles east of here. Rav, do you want to give them the details?'

Rav nodded. 'The pilot's name is Barry Osmin.'

'Good Mexican name,' Spud said.

'He's American, a geological surveyor. At least, that's his cover. He works freelance for the oil companies, spotting likely drilling sites, that kind of thing. Keeps his Cessna at this airfield, has fifteen to twenty flying hours a week. Once a month, regular as clockwork, he takes a night flight, leaving the airfield at approximately 0200 hours. He flies east along the Rio Grande – the northern edge of the US border – for about ten minutes, then we routinely lose him from the radar picture. He reappears at the same point about an hour later and returns to the airfield.'

Danny knew what the pilot was doing. 'He's losing height quickly so he's off-radar, then he's heading over the border to deliver the money.'

'That's our best guess, boy,' Kleinman said. He stood up and walked over to one of the maps on the wall. 'Given the timings, the only airfield in range is this one.' He pointed to a red dot on the map, about ten miles south of the border.

Tyson shook his head. 'Cessna like that, decent pilot, you don't need an airstrip. You could land it on a road or anywhere.'

'Sure,' Kleinman said, sparking his lighter. 'But we don't think so. The cartel doesn't need to be so covert. They'll have bribed or threatened whoever they need to make sure the money gets unloaded. It's precious to them, so we're pretty sure they'd put the plane down on a decent runway, for safety.'

'How much is the plane carrying with each run?' Spike asked quietly.

'Hard to tell. At a guess, I'd say about 20 mill.'

Tyson gave a low whistle. 'Worth a bit of aggro then,' he said. 'Old Z1's gone up in the world since I knew him.'

'So why haven't you hit it before now?' Spud asked.

'Because there's no point unless it's part of a coordinated strategy, boy. The Zetas need to know that somebody is systematically going after their money. The plane is only one of two initial targets you'll be going after. You'll remember I told you the cartel has different methods of smuggling product across the border?'

'Drug catapults,' Danny recalled. 'Drones.'

'Right. They're not going to use those two methods to move cash back into Mexico, but in addition to light aircraft, they also use the tunnels they've dug under the border. Ordinarily, by the time we locate these tunnels the cartel has moved on to new ones. Past few days, we struck lucky. We've had surveillance on a Zeta sicario, name of Jesús.'

'Halle-fuckin'-luia,' Spud said.

'We believe he knows the location of one of these tunnels, and the time and date of a major transportation of drug money from the US side to the Mexican side.'

'These tunnels really go under the Rio Grande river?' Danny asked.

'In a few instances, yes. You need to pick this guy up and encourage him to be ... how can I put it ... forthcoming about everything he knows. I guess that means making him more scared of you than he is of his Zeta paymasters.'

'I think we can manage that,' Spud said.

'When's the next light aircraft run?' Danny said.

'Tomorrow night, 0200 hours. The guys can give you all the intel you need. I'll leave it up to you how you want to hit the money, but if the aircraft itself needs to run into any . . .' He took a moment to search for the right words. 'Any *technical* difficulties, it needs to happen in Mexican airspace, not ours. In the meantime, our Zeta sicario is due in San Antonio tomorrow at midday. He supplies a suburban soccer mom, name of Claire DuPré, with a regular package of heroin in return for favours of a sexual nature. I suggest you pick him up when he's at his most vulnerable, if you take my meaning?'

Rav Patel sniggered. 'I'll play you the tape of their last get-together,' he said. '*Then* you'll get his meaning.'

'What's the location of the San Antonio meet?' Danny asked.

'The DuPrés' house,' Kleinman said. 'Rav, play the tape.'

'Close your ears, Snowflake,' Tyson said. 'Save your blushes, huh?'

'Cut it out, Tyson,' Danny said angrily as Rav turned to his computer and started a recording. A woman with a pure American accent, a guy with a Mexican inflection.

– *Did you bring it?*

– *Where is he?*

– *Away on business. Vancouver.*

'Move us to the relevant part, Rav.'

Rav shrugged, but did as he was told.

– *You'll be back, right?*

– *Three days, bitch. Same time, same place. And you'd better up your game – that was a definite six out of ten.*

'You know,' Spud said quietly, 'I don't think him and me are ever going to be friends.'

'Do you have pictures of the house?' Danny asked. 'Layouts?'

Again, Kleinman turned to Rav, who handed over a package of photographs. Danny laid them out on the table. They showed a well-heeled, expensive suburban house. Palm trees on the front. A very neat, well-manicured lawn with diagonal stripes. White Range Rover in the drive.

'Sweet,' Spud said.

Danny was scanning the photos of the house for possible entry points, but his eyes were attracted to something else. At the front of the lawn was a small wooden sign staked into the grass, only a few inches high. It said 'RealGreen'. He pointed at it. 'What's that?'

Kleinman looked. 'Lawn care company,' he said. 'They put their signs on each lawn they look after. Like, advertising.'

Danny turned to Rav. 'I need you to go into town first thing, find one of those places that prints up T-shirts. Get four with "RealGreen" printed on them. Big letters. You can do that?'

Rav nodded. 'Sure.'

'I'll need to know the name of the woman's husband and kids.'

'Not a problem.'

Danny looked over at Spike. 'We need to get an IED on board that Cessna before it takes off. Remote detonation. What do you need?'

Spike walked up to the table and took another look at the picture of the Cessna. His fingers absentmindedly touched the acne on his face. 'Four-inch stick of military-grade C4,' he said. 'Three active mobile phones . . . Detonator . . .' His eyes narrowed for a moment. 'Get me a small emergency first aid pouch from a fishing tackle place.'

Danny looked at Kleinman. 'You got it,' the CIA man said.

'We'll need two sets of old mechanics' overalls,' he said. 'And two of us need to cross the Mexican border to get eyes on the airfield where our guy puts the Cessna down.'

'Leave it with me,' Kleinman said. 'I suggest we RV at 0600 tomorrow morning for an update.'

'Roger that,' Danny said

'In the meantime,' Kleinman said, 'do you have any further questions?'

'Yeah,' Spud said. 'I've got a question. Where do we get something to eat? Apart from the four dicks of death. I'm Hank Marvin here.'

A flicker of annoyance crossed Kleinman's face, but he let it pass. 'Rav or Michael will fetch you whatever you need, boy,' he said. 'In the meantime, I suggest you make yourself comfortable in your rooms. Tomorrow's going to be a busy day.'

'Abduct a Zeta hitman, blow up a plane.' Spud checked the items off on his fingers. 'All in a day's work,' he said. 'Right, fellas?'

Danny's room was about as sparse as he expected it to be. Like in the ops room, the windows were blacked out, and the light from the one bare bulb was very dim. A single bed, a bathroom that was clean but basic, with a new bar of rough soap and some shaving foam, a razor and some traditional razor blades in the bathroom cabinet. A thin layer of dust on all the surfaces. Cobwebs in the corner. Kleinman had clearly seen to it that no cleaning staff would be around to trouble them. Not that it mattered. This was luxury compared to some of the places he'd operated out of. The clothing and boots the CIA man had promised them were stashed in cardboard delivery boxes. Danny was just rummaging through them when there was a knock on his door. He opened it. Spud was standing there.

Spud yanked a thumb backwards to indicate they should talk outside. Danny understood why. They were supposedly on the same team as the CIA guys, of course, but it was beyond question that their rooms would be bugged and the two intel guys would be monitoring their conversations. If Danny had been in their shoes, that's what he would do.

He followed his mate out into the car park in front of the motel. It was still hot out. 'Did you notice how the old boy's hand trembled when he held up that photo of Z1?' Spud asked.

Danny nodded. 'He knows the guy. I'd bet my house on it.'

'Yeah? Well I've seen the state of your house.'

Danny grinned. It was good to have Spud along. His sarcastic comments had a way of taking the heat out of any situation.

'Anything else he's not telling us?' Spud said.

'He's a spook,' Danny said. 'There's a whole shitload he's not telling us. Just like you told Spike. And talking of Spike . . .' Danny chose his words carefully. 'He's up to sorting this IED, right?'

'Are you kidding me? I told you – Spike's a fucking genius at all that shit. Ignore Tyson. He's just stirring.'

Danny nodded, but didn't reply. Rav Patel was walking across the car park carrying an armful of pizza boxes. He grinned at them. 'Bon appetit, gentlemen,' he said. He handed the pizzas over to Spud, then sauntered back toward the ops room. Halfway there, he stopped and looked back over his shoulder. 'RealGreen, right?'

'Right.'

He returned to the ops room, whistling tunelessly.

The old man had only one hope. So he tried not to look at the clock above the fireplace too often.

He was finding it difficult to keep track of time. Sometimes he would look at the clock and an hour had passed. Sometimes only ten minutes. He had spent the worst night of his life with his two captors. They didn't let him leave the front room, except to go to the toilet. Even then they made him keep the door open, and laughed cruelly when he was unable to go. He tried to explain that he needed a laxative from the chemist. They told him not to be so stupid. That if he didn't shut up, the only way he'd be leaving this house was in several pieces, in bin liners.

He had drowsed on the sofa during the night while the two men took turns watching him. He was terribly cold, and woke every ten minutes from shivering. His head hurt from where he'd hit it, and his lips tasted of blood where the men had ripped off the duct tape after taking their video of him. He was very hungry, but the men didn't offer him any food, and just the occasional mouthful of water to keep him alive. They helped themselves to whatever was in his fridge.

And as the following day passed, they grew more and more edgy. Every couple of hours there would be a phone call. The old man couldn't hear what was being said at the other end, of course, but his two tormentors kept repeating the same message. 'But we can't keep him here.' 'Someone will come.' 'We need somewhere to move him to, if you want the old bastard alive.'

To each other, they said: 'If anyone comes, we keep quiet. Don't answer the door.'

Ten minutes ago there was a different call. He heard one of the men say, 'OK, we'll get him in the car as soon as it's dark.'

He felt a surge of panic as he heard that, and looked at the clock again. Five minutes to four. The light was failing outside.

He bowed his head. If they knew he was clock-watching, they might realise he was waiting for someone.

Which he was.

The young man. Benjamin. A volunteer from the local church. He was only eighteen, and his wispy goatee beard didn't make him look any older. The old man looked forward to his visits. A half-hour chat and a cup of tea with someone made all the difference when you lived alone.

He was always punctual. Four o'clock. On the dot.

The old man allowed himself a quick glance at the clock. Two minutes to four.

'I need the lavatory,' he croaked.

'For fuck's sake, old man. You're bunged up. Just sit there and keep your mouth shut.'

'Keep your arsehole shut, and all,' the other man laughed.

'I think . . . I think I'm going to dirty myself.'

Both men looked at him in disgust. The old man glanced at the clock again. One minute to four.

'I did him last time,' one of the men said. 'It's your turn.'

'I don't see why we can't just plug him now.'

'Just take the old fucker upstairs, will you?'

The old man found it hard to stand up. Nobody helped him. By the time he was finally on his feet, his reluctant toilet companion had already moved to the hallway and was standing at the foot of the stairs, a couple of metres from the front door. The old man walked painfully toward him. Every muscle ached. His legs trembled.

He was halfway across the room when the doorbell rang.

The old man stopped. The guy by the stairs appeared in the living room doorway. The other man stood up. They stared at each other for a moment.

Silence.

'Expecting someone?' the guy in the front room breathed dangerously.

The old man didn't reply. The bell rang again, and there was a rap on the door.

'I think he saw me through the glass,' the guy by the door whispered. 'We need to open up. He ain't going away.'

The other man walked up to him. He had his gun, and he rested it hard against the old man's neck. 'What's their name?' he said.

'Ben ... Benjamin.'

'Who is he?'

'He ... he comes and has a cup of tea with me.'

'Do you want him to walk away with his brains still inside his skull?'

'Yes ... but ...'

'Then you tell him we're from the council. Checking everything's alright. Got it?'

The old man nodded.

The man with the gun looked toward his mate. 'Open up,' he said quietly.

The guy turned to the front door. The old man couldn't see him now, but heard him undoing the latches and opening up. 'You must be Benjamin!' he said brightly. 'Come on in, he's waiting for you. Kettle's on.'

'*Call the police!*' the old man shouted as loud as his feeble voice could manage. '*Benjamin ... call the ...*'

Everything happened so quickly. The man with the gun jabbed his elbow hard into the old man's chest, knocking him, winded, on to the floor. There was a scuffling at the doorway. Within five seconds the old man heard the door slam shut and, to his horror, saw his friend Benjamin being hauled aggressively into the room. Benjamin seemed too surprised to struggle or make a noise. He didn't understand what was going on.

'No blood,' said the guy who had knocked the old man down. He said it sharply, like he was worried.

He didn't need to be. His mate hooked one arm around Benjamin's neck. Benjamin made his first sound: a strangled, choking noise. It didn't last long. His attacker thrust the palm of his free hand hard against the side of Benjamin's head. His head tilted grotesquely several degrees. There was a nasty crack. Benjamin's body went limp. His attacker let him slump gently to the floor.

The old man heard nothing but the clock ticking on the mantelpiece.

Then the guy with the gun was in his face, kneeling down and hissing. 'You stupid, *stupid* old git,' he said. 'Try something like that again, we'll be shoving you in a hole with your mate Benjamin.'

He turned to his friend. 'We'll have to get rid the body,' he growled.

Then, suddenly losing his temper, he kicked Benjamin's corpse hard in the ribs. 'Fuck!' he spat. '*Fuck!*'

His mate was scowling too. 'Who's going to tell Aiden Bailey?' he asked. 'Jesus, this is a fuck-up . . .'

The two men stared at each other.

'Just get the body packaged up,' said the guy with the gun. 'We'll move it after dark.' He looked down at the old man, who couldn't stand the heat of his stare.

He put his face in his hands and started to cry.

The village of San Cristobal had a population of just over two thousand. It nestled at the foot of a hill twenty miles south of Nuevo Laredo, and was by far the poorest in the region.

There was a grand old municipal building on the centre square, painted yellow and red. It doubled up as an administrative centre, a doctor's surgery and a food bank. On the other side of the square was a timber-framed Catholic church, with a large wooden crucifix set outside it. These were the only two buildings of note in San Cristobal. Every other structure was a shack. Breeze-block exterior walls. Tin roofs. The village sat under a nest of humming electricity pylons. Some of the inhabitants had painted their tiny houses in bright, vivid colours. Others were covered with spray-paint graffiti. There was no car in this village less than fifteen years old.

It was an ugly village, but softened slightly by the setting sun. Kids played with pebbles in the dusty streets. Older men in dirty T-shirts and baseball caps sat on low concrete walls smoking roll-up cigarettes. Teenage girls paraded in brightly coloured, home-made dresses. Young men cat-called them, but they didn't seem to mind.

Everything changed when six vehicles appeared on the hillside, their headlamps glowing in the dusk as they descended toward the village. The old men barked at the kids to get inside. The teenage girls disappeared back to their houses. The boys forgot their shows of bravado and did the same.

By the time the convoy reached the village, the streets were practically empty. The vehicles – shiny black SUVs that looked quite out of place in San Cristobal – parked in the centre square, outside the church. Men emerged. They carried guns. Some had rifles slung across their chests. Others had handguns in uncon-cealed holsters. Across their faces, many of them wore black bandanas printed with white skulls. They all had a swagger – none more so than one man who, when he blinked, revealed fake eyes tattooed on his eyelids.

He stood by the large wooden crucifix and slowly looked around the deserted centre of the village. There was still nobody outside. He addressed his men. 'One each,' he said.

The men nodded and dispersed from the village square in many different directions. The man with the tattooed eyelids leaned against his vehicle and lit a cigarette. He glanced at his watch, then started to whistle tunelessly. He heard someone scream in the distance. He stubbed out his cigarette and lit another.

It took about three minutes for the first of his men to reappear. He had a villager at gunpoint – an old guy with light hair and a leathery face. 'In the church,' he instructed, and his guy poked the old guy in the back with the tip of his weapon and nudged him toward the entrance of the church. By this time, two more of his men were entering the square from different directions. One had a younger man at gunpoint, who stumbled ahead of him, clearly sick with terror. The other had one of the young girls in the brightly coloured dresses. She was crying. The man with tattooed lids eyed her up and down as his guy forced her toward the church.

Within five minutes, each of his guys had grabbed a villager and forced them into the church. The door was shut. Five of the gunmen surrounded the building. There was shouting across the village. Wailing. A few of the braver villagers had appeared at the perimeter of the centre square. Ten or fifteen. A couple of the braver ones – men in their twenties – edged on to the square itself. 'Get out of here!' one of them shouted. 'We don't want you here!'

The guy with the tattooed eyelids walked toward them. They stuck together, chins jutting out. 'We said get out of here!' one of them shouted. The guy stopped when he was two metres from where they were standing. Then he withdrew his handgun. Unlocked it. Without hesitation, he pointed it at the head of one of the young men. He fired. The gunshot echoed across the hillside as a round slammed into the young man's forehead, cracking away part of his skull and spattering his companion with blood like paint flicked from a brush. The young man collapsed heavily to the ground. His companion staggered back. The guy with the tattooed eyelids pointed his gun at the head of this second man. Fired again. Turned his back immediately and was walking back toward the church by the time his second victim had hit the deck.

He went directly to the trunk of his vehicle. Removed four large, heavy jerrycans full of petrol. Handed three of the cans to three of his men. They used it to douse the wooden walls of the church. Front, back and sides. While he was glugging fuel against the wooden front door, it opened and one of the prisoners started shouting at them. It earned him a fierce crack to his left cheekbone with the butt of a rifle. The door didn't open again.

But the sound from inside grew louder. Men were shouting. Women were screaming. Children were crying. It started to get on his nerves.

When all four jerrycans were empty he piled them up by the front door. The men all stepped back. Several of them had their phones out, videoing the church. The man with the tattooed eyes waited until he was ten metres away, then lit a third cigarette.

He took several deep drags. He blew gently on the end to ensure the tip was burning properly.

Then he threw it toward the jerrycans.

The fuel vapour ignited even before the cigarette hit the cans.

An impenetrable circle of flames immediately surrounded the church. They were silent for a few seconds, but then started to crackle as the wooden structure – bone-dry from the Mexican heat – started to combust. Within a minute, the noise of the flames drowned out the sound of the people screaming inside. There were still screams and shouting from the surrounding village, but several of his guys were now directing their rifles towards the perimeter of the square. Nobody dared approach, for fear of ending up like the two corpses still bleeding out on to the dusty ground.

The flames licked higher up the walls of the church. Clouds of smoke billowed up into the air. He thought that, maybe, he could hear somebody screaming. Any minute now, he knew, they would try to escape from the church, but that was okay. He was facing the main entrance, his handgun ready. The remainder of his men had surrounded the building and were covering every possible exit point: the windows and the door at the rear.

He was right. Barely thirty seconds passed before the front door opened. There was a belch of thick smoke and a figure appeared silhouetted behind the flames. Adult, by the look of it, but he couldn't immediately tell if it was male or female. The figure sprinted out of the church. Male. His hair was on fire. He was screaming wildly. The gunman waited until he was ten metres clear of the church before raising his weapon.

He shot once. The figure went down.

He turned to a couple of his men. 'That one will do,' he said. A couple of his guys sauntered back to their vehicle. When they returned to the body, one of them was carrying a heavy-duty hacksaw. The corpse's hair had burned away now, though the head was still smouldering. The guy with the hacksaw bent down, placed the blade against the man's gullet and started to saw. He was as nonchalant as if he was doing a straightforward home repair.

The man with the tatooed eyelids turned his attention back to the church. Opening the door had been a bad move by the dead man. A backdraught had sucked the fire into the church itself. Within a couple of minutes, all the exterior walls were covered with flame. The roof itself was smouldering. Part of it had collapsed. There was no chance of anyone escaping now. If the heat hadn't got them, the smoke certainly would have. The guys surrounding the church, who had done this before, knew that too. They lowered their weapons and were sauntering back toward the vehicles. Cracking jokes. Laughing. Watching their video footage of the burning church as they walked. The guys holding the perimeter square held on for a minute or so longer, but soon they too were returning to the convoy.

Nobody needed to give any kind of instruction. They all simply climbed back into their vehicles, as relaxed as if they'd just stopped off for a cup of coffee. The man with the saw was stuffing the decapitated head into a regular supermarket plastic bag. His hands were covered in blood, and he looked at them with annoyance, before wiping them on his clothes and carrying his gruesome package back to one of the vehicles. He didn't look back at the decapitated body lying on the ground.

The convoy drove off through the village, back toward the hillside, in the same order in which it had arrived. Its evening's work was done.

The villagers waited until the convoy had left the village before they dared to enter the church square again. Two sets of parents collapsed by the bodies of their sons, whose faces were now unrecognisable from the entry wounds. A wife knelt by the decapitated body of her husband, wailing desperately. The remaining villagers approached the church, but they couldn't get closer than fifteen metres because the flames were still fierce. Those who had family inside fell to their knees, distraught and broken. Those who did not stared at each other in disbelief and, as the burning church collapsed in on itself, uttered the same word to each other, over and over again.

Por qué, they said.

Why?

SATURDAY

NINE

Danny slept lightly behind the locked door of his motel room. His sleep was disturbed. He saw his daughter in the cockpit of a light aircraft that exploded a moment later. He saw the drug-squalid flat where he'd found his brother, but now a Mexican sicario called Jesús was sprawled on the sofa.

At approximately 0400, he heard a vehicle pull up outside the motel. A car door slammed. Two minutes later, the car drove away.

He got out of bed at 0500 exactly. It was completely dark in the room, thanks to the cardboard-covered windows, so he switched on the bedside light, which he covered with yesterday's T-shirt to keep the glare down. A hundred press-ups, a hundred sit-ups. Washed. Pulled on some of the Duluth Trading clothing Kleinman had supplied – sand-coloured jeans and a checked shirt. His body armour was leaning up against one wall. For a moment he considered wearing it, but rejected the idea. Body armour would look too bulky, too obvious. They were about to operate in a suburban residential area. It would make him stick out.

He unlocked the door to his room at 0555 hours. Spud was already outside the motel, silhouetted in the dawn light as he looked toward the main road. Very few cars. His mate looked over at Danny and nodded. There was no need for any pleasantries. It was time to get working.

Spike and Tyson appeared thirty seconds later. Together the unit entered the ops room.

Hernandez was asleep in one of the army cots. He didn't stir as they entered. For all Danny knew, Kleinman and Rav could have been up all night. They were wearing the same clothes, and the

97

room smelt even worse than when they'd arrived. There was a tray of coffees in Dunkin' Donuts packaging on the table, and another tray containing the doughnuts themselves. Kleinman made a 'help yourself' gesture, while sparking his lighter with one hand. The unit did just that.

Rav held up a T-shirt. Large. Pale green. The 'RealGreen' logo, just as Danny had seen it on the lawn sign, was printed across the chest. He had to hand it to the CIA – they moved fast. He figured the vehicle he'd heard in the night was delivering the gear he'd asked for. 'Your overalls are in the weapons room,' Rav said. He looked at Spike. 'You'll find everything you asked for there, too. I've got radio sets and wireless earpieces for you. They're tuned in to the listening devices we've planted in the house, so you'll be able to hear everything that's going on in there.' He gave them a salacious grin, which none of the SAS men returned.

Danny turned to his team. 'Spike,' he said. 'You're staying here.'

Spike visibly flushed. 'What? What are you talking . . .?'

'You need to construct your IED. Without that, tonight's hit on the plane is a no-go. Take your time, make sure it works.'

'Leave the big jobs to the big boys, Snowflake,' Tyson said.

Before Spike could continue the argument, Danny addressed Kleinman. 'What's the deal with the border crossing?'

'The only official border crossing is the one between Laredo on the US side and Nuevo Laredo on the Mexican side,' Kleinman said. 'There's too much surveillance there and I don't want your faces cropping up on CCTV imagery. Facial recognition is too good. We've made contact with some tame US border control agents. They have vehicles patrolling those parts of the border that aren't fenced or at a road head. We're in the process of arranging an RV with them for you. They'll get you across.' He looked at his watch, then threw Spud a key. 'That's for the cargo unit in the back of the Tahoe. It'll be cosy, but big enough for your guy. It's about a three-hour drive to San Antonio. You need to get ready.'

It didn't take more than ten minutes for Danny, Spud and Tyson to prepare themselves. They removed their shirts and strapped on the radio packs that Rav handed round. Then they moved into the weapons room, where they each selected a body holster before turning their attention to the handguns. Danny chose a compact HK45C, which he loaded with a full 10-round clip. Spud and Tyson both selected a Sig Sauer P226 9mm. Danny and Spud took a spare magazine, loaded. Tyson brazenly took three. There was an aftermarket for good ammo, and it wasn't unknown for a certain type of Regiment guy to make a few quid on the side flogging excess ammo. Tyson was that type. Grabbing all he could get was hard-wired in him.

Once they'd strapped on their weapons and radios, each man grabbed a fistful of cable ties, essential for a hard arrest, then donned the RealGreen T-shirts. They were extra large – baggy enough to conceal the bulges of the firearms underneath, at least to the untrained eye. For now they put their regular shirts back over their T-shirts, and they looked once more like three ordinary guys. Kleinman gave them directions to Claire DuPré's house, along with the keys to one of the armoured Tahoes outside the motel.

'You wanted the names of her husband and children,' Rav said when they were nearly ready to depart. 'He's called Donald – Don DuPré. The children are Charlie and Chelsea.' He paused, looking as if an unpleasant thought had just hit him. 'You guys aren't going to mess with the kids, right?'

Danny, Spud and Tyson gave him a steady look. None of them answered. Danny turned to Spike. He hadn't spoken since he'd been told he wasn't joining them. Like he was sulking. Well, he could sulk all he liked. Getting an explosive device on to the Cessna that evening wasn't going to be straightforward. Spike needed to get his part right, and that meant not rushing it. 'We'll be back by 1600 hours,' Danny said. 'Make sure you're ready by then.'

'And try not to blow the motel up, Spike, there's a good lad.' Spud winked at him. Spike simply glowered back.

Danny turned to the others. 'Let's move,' he said.

⋆   ⋆   ⋆

By 0630 hours Danny, Spud and Tyson all needed their sunglasses, and the aircon was on full. Danny drove along the highway at a steady 55 mph. He had memorised the directions to the suburb of San Antonio where they were heading, and the road was clear. But he counted three police cars in the first half hour of travel, and the last thing he wanted was to be pulled over for speeding. A call to their CIA handler would get them out of any kind of infringement, of course, but they couldn't afford a delay. The tape of Jesús talking to his junkie soccer mom had stipulated 'same time, same place', and as Kleinman had told them, that meant they had to be ready for their target at 1200 hours.

Not a problem. It was just shy of 1000 when their beaten-up but souped-up Tahoe drove down the road in which Claire DuPré's house was situated. They identified the house from its photo immediately. The two gently swaying palm trees. The RealGreen placard. No sign of the white Range Rover. Dany figured it was in the adjoining garage. They only drove past the house once – it was deeply engrained in Danny from more surveillance sessions than he could remember that repeated drive-pasts were a red light to anyone with eyes on. They pulled up fifty metres beyond the front yard. From here, they could watch the comings and goings in the house in the rear-view mirror. They were also close enough to get there fast.

'Reckon I'd top myself, if I lived here,' Spud said after they'd been sitting there for half an hour. Danny knew what he meant. The sky was a clear blue, the weather was warm, the houses were big and the parked cars were flash. But nothing was *happening* in this wide, perfect residential street. There were no pedestrians. No traffic. It was a ghost town.

The outside temperature rose. The inside of the Tahoe became an oven. Danny kept eyes on the DuPré residence in the rear-view mirror. It showed no signs of occupancy. Even the wooden shutters were closed, both on the ground floor and the first floor. At 1130 hours, they switched on their radio packs and inserted their covert earpieces. Silence, except for the occasional sound of an interior door opening and closing. Danny had an image of Claire DuPré pacing the rooms of her house, waiting for her visitor.

Their target arrived at 1155 hours. Danny didn't need to see his face to realise it was him. A gleaming black Range Rover stormed up the road, music pumping through its windows. As it sped past the unit's Tahoe, Danny got a glimpse of a young man with a black and white bandana tight round his forehead. The wheels of his vehicle screeched slightly as he came to a clumsy halt outside the DuPré house. The music died. He slammed the driver's door hard as he exited the vehicle and swaggered across the immaculate front lawn, holding a brown envelope in his hands.

'What a cunt,' Spud said.

'Hundred carat,' Danny agreed.

'A hundred carat cunt,' Spud grinned. 'Imagine that.'

Danny smiled. Tyson didn't. 'He's got a weapon,' Tyson said, eyeing the target in the Tahoe's side mirror, 'tucked into the back of his jeans, under his baseball top.'

'Got it,' Danny agreed.

As their target rang the bell, they heard the noise in their earpieces. The front door opened almost immediately. The target entered the DuPré house, and they heard the door closing. The conversation inside the house was relayed into their earpieces.

— *The fuck you wearing? I thought I told you to raise your game.*

— *I . . . I thought you'd like this.*

— *You thought wrong. Maybe I'll take this shit somewhere else . . .*

— *No . . . no, I . . . come on, baby . . .*

'There was me thinking this was going to be one for the wank bank,' Spud said.

'When the time comes, I get to plug the fucker,' Tyson growled. All three men were removing their shirts to reveal their RealGreen tops.

'Join the queue,' Danny said. 'But no-one plugs anyone yet. We need to get Romeo back to the motel . . .'

By the sound of it, Romeo was getting busy. They heard a clattering sound over the radio, and a small whimper. It sounded as though their target was getting rough with Claire DuPré.

'Let's do it,' Danny said. He turned on the Tahoe's ignition and performed a U-turn so they were facing back toward the DuPré house. He approached it at a normal speed. No boy racer antics, for two reasons. It kept him in control of the vehicle, and it stopped them drawing attention to themselves. They pulled up outside the house. 'Positions,' Danny said.

Each man reached under his shirt, removed their weapon from their holster, cocked them and locked them, then stowed them down the back of their trousers, just as Jesús had done. They exited the car. Spud took up position at the front edge of the lawn. He bent down, as though examining the grass. Tyson walked up to the black Range Rover. If their target tried to run, there was a high likelihood he would try to get to his vehicle. With Tyson standing between him and it, that wouldn't be straightforward.

Danny approached the door. In his earpiece he heard porno sounds. Claire DuPré was obviously putting on a show for her dealer.

He rang the doorbell.

The porno sounds stopped.

— *Fucking leave it.*

— *What if it's my . . . You have to hide . . .*

She sounded terrified.

— *I ain't hiding,* puta.

Danny rang the bell again, twice in quick succession. There was a pause of twenty seconds. From the corner of his eye, Danny saw the shutter of the room adjacent to where he was standing flick open.

— *It's the lawn people.*

The relief in her voice was clear.

— *The what? What the fuck's the lawn people?*

— *They look after . . . It doesn't matter . . . I'll get rid of them . . . they're not supposed to come today . . . I'll get rid of them now . . .*

— *Do it quickly.*

A hard arrest needed to be just that. Hard. Danny listened carefully for footsteps on the other side of the door. When he heard them, close, he pulled his weapon out of his jeans and unlocked the safety.

Claire DuPré was talking even before she opened the door. Danny heard her voice additionally in his earpiece. It was reedy and trembling. 'We didn't call you,' she said. 'It's not convenient today, you'll have to come back another . . .'

As she spoke, she opened the door.

Danny didn't hesitate for a second. In one movement he thrust the door open as hard as he could, removing the handgun from the back of his jeans. He burst into the house. Their target was sitting on an upholstered chaise longue at the far side of the large entrance hall. Distance ten metres. His trousers and underwear were round his ankles. His firearm was lying by his feet on the marble floor. Danny immediately identified it as a Glock 43 9mm semi-automatic. The brown envelope he'd been carrying was resting next to him. For a few precious seconds he seemed more concerned about pulling his baggy baseball top over his dick than defending himself. Danny used that time to rush toward him, his weapon firmly fixed at his target's chest. He'd covered half the distance by the time the target seemed to understand what was happening. He forgot about his modesty and suddenly reached down for his own weapon.

Too late.

Danny was there. He didn't want to lay down a round if he didn't have to, so he used his advantage of height to kick the base of his heavy boot flat into his target's face. There was a snap as the nose broke. The target slammed violently back on the chaise longue and cracked his head against the wall. Blood streamed down his face. Danny kicked his firearm backwards. It slid across the shiny floor. He glanced over his shoulder. Spud and Tyson were there. Tyson had grabbed the woman and slammed one hand over her mouth to stop her making a noise. She was semi-naked, dressed only in black underwear and a negligee. Her eyes were wide and terrified. Spud closed the door quietly, then reached into his rucksack as he hurried toward Danny and the target.

Danny grabbed the target by his neck. He forcefully pulled

him up, then threw him face down on to the ground and pulled his arms behind his back. Spud handed him a sturdy plastic cable tie, which Danny used to bind the target's wrists. The target shouted something in Spanish. Danny wasn't having it. He thumped the back of his target's head so his bleeding face slammed against the hard marble floor. That shut him up. He rolled him on to his back, removed the bandana he was wearing round his forehead, scrunched it up into a ball and forced it hard into the target's mouth. While he did this, Spud was binding his ankles with another cable tie. The target's trousers were still down, his dick still exposed. 'I'd heard Mexicans were hung like a fucking cocktail sausage,' Spud said. 'Turns out it's true, huh?'

'Give me the hood,' Danny said. Spud reached into his bag and pulled out a black hood with a drawstring at the hem. The target started shaking his head and making frightened, strangled noises. Danny ignored that as he pulled the hood over his head and tightened the drawstring so it wouldn't fall off. Danny decided to leave his trousers down. A bit of humiliation went a long way in keeping a prisoner compliant.

He and Spud stood up. Spud went to reclaim the target's weapon, which he immediately made safe before removing the magazine. Danny strode up to where Tyson was restraining the woman by the door, his hand still over her mouth. She wasn't struggling. She was completely paralysed with fear.

'Listen carefully,' Danny said. 'That man is a known drug dealer. We have photographic evidence and audio recordings of your meetings with him. If you mention a single word of what's happened today, that evidence gets handed directly to your husband Donald, your son Charlie and your daughter Chelsea. Got it?'

She nodded vigorously.

Tyson removed his hand from over her mouth. She instantly dissolved into great racking sobs, hiding her face in her hands. The target was squirming on the floor, unable to stand up, squeaking with terror. Danny turned to Spud. 'Open up the garage,' he said. And to Tyson: 'Move the vehicles. Back the Tahoe up to the garage door. We'll load him into the trunk from there.'

His unit mates nodded. Tyson exited from the front, shutting the door behind him. Danny heard him whistling as he walked away from the house. Spud left the entrance hall in the direction of the adjoining garage. Danny made to follow him. He walked over to the target and his eyes fell on the brown envelope which had fallen to the floor in front of the chaise longue. He grabbed it, then leant down to lift up the target and put him over his shoulder.

'Wait!'

The woman was still standing by the door. She looked ghoulish. Her eye make-up was streaming down her cheeks. Her skin was white.

'The . . . the package. It's mine. Give it to me.'

Danny looked inside the envelope. It contained three ziplock bags, each with a quantity of white powder with a faint brown tinge. Danny felt a surge of distaste as he remembered Kyle's disgusting apartment. It sickened him that, despite everything, this woman – abused, humiliated and desperate – was still thinking of nothing but her next hit. He wanted to take the poison away with him, for her own good.

But that wasn't the right operational call. If she was desperate for her junk, Claire DuPré could make things difficult for the unit. Start screaming. Run out the house semi-naked, trying to grab her drugs.

No. The right call was to give her the package. Let her disappear quietly upstairs.

He threw the package across the marble floor. It slid toward her. She stumbled toward it, a horrible hunger in her eyes. Bent down to grab it. With a final, animal-like glance at Danny, she scurried through a door on the far side of the room.

Danny heard the sound of the Tahoe reversing up the drive toward the garage door. He bent down and felt inside the pocket of the target's rolled-down jeans. His car keys were there. Danny took them. He grabbed their wriggling target and put him over his shoulder, fireman's lift-style. 'Alright, Jesús,' he said. 'Piss yourself and I'll cut your dick off. There'll be no second coming for you.' The target wriggled some more, trying to escape from his ignominious position. But he wasn't going anywhere. Danny followed Spud's route out of the entrance hall. He carried the target through an immaculate, expensive kitchen, on the far side of which was a door leading directly to the adjoining garage. A white Range Rover was parked in here – Danny recognised it from the photographs of the house – and Spud raised the up-and-over garage door. Tyson reversed the black Tahoe up to it and was now opening the trunk. Danny kept back for a minute while Spud checked nobody was watching from the street. He gave Danny the nod. Danny carried the target up to the open trunk. The cargo unit was open. Danny forced his prisoner inside. He wriggled and squealed more than usual. Tyson leant in. When he straightened up again, he had Jesús's wallet. As Danny shut the cargo unit, and the prisoner's squeals became muffled as he locked it and then closed the trunk, Tyson rifled through the wallet, pulling out a thick wodge of American dollars. 'Finders keepers,' he muttered.

'Let's get out of here,' Danny said. He handed Spud the target's car keys. 'Follow us. We'll find a parking lot to dump his vehicle in.'

Tyson took the wheel of the Tahoe. He edged it forward so they could close the garage door. As Danny approached the passenger seat, he saw a neighbour on the far side of the road, watching them. He gave her a wave and a bright smile. The neighbour didn't return it, but walked on, seemingly unsuspicious. Why would she be? They were just three regular lawn guys, loading up.

As they drove down the driveway, Danny could vaguely hear the target bumping around in the back. Experience told him he would quieten down within about ten minutes.

If he didn't? That was his problem.

They indicated left. Danny looked back toward the house. He wasn't certain, but he thought he saw the figure of Claire DuPré at the half-open shutters, her gaunt, ghostly face looking out. As they drove away, he had the impression that she collapsed where she stood.

In a tiny part of his mind he wondered if he shouldn't have handed over the junk. But he soon rid himself of that thought. He wasn't a social worker. He was a soldier, and he had a job to do.

They dumped the target's vehicle in a Walmart parking lot twenty minutes from the DuPré house, knowing it would likely be a couple of days minimum before anyone reported it as abandoned. They were back at the motel at 1530 hours. The Texan sun was oppressively hot. That played to their advantage. Nobody would venture outside in this kind of heat unless they had to. The lot in front of the motel was as deserted as it was the previous night. They could transfer their prisoner without worrying about anybody seeing.

Kleinman was waiting for them in the scant shade cast by the motel's frontage, sparking his lighter as usual, though he still didn't have a cigarette. They hadn't been in touch. Danny simply assumed their vehicle was fitted with a tracking device, so he knew to expect them. As they approached the building, the CIA man opened the door of the bedroom at the far end of the strip. Tyson pulled up outside it with the car facing away from the motel. The unit got out of the vehicle. Danny opened the trunk. As he predicted, the target had fallen silent shortly after leaving San Antonio. When Danny unlocked the cargo unit, and the light flooded in, he started wriggling and squealing again. He sounded even more frightened this time. It crossed Danny's mind that he possibly thought he'd been picked up by a rival cartel. In which case, he'd be expecting the same treatment he'd dished out himself. Danny saw no immediate need to tell him any different. Let the fucker sweat it out for a bit.

Danny took his arms, Spud took his feet. They manoeuvred him into the bedroom where Kleinman was waiting for them, an enquiring look on his face. 'In the tub,' Danny said. They moved him into the bathroom and dumped their bound, hooded, wriggling target into the bath.

'You sure you got the right guy?' Kleinman said critically. 'Doesn't look like a Zeta hitman to me.'

'Don't expect them all to be like that, kiddos,' said Tyson, who had appeared in the doorway. 'My guess is this fella's pretty low down the food chain. When the big boys come out to play, things'll get tougher.'

They moved out into the bedroom. 'We'll question him about the location of the tunnel tomorrow, once he's had chance to get a bit more fucked up in the head,' Danny said. 'Someone needs to watch him while we're on the job tonight.'

'Rav and Michael can do a rota,' Kleinman said.

He left them for a moment, then returned with Hernandez who, as usual, barely made eye contact with the unit, let alone spoke to them. He appeared less than thrilled to be on guard duty.

'Our guy stays in the tub,' Danny said. 'If he needs to piss or shit, he does it there. Keep the hood on, keep the wrists and legs strapped. Don't let him out for any reason. If he starts to make a fuss, whack him over the head. If he starts to fall asleep, spray him with a cold shower. I want him sleep-deprived when the time comes to question him. Got it?'

Hernandez inclined his head and disappeared into the bathroom.

'Where's Spike?' Danny asked.

'In the ops room with Rav,' Kleinman said. He led them from the bedroom, locking the door on the outside. They followed their limping CIA contact to the other end of the motel. Rav was sitting at the desk, headset on, staring at his computer screen. He barely looked up as the unit entered. The adjoining door to the weapons room was open. Spike was in that room, surrounded by their miniature arsenal. He'd set up a small table in the middle of the room. There was a reading lamp shining down on the table, on which was resting a soldering iron, a roll of solder, some small screwdrivers and a magnifying glass. And additionally, the fruit of Spike's morning's work.

He had constructed a neat little package. It comprised an old-fashioned flip-to-open cell phone handset. The front casing was removed to reveal the guts of the phone. Two wires were soldered into the circuitry. They were connected to a small detonator, whose prongs were inserted into a four-inch stick of C4 military-grade explosive. A simple but effective device. A call to the cell phone would activate the detonator, and that small stick of explosive was easily enough to bring down a light aircraft like the Cessna.

Spud eyed the device a bit nervously. 'No chance of anyone dialling that mobile number by mistake, mucker?'

'It's switched off,' Spike said, without looking up. He sounded as resentful as he was that morning. 'Do you have to do that? It's getting on my tits.' Kleinman was sparking his lighter again, no cigarette in sight.

'Reformed smoker,' Kleinman said. 'What can I tell you? It keeps my hands busy.' He carried on sparking.

Danny approached the table. 'What's all this?' he asked. In one corner was the guts of a second cell phone. The battery was removed and the circuit board was snapped in two.

'Failsafe . . .' Spike said curtly.

'What do you mean?' Tyson asked. He looked very interested.

Finally Spike looked up. 'It's a break phone,' he said. 'A simple way of making the call that activates the detonator less easy to trace. I've set up call forwarding from the smashed-up phone to the detonator phone. When we want to activate the detonator phone, we call the number of the smashed-up phone. It forwards the call, and anyone trying to trace the call that caused the explosion will think this phone made it . . .' He prodded the broken circuit board. 'Not the phone that made the original call.'

Spud grinned. 'On it like a car bonnet,' he announced to nobody in particular. 'I told you he was a genius. Fucking psycho, but a genius.'

'Kids and technology,' Tyson said, earning himself a dark look from Spike as he produced the emergency first aid pouch that he'd asked Kleinman to supply. It was made of a black canvas material, no bigger than a hardback book and perhaps two inches thick. It had the words *First Aid* written on the front in big white letters, and a zip to open it. Spike unfastened the zip and carefully slid the explosive device into the pouch. 'We need to get it under the pilot's seat,' he said. 'If anybody finds it, they'll just assume it's part of the aircraft's regular ...' His sentence trailed off into nothing.

'Are you sure there's cell phone service on the Cessna's expected flight path?' Danny said.

Spike nodded. 'Rav checked. So long as the aircraft flies below radar height, which we know it does, it'll be ...'

'Good work,' Danny said. He turned to Kleinman. 'Have you finalised the border crossing for tonight?'

'It's all in hand, boy. I just need to know which of you is crossing over into Mexico.'

'Spud and Tyson. Spike and me will infiltrate the airfield, get the IED on the Cessna before it flies.'

Kleinman removed his glasses and started cleaning them on his sleeve. 'Good,' he said. 'I have to say, gentlemen, so far I'm pleasantly surprised. I wasn't thrilled at the idea of using a British team for a job this delicate. I'm pleased to say you're proving me wrong. I hope it continues.'

As he said it, he couldn't stop his eyes flickering at Spike. Spike jutted his chin out, and looked as if he was about to say something. He didn't get the chance. 'You're going to need precise timings and locations for this evening's operation,' Kleinman said. 'And I'll need to talk you through the plan for the border crossing. Rav'll get us some food. We'll eat while we talk.'

He limped back into the ops room. The unit followed.

TEN

Docklands, London.
0037 hours GMT.

Delta Team call sign Yankee Bravo Nine had arrived at RAF Northolt with nothing but the clothes they were wearing and a fresh set of civvies. A driver affiliated to the American Embassy in London had met them and delivered them promptly to their safe house: a penthouse apartment in the Docklands region of east London. Nobody was waiting for them here, but there was a full complement of all the military hardware they could possibly require. Rifles. Handguns. Ammunition. Body armour. Night sights. Comms equipment. Med packs. Everything discreetly delivered by somebody whose face they knew they would never see.

It meant they could get to work immediately.

And that was a good thing, Tam Garrick thought to himself. Because the sooner they completed their op, the sooner they could get the hell out of London.

Tam had *never* liked London. Operating in London was like operating in a grey box.

And the food. *Jesus*, the food.

Bumping into SAS man Jack 'Tyson' Fletcher hadn't helped things. There was something about that guy Tam didn't trust. Tam knew a bit about him. How he'd been stationed out in Mexico back in the day. It wouldn't surprise him if that was where he and his SAS unit were heading back to now. But Tyson also had a bit of a reputation out in Afghanistan. Rumours going round that he was on the take from some of the elders who had a financial

111

interest in the Taliban's heroin operations. And when he'd tried to pump them for information back at the RAF base, the rest of Tam's team – Brooks, Webb and Dixon – instantly took the same view. They were pissed enough at having to engage in low-level operations in the UK. Being touched up for info by a questionable Regiment dude hadn't helped matters.

Yeah. Sooner they could get this op squared away, the better.

Which was why they now found themselves on the southern bank of the Thames. To their left, the Queen Elizabeth Bridge glowed in the twilight, its lanes rammed with lines of white headlamps and red brake lights. The river was busy too. Several freight ships were heading into the docks, but there were pleasure boats and police vessels also moving in both directions. Cranes towered above the water and even now, at this late hour, one of them was lifting metal storage containers the size of a semi-trailer off the deck of a grimy-looking merchant vessel. This dock was a 24-hour operation.

The Delta unit were on the fringes of a storage area. Here, approximately fifty of these vast metal containers were lined up, ready to be winched on to lorries for the next part of their journey. Security was moderate. The storage area that housed the containers was about a hundred metres by fifty, protected on three sides by a high mesh fence and on the fourth by the river itself. There was a wide entrance on the near side of the fence, with a vehicle barrier, a small security hut and several guys milling around smoking. It would be difficult to gain covert access to the storage area, but not impossible. They could make a waterborne entrance from the river. They could find an area of fence to cut through. Chances were they could even talk their way through the security barrier. Tam decided, however, that none of these options was necessary. They could watch from outside the fence. He left Brooks and Dixon in their vehicle on the main road just opposite the security entrance – their disabled parking badge meant they wouldn't get moved on by the police. Webb was watching the storage area through the fence on the eastern side. Tam himself had walked west. From here he could see the security entrance a hundred metres away, and had a good view of most of the storage containers, carefully stacked and laid out.

The intel they'd been given was very clear. A delivery vehicle would be picking up from this location between midnight and 0100 hours. Tam was calculating that, this being an unpopular time for some fat-ass delivery driver to make their pick-up, it would be straightforward to identify their target.

So far, so good.

It was 0037 hours. An unmarked white Transit had just pulled up at the security entrance. Tam was immediately suspicious of it – not just because of the late hour, or because it arrived in the time window they'd been told to expect. It took a semi-trailer, or what the Brits called an articulated lorry, to move these storage containers wholesale. A van like that could only be collecting individual items from one of the containers. Not a smoking gun in itself, but enough for Tam to pay some attention to this new arrival.

'You watching?' he said into his radio mike.

'*You bet,*' came Webb's reply through his covert earpiece.

The van sat at the security entrance for thirty seconds. The barrier raised and it moved inside the perimeter. The driver seemed to know where he was going. The van curled round toward the eastern side of the storage area. Tam lost eye contact. 'You still have it?'

'*Roger that.*'

Tam started walking briskly around the perimeter toward the security entrance, his hands plunged into the pockets of his heavy coat, which completely camouflaged his fully loaded ops vest. His fingers touched a metal object about the size and weight of a Zippo lighter. He affected a slight stagger.

Distance to the entrance: fifty metres. Webb's voice crackled in his ear. '*I've lost visuals. The vehicle's pulled up at the end of one of the storage containers. I can only see its nose. Two guys exiting. I think they're loading something up into the back.*'

Tam slowed his pace to more of a shuffle. He wanted to arrive at the security entrance at the same time the vehicle left. He stopped to light a cigarette that he would never smoke but which bought him a bit of time and made him a little less noticeable.

Just a liquored-up black dude, staggering around.

Three minutes passed.

Four.

'*Target's on the move,*' said the voice in his ear.

Tam increased his pace. In his peripheral vision he saw the vehicle heading back toward the security entrance. Distance: ten metres. The barrier was already open. The Transit vehicle was accelerating toward it. Tam was on a collision course.

Ten metres.

Five.

The vehicle passed the barrier. Tam stepped out into the road in front of it.

The driver hit the brakes heavily. The van screeched to a halt barely a metre from where Tam was staggering in the road. He stumbled and fell, entirely on purpose, hitting the ground just shy of the vehicle's wheel arch. He heard the driver's door open and pulled the metal object out of his pocket. It was heavily magnetic. Tam stuck it quickly on the underside of the wheel arch. Then he started shouting at the top of his voice, slurring with a passable British accent. 'You fucking idiots! Look where you're fucking going!'

He scrambled to his feet and staggered around in the glare of the vehicle's headlamp. Two burly guys in leather jackets – they almost looked like twins with their shaved heads and flat noses – emerged from the vehicle. One of them grabbed Tam by his coat collar and pushed him heavily back on to the pavement.

'Take your hands off me!' Tam screamed at them as he fell heavily against the perimeter fence of the storage area.

'Stupid fucking spade,' the driver of the vehicle growled at him. 'Wish I'd fucking hit you now. One less to worry about. Why don't you fuck off back to Bongo-bongo land.' He and his companion climbed back into the vehicle. Both guys slammed their doors shut. The vehicle screeched away.

'*Nicely done,*' came Webb's voice over Tam's earpiece.

Dead-eyed, Tam watched the Transit disappear into the traffic. 'We tracking those motherfuckers?' he said.

'*Sure are, bud,*' said Brooks from the unit vehicle. '*Sure are.*'

Back in the Delta unit's armoured vehicle, Tam sat in the passenger seat. Brooks was driving, Webb and Dixon sat in the back. Their GPS tracking screen was fitted to the dashboard, and they were following the Transit at a distance of about half a mile through areas of London he'd never heard of before. Woolwich. Bexleyheath. Swanley.

'Makes Al-Anbar look like Fifth fuckin' Avenue,' Webb drawled in the back.

They crossed over the M25 and, ten minutes later, found themselves driving down a quiet, dark country lane. A heavy mist had descended. Trees on either side. No other vehicles on the road. Not this time of night. It was a good location for what they had to do.

'Hit the gas,' Tam told Brooks.

Brooks accelerated from fifty to seventy. The GPS screen told Tam the gap between them and the target vehicle was closing. A minute later, the red tail lights appeared briefly on the road ahead, before disappearing round a bend. They kept their speed up. When the road straightened out and the tail lights appeared again, Tam estimated a gap of fifty metres. They closed it down in twenty seconds and were almost bumper to bumper before the Delta vehicle swung out and overtook. The white Transit sounded its horn as Brooks took the middle of the road and started to bully the Transit into slowing down. In his wing mirror Tam saw the vehicle trying to overtake, but the road was too narrow and Brooks was too good a military driver to allow that to happen. Gradually both vehicles came to a halt. As it did so, he was aware of Webb and Dixon in the back winding down their windows.

There was no need for Tam to issue instructions. This was a parade-ground manoeuvre. The Delta unit knew the importance of hitting hard and fast. The drivers of the Transit could be armed. It was imperative they be neutralised before they could do the unit any harm. Tam unholstered his side arm and waited for Webb, who was sitting directly behind him, to open his door. Only then did he exit the vehicle. From behind the protection of the door, he aimed his weapon through the open window and, with two precise shots, took out the headlamps of the Transit. He directed a third shot to the top middle of the van's windscreen. A spider's web splintered across the entire sheet of glass, to serve two purposes: to obscure the view of the driver and his passenger, and to properly put the shits up them. Tam guessed they were probably cringing behind the dash about now.

'Go!' he shouted.

Webb and Dixon moved from their back seat positions and sprinted to either side of the Transit van. In a couple of seconds they had opened up the doors and were now dragging the driver and passenger out of their seats. Tam heard the thud as they landed heavily on the road. Webb and Dixon started screaming at them. 'Get your hands behind your backs. Hands behind your fucking backs, assholes!' In just a few more seconds their wrists were tightly bound with cable ties. Webb and Dixon dragged them up to their feet and hustled them roughly to the side of the road.

'Get them behind the tree line!' Tam barked. 'We'll sort the vehicles.'

There was the sound of muffled scuffling as Webb and Dixon moved the prisoners away from the road. Tam slammed the doors of the unit vehicle shut. Brooks pulled over onto the left-hand side of the road. Tam himself jumped behind the wheel of the Transit van. The engine was still turning over. He knocked it into reverse and, using the wing mirrors and the red glow of the tail lights, quickly backed up into a gap in the trees beyond the verge. He stopped about fifteen metres beyond the tree line, killed the engine and jumped out. There was a thick blanket of mist swirling on the forest floor. He was aware of Webb and Dixon about fifteen metres away into the woodland, and knew he could trust them to keep the two prisoners quiet and compliant. Brooks joined him. Wordlessly, they moved to the rear of the Transit and opened up the back doors. Both men were carrying pencil-thin black flashlights. They shone them into the van.

'Mattresses,' Brooks said.

Sure enough, their torch beams fell on eight mattresses, stacked on their sides. They looked new – wrapped in clear plastic.

'Like hell,' Tam said. He jumped up into the back of the van and pulled a black-handled utility knife from his ops vest. He selected a mattress at random. Holding his torch between his teeth, he cut open the plastic wrapper. Then, with one deft slice, he cut into the mattress itself. He was aware of Brooks looking over his shoulder as he parted both sides of the opening.

'Last time I did that,' Brooks said, 'she was wetter than an otter's pocket.'

Tam ignored the comment. There was foam stuffing inside the mattress. But he didn't have to pull out too many handfuls to get to what it was really concealing. A moment later, he pulled something out. He held it up to show Brooks. 'I'm thinking this won't give you the most comfortable night's sleep,' he said.

It was a set of military-grade night-vision goggles. Top of the range: a Kevlar helmet fitted with four NV tubes that would give full peripheral vision. Tam estimated he was holding seventy-five thousand dollars' worth of kit in that helmet alone.

'Let's go talk to our boys,' he said.

They jumped down from the van, slammed the doors shut and hurried round to where Webb and Dixon were standing over the two prisoners. Tam shone his flashlight directly into their faces. They winced from the fierce beam. Tam selected the driver who, just an hour ago, had hurled abuse at him and pushed him against the perimeter fence of the storage area. He was cheek-down against the ground. Tam caught a whiff of urine. He knelt down beside him, keeping the flashlight beam shining directly in his eyes. He rested the butt of his handgun against the man's head.

'You want to know what kind of weapon I've got pressing into your skull right now?'

The guy didn't reply.

'It's a Heckler and Koch HK45,' Tam told him. 'Compact, but hard-hitting. If I release a round now, it's going to go straight through your head and several inches into the ground. It's your call, asshole, but my advice is to answer my questions.'

'Who are you?' the guy breathed.

Tam knew he shouldn't really answer, but it didn't much matter. This guy wasn't going to see sunrise. 'Ah, you know,' he said. 'Just some stupid fucking spade on his way back to Bongo-bongo land.'

'Jesus . . .' the guy gibbered. 'Mate, I'm sorry . . . I didn't mean nothing by it . . . I didn't think you was a Yank . . .'

'I've heard worse from five-year-olds, asshole. You think I give a baker's fuck what a low-life like *you* thinks?'

The guy shook his head.

'What have you got in the back of the van?'

'M . . . mattresses. That's all, just mattresses.'

'And in the mattresses?'

'I don't know. They didn't tell me. I just had to pick them up.'

Tam considered that for a moment. Was he telling the truth? Maybe. Maybe not.

'Let me enlighten you,' he said. 'Those mattresses are stuffed with high-grade military equipment. That shipping container you took them out of was last registered on the east African coast. Know where east Africa is, asshole?'

The guy nodded again, desperately.

'Good,' Tam said. 'Now we're getting somewhere. You know where this military equipment is *headed*?'

A terrified shake of the head.

'To terrorist cells in the United States. That's where we come in, asshole. Do you know what guys like us do to guys like you who help terrorists on US soil?'

Another shake of the head.

'Oh,' Tam said, affecting a note of disappointment. 'Well, let me show you, huh?' He looked toward Webb and Brooks. 'Pull him up,' he instructed. His team mates grabbed one arm each and yanked the guy to his feet. Tam moved over to where the second guy was lying face down on the ground, with Dixon standing over him. He extended his right arm and pointed both his weapon and his flashlight at the man's head. Then he fired.

The suppressed round made a knocking sound as it left the barrel. It slammed into the target's skull. The flashlight illuminated the pink mist as a cloud of blood, bone and brain matter exploded on to the surrounding ground. It was immediately accompanied by the sound of retching from the driver, a couple of metres behind Tam.

Tam turned to face him again, once more shining his torch directly into his eyes.

'I've got good news. I don't believe for a single second that a dumbass like you is the brains behind a major weapons-smuggling operation. That's good news isn't it, asshole?'

The guy retched again.

'So all you got to do is tell me,' Tam continued in a deathly quiet voice, 'who you're working for.'

The driver could barely stand up. His knees kept going. He had vomit down his front and over his chin. He tried to say something, but couldn't get the words out.

Tam stepped closer to him. Made sure he could see the barrel of the handgun through the glare of the flashlight beam.

'I can't hear you, shit-for-brains,' he said in a sing-song voice. 'Who ... are ... you ... working ... for?'

'B ... Bailey ...' the driver stammered. 'Aiden Bailey.'

Tam smiled. 'There,' he said. 'That wasn't so hard, now was it?'

He lowered the flashlight and the weapon. Then he nodded at Dixon.

'You want to do him, bro?' Dixon said. 'After that shit he said?'

But Tam didn't care about that stuff. He turned his back on the driver and, as he walked back toward the white Transit, heard two sounds: the thump of Dixon throwing the driver back down to the ground, and the brutal knock of a suppressed weapon delivering a round to his head.

A thick, impenetrable silence fell over the forest. The guys went about their work silently. Dixon and Brooks carried the corpses of the two men back to the white Transit. Stuffed them into the back alongside the mattresses full of military gear. Tam and Webb went to their unit vehicle and recovered a couple of full jerrycans. They carried them back to the white Transit and soaked the bodies and the mattresses with gasoline. Once the cans were empty, Dixon placed a small remote detonator in the van. There could be military-grade explosives in there, so they needed to put some distance between them and it before igniting the fuel. They hurried back to their unit vehicle and retook their seats. Brooks pulled out into the road and hit the gas. They put two hundred metres between them and the white Transit before Tam gave the instruction: 'Blow it.'

Dixon clicked the detonator. In the rear-view mirror, Tam saw a sudden glow above the tree line. But no sound.

He pulled out his encrypted sat phone. Dialled a number. A featureless male voice answered immediately. '*State your identity.*'

'This is Yankee Bravo Nine,' Tam said. 'We have a name.'

'*Go ahead.*'

'Aiden Bailey. Alpha, India, Delta, Alpha, November. Bravo, Alpha, Indigo, Leo, Echo, Yankee.'

'*Copy that.*'

'Requesting all intelligence on his current location,' Tam said.

'*Understood*,' said the voice. '*Wait out. We'll find him.*'

The line went dead.

ELEVEN

2300 hours.

The unit was preparing to split up.

Danny and Spike were heading to the airfield from which the Cessna was expected to fly. Spud and Tyson were heading over the border. They were to dig in near the aircraft's landing strip and, when they could see the aircraft coming in to land, give the order to detonate Spike's IED. Once they'd confirmed the aircraft had gone down, they could bug out.

All in a night's work.

Before leaving, Danny checked in on their Zeta prisoner. He was still huddled in the bath, arms and legs bound. He had soiled himself – there was urine and runny faeces in the bathtub, and a terrible stench in the room. Hernandez was sitting on the toilet seat, flicking through his phone. He gave Danny a sour look as he entered. At the same time, the target started making a frightened, squealing noise. He was obviously scared what the arrival of someone in the room might mean. Danny removed his side arm from his body holster, held it by the barrel and cracked the handle down on the prisoner's hooded skull. That shut him up.

Back outside, the others were waiting. Spud and Tyson were wearing sets of the hardwearing work clothes Kleinman had supplied. Sturdy boots. Body armour. They were stashing their rifles and military Bergens into the trunk of the Tahoe that had Mexican plates. The Bergens each had two empty water canteens in the side pockets. Kleinman was going over some last-minute details. 'You have the coordinates of the RV point. It's only forty-five minutes from here. The border control guys will meet you at . . .'

'They'll meet us at 0015 hours,' Spud said. 'Yeah, we got it, buddy.' He looked over at Tyson. 'Ready to get wet, brother?'

Tyson nodded. 'Laters masturbators,' he said. He winked at Spike like a patronising uncle, then gave Danny a slightly unfriendly nod. They climbed into the vehicle and drove off.

Spike, like Danny, was dressed in the blue mechanic's overalls that Kleinman had given them. They were artfully spotted with oil and smelled of sweat and turpentine. The only difference between these and a regular pair of overalls was the tear in the side pocket, which allowed them access to their side arms. Each man had a covert radio earpiece, and a chest mike hidden under their overalls. Like Spud and Tyson, they had stashed their longs in the trunk of their vehicle. With luck they wouldn't need them, but Danny wasn't prepared to rely on luck alone.

'IED?' Danny checked with Spike.

Spike held up the old rucksack he was carrying.

'Then let's go,' Danny said. He looked at Kleinman. 'We'll RV back here at 0400 hours.'

'Sure,' Kleinman said. 'All things being equal.'

'What's that supposed to mean?'

'Nothing,' Kleinman said mildly. He turned his back on them and walked back toward the ops room. Danny could hear the sound of him sparking his lighter.

'What is it with that guy?' Spike said. 'It's like he doesn't think we know what we're . . .'

'It's just a Yank–Brit thing,' Danny said. 'You get used to it.' But he followed Kleinman with his eyes. There was something about the guy that grated. Maybe it was just that he was a spook. Danny didn't have a great track record with spooks. He turned back to Spike. 'I'll drive, you navigate,' he said.

The directions Kleinman had given them soon took Danny and Spike away from the built-up area around the outskirts of Laredo and into the bleak, baked Texan desert. Their faces glowed dimly in the light from the dashboard, and the landscape to the side of the road passed by in a blur. Danny kept his eyes on the road and in the rear-view mirror, but was aware of Spike giving him the occasional, apprehensive look. Once or twice Spike almost spoke, but then seemed to think better of it.

'Spit it out,' Danny said.

There was a pause. Spike looked down at his map. 'The road forks to the left in about a mile,' he said. A redundant instruction, because Danny had memorised their route.

'You're still pissed off,' Danny said, 'because I told you to stay at the motel instead of coming to pick up our Zeta boy?'

No reply.

'Get over it,' Danny said. He had no time to mollycoddle a sensitive unit member. 'If anyone else was i/c the package for the Cessna, they'd have stayed back to sort it too. You're a good soldier. I can tell that.'

Spike nodded. 'How long have you known Spud?' he said.

'Long enough.'

'He talks about you a lot.'

'We've *been* through a lot.'

'Is he your best friend?' It was a strangely childish question.

'Sure,' Danny said gruffly. 'If you want to call it that.' Truth was, 'best friend' didn't come close. But it was impossible to explain.

Again, Spike looked like he was going to say something. But he didn't. Just looked out the passenger window for a few seconds, then back to his map.

Estimated journey time to the airfield: thirty minutes. They made it in twenty-five. 'It's over the brow of that hill,' Spike said, pointing to a hill about half a mile distant. Danny hit the brakes. SOPs dictated they should cover the remaining ground on foot. He killed the headlamps and made a quick three-point turn so the vehicle was pointing in the right direction if they had to extract quickly. Then he pulled over to the side of the road. He and Spike exited the vehicle. Danny removed his M16 from the trunk, double-checking the image-intensifying night-vision sight he'd fitted to it. Spike took his discreet IED, stashed into the patched-up old rucksack that suited his oil-spattered overalls.

They checked their covert radios were fully operational, then Danny secured the vehicle, slung his weapon over his shoulder and, together with Spike, ran the remaining half mile to the brow of the hill, hitting the ground and crawling as they came to the crest. Their destination lay on the desert plain ahead of them.

It was the third airfield Danny had seen in the past forty-eight hours, and by far the smallest. Distance: two hundred metres. There was a perimeter fence of sorts, but it might as well not have been there, since there were several gaps in it, large enough to drive a vehicle through. The road itself drove straight into the airfield. There was no checkpoint or reception area. There was a single-storey building on the western edge of the field, with a couple of refuelling vehicles and several regular cars parked outside. A hangar sat on the opposite, eastern side. Danny counted three light aircraft parked outside it. The runway itself ran through the centre of the airfield, north to south. It was poorly lit, at least in comparison to the military runways he was used to.

Spike had taken a night sight from somewhere about his person. He scanned the airfield for a minute. 'See those three light aircraft,' he breathed.

'Roger that.'

'Our Cessna is the one in the middle. I can read the registration . . .'

Danny picked it out. He estimated the aircraft were about thirty metres from each other, wing tip to wing tip.

'Any sign of personnel?'

'Not by the aircraft I can see. Three people having a smoke by the other building. All male.'

Danny squinted. He could make them out with the naked eye, but not clearly.

'How are they dressed?'

'Two of them in regular civvies. One in mechanic's overalls.'

Danny nodded. 'We'll watch for another five minutes,' he said. 'That'll give us a better idea of the probable movement of personnel.'

But if anything, the next five minutes suggested there would be even fewer problems approaching the Cessna than Danny had anticipated. The three guys loitering by the low building disappeared back inside. The only movement now was a night bird of some description that came to settle on the top of the hangar.

'Give me the sight,' Danny said when the five minutes were up.

Spike handed it over. Danny put it to his eye, but this time concentrated on the ground outside the perimeter fence of the airfield. The NV capability of the night sight lit it up clear and sharp, although with a faint green tinge. It was standard semi-arid terrain. Flat. Hard-baked. Patches of low scrub here and there. Nowhere particularly useful as an OP, with the exception of a gorse bush, perhaps a metre high and two metres wide, situated thirty metres from a gap in the perimeter fence on the eastern side of the airfield, just shy of the hangar. Danny pointed it out to Spike. 'I'll dig in there,' he said. 'I'll be able to cover you until you get past the first aircraft.'

'What if someone challenges me?'

'Front them up. Tell them you're there to check the landing gear on the Cessna.'

'If they don't believe . . .?'

Danny stopped himself from giving him an exhausted look. 'You'll come up with something. How long do you need to plant the device?'

'Just a few seconds,' Spike said. 'They never lock these planes. It's just a matter of putting it under the pilot's seat. I'll switch the detonator phone on before I make my approach . . .'

Danny nodded his approval. 'Let's move,' he said.

0010 hours.

Spud had his handgun on his lap. Cocked and locked. He knew this off-road border territory was potentially dangerous. He didn't need Tyson to tell him that. Not that it stopped him. 'It's mainly just poor Mexicans making illegal border entries,' Tyson said, two hands on the wheel, eyes on the road ahead. 'They cross the Rio

Grande on crappy little boats, or even try to swim across. But you can bet your boots there'll be narcos making the crossing too. Low-grade mules mostly. The bosses wouldn't risk anyone important. It's that lot you need to look out for, though. High, most of the time. Fucking unhinged.'

'Give that man a first-class degree in stating the bleedin' obvious,' Spud said.

'Fucking Kleinman. There's a perfectly good border crossing at Nuevo Laredo. I bet he doesn't get his arse wet wading across the fucking river every time he wants to get into Mexico.'

'If I had a limp like that,' Spud said, 'I'd stay clear of a deep puddle, forget about the Rio Grande.' He sniffed. 'There's something about that guy,' he muttered. He glanced at the GPS unit fitted to the dashboard. 'Two klicks on the right.'

'That Danny Black wanker likes the sound of his own voice, and all.' Tyson sniffed. 'You think he's up to unit command?'

Spud glanced at him. Truth was, Danny Black had saved his life more times than he could count. They were like brothers. 'Yeah,' he said. 'I do. Word of advice – if you're going to slag Danny off, do it on someone else's time, not mine.'

Tyson shrugged. 'Quite the bromance,' he said.

'And lay off Spike while you're at it. Keep talking to him like that, one day he's going to have a fucking pop at you. Wouldn't blame him, either.'

'Reckon I'll take my chances,' Tyson replied.

They fell into a momentary silence, then Spud said: 'There.'

Two hundred metres up ahead, parked on the side of the road, was a vehicle. Amber and red roof lights flashing silently. Tyson braked gradually and came to a halt right behind it. Spud holstered his weapon and exited the vehicle. It was a white off-roader, with a diagonal green stripe along the middle and the words *Border Control* clearly marked. The driver wound down his window as Spud walked up alongside it. Uniform. Hispanic features. Zero sign of friendliness. The smell of fast food emerged from inside the vehicle, and Spike could barely make out the driver's colleague in the passenger seat.

'I guess you're the package we've been waiting for,' the driver said.

'I guess we are,' Spud replied.

'Keep to our tail. We stop, you stop. You got that?'

'Doesn't sound too complicated.'

'We're going off-road. You'll need to drive carefully.'

'No shit, Sherlock.'

The driver gave him an unfriendly look, then wound up the window again. Spud returned to his seat just as the border control vehicle pulled out. 'He told us to drive carefully,' he said, removing his side arm from his holster and lying it on his back once more.

It wasn't a good night for covert manoeuvres, Danny decided. A half moon hung in the clear sky, providing enough light to cast a faint shadow on the dark ground. The stars swirled impressively. However, their brief surveillance of the airfield had not identified any dedicated security looking out into the desert. Moreover, any of the regular personnel on-site would be unlikely to see Danny and Spike approaching, since they would be looking out from an illuminated area, likely without the benefit of any spotting devices.

They crested the hill and jogged toward the bush Danny had identified. Distance: a hundred and fifty metres. They covered it in thirty seconds. They crouched down behind it, while Danny unstrapped his rifle and Spike removed the IED from his rucksack. Danny watched a little apprehensively as Spike powered up the cell-phone detonator. The four-inch stick of C4 to which it was fitted would be enough to take out anyone within a 30-metre radius. The cell-phone screen glowed in the darkness. Spike nodded with satisfaction, flipped the phone closed and replaced the device into the innocent-looking first aid pouch, which he then stashed back in the rucksack.

Danny lay on his front, the bush just to his right, his rifle on the ground ahead of him. He rested the end of the barrel on a small hinged bipod he'd taken from his pack, and put his eye to the image-intensifying NV sight. The delicate crosshairs were centred on the edge of the runway. He panned right. The three smokers were no longer outside. He panned left. A blur, then the sight settled on the nearest of the three planes: its white body appeared clear and sharp.

'Go,' he told Spike, without taking his eye from the sight.

He sensed Spike getting to his feet and heard his footsteps as he walked round Danny. His unit mate came into his field of view a second later, a hulking silhouette jogging toward the perimeter fence of the airfield, growing smaller as he approached it.

Silence.

Danny kept totally still, his eye to the sight, his finger to the trigger. He hoped there would be no need to use it.

Forty-five seconds passed. Spike arrived at a gap in the perimeter fence. He stopped momentarily. Danny allowed himself to pan left and right, checking for personnel. Nothing.

'Clear,' he said into his radio.

No reply, but Spike moved immediately across the line of the perimeter fence, toward the first of the three aircraft.

Danny panned left.

Clear.

Right.

Clear.

Left again.

He stopped.

Shit.

'Company to your ten o'clock,' he said.

A figure was emerging from the aircraft hangar. Danny had a direct line of sight toward him, through the gap in the fence. He was walking toward the first aircraft, just like Spike.

'Get down,' Danny hissed.

'*Too late,*' Spike breathed over the comms. '*He's seen me.*'

Danny followed the guy with his sights, the crosshairs directly covering his target's chest. He looked like a mechanic, dressed similarly to Spike. Distance between the two men: fifteen metres.

Danny heard the man's voice, muffled, over Spike's chest mike. '*Hey, pal, can I help you?*' A slow, suspicious Texan drawl.

Danny had to hand it to Spike. He was good. Didn't hesitate for a second. He managed to affect a slight American accent as he replied, '*Yeah, they asked me to check the landing gear on this* . . .'

The man was still walking toward Spike. Danny followed, his crosshairs not veering from the man's chest. But as he continued to approach Spike, Danny's line of sight was obscured by the perimeter fence. He could see through the wire, but there was no way he could guarantee a direct shot if he needed it.

'*What you talking about?*' The guy's voice was more challenging now. Aggressive. '*Who told you?*'

'*Barry. Barry Osmin, the pilot* . . .'

'*Yeah, well, it's the first I've heard of it. I'll call him now* . . .'

'Put him down,' Danny breathed.

It happened in under five seconds. Danny saw it all clearly through the night sight. The mechanic had put himself within a metre of Spike's reach. The young SAS soldier moved incredibly quickly. He grabbed the back of the mechanic's neck with his right hand, then made a spear out of the fingers of his left hand. He rammed those fingers, at an angle, just to the side of the mechanic's larynx. Hard. Sharp. A training-ground throat strike, perfectly and violently executed. Danny knew if the blow was hard enough, it would kill the mechanic in an instant. Slightly softer, and it would put him under for a good twenty minutes. He watched as Spike lowered the man's limp body to the ground, and he remembered how highly the guys in the training wing had spoken about Spike's skills in unarmed combat. They weren't wrong. He watched Spike bend down and check the pulse. '*He'll be okay,*' came the report over the comms.

The trouble with putting a guy down, though, is that sometimes it causes more problems than it solves. They couldn't leave an unconscious mechanic where he was likely to be found. Danny was already panning the area through his rifle sight, checking there were no more personnel in Spike's vicinity likely to have seen what had happened, or stumble across the mechanic while Spike did his job.

'The area's clear,' he said through the radio. 'Deliver your package, then get your man off-site.'

Spike didn't need telling twice. He left the mechanic on the ground and strode toward the Cessna. Danny lost sight of him as he walked around the far side of the aircraft, but over the radio he heard the Cessna door opening, then the sound of Spike scratching around as he placed the IED under the pilot's seat, then the door closing again. It had taken him no more than twenty seconds to plant the device. He reappeared in Danny's sights. Danny panned the area again.

'Clear.'

Spike walked back toward the position of the mechanic. He bent down, easily picked the guy up and slung him over his right shoulder. He jogged toward the perimeter fence while Danny continued his surveillance of the airfield. As Spike cleared the perimeter, he upped his pace, running toward the relative security of Danny's position. Danny realised he was sweating badly. His skin was slippery against the hard metal of his trigger.

Thirty seconds later, Spike reached the OP. He dumped the mechanic on the ground, where he landed with an unpleasant thud.

Danny and Spike looked at each other. There was no need to state the obvious: a missing mechanic could scupper their evening's plans. If anybody came looking for him, things could go noisy.

'What do we do?' Spike said.

'We stay put,' Danny told him. 'Keep eyes on the Cessna. Make sure it gets in the air. Stay in contact with Spud and Tyson, and when they confirm the aircraft's in Mexican airspace ...' He left it hanging.

'And him?' Spike nudged the mechanic with his foot.

Danny shrugged. 'We'll tie him up. Guard him until the Cessna's taken off. When we bug out, we'll dump him by the road somewhere. It won't matter by then.'

Spud's cheek twitched. 'You think the pilot's got a family?' he asked quietly.

Danny gave him a hard look. A look that said: don't start think-ing that way, kid. Not in the middle of an op. He checked his watch. 0030 hours. Kleinman had said the plane would depart at 0200.

'Get down,' he told his unit mate as he took some cable ties from his pack to deal with the mechanic. 'We've got 90 minutes to sit this out.'

The desert terrain was rough. Uncompromising. But Tyson was a good driver. Better than the guy in the border control vehicle they'd been following for the past twenty minutes. They were now driving through a narrow ravine, fifteen metres in width, sides about five metres high. The ground was littered with rocks. Reminded Spud of dried-out wadis in the Middle East.

The vehicle ahead stopped suddenly. The red of its brake lamps illuminated Spud and Tyson's faces. Spud clutched his handgun a little tighter.

'Problem?' Tyson muttered.

'I'll check it out.'

Spud exited the vehicle. So did the two border control agents. He followed them to the front of their vehicle. He saw immedi-ately what had made them stop. Lit up by the vehicle's headlamps was a body, face down in the dust. It had obviously been there for some time, because Spud could make out the unmistakable stench of sun-rotted flesh.

The two border guards displayed no emotion. They simply grabbed the body's arms and legs and dragged it to the side of the road. 'Migrant,' the driver said to Spud as he moved it. 'They swim across the Rio Grande, exhaust themselves, then collapse on this side. We'll call it in when you've finished your little excursion.' They laid the body back down again. 'The river's five hundred metres from here,' he said.

'We'll leave our vehicle here,' Spud said. It was a good place. The ravine meant the Tahoe wouldn't be visible from the plain above, or from the river. They took their packs and weapons from the trunk, then climbed into the back of the border control vehicle. It trundled up out of the ravine. Spud and Tyson set eyes on the Rio Grande. The bank was a hundred metres away, and the moon reflected brightly off the water, which was perhaps fifty metres wide. The water appeared to be slow-moving, but Spud knew the undercurrents could be strong. Flat terrain on both sides. Exposed. Hardly the best place for a covert crossing, but there didn't seem to be anyone else around.

The patrol vehicle stopped. The driver looked over his shoulder. 'It's probably neck-high,' he said. 'Most illegals choose a shallower stretch about twenty miles west of here.' He shrugged. 'Rather you than me,' he said.

Spud exited the vehicle, grabbed his Bergen and opened it up. Everything inside was stashed within a waterproof plastic lining with a ziplock seal at the top. It would keep his gear dry, and the trapped air would act as a flotation aid as they crossed the river – as would the empty water canteens in the side pocket. Spud took a night sight from his pack. He scanned the open ground between the vehicle and the river bank. Just the plain, semi-arid terrain they were used to. He panned round. No sign of any movement. He looked across the river. A vehicle was waiting on the far bank, about thirty metres from the water's edge, just as Kleinman had told them there would be. It was empty, so far as Spud could tell.

He stowed the sight and carefully sealed the ziplock bag before closing the Bergen. The others had all exited the vehicle. 'You'll stay here until we've crossed? Keep any other border control guys off our backs?'

The guy nodded.

'Best estimate for our return crossing,' Spud continued, 'is 0400 hours. You'll be here then?'

'Sure,' said the border control guy. 'But if you're late . . .' He left it hanging. 'When you get to the far side, head south for a mile and you'll hit the road you want. There'll be no police presence when you're there. Which may or may not be a good thing.'

'What do you mean?'

The driver gave him a piercing look. 'Cartel boys. You want my advice? Don't stop for them.'

'Roger that,' Spud muttered. He turned to Tyson. 'Let's move,' he said.

They jogged down to the water's edge in single file, their packs firmly strapped to their backs and their rifles slung round their necks. Spud entered the water first. He could immediately feel a current around his ankles. Weak, but he knew it would grow stronger as the water got deeper. The water was cold. By the time he'd waded ten metres across, he was thigh-deep and he noticed his body temperature dropping dramatically. He looked over his shoulder. He could make out the silhouette of the border patrol vehicle in the distance. At the water's edge, Tyson was down on one knee, rifle engaged, scanning the far bank for any sign of hostile activity. He had Spud's back. Spud waded deeper, steeling himself firmly against the current. His muscles felt slow because of the temperature, and it was a strain to push himself toward the far bank. Although his Bergen gave him a little extra buoyancy, once or twice he lost his footing, got swept a couple of metres downstream. But he righted himself again, even as the water lashed against his neck.

The crossing took five minutes. He emerged on the other side, water dripping from his sodden clothes pack and sluicing out of his weapon. Even though his limbs were chilled, he didn't hesitate. As he made the water's edge he put himself down on to one knee with his back to the river, engaged his weapon and then held up one hand to indicate that Tyson should cross. He panned across the flat Mexican terrain, checking for movement, for threats, the border patrol guy's words ringing in his ears. But there was nothing, and five minutes later Tyson emerged from the water. When Spud looked back across the river, he saw that the border control vehicle had gone.

'Dickheads,' Spud said. 'They were supposed to stay there.'

'Kleinman,' Tyson muttered. 'All mouth, no fucking trousers.'

They were on their own. Still dripping wet, they jogged toward the vehicle. It was a beaten-up old saloon. Nothing like the pimp-mobile they'd left on the US side of the river. They stowed their packs in the back seat and their longs between the driver's and passenger's seats. The keys were in the ignition. Tyson took the wheel. Ignoring their soaked clothing, they headed slowly south over the hard-baked terrain. The moon was bright enough for them to keep the headlamps off. After ten minutes, as the border control officer had promised, they hit an east–west road. It was substantially less well kept than the last road they'd encountered on the American side of the border.

'*Bienvenida a México*,' Tyson said. 'It's good to be back.' He flicked on the headlamps, hung a left and headed east.

0145 hours.

'We've got a new arrival,' Danny said.

He and Spike donned black balaclavas. The mechanic woke up, whereupon Spike shoved a rag in his mouth to keep him quiet. Better, though, that he didn't get the opportunity to fix Danny and Spike's faces in his mind. Hence the masks.

Now a vehicle was approaching the entrance to the airfield. Through the night sights, Danny saw it was a Hilux, though he couldn't tell what colour. It crossed the perimeter without anyone stopping it, or even observing it – all personnel were still in the low building on the western side. The Hilux swung across the airfield and headed toward the three aircraft. It pulled up by the nose of the Cessna. A figure emerged. Danny zeroed in on him. Tough to make out his features in profile, even with the image-intensifying sight, but he was certain he recognised the pilot Barry Osmin from the photo Kleinman had shown them. 'Positive ID,' he said. 'Get Spud on the line.'

As Spike pulled out the encrypted sat phone Kleinman had supplied them with, Danny kept eyes on the target. He headed straight to the trunk of his vehicle and was in the process of removing a suitcase. It was obviously heavy. He hauled around to the far side of the Cessna. Danny lost visual. When he came back into view, he no longer had the suitcase, but unloaded a second from the trunk.

Spike spoke into his sat phone. 'The bird's getting ready to fly,' he said. 'Are you comfortable? Over.'

Spud's voice came over the loudspeaker of the sat phone. '*Roger that, we have an excellent position for birdwatching. Over.*'

'Keep the line open,' Danny said without taking his eye off the pilot, who was now loading his third suitcase into the aircraft. He returned to the car, closed the trunk and moved the vehicle alongside the hangar. Then he returned to the aircraft and climbed up into the cockpit. A minute later, the Cessna was taxiing over to the runway. There was still no sign of personnel on the aircraft. Either this flight was so regular as to be of no interest, or they'd been told to make themselves scarce. Whatever the truth, the Cessna encountered no obstructions. It accelerated down the runway, lifted into the air. As it gained height, it flew directly south.

'The bird has flown,' Spike said into the cell phone. 'Repeat, the bird has flown.'

Danny kept eyes on the aircraft until it disappeared from sight. The he turned to look at Spike. His unit mate had removed the old-fashioned cell phone he was going to use to detonate the device, and was in the process of powering it up. He kept his hand over the screen to stop the glow from emanating.

'Ready?' Danny said.

'Ready,' said Spike.

If the airfield from which the Cessna had taken off was small-time, the airfield where it was scheduled to land was positively homespun. A rough landing strip in the middle of a flat desert plain three hundred metres from the road head. A small building, little more than a shack, halfway along the strip, about fifty metres to the eastern side. The vehicles that had congregated around it, however, spoke of money. Five black SUVs, well appointed, surrounded by a total of eleven men, each of whom was openly carrying an assault rifle.

Spud and Tyson were still damp from the river crossing. They had left their vehicle in a depression in the terrain a mile to the north of the road head. Then they skirted round the airstrip to dig in at the south end of the runway, a hundred metres from it. Here, there was a dilapidated building – three remaining walls, no roof – that afforded them cover to put in surveillance on the runway. Tyson lay on his front in the doorframe, rifle engaged and aiming toward the point where the narco vehicles had parked. Spud looked through what was once a window frame, camouflaged by the darkness, looking out toward the airstrip through his night sight. The sat phone with the open line to Danny and Spike was at his feet. He'd stuck a strip of duct tape over the screen to shield the glow.

Time check: 0220 hours.

The armed men by the cars looked relaxed. Chatting. Smoking. Spud could tell they'd done this before and were in no way concerned that they would be disturbed, or challenged, or that anything would go wrong.

Think again, dickheads, Spud said to himself.

'He's coming,' Tyson said.

Spud panned up to the airspace above the landing strip. Tyson was right. In the distance, flying low, was a light aircraft. It was maybe a couple of klicks out. 'We have eyes on the bird,' Spud said, loud enough to be heard over the sat phone. 'She's in Mexican airspace.'

'*Roger that,*' came Danny's voice from the other end. '*On your command.*'

Spud gave it a moment. No operational reason, other than wanting to put the shits up the wankers by the cars.

Ten seconds passed.

Twenty seconds.

'Okay,' Spud said into the cell phone. 'Fireworks.'

'*Fireworks.*'

'Light it up,' Danny instructed.

Spike nodded. He put the old handset on speaker. Keyed in a number. Pressed *Call.*

'*Light it up.*'

Spud realised he was holding his breath as he watched the aircraft.

The explosion, when it came, was spectacular.

It came in two waves. The initial blast ripped the cockpit open like a sinister metal flower coming into bloom, silhouetted against the night sky. A dull boom hit Spud's ears a couple of seconds later. The aircraft had barely started to fall from the sky, however, when the fuel tank exploded. The Cessna was suddenly a blazing fireball of dark orange flame and black smoke. The noise of this second explosion was five times as loud as the first, and it illuminated the entire airstrip as it fell spectacularly to earth, its forward momentum giving it a steep downward arc. Seconds later, it smashed on to the airstrip.

Spud found himself grinning. 'Attaboy, Spike,' he said. He turned his attention to the armed men. They were fiercely illuminated by the burning aircraft. Without exception, they were sprinting for their vehicles, clearly desperate to get the hell out of there. He glanced down at Tyson, then back at the Cessna. 'Beautiful evening,' he said.

'Absolute fucking cracker,' Tyson said.

The Zeta vehicles stormed from the site, their engines high-pitched and urgent over the crackling blaze of what remained of the Cessna.

SUNDAY

TWELVE

The night shifts were always the busiest. Sure, during the day every hour of a doctor's time was spoken for. But it was at night that the hospital tended to enter crisis mode. The triage area was the busiest thousand square foot in Nuevo Laredo. The emergency room was in constant use. The day shifts were set aside for appendicitis and broken limbs. The night shifts were a conveyor belt of gunshot wounds.

So when Ana Rodriguez left the hospital at 6 a.m., she was exhausted. The streets, bathed in the early morning light, were empty. It was Sunday. She negotiated them numbly, automatically. She wanted nothing more than to get home, and collapse into bed next to her little boy Miguel.

She turned into her road at 6.17, two minutes earlier than usual. She recognised one of her neighbours – a woman about her age, whose name she didn't know – walking her dog along the pavement. The dog seemed jumpy. The woman caught her eye, but then looked away quickly.

Ana was accustomed to that reaction.

Sleepily, almost on autopilot, she turned left into the front yard of her house.

She hit the brakes and came to a sudden halt.

In most respects, everything was as she had left it. The dog bowl on the porch. The outdoor light still shining.

But in one respect it was very different.

There were two cars parked in the yard. Facing away from the house, toward the exit. Black SUVs. Tinted windows. Five Mexican men. Two leaning against each of the SUVs. The fifth standing in the porch. They were well built, broad-shouldered. Each of them had a chilling deadness in their eyes. They all stared unblinkingly at her. One of them was holding two lean mongrel dogs on chains. They were straining and, at the sight of Ana, gave a low growl. She saw their teeth were tipped with metal, as though they had fillings. The old van, which she sometimes used as a makeshift ambulance, that she'd left with the Zetas three nights earlier, was parked on the left-hand side.

Ana felt a sudden wave of cold nausea. She put one hand to her mouth in case she was sick. But she managed to hold it in, and whispered one word to herself: 'Miguel ...'

She fumbled for the car latch and exited the vehicle without even bothering to turn the engine off or close the door behind her. As she hurried up to the front door, her skin prickled as she passed each of the men leaning against their vehicles, who burned into her with their eyes.

She reached the porch. The fifth man stood in front of the door, blocking her way. He stank of body odour. With a jolt, she realised she recognised him. He was the man from the other night. The one with fake eyes tattooed on his eyelids.

'Where ... is ... my ... son?' Ana hissed. 'If he's been harmed in *any* way, I swear I—'

The man raised a finger and pressed it to her lips. 'Save it, *señora*,' he said. 'Save it for Z1.'

Ana knocked the man's hand away. 'Don't touch me,' she said, pushing past him. As she opened her front door, she looked over her shoulder at the man. 'And his name is Augusto,' she said.

She hurried into the house and slammed the door behind her. Her whole body was shaking. The scene that awaited her didn't help.

Miguel was in his pyjamas, sitting at the table. He had a lollipop in his mouth, which, when he saw his mother, he guiltily removed and placed on the table next to Buzz Lightyear with the missing left arm. Next to him was a man in late middle age, black cropped hair, pencil moustache. He wore a white vest that revealed his strong upper arms, covered in tattoos. He had put on weight since

Ana had last seen him. His face was jowly, his fingers fat. On the table in front of them was a handgun, stripped down into its constituent parts. The man was holding the barrel, showing it to Miguel. On the near side of the table was an expensive-looking Chanel shoulder bag. Black, with gold coloured accessories. It bulged slightly. There was something inside.

The man looked over at Ana, as if surprised they had been interrupted.

'Say good morning to your mother, Miguel,' he said, in a hoarse voice that was not much more than a whisper.

'Good morning, Mother,' said Miguel.

Ana was still shaking. 'Come here, Miguel,' she said.

The man nodded at the boy. 'Do as your mother says.'

Miguel climbed down from the table, grabbed Buzz Lightyear and walked across the room to Ana, who held him fiercely. 'What are you doing here?' she said to the man.

He didn't answer immediately. He stood up and started clunking the pieces of the handgun back together again. Finally he spoke. 'A boy should know how to strip down a weapon,' he said.

'No, Augusto,' Ana said. 'A boy should *not* know how to strip down a weapon.'

A flicker of annoyance passed over the man's face. But then he smiled and continued to assemble the firearm. 'If one of the men outside called me Augusto,' he said, 'I would have them hanged.' He clunked the magazine into the assembled firearm. 'And flayed,' he said, almost as an afterthought.

'What are you doing here?' Ana repeated. 'I thought you spent all your time in your precious safe house.'

'A brother cannot visit his own sister?'

'You are no brother of mine.'

Augusto showed no emotion. He walked around the table and toward Ana and Miguel. 'That's not what you suggested to my men two nights ago,' he said quietly.

Ana backed away from him, still clutching Miguel. Her back was against the door now. 'They were going to rape me,' she breathed. 'Have you changed so much that you will let your men rape your own sister?'

'I thought I was no brother of yours.' Augusto stood one metre away from her and Miguel. His face turned blank again. 'Last night,' he said, 'my men visited a small village called San Cristobal, twenty miles south of here. Would you like to know what they did there?'

Ana shook her head.

'They selected ten of the villagers. They imprisoned them inside the village church. Then they set fire to it. When the prisoners tried to escape, they shot them.'

Silence.

'Would you like to see the video? It's very entertaining.'

'No.'

'Then would you like to know what their crime was?'

Ana said nothing.

'There was no crime,' Augusto continued, without taking his eyes from her. 'Their death was *your* punishment, for what *you* did the other night. Their blood is on *your* hands.'

She stared at her brother in horror.

'From now on, you will only provide medical help to members of the Zeta cartel. If I hear that you have disobeyed this command, another ten innocent people will die in the same way. Every time you threaten my men as you did the other night, another ten.' He took a step closer. 'I have previously made it known,' he whispered, 'that you and Miguel are not to be touched. I have allowed you to live away from my protection, rather than take my nephew under my wing where he should be. You ought to be grateful. Instead, you throw my kindness back in my face. It ends today. Is that understood?' Ana said nothing.

'Is that understood?' Augusto repeated.

'Yes,' she breathed.

Another step forward. Their faces were inches apart.

'Yes what?' he whispered.

Ana swallowed hard. 'Yes, Z1,' she said.

He nodded slowly. Wet lips. That black, mirthless stare. Ana, terrified, found herself trying to remember what he'd looked like as a child. She couldn't.

He stepped back. A grin spread across his face. He reached out and ruffled Miguel's hair. 'He's a good kid,' he announced. 'Good genes. Me? I'm a proud uncle. Miguel, you want to come and work for your uncle when you're older?'

Miguel didn't reply, but that only seemed to please Augusto more. 'A good kid,' he repeated. He looked over to the table and pointed to the Chanel bag. 'For you,' he said. 'A small gift, from brother to sister.' He lowered his voice. 'For you, Ana. Not for the boy. Now move out the way.'

Ana stepped aside. Anything to get him out of there.

She didn't turn round until she heard the door shut. Only then did she let go of Miguel, who ran into his bedroom. Ana looked through the window out into the front yard. There was no sign of Augusto. He had clearly already climbed into one of the cars, as had all his men with the exception of the guy with tattoos on his eyelids. He was standing by the open driver's door of one of the vehicles, looking directly at Ana through the window.

He closed his eyes to reveal their tattooed counterparts. Then he opened them again, inclined his head to Ana, got behind the wheel of the vehicle and drove away.

Ana watched him go. The sickness hadn't left her stomach. She turned and stared at the Chanel bag on the table. She found herself both repelled by and horribly drawn to it. She didn't move for a full thirty seconds. She was holding her breath when she finally approached.

There was a smell coming from the bag. Putrid. Rotten. Part of her mind shrieked at her not to open it. But she also felt as if someone else was controlling her body as she reached out and unbuckled the golden clasp.

She opened the bag.

Immediately, she wanted to vomit.

A severed head stared up at her. Its eyes were open, and even in death it managed to express the untold horror of what had gone before. The skin was waxy, yellow and blood-spattered. The hair was matted. There was movement around the nostril: a maggot, crawling its way out of the sudden light. Ana couldn't tell if it was male or female. She didn't want to know. She clasped the bag quickly shut again. Put one hand over her mouth to stop herself from being sick.

She staggered back from the bag, unable to take her eyes from the monstrous contours its innards made on the fabric. The room seemed to spin, and for a moment she thought she might fall. She didn't. Instead, she rushed over to the wooden sideboard. She opened the cutlery drawer to the back of which she had duct-taped her handgun. But she didn't pull it all the way out. Instead, she lifted the cutlery tray and, with trembling hands, felt underneath it for a small piece of paper, folded in two. She opened it up and read what was written on it. A US cell-phone number.

She stared at it, nervously chewing on her lower lip. She looked over her shoulder, first at the Chanel bag, then at the door to the bedroom. Then back at the paper.

She realised she had never been so scared. It was as if the fear was an actual substance, a cold liquid pumping through her veins.

She needed help. *Santa Maria*, she needed help.

It had been offered to her years before and she had turned it down. But she couldn't turn it down any longer.

She fetched her phone and, with sweating, shaking hands, dialled the number. It rang three times. Then an American voice answered.

'*Kleinman,*' it said.

THIRTEEN

Danny and Spike had driven thirty miles from the airfield with the trussed-up mechanic bundled in the back of their vehicle before Danny pulled up by the side of the deserted road and let him out. They had nothing against the guy. He was just in the wrong place at the wrong time. Danny had cut off the cable ties binding his wrists and they wordlessly left him by the roadside. They only removed their balaclavas when he was well out of sight.

They were now turning into the parking lot outside the motel. It took them nearly five hours to return as, having dumped the mechanic, they doubled back on themselves several times to check they weren't being followed. Danny had already clocked Kleinman standing outside the bedroom set aside as an ops centre. He thought he could see an orange spark as the CIA man flicked his lighter. He resisted the urge to accelerate across the lot, bringing the car to a careful, unobtrusive stop in front of the motel. He turned to Spike. 'Good work,' he said.

Spike didn't look as pleased as Danny expected him to. Embarrassed, if anything.

They alighted. Danny took the lead, striding straight up to Kleinman.

'Spud?'

'We're tracking their phones,' Kleinman said. 'They've made it back across the border.'

Danny allowed himself to relax a little. He hadn't made phone contact with the rest of the unit. He knew they would be focused on getting away from the Mexican airstrip without being spotted by any cartel personnel. There was nothing he could do to help them with that, and making contact could be a distraction. It was good to know they were back on US soil. 'Is our cartel boy still where we left him?' he asked.

Kleinman nodded.

'You questioned him?'

'No.'

Good, Danny thought. The kid would have had several hours sitting trussed up in his own filth to get himself good and worked up. He turned to Spike. 'Come with me,' he said.

Spike, who'd remained very quiet, nodded.

'You too,' Danny said to Kleinman, but the CIA man was already heading toward the room where the Zeta prisoner was being held, sparking his lighter as he went.

He was in a worse state than Danny expected. The stench in the bathroom was disgusting. He had obviously soiled himself several times more. His arms and legs were still bound, his head still hooded. He was shaking heavily, even though it was warm in the room.

Breathing through his mouth to stop the disgusting smell getting up his nose, Danny leaned over and pulled off the hood. The cartel boy winced from the light, then forced his eyes open and took a moment to focus. When he recognised Danny standing over him, he started to squeal like a pig and writhe around in the mess in the bath. A frightened animal trying to escape, but with no place to go.

Danny stared darkly at him, ignoring his pathetic struggling until he fell still and silent, apart from the occasional terrified whimper. Then he bent over and ripped the tape from around his mouth. His lips were bleeding. More blood had congealed under his broken nose. He gasped noisily. Danny pulled his handgun, made a show of cocking and unlocking it, then leaned over and rested the barrel against the prisoner's skull. 'Your cartel buddies think they're pretty sick, huh?'

Jesús said nothing. Danny grabbed his hair with his free hand and forced the barrel of the gun into his prisoner's mouth. Jesús gagged. He seemed to be trying to say something, so Danny removed the gun. 'They think they're pretty sick, huh?' he repeated.

'Yes, sir,' Jesús replied. 'They think they're pretty sick.'

'Next to me and my friends,' Danny said, 'they're pussies. What are they next to me and my friends?'

'Pussies, sir,' Jesús said.

'Got it in one.' Danny looked over his shoulder at Kleinman, who was standing in the doorway to the bathroom. 'Fire away,' he said.

Kleinman limped further into the room. Looked grimly down at Jesús through his little round glasses. 'There's a Zeta tunnel leading under the Rio Grande,' he said. 'The entrance is in a meat-packing facility on the American side of the border. The exit is in a storage warehouse on the Mexican side. The Zetas use this tunnel to move drug money from the US back into Mexico. You are now going to tell us when the next shipment of money will be transported across the border.'

'My friend here missed a bit out,' Danny said. 'By the time I've finished with you, you'll be *begging* to tell us when the shipment is.'

The Zeta sicario closed his eyes. 'Tonight,' he whispered.

Danny and Kleinman glanced at each other.

'What time?' Danny said.

'Midnight,' Jesús breathed. 'They ... they do it on Sunday nights because there are no workers at the factory.'

'How many people are involved?'

Jesús breathed deeply. Shakily. 'Six,' he said. 'Three on this side, three on the Mexican side. There are rails in the tunnel ... a cart on a pulley system. They load the money into the cart, then walk with it while the three people on the Mexican side wind the pulley system to pull the cart along the tunnel. There's a car waiting at the warehouse to take the money on.'

'How long does it take?' Danny asked.

'About an hour, sir.'

'And the meat-packing factory is deserted when they make the run?'

'Yes, sir. We pay the owners off, sir.'

Danny shoved the barrel of his gun back into Jesús's mouth. 'You know what happens if you're lying to us? You're not fucking going anywhere. If there's anything else you want to tell us, now's the time.'

Jesús shook his head violently, his eyes bulging. Danny removed the gun and turned to Spike. 'Tape him up again,' he said. 'Get the hood back on. He stays here in case we need any more intel.' He looked at his watch. 0700 hours. 'Where the hell is Spud?' he muttered.

When Spud and Tyson finally arrived, it was midday. They were dirty and stank of stale river water, but were grinning nevertheless. Spud high-fived his cousin. Even Tyson was grinning. A successful op left everyone with a good feeling. This was one of those moments.

'What kept you?' Danny asked.

'We took the long way round in case we were being followed,' Spud said. He gave Kleinman a slightly edgy look. 'Your border control muppets had fucked off when we got to the river. We had to make the crossing without anyone keeping eyes on. In daylight.' He turned to his unit mates. 'You want something done properly . . .'

'We've got a problem,' Rav interrupted.

Everyone fell silent. They turned to Rav, who was staring at his screen, a confused look on his face.

'What?' Danny demanded.

'I've just accessed the Federal Aviation Authority's systems,' he said. 'It was an American pilot so they had agents at the crash site within an hour.'

'What's the fucking problem?' Tyson pressed.

Rav looked up at them. 'There was no money on the aircraft,' he said.

Silence.

'That's impossible,' Spike said. 'We saw the pilot loading it up. It was in suitcases. Right, Danny?'

'Right,' Danny said. 'There were definitely suitcases.'

'Trust me,' Rav said. 'Those crash site guys are forensics geniuses. If there were traces of currency at the site, they'd have listed it.'

Nobody spoke. The buoyant mood among the unit had suddenly deflated.

Spud broke the silence. 'Look,' he said, 'I saw the plane go up. It was a fucking fireball. Hardly surprising there was no trace of the money. It went up in smoke.'

Rav didn't appear convinced. He exchanged a long look with Kleinman. Danny knew what they were thinking. If there was no money on the flight, did it mean the Zetas knew the aircraft was going to be hit? Had they sacrificed their courier because they knew he was under surveillance?

And if so, who tipped them off?

'Seriously,' Spud continued. 'It was napalmed. The whole point was to destroy the money, wasn't it? How much C4 did you put in that pouch, Spike?'

'Enough,' Spike said. 'It wouldn't surprise me if there was no sign of—'

'We'll monitor the situation,' Kleinman interrupted, in a voice that brought an end to the conversation. His eyes met Danny's, but he quickly turned to the documents spread out on the ops room table.

Danny and Spike were examining maps and satellite imagery of that part of the border where the cartel's tunnel was situated. Danny tried to dispel the air of sudden uncertainty in the room as he briefly explained the intel they'd received from Jesús to Tyson and Spud, before turning back to the imaging. He indicated a rectangular building on the northern edge of a narrow stretch of the Rio Grande, about thirty klicks east of their current location. 'This is the meat-packing facility,' he said. He pointed at another similarly sized building on the Mexican side of the river. 'That's the warehouse. It's a major engineering feat getting a tunnel under that river. My guess is it'll be pretty narrow. We don't want to get caught up in there. I suggest we get to the meat-packing facility several hours in advance, then engage the three guys delivering the money before they have a chance to get it in the tunnel. Agreed?'

Spud, Tyson and Spike nodded. Everyone seemed more focused, now they were talking tactics.

'I want at least a two-hour set-up,' Danny said. 'That means arrival at 2200 hours. Kleinman, can you get a drone up over the warehouse on the Mexican side by then? I want advance notice of anything unexpected.'

'I'll see what I can do, boy,' Kleinman said.

'When the men arrive, we whack them and burn the money,' Danny said. He happened to be looking at Tyson at the time. He saw him wince at the thought of all that cash going up in smoke, but his unit mate didn't say anything so Danny continued. 'Right now, we need to get some shut-eye,' he said. 'We leave at 2030 hours.'

Back in his room, Danny slept only fitfully for a couple of hours. At 1500 he gave up the pretence. He got out of bed, splashed cold water on his face and let himself out of his room, wincing slightly as he opened the door to the bright Texan afternoon light. His plan was to check on Jesús, but as he stepped outside he heard voices to his right. Rav. Kleinman. There was a faint smell of tobacco on the air.

He moved silently along the motel strip, past the door into the ops room, to the corner of the building. He couldn't see the two men, but it was clear at least one of them was having a cigarette break just a couple of metres from where he was standing.

And they were talking about him.

'He seems capable,' Kleinman was saying. There was the familiar grating sound as he sparked his lighter. 'I had my doubts at first. His file is impressive, but suggests a tendency to follow his own muse from time to time. But he's decisive and seems to know what he's doing. Everything's gone according to plan so far. Not that I wouldn't prefer an American team, but ...'

'I don't know, boss,' Rav said. 'That FAA report doesn't stack up. I've read a million of them. They'd have detected the money.'

'Perhaps,' Kleinman said mildly. 'Perhaps not.'

'Don't tell me you haven't had the same thought as me,' Rav said.

There was a pause. 'I don't quite follow you, boy.'

'I don't trust that guy Tyson. Have you seen his resumé? He got pretty close to the Mexican special forces operatives who became Zetas. He knows Z1, for chrissakes. And his file isn't exactly spotless. Plenty of our boys out in Afghanistan seem to think he was on the take from the Taliban's heroin operation.'

Another pause. 'You're over-thinking things. The Pentagon have had direct contact with SAS headquarters in Hereford. Each member of that team has been thoroughly vetted.'

'Yeah, well even the Five-Sided Puzzle Palace gets things wrong from time to time.'

'Certainly,' said Kleinman. 'And the same goes for FAA forensic teams. I know we'd all prefer an American team on the job, but that option's not open to us. Let's not start inventing bogeymen, okay?'

Danny didn't hang around to hear any more. The conversation was clearly coming to a close. He didn't want Kleinman and Rav to know he'd overheard them. He slipped silently back into his room, where he sat on the edge of his bed for a moment, mulling over what he'd just heard. Could Rav possibly be right? Tyson? Dirty? Danny thought back to Aiden Bailey's party at the Emirates Stadium. It was true he was surprised that Tyson should be on first-name terms with a guy like Bailey. Danny knew better than most there were men in the Regiment who comfortably walked both sides of the line dividing the legal and the illegal. But Tyson? In the pockets of the Mexican cartels? It just didn't stack up.

The plane hit had been a success. Rav was chasing shadows. As for Danny, he needed to remember the first rule of a successful operation: you trust your team.

That was exactly what he intended to do.

★   ★   ★

Tam Garrick and the rest of team Yankee Bravo Nine had returned to their Docklands base immediately after the hit. They'd cleaned up – Tam used a whole tub of Swarfega to get the blood spatter off his hands and face – got some food down their throats and caught some sleep. As the morning wore on, Tam kept one eye on the BBC News 24 channel to see if there were any reports of a burned-out Transit van in a forest on the outskirts of London. There were none. Maybe it hadn't been found. Unlikely. Or maybe somebody was hushing things up.

Yeah. Someone was hushing things up.

The call came through at three in the afternoon. The same monotone voice Tam had spoken to as they left the scene of the hit. '*We've got him. Check your secure server.*' Nothing more.

Tam opened up his laptop – a tough, rugged machine with a dented metal casing. He opened the browser, allowed the inbuilt camera to take a shot of his iris and, once his identity was confirmed, navigated to the folder waiting for him on the server.

'Aiden Bailey,' he muttered. His unit mates were standing around the table, viewing the screen over his shoulder. Tam had clicked on an icon that brought up a black and white photograph, taken with a telephoto lens. Aiden Bailey wasn't a very impressive-looking man. About five foot eight, squat shoulders, round face. He had a good tan and wore an open-neck shirt with a chunky medallion round his neck. The photo showed him walking toward the camera, a cell phone to his ear. A blonde woman in high heels was tottering along behind him.

A second photo showed the frontage of a building. Brown brick, three storeys high. There was a rather tatty sign above the entrance. In garish red lettering it said: *Paradise Gym*. A sign in one of the blacked-out windows read: 'Open seven days a week till late'.

'That, my friend,' said Webb from over Tam's shoulder, 'is a gay gym.'

'I heard you were an expert,' Tam said. There was a silence as his joke failed to find its mark.

Tam's cell phone rang again. He answered it and put it on speaker so the rest of the team could hear it. 'Thanks for the dirty photos,' Tam said.

The humourless voice ignored that comment. *'Aiden Bailey is known to the UK security services,'* it said. *'He has a number of illegal operations. As far as the British are concerned, he specialises in protection rackets and extortion. MI5 cut him some slack because he is blackmailing several Members of Parliament and at least one police commissioner. It suits their purposes because they can then counter-blackmail the same people. If Aiden Bailey does indeed have a sideline in exporting military hardware to terrorist groups in the US, the British are unaware of it. We need evidence of these activities if we are going to extradite him.'*

'So what's the deal with the Paradise Gym?' Tam asked.

'Bailey has various offices and centres of operation. Most of them are in expensive office blocks. They're just fronts. We believe this to be the true nerve centre of his operation. He has already entrapped three Conservative Members of Parliament by taking photographs of their homosexual trysts at the Paradise Gym. There is a suite of offices on the third floor and Bailey's people spend more time at this location than any of the others. You should start your search for evidence here.'

'Why don't we just find this motherfucker,' drawled Webb, 'and put a round in his skull? End of problem.'

'Negative,' said the voice. *'You need something more solid than the word of another criminal.'*

'What if we get the evidence?' Tam said. The idea of some London hood sending weapons into the US made his trigger finger itch.

'If it's watertight, you have the go-ahead for a hit. But under the radar. We don't want a firefight on a London street and we don't want the UK authorities to know you're involved. If it happens, it needs to look like an inter-gang thing. If the British find out we're targeting UK citizens there'll be a shitstorm.' There was a pause. *'So that means no more camp fires in British forests. Is that understood?'*

The men looked at each other. 'Understood,' Tam said.

'You can expect Bailey's guys to be on a war footing. They've lost two men already.'

'Understood. What's the location of the Paradise Gym?'

The dry voice gave them a precise address.

Now the unit was in position in the environs of a broad, busy road back in east London. Here, the Paradise Gym was sandwiched between a large second-hand clothes shop and a bustling café. On the opposite side of the road was a recreation area – a skate park strewn with graffiti, and a children's playground populated by youths who hadn't been children for a long time. This was where Brooks and Dixon were situated. They were dressed in hoodies, trainers and tatty raincoats – clothes that made them as good as invisible, but also hid their covert mikes and earpieces as they loitered on the far side of the road from the gym, carefully watching any comings and goings.

There was heavy, driving rain. The raincoats did a half-decent job of keeping them dry, but they were well used to operating in more hostile conditions. Tam and Webb were working together. They were not observing the front of the Paradise Gym. Instead, they recce'd the back of the building. Here there was a shabby rear entrance, its doors locked with a heavy chain. Two large, overflowing bins stood sentry on either side, and a security camera covered, Tam estimated, a semicircle outside the entrance with a radius of approximately seven metres. A terrace of high, rundown east London buildings faced the rear entrance across a deserted cobbled street, strewn with litter and only ten metres wide. A dark, claustrophobic space. If they wanted to conduct surveillance here, they needed to find a satisfactory OP. They'd stick out simply loitering in the road.

The buildings on the opposite side of the road looked deserted – some were even boarded up. It crossed Tam's mind that they could break in to one of those and observe the rear entrance from a window opposite. He quickly decided against that idea. Just because the buildings *looked* deserted, it didn't mean they *were* deserted. There could be squatters or even genuine residents behind that grimy facade.

Instead, he looked up.

Whenever Tam was operating in an urban environment, he was always struck by how infrequently people looked up. They were forever looking over their shoulders, but they so often seemed oblivious to the fact that a whole world existed above their heads. As he and Webb stood out of the rain in a dark doorway on the same side of the street as the back entrance to the gym, he checked out the roofline opposite. The buildings were three storeys high, but flat-roofed – there was no sign of a ridge. Instead, the brick facade of the building was topped with what looked like a low wall. There were bricks missing here and there, and a single protective line of barbed wire.

'I'm going to look for a way up,' he told Webb.

He stepped out into the cobbled street, into the rain, his hood over his head, his standard civilian rucksack slung over his right shoulder. He strode past the rear entrance to the gym and continued fifty metres along the road. He passed nobody, except a homeless guy huddled out of the elements in another doorway, swathed in several dirty blankets. There was an alleyway on his left, ten metres from the end of the road. Tam spotted a black metal exterior staircase. The rain was splashing heavily off the treads. Tam hooked a left and strode toward the staircase. Unobserved, he climbed it. It led to a fire door on the side wall of the top floor of the terrace. The platform at the top of the stairs was surrounded on two sides by a metal grille, two metres high. Tam looked down. Checked he was unobserved. The alley was deserted in the teeming rain. He clambered up the inside of the grille and hauled himself over the edge of the roofline.

The roofs along the terrace were flat, as he expected. A couple of inches of water had already pooled where he was standing. A half-metre wall divided each of the buildings along the terrace. Tam kept back from the front edge of the building so he could not be seen from the road, and jogged back toward the section of roof that overlooked the gym. He crouched down behind one of the gaps formed by a missing brick, then removed a spotting scope from his rucksack. He rested it in the gap, then looked through the lens on to the street below. He could make out Webb, still standing in the doorway. More importantly, he had a full view of the rear entrance to the gym. Anyone came in or out of that place, Tam would have eyes on. With Brooks and Dixon watching the front, and Webb positioned down at ground level, they would soon be able to build up a picture of the comings and goings at this seedy gym. They could choose the correct moment to gain access, strip the place down and search for evidence. If they were lucky, they might see that motherfucker Bailey entering. Tam was as happy to avoid a confrontation as start one if that was the best outcome for the op, but a little bit of him relished the idea of nailing the bastard who thought moving illegal weapons into the US was a good idea. If getting the green light to do that meant lying here on the rooftop under the pouring rain for forty-eight hours, so be it. It was just part of the job.

'In position,' he said into his covert radio.

Three separate American voices responded with the same phrase: '*Roger that.*'

FOURTEEN

2130 hours.

Danny had the wheel. Spud was in the passenger seat. Spike and Tyson were in the back.

They wore fresh, sand-coloured clothes. Body armour. The trunk of their vehicle was rammed with equipment. M16s. Infrared sights. Several boxes of ammunition. Scopes. Helmets. NV equipment. Everything they needed for a hit. It was a simple plan. Drive to within a mile of the meat-packing facility. Leave the vehicle. Make a covert approach and check, from a distance, that the facility was deserted, as Jesús said it would be. Infiltrate the facility and wait for their targets to arrive. If everything went as it should, they'd be dead before they even knew they had company. Easy. The unit would destroy the Zeta money before they had time to get into the tunnel, and be back at the motel by midnight.

Darkness would fall at approximately 2230 hours. For now the setting sun softened the Texan terrain. As they drove along a deserted road through the semi-arid landscape, Danny occasionally caught a glimpse of the Rio Grande glittering red in the distance off to his right. It would disappear as soon as he saw it, however, as the terrain undulated.

'Let's get off the road,' Spud said finally. 'We're about two klicks out.'

Danny nodded, slowed down and pulled off the tarmac on to the hard-baked terrain to its northern side. The Tahoe's suspension was good, but it was still a jolty drive over the rough ground as Danny headed toward a mound approximately fifty metres away. It was big enough to hide the vehicle behind and ensure it would remain unobserved from the road. Anyone approaching off-road from the north would see it, but that was a risk the unit would have to take. There was nowhere else to secrete it.

They alighted and silently went about the business of preparing themselves. Each man fitted his kevlar helmet, complete with four-tube ground-panoramic NV goggles. They strapped knee pads to their dominant knees – the right for Danny, Spud and Tyson, the left for Spike. They tightened the straps on their ops waistcoats and checked over their weapons and personal comms systems. They strapped their sand-coloured Bergens to their backs, and Spud took a piss. Within five minutes they were ready to go.

The sun had almost set. Danny knew they would be very hard to make out against the arid backdrop of the terrain, if anyone was watching in the darkness. They still moved carefully. Patrol formation. Spud led. Danny second. Then Spike. Then Tyson. They kept a distance of ten metres between them, and jogged at a steady, even pace. Danny clutched his rifle as he moved, and panned left and right, hyper-alert to any potential threat. He saw nothing but the parched brush of the semi-arid landscape. Undulating terrain. A gibbous moon rising in the sky to the south. Even though night was falling, it was still hot – high twenties – and he was soon sweating.

They'd been jogging for ten minutes, and were moving up a slight incline, when Spud suddenly stopped and raised one hand. Danny instinctively fell to one knee. Raised his weapon, panned left and right. He knew Tyson and Spike would be doing the same behind him. Up ahead, Spud crouched low and crawled to the brow of the incline. He looked south, then Danny heard his mate's voice in the earpiece. *'We've got a problem.'*

'Keep your positions,' Danny told Tyson and Spike over the comms. He lowered his own weapon and crawled up to the brow, where Spike was lying on all fours. He looked south, and immediately saw what Spud meant.

The meat-packing factory – their destination – was 500 metres away over open ground. Beyond it, the reflected moon on the surface of the Rio Grande. The factory itself was a single building. A huge, prefabricated shed. Its short end was facing them, and was at least seventy-five metres wide. A line of trucks were parked along the right-hand side – Danny couldn't see how many. On the opposite side of the building was a shed. Danny assumed that was a generator housing since he couldn't see any electricity lines going in.

None of this was the problem.

The problem was the SUV parked in front of the building, its headlamps on and shining almost directly toward them. And the huge main door to the building, slightly ajar, light leaking out from the gap.

'Shit,' Danny breathed.

Jesús had said the facility would be deserted.

Jesús was wrong.

Or lying.

He pulled a spotting scope from his ops waistcoat. Directed it toward the SUV. It was difficult to see anything clearly because the headlamps were shining in their direction. But he managed to make out silhouettes moving behind the car. It looked like they were taking something out of the trunk. He watched as two, maybe three, figures carried their package toward the door. They disappeared inside.

'We're too late,' Danny growled.

Spud looked at him. He had a sharp eagerness in his eyes. 'We can still take them, mucker,' he said. 'They don't know we're here. If we advance now, we'll have the element of surprise.'

Danny's eyes narrowed.

'C'mon mucker,' Spud breathed. 'If they're anything like that Jesús cunt, it'll be like shooting fish in a barrel.'

Danny looked back over the open ground. There was no sign of any other hostiles. And Spud was right. If they reached the facility before the cartel boys got their money into the tunnel, everything should be relatively straightforward.

So what was stopping him?

'Why are they early?' he breathed.

'Who cares, mucker? If they thought we were going to be here, they wouldn't have turned up at all.'

Danny gave it five seconds' thought. 'Okay,' he said. 'Let's do it.'

He looked back toward Tyson and Spike and gestured at them to join him and Spud. Neither man had any objection to advancing on to the target. They edged forward in a leapfrog formation. Danny and Spud led, moving fifty metres toward the facility but at a slight angle so they were veering away from the field of the SUV's headlamps, while Spike and Tyson covered them from the brow of the incline. Then Danny and Spud hit the ground and covered while Tyson and Spike caught up and advanced another fifty metres. Within ten minutes they had silently covered the open ground and were positioned thirty metres from the western corner of the facility. The large door to the building was still maybe half a metre ajar. Light was still spilling from it. Danny could smell the river, now no more than a hundred metres away.

They listened hard for a moment. Danny thought he maybe caught the sound of a voice from inside the facility, but he couldn't be sure.

Tyson and Spike dropped down on to one knee. Tyson covered the entrance, Spike the long side of the facility leading down to the river. Danny and Spud advanced side by side, weapons engaged and pointing directly at the entrance to the building.

Twenty metres.

Ten metres.

Five.

They stopped. Danny held his breath and listened hard. He saw three guys from a distance, but there could be more. If he could make out voices, he could estimate how many they were up against. But there was nothing.

He turned to Spud. Pointed to his mate, then to the door. Spud understood the signal and advanced to the corner of the doorframe. Stopped. Waited for Danny to follow.

Which he did.

Stood in the open section of the door frame, his shadow

stretching out behind him. Held his weapon with one hand and displayed three fingers to Spud.

Two.

One.

They advanced into the facility with a single movement. Danny took in everything with one glance. The facility was a single room, about a hundred metres in length. It was well air-conditioned. Along the left-hand side of the facility was a line of cold-storage units. Along the middle, a single steel work counter stretching almost the whole length of the facility. In the corner to Danny's left, a collection of metal trolleys. To the right, an immense shrink-wrapping machine. The place stank of dead meat and disinfectant.

And at the far end of the facility was a man. Just one.

He was short. Young, probably not more than eighteen. An intricate tattoo on one side of his face. It was quite clear he hadn't expected anybody to arrive. He was armed, but his weapon was slung casually across his front. He was smoking a cigarette and didn't seem to have noticed the arrival of two heavily armed guys in the facility.

That didn't last long.

By the time Danny had the target in his sights, the guy had dropped his cigarette and was fumbling for his weapon. Danny had his crosshairs settled precisely on the target's head. At the last moment, he lowered his weapon slightly so he was aiming for the right shoulder. He needed information. Hard for a guy to talk with a round in his skull.

He fired.

The suppressed knock of his weapon echoed slightly around the facility. The target hit the ground behind the long metal work counter. Out of sight. His screams, however, were sickening. They echoed far more resoundingly than the gunshot had. Danny panned round, on high alert for the guard's mates, but there was no sign of them. 'Get in here,' he said sharply over the comms. He advanced quickly along the left-hand side of the work counter, weapon still engaged, an extension of his body. In his peripheral vision he was aware of Spud moving along the right-hand side of the counter, his weapon panning left and right, searching for threats.

He was halfway along the building. The target's screams were worse. It sounded an alarm bell in Danny's head. Normally, after the initial pain, the screams faded. He sensed that the target was trying to make it sound as if his condition was worse than it was.

Nice try, Danny thought.

He was three metres from the end of the worktop. The target was on the ground at the very end. Danny could see part of his foot. In his head, he pictured the target lying on the ground, clutching his wound with one hand, and maybe a pistol with the other. He would be trying to decide from which side of the counter the enemy would be approaching . . .

Danny looked across the worktop at Spud. Gave him a nod that carried with it a whole set of instructions. Instructions he knew Spud would instinctively understand. Danny edged forward. He was at the very end of the worktop now. One more step, he'd be in the target's line of fire. He knocked the edge of the work counter with the butt of his weapon.

Instantly, the screaming stopped. Rounds flew from the end of the counter across the path that Danny would take if he continued to walk. But Danny didn't do the walking. Spud did. He stepped to the end of the counter, aimed his weapon down and to his left and fired a single shot. The target's gunfire stopped. The screaming started again. Danny held his position as Spud moved round to the end of the worktop. He leaned down, picked up the bleeding target and hurled him face down on to the metal worktop.

The guy was a mess. As butchered as the carcasses that normally found their way into this meat-packing facility. He had bullet wounds to both shoulders. His tattooed face was smeared red and he was heavily bleeding out on to the metal worktop. After just a few seconds, blood was dripping down its edges. The screaming was replaced by a desperate, shaking whimpering. He didn't have long.

Danny looked right. Tyson and Spike were advancing along the counter, one on either side, twisting their bodies to aim their weapons all around the facility. Standard operating procedure, checking for unseen hostiles, but Danny knew if they hadn't come under attack by now, there was no one to do it. 'Talk to him,' Danny called to Tyson. 'We need to know how long since his mates went down the tunnel . . .'

A moment later Tyson was alongside the bleeding, shaking cartel boy.

'Tell him we'll give him medical attention if he tells us what we want to know,' Danny instructed. He earned himself a withering look from Tyson. An 'I have done this before' look. Tyson bent over and started muttering something in Spanish into the ear of the dying target. He spoke quickly but quietly. Danny watched the target's eyes roll. He wondered if he could understand anything Tyson was saying.

Danny looked left. He saw what the guy was guarding. A large trap door in the floor. To one side, a sheet of vinyl flooring that had clearly been used to hide it.

The guy mumbled incoherently in Spanish. Tyson looked up. 'They've been in there for fifteen minutes. He says it takes about twenty minutes to get the money across.'

'How many guys?' Danny demanded.

'Four, including him.'

Danny nodded. 'Finish him,' he said. He strode toward the trap door and wasn't looking at the prisoner when he heard the shot that quietened him for ever, and the thump as he slid off the metal counter on to the floor. Instead, Danny was aiming his weapon at the closed trap door – as if it might burst open at any moment.

He considered his options.

Option one: retreat now. Get back their vehicle and floor it back to the motel. Pump Jesús for more intel about Zeta money runs. Danny dismissed that. Jesús was a dead end. His intel was flawed.

Option two. Wait here for the Zeta delivery boys to return. Take them out as they emerged from the trap door. Pointless. Their objective was to hit the money, not the personnel.

Option three. Enter the tunnel. Go after the money. Do what they came here to do.

'You thinking what I'm thinking, buddy?' Spud said. He'd joined Danny by the trap door.

Danny narrowed his eyes. 'No,' he said. 'We don't know what's down there. We retreat.'

'Fuck that,' Tyson said. 'We can take them.'

'He's right,' Spud agreed. 'Get on the blower to Kleinman. See if his drone's picked up anything we can't handle on the other side.'

Danny hesitated. He pulled his encrypted sat phone from his ops waistcoat. Speed-dialled a number. It was answered immediately. Kleinman's voice. '*Go ahead.*'

'We were too late,' Danny said. 'They were already here. One target down. The remainder are in the tunnel.' He paused. Glanced at the fierce, eager faces of his unit mates. 'Is your drone picking up any movement of personnel on the far side of the river?'

'*Negative. We saw one vehicle entering forty-five minutes ago. Probably arriving to pick up the money. That aside, it's all quiet on the south side of the river.*'

Time to make the decision.

'Permission to go after them,' he said.

There was a moment of hesitation at the other end. Danny sensed Kleinman was uncertain. He understood why. This had turned into a purely reactive operation. They were fighting blind.

'*Go ahead,*' Kleinman said finally.

'Okay. We're going in.'

'*Black.*'

'What?'

'*Be careful. Those tunnels are temporary. They're known to collapse. Any violent vibrations . . .*'

'Understood,' Danny interrupted. There wasn't time for a long conversation. He killed the phone. He looked at his team. 'We need one guy here, covering the entrance,' he said. More options entered his thinking. Clearly he wanted Spud by his side. And for the briefest moment he recalled the conversation he'd overheard at the motel. *I don't trust that guy Tyson ... his file isn't exactly spotless ...*

Danny quickly divorced himself from that thought. It was just paranoia. The truth was, the decision about who was to stay behind and guard the entrance to the tunnel made itself. He turned to Spike, the least experienced of their team. He prepared himself for an argument, but an argument didn't come. 'I'm on stag, I know,' Spike said. He turned his back on the others. Spud's gaze lingered on his cousin for a moment, but he said nothing.

Danny and Tyson approached the trap door. Bent down and grabbed the hinged rungs that were flush with the floor. Lifted the door. A damp, earthy smell immediately hit Danny's senses. There was a vertical drop of about three metres, and a metal ladder leading down. Only enough room for one man to descend at a time.

Danny recalled the map he'd seen of the area. 'It's about a hundred metres,' he said. 'A couple of minutes to cross. If the Zetas are moving money, they'll be slower. Maybe fifty metres ahead of us. We might get to them before they leave the tunnel.'

The guys nodded. Nothing to add. Danny took the lead. Felt his pack scraping against the side of the wall as he descended. When he reached the bottom of the ladder, it was dark even with the light spill from the top of the hole. He engaged his NV goggles. The world turned grainy, but illuminated. The tunnel headed south toward the river, just as he'd expected it to. It was about three metres wide and two metres high. Enough headspace to walk without hunching, but only just. There were two narrow-gauge rails on the ground and a slightly wonky timber beam across the ceiling of the tunnel, held up by two more beams on either side. It looked distinctly Heath Robinson, and Danny had to suppress a prickle of claustrophobia.

He looked up. Gave a thumbs-up to indicate that Spud and Tyson should follow. Stepped forward several metres into the tunnel, his weapon engaged.

Even with his NV goggles, he could barely see anything. The goggles were designed to pick up ambient infrared light. Here, metres under the ground, there was none. He flicked on the infra-red beam of his weapon's sights. What looked like a narrow laser beam sliced through the darkness up ahead, invisible to anyone without NV capability. The tunnel took a downward incline. The narrow-gauge tracks disappeared to a point in the distance. There was a support beam every five or ten metres. They didn't look at all trustworthy or well engineered. Danny made a private bet with himself that the upper echelons of the Zeta hierarchy would never find themselves in such a dangerous place as this.

Two more laser beams cut through the air from behind him, telling him Spud and Tyson had made it down into the tunnel. As Danny advanced, the beams occasionally disappeared as their path was blocked by his body. He started to jog. His footsteps were curiously deadened by the vast quantity of earth surrounding him.

Earth *and* water, he told himself when he'd advanced about fifty metres and the tunnel had levelled out. They must be under the river by now. He put from his mind the thought of all that water above him. Kept driving forward. Searching. Listening. Expecting any moment to see movement up ahead.

There was none, except for the occasional scurrying of rodents at his feet. The smell had changed. Oil. Droppings. It was bitingly cold.

Gradually, the tunnel started to incline upwards. Danny felt a mixed sense of relief – they had probably passed under the river – and apprehension – where the hell were their targets?

He stopped suddenly. The view up ahead had changed. About twenty metres away, Danny could see the end of the rails. There was a cart sitting there – it reminded Danny of the railroad carts he'd seen in cowboy movies he'd watched as a kid. It was empty. There was no sign of enemy personnel.

Silence. He sensed Spud and Tyson at either shoulder.

Danny's heart pumped heavily. He was glad of it. It heightened his senses. Raised his level of alertness.

Kleinman had told them only one vehicle had arrived at the Mexican warehouse. Did that mean they still had the element of surprise? Could they still make the attack?

He moved forward. Reached the end of the tunnel. In the enhanced peripheral vision of his NV goggles, he saw the final support beam was reinforced by what looked like small sandbags. There was a ladder here, just as there had been on the American side, except this one was concreted to the wall of the hole leading upward.

Danny paused. Switched off the IR beam from his sights. The laser disappeared. Spud and Tyson did the same. He looked up. The exit to the hole, two metres above his head, was open. He could just make out the rectangle of the opening. But there was still very little ambient infrared light, which told him the lights in the warehouse were off.

He breathed steadily and deeply. A conscious, determined choice to keep his nerves calm and his thinking clear. Climbing up that ladder was a risk. If anyone was covering it with a weapon, Danny would be exposed. They'd be sitting ducks if anyone was waiting for them.

He paused for a second. Then he unstrapped his helmet. Removed it. Unclipped his weapon. Held it vertically with the helmet propped on the end. Climbed two rungs of the ladder, one-handed. Raised his weapon vertically so that just the top of the helmet was exposed a couple of inches above the line of the trap door.

Waited.

Nothing happened.

He lowered the helmet. Jumped off the ladder. Strapped the helmet back on again. Re-clipped his weapon to its lanyard. Re-activated the infrared beam. Turned to his unit mates.

'We should retreat,' he said. 'Something's not right. It's dark in the warehouse. No noise. Why, if the targets are operating there?'

He turned to Tyson, seeking his opinion. 'They'll be outside the warehouse,' Tyson said. 'Loading the money into their vehicle. We can nail them if we move quickly.'

'Agreed,' said Spud.

Two to one. Danny was outnumbered. He hesitated for a moment. Then he turned his back on his mates and quickly climbed the ladder.

As he emerged from the tunnel, he rolled quickly over the lip of the hole, ending up in the firing position on one knee. He panned round, allowing the infrared beam to illuminate his surroundings.

There was a lot to take in.

They had emerged against the long edge of a large hangar-cum-warehouse, similar in size to the meat-packing factory on the other side of the border. It was clearly used as some kind of vehicle repair facility. Ten metres to Danny's eleven o'clock a car was jacked up, two metres in the air. Straight ahead of him was a workbench, seven or eight metres long, with tools hanging from its edge. A few metres beyond that was a line of vehicles. Their trunks were open, as if they were waiting to be filled. Dotted around the hangar were large piles of storage boxes, welding stations and various collections of oil drums. It briefly crossed Danny's mind that a welded oil drum would be a good storage container for a pile of illicit cash.

He was aware of a second infrared beam as Spud emerged from the tunnel. By now he had clocked several industrial spotlights on tripods about five metres high. Approximately ten of them, at even intervals around the perimeter of the hangar. Spud settled down on to one knee, six metres to Danny's one o'clock.

A third IR beam panning round the space told him Tyson was in position. He was in the firing position ten metres to Danny's three o'clock. Danny located the exit at the end of the hangar, thirty metres away to his ten o'clock. It was closed, though his NV picked up the faint rectangle of the doorframe where the ambient light from outside was leaking through.

Everything was still.

Silent.

No sign of the money. No sign of the cartel runners.

It didn't stack up.

If their targets weren't here, why were the cars lined up like that, ready to take the money?

'This isn't right,' Danny breathed. His instincts were screaming at him. What if Rav had been right about the money on the Cessna? What if the Zetas had been tipped off that the plane was going to be hit?

They'd made the wrong call advancing through this tunnel.

'Agreed,' Spud said, a biting tension in his voice.

'Get back down the tunnel. *Now!*'

It was as if his words had flicked a switch.

There was sudden movement. It came from Danny's one o'clock, from behind the line of parked vehicles with their trunks open. He knew they were dogs, even though he couldn't see them clearly. They were fast. A blur. Out of pure instinct, Danny twisted his body, and his weapon with it, to take out the threats. He had just enough time to see the dogs were going straight for Spud before everything turned to shit.

There was a click. A hum. In an instant, Danny was blinded. His vision was filled with a hot, painful white light. It stabbed his retinas.

He knew exactly what had happened: all the industrial spotlights in the hangar had been switched on. A deliberate tactic to burn their night vision. His reaction was immediate. He ripped the NV goggles from his head, just as he heard a piercing roar of pain that he knew came from Spud. There was a vicious snarling sound and Danny knew for absolute certain that the dogs had attacked his mate.

But he *still* couldn't see anything. The blinding white light had compromised his vision. It was blotchy. Fully burned out. The hot white of the spotlights didn't help. He staggered back, just as he heard the rough bark of two rounds being released. He instinctively knew they came from an AK and an Armalite AR-15 respectively. He also knew if he hadn't staggered back a couple of paces, he'd have taken a direct hit. He sensed a round ricocheting on the ground a metre in front of him.

There was a muzzle flash almost directly to his twelve o'clock. His only indication of where the threat was coming from. He raised his weapon and fired a burst in that direction. There was a blistering sound of rounds against metal and glass – he knew he'd

171

hit the vehicles and he swore inwardly. It would be obvious to anyone watching that his aim wasn't true.

That he was an easy target, with no cover.

More incoming. Danny felt impact. A round had hit the ceramic of his body armour, knocking the air from his lungs. He was flung, gasping, to the ground just as he heard, over Spud's screaming and the horrible snarling of the dogs, Tyson's voice: *'Get back to the tunnel! Back to the fucking tunnel!'*

But now it had truly gone noisy. Danny's vision was beginning to repair itself. He could see a blurred silhouette that was Spud, writhing on the ground, the two dogs still attacking. One of them had Spud's arm in his jaws. The other was snapping at Spud's face. Danny saw a metallic glint coming from their teeth – it meant they'd been coated with titanium to make their bite more brutal. A second blur was Tyson, crawling toward the tunnel.

Danny hauled himself back up into the firing position. He could see targets now. Fifteen, maybe twenty. They emerged from behind the line of vehicles, from behind storage boxes and the jacked-up car.

They were everywhere. Danny knew his only chance of survival was to return fire. Without his body armour, he'd already be dead. Aggressive counter-fire was his only chance. He let loose another burst, panning round in a blind attempt to hit as many enemy targets as possible. The blurry figures disappeared, their fire suppressed, but Danny couldn't tell if he'd hit them or forced them down into cover. He raised his weapon, set it to semi-automatic and aimed a round at one of the spotlights. It found its mark. The light fizzed and burst noisily, showers of sparks falling from the bulb.

Danny quickly turned his attention to Spud. He directed his weapon at the dog that was snapping at Spud's face. Laid down a single round. There was a slam and a whimper. The dog collapsed.

But in the time he had taken to eliminate the pit bull, the enemy figures had reappeared. Danny was under fire again. Heavy fire. A second round hit the ceramic of his plate hangars. He managed not to fall this time, but he was on borrowed time. He returned fire, staggering back to the tunnel.

'*GO!*' he heard Spud's agonised voice roar. '*FUCKING GO!*'

Danny had no choice. He staggered back, returning fire as best he could, knowing this was his only chance of avoiding a round. Some of his semi-blind bursts of rounds must have hit their mark, because he heard the sound of men screaming in pain. But if they were screaming, it meant they were only wounded – and there was still incoming fire. When he reached the hole that led down to the tunnel, he simply jumped backwards, landing heavily and awkwardly two metres below.

'Tyson!' he yelled, aiming his weapon up toward the hangar. 'Tyson, where the hell are you?'

'*Get back here!*' Tyson roared from further inside the tunnel.

'Spud!' Danny shouted. 'He's still up there. We need to get him ...'

'Get back here!' Tyson repeated.

'We're not leaving Spud there.'

Suddenly, Tyson was there. He grabbed Danny by the shoulders and spun him round. He too had raised his NV goggles, and his face was dripping with sweat and dirt. His eyes were a bit wild. 'Listen to me,' he said, his voice low and urgent. 'Spud is dead. Did you get that? *Spud is dead.* And if we don't move in the next ten seconds, so are we. This exit is booby-trapped. We *have* to bug out.'

The gunfire in the hangar had stopped. There was no sound of Spud's screaming.

Danny felt his stomach turning over.

'*Now!*' Tyson said.

He flicked his NV goggles down. Turned his back on Danny. Started to run back down the tunnel.

'How do you know it's booby-trapped?' Danny shouted.

'Follow me.'

Danny was torn. Torn between going back for his mate and his instinct for survival.

He flicked down his NV. Followed Tyson back into the tunnel. Caught up with him at the first support beams. The ones padded with what looked like sandbags.

Only now, facing them from the other direction, he saw these sandbags had cables running from them.

Explosives.

The implications of the past few minutes crashed in on Danny. The cartel had been expecting them. They *knew*. It was a set-up. Tyson was right. If they returned to the hangar, they'd draw fire. And the tunnel was booby-trapped for a reason. The cartel knew it was compromised. It was no longer any good to them. Which meant they wouldn't hesitate to destroy it.

'*Run!*' Danny hissed. But Tyson was already moving. Sprinting north, down the incline. Danny followed, genuine sickness in his gut. The roughly hewn walls of the tunnel passed his peripheral NV vision in a blur. Their sprinting footsteps gave a dead thump. Any moment now, Danny thought. Any moment now the booby trap was going to blow. He tried not to let the crippling sense of claustrophobic panic slow him down. Tried not to imagine the crushing horror of the tunnel collapsing on top of him. The water flooding in.

How long did he have? If the cartel were going to detonate the explosions, they would need to evacuate the hangar first. That quantity of explosive would wipe them all out otherwise.

It would take them a minute at the most.

Which gave him about twenty seconds.

He estimated he was only at the halfway mark. Tyson was ten metres ahead of him. He forced himself to run harder.

Ten seconds . . .

Tyson tripped. Danny stopped just in time to avoid stumbling. He bent down. Grabbed Tyson's arm. Pulled him to his feet.

Which was when they heard it.

The explosion was muffled, but still loud. The shock wave, focused by the narrow tunnel, hit them like a bullet. They were two metres from the nearest timber beam. It shifted a couple of inches. A shower of dirt fell on them.

'*MOVE!*' Danny bellowed, pulling Tyson to his feet and pushing him along the tunnel.

He didn't look back. Didn't *dare* look back. It would waste time they didn't have. But he could hear a dreadful, rushing, roaring sound behind him. He knew the tunnel was collapsing at the Mexican end. And once that party started, it wasn't going to end until the whole tunnel was destroyed ...

Dirt was raining down on them now. It was in Danny's mouth and was blocking the tubes of his NV goggles. He ripped them from his face again, and instantly regretted it because now the dirt was in his eyes. He felt moisture. Water was coming in from somewhere. He couldn't tell how far ahead Tyson was. It was too dark. The air was too thick.

The tunnel, however, was inclining upwards. He surged forward. Behind him, there was a terrific, terrifying crash.

More dirt and dust.

Water at his ankles.

Run.

He could barely breathe. Each intake of breath caused dirt to catch in the back of his nose or throat. It was like drowning.

Run.

He kept his eyes half open. With a sudden surge of relief, he thought he could see light up ahead. Hard to tell the distance. Fifteen metres? Maybe twenty? All he could do was keep pushing on.

'Danny!'

He couldn't tell if it was Tyson's voice or Spike calling to him. It was muffled by the collapsing tunnel. He looked down and realised he was wading through water up to the knee. It was like treacle. Danny grasped for the light. The intervening distance seemed to close only in slow motion. Like in a dream, where his legs wouldn't carry him fast enough to escape some unseen terror. It seemed to take an age to close it down to ten metres.

To five.

He saw Tyson. His unit mate was halfway up the ladder. The water was waist-high. Surging and sucking. Danny lost his footing. Slipped back. There was water up to his neck. He had to swim. Thrust himself forward with huge, powerful strokes. There was barely a foot between the water line and the top of the tunnel.

Until suddenly he burst through into the entrance hole that led up to the trap door. The ladder was still there, though it had slipped. Danny threw himself on to it. Climbed the rungs two at a time. Looked up. He saw Spike there, leaning down, holding out both hands. Danny stretched upwards. Felt Spike clutch his right arm. Launched himself up from the ladder just as he felt his unit mate pulling.

A second later, he was scrambling out of the hole. He collapsed on to his knees, coughing so badly and with such a hoarse bark that he thought he might bring up blood any second. He was aware of Tyson doing exactly the same, just a couple of metres away from him.

His head was spinning. On the edge of his consciousness he was aware of Spike shouting. 'Where's Spud? *Where the hell's Spud?*'

Danny inhaled deeply. He looked up. Spike had his weapon engaged and was pointing it back down the length of the facility. Tyson was still on his knees, bent double. Danny felt a torrent of hot fury boil through him. It was almost as if somebody else was in control of his body. He hurled himself at Tyson and somewhere, in the corner of his brain, he heard Rav's voice. *I don't trust that guy Tyson . . . his file isn't exactly spotless . . .*

He found himself grabbing Tyson by the neck. Pulling him up to his feet and throwing him against the metal workbench where the dead cartel fighter was splayed out. 'They knew we were coming!' he bellowed. 'Did you tell them?' He pulled his handgun and pressed it against Tyson's head. '*Did you tell them?*'

'What are you *talking* about, Black?' Tyson spat back at him. 'Are you fucking *insane?*'

'*Then what the fuck was that about?*'

'Jesús goes missing. The Zetas get jumpy. They put on extra security . . .'

Danny stared at him. He realised Tyson was right. They should have predicted this.

'What's going on?' Spike shouted. 'Where the hell is Spud?'

Spud. The image of his mate flashed through Danny's brain. Spud, lying on the floor, one dead pit bull by his side, another with its jaws locked ferociously around his forearm.

He clenched his eyes shut. Felt the water dripping heavily off his clothes. Tried to think clearly. Had Spud still been alive when Danny threw himself back down into the tunnel? Danny thought so.

But why?

Why hadn't the cartel gunmen just taken him out? He was a sitting duck.

'Where's Spud?' Spike demanded for the third time.

Had they just been leaving him to the dogs?

'What the fuck do you think?' Tyson barked. 'He's fucking KIA.' Tyson turned to Danny. 'We need to get out of here.'

Or did they have other plans for him?

'No,' Danny said. He turned to the others. Tyson looked a mess – filthy, wet, battle-worn. Spike looked properly scared.

'What are you talking about?' Tyson barked.

'He's not dead. They could have shot him. They didn't. They're keeping him. It's what they do – make an example of their enemies.'

'Bullshit,' Tyson said. 'They didn't shoot him because he was down and they were concentrating on us.'

But Danny wasn't listening. He strode up to Spike. 'Give me your sat phone.'

Spike grabbed his handset from his ops waistcoat and handed it over. His hand was shaking and he looked as sick as Danny felt. Danny speed-dialled Kleinman. The call was answered immediately. Kleinman sounded stressed. '*What the hell . . . there was some kind of explosion . . .*'

'Where's your drone? Do you have eyes on?'

'*Yes. It's a shitstorm there. What happened?*'

'They've got Spud. Find out what vehicle he's in. Follow it.'

'*It's not that simple, Black. We have to . . .*'

'Follow it!' Danny barked.

He killed the line. He was halfway to the exit. Running. Tyson and Spike were on his shoulder. He holstered his handgun and raised his rifle as he ran. At the exit to the meat-packing factory, he stopped for a moment at the half-open door. Knelt down into the firing position and laid down two rounds. He jabbed his finger forward. Spike and Tyson understood the instruction and advanced outside. Danny heard each of them fire a warning round before he himself advanced into the darkness.

Everything was still. The cartel vehicle was sitting outside. Its headlamps were still on, its trunk still up. Danny ran up to it and checked the ignition. The keys were still there. 'Get in,' he told the others, before closing the trunk. 'Tyson, drive. Get us back to our vehicle.'

He climbed into the passenger seat as Tyson took the wheel and Spud got into the back. He speed-dialled Kleinman again. 'Well?' he said, before the CIA man even had time to answer.

'*They've got him,*' Kleinman said. '*At least I think it's him – they've got someone hooded and tied. He's in one of their vehicles and they're driving south in convoy.*'

'Keep on him,' Danny said. 'If you lose him, he's a dead man. I need to know his exact destination. Is that understood?'

'*You're to return to unit base immediately, boy. You get that, right? This could be an international incident.*'

'You want an international incident, Kleinman? See what happens when I cross the border using my assault rifle as a passport.'

'*No!*' Kleinman's voice was sharp.

'Then listen to me, and carefully. To hell with the operation. To hell with killing Zetas. We're going after Spud, whether you like it or not.'

Silence. Then: '*Get back here now. We're tracking him. We'll make a plan, you have my word.*'

Danny hesitated. Every instinct told him to go after Spud immediately. But the logistics were more complicated. They needed Kleinman's help – both to track Spud's location, and to get across the border. 'Trust me, Kleinman, if you lose that convoy, you'll have more than a fucking limp to show for it,' he said. 'We're on our way back. Make arrangements for us to get across the border immediately.'

He killed the phone again. Then he turned to Tyson. 'Fucking drive,' he said.

MONDAY

FIFTEEN

London.
0600 hours GMT.
Tam's bones ached.

He'd spent all night in position, on the rooftop, keeping eyes on the back entrance to the Paradise Gym. The rain stopped at midnight, but his hair and the bottom of his trousers – those parts of him that weren't protected by his raincoat – remained damp until the small hours. He was dry now, but he was still cold, tired and thoroughly pissed.

And he still had eyes on.

There were some comings and goings throughout the night. A couple of shifty-looking guys turned up at about 0130 hours. One of them left half an hour later. Tam knew from the voices of his unit mates over the comms that the front entrance to the gym was busier than the back. 'Jeez,' Webb said just before 0300 hours, 'this is muscle Mary central. You'd think these fellas would have fucked themselves dry by now.'

But no. The Paradise Gym clearly did a good trade at night.

The clientele started to drift away at dawn. At 0430 someone put a load of trash on to the pavement outside the gym. At 0500 a refuse lorry made its noisy, beeping way along the street to pick it up. So Tam wasn't surprised to see an SUV pull up outside the rear entrance at 0610 hours precisely.

Not surprised. But suspicious.

There were three things that made him pay attention to this vehicle. The first was its expense. It was a new BMW X5 with all the trimmings. Stainless steel engine guard. Titanium-effect grille bars. In Tam's experience, bad guys made this mistake every day of the week. Showing off their wealth, instead of choosing the right disguise for the right environment. That X5 would look fine in a better part of town. Out here, in this dingy backstreet of east London, it stuck out.

The second alarm bell was the slight green tint of the windscreen. Toughened glass. Hardly your regular optional extra.

And the third alarm bell was caused by the bulges under the jackets of the two guys who climbed out of the vehicle once it was parked up on the sidewalk, its hazard lights flashing. Tam spoke quietly into his comms. 'We have movement of armed personnel to the rear of the building,' he said.

Tam focused in on the faces of the two guys. They didn't look British. Hispanic, if anything, though Tam didn't jump to conclusions. He knew skin colour was a poor indicator of nationality. He considered himself to be as American as apple pie, though plenty of people disagreed. Still, there was something about these two guys. They seemed somehow uncomfortable in their environment. Tam would have bet pretty much anything that they weren't UK nationals.

One of them stood on the sidewalk, looking up and down the road, clearly keeping watch. The other opened up the back of the X5. He called to his companion and together they pulled out a large flight case. It was evidently heavy. As they moved it to the back entrance of the gym, they had to shuffle awkwardly with its weight.

Tam spoke into the comms. 'Our guys are making a delivery,' he said. 'I'm going to stick my neck out and say it's not a consignment of poppers.'

The two men dropped the flight case down on to the sidewalk. One of them thumped hard on the door. It opened almost immediately. The guys lifted the flight case and carried it into the building. Their vehicle still had its trunk open. Its hazard lights were still blinking. The guys re-emerged thirty seconds later. Shut the door behind them. Closed the trunk. Climbed into the vehicle. Killed the hazards. Drove off. They'd been on-site no more than two minutes.

'Okay,' Tam said. 'Call me nosy, but I'd like to see what's in that box.'

'*You want to see what's in the box, bud,*' Webb said over the comms, '*you can go hang with the ring snatchers.*'

'You seen anybody go in, last couple of hours?'

'*Negative. It's still early.*'

True that, Tam thought. 'Let me know when the ring snatchers start turning up.'

'*Roger that.*'

Tam kept his position. Eyes on. Didn't move.

The drone footage was monochrome, grainy and indistinct. But it was enough to show that Spud was alive.

Just.

The remaining three members of the unit stood round Rav's screen. It was divided into two sections. The left-hand side showed several still photographs, taken by the drone above the warehouse and saturated by the green haze of NV filters. The blast-damaged warehouse. A hooded man – Spud – being dragged to a car. Several cartel boys, clearly wounded, being carried by their accomplices. A six-car convoy heading west from the facility by the river. They appeared to be heading to the conurbation of Nuevo Laredo, directly across the border from the nearby US town of Laredo.

The right hand of the screen showed the convoy in real time. A map was superimposed on to the screen. The convoy had penetrated the outskirts of Nuevo Laredo, just across the Mexican border and probably twenty miles from the unit's current position. Now it was heading to an area on the south-western side. There were narrow, criss-crossing streets, and more traffic than Danny would have expected at that time of night. After ten minutes, the convoy hooked a right down a very small side street and came to a halt at what looked like a solid wall. Danny's mind was turning over, calculating, observing every square inch of the screen, taking in very precisely the environment Spud was about to find himself in.

On the other side of the wall was a square. Surrounded on three sides by buildings and no obvious way in. The square itself was in fact rectangular. Danny estimated it was forty metres wide by eighty metres deep. It was hard, because of the darkness, to discern the geography inside it, but it looked to Danny like the northern half of the square, opposite the entrance, was thick with trees – an intense patch of urban greenery surrounded by concrete. There also appeared to be a couple of low buildings on the northwestern and northeastern corners. The roofs of these buildings were just visible because here there was no canopy. The convoy was on the south side of the enclosure.

'We have five per cent power on the drone,' Hernandez said.

'How tall are those buildings?' Danny asked.

'The entrance to the square, where the convoy is now, is on a narrow road called Avenida Hidalgo,' Kleinman replied, sparking his lighter with more vigour than usual. 'It's a built-up part of town. I'd say five storeys, maybe six.'

'Occupied?'

'Probably.'

'Do we have rappelling gear?' Danny pointed toward their store room.

Kleinman shook his head. 'We can get it, but ... twenty-four hours.'

'Forget it.'

After a few seconds it became clear that the wall at which the convoy had stopped was in fact not a wall but a long, sturdy gate. It was hinged on the left-hand side, as you looked from the street. It swung open and the convoy entered the square. Stopped. The gates swung closed again.

'Can you zoom in?' Danny said.

Rav, who had wisely barely said a word since the three SAS men had stormed into the ops room, tapped on his keyboard. The field of view grew closer, the image grainier. They watched as the car doors opened. Men emerged. Danny focused in on the blurred image of two guys pulling a third from the rear of the second vehicle. The indistinct figures dragged their prisoner toward the northwest of the square, but Danny soon lost sight of them among the thick trees.

'I can switch to thermal imaging view,' Rav said. 'It'll use more power, but . . .'

'Do it.'

Rav clicked his mouse.

'Three minutes,' Hernandez said.

The screen changed. Heat spots of red and yellow appeared within the square. Danny could see Spud was still being accompanied by two guys toward the northwestern building. The rest of the square was deserted, apart from the area around the entrance gate. Here, the vehicles produced substantial heat spots. Around them, Danny counted six guys.

'Two minutes.'

There was movement. They seemed to be helping other men out of the vehicles. The wounded? Danny reckoned so. They started moving slowly in pairs toward the other building on the northeastern side of the square. It took about a minute to install three of the wounded Zetas in that building.

'Thirty seconds.'

The men helping them returned to the convoy. Most of them climbed into the vehicles. The gates opened and the convoy left. Danny quickly counted up the remaining personnel in the square. Spud and one guard in the northwestern building. Three wounded Zetas in the northeastern building. Two guards at the gate.

The screen suddenly went blank. 'Okay, we've lost power,' Rav said.

'Why haven't they killed him yet?' Danny said.

'He's valuable,' Kleinman replied. 'Spud's clearly an SF soldier. It would suit the Zetas' vanity to show off that they've caught him. They'll have something special planned for him, I'm afraid. I think they'll move him from that city centre location once they've decided exactly what to do with him. My guess is they'll move him tomorrow, after dark.'

'Why?'

'Because if they were going to get him out of Nuevo Laredo tonight, they'd be doing it now. It'll be impossible for us to track him once he's out in the countryside.'

'So we hit them today,' Danny said. 'We need a chopper. We can fast-rope into Spud's location ...'

'That's just not going to happen, Black,' Kleinman said. 'An operation like that needs to be authorised from the White House. If you think the Oval Office is going to risk an operation like that on Mexican territory ...'

'What about Mexican law enforcement?' Tyson said. 'The regular police are in the pockets of the cartels, but the *Federales* know what they're doing.'

Kleinman gave him an 'are you an idiot?' look. 'You think the CIA is going to let the *Federales* know UK special forces are operating on Mexican soil with the blessing of the US? Forget it, buddy. In any case, the *Federales* need to keep their powder dry. They wouldn't chance a confrontation with the Zetas unless there was definitely a high-value target on-site.'

'I disagree,' Tyson said. 'I've known some of those guys. They hate the cartels.'

'Of course they do. But for a handful of sicarios, the risk–reward ratio doesn't stack up. And even if it did, and even if there was a remote possibility that my handlers gave the green light to tipping off the *Federales*, those guys would just turn up and shoot everyone on sight. They won't differentiate between your guy and the Zetas. They'll kill everyone on-site.'

'Then we do it ourselves,' Danny snapped back. 'Can your border control units get us into Mexico?'

'That will take ten to twelve hours to arrange.'

'*Jesus!*' Danny slammed his fist on the table. 'We haven't *got* ten to twelve hours. If Spud dies, Kleinman, it's on you.'

Kleinman removed his glasses and cleaned them on his tie. He spoke mildly, but there was a tear of sweat on the side of his face. He put his glasses back on and peered at them with his watery eyes. 'Your quickest option is a regular border crossing,' he said.

'They'll have a vehicle full of hardware,' Rav protested. 'If they get searched by border control or *Federales* ...'

'It's still the quickest option, boy. And they're leaving the US, not entering it, which means the checks will be fewer and further between. But I don't like it. There are cameras ... facial recognition—'

'Jesus, Kleinman,' Danny snapped. 'Don't you care we're a guy down? What's your fucking problem?' He paced the room for a moment, trying to straighten out his thoughts. 'We'll do the border crossing. To hell with the cameras. We'll head straight for the location.' He realised his two unit mates were staring at him. 'What?' he said.

'Look at it, Black,' Tyson said. 'It's daylight. It's surrounded by high buildings. Spud's got a guard with him. If those gates are as sturdy as they look, you're going to need a hefty charge to blast them open. The guy watching Spud is going to nail him the moment he hears that happen.'

'Are you telling me you're happy to leave him to those animals?'

'No,' Tyson said. 'I'm saying we need a scalpel, not a hammer. We need to infiltrate that square covertly, otherwise Spud's dead in a second. We need to do it quietly, and we probably need to do it after dark. Right, Spike?'

Spike nodded, but didn't say anything. He looked uncomfortable with the disagreement.

'It's blocked off on four sides,' Danny said flatly. 'We can't grapple down, we can't fast-rope in. There's no way of gaining access to the square apart from through that gate. You reckon those two guards are going to open up just because we ask them nicely?'

There was a tense silence as Danny and Tyson stared at each other.

'I think maybe they will,' Kleinman said quietly.

The Regiment guys turned to look at him. He had his back to them, and was staring at a map on the wall.

'What do you mean?' Danny said.

Kleinman turned round. Glanced at Rav and Hernandez. 'Ana Rodriguez,' he said.

The other two CIA guys looked uncomfortable.

'The Zetas have wounded men,' Kleinman said, as if that explained everything.

'For *this*?' Rav said. 'You're going to use her to get one guy out? Boss, Langley are *not* going to see that as a good cost–benefit . . .'

'What are you talking about?' Danny interrupted. 'Who the hell is . . .'

'She's an informant,' Kleinman said. He limped away from the map into the centre of the room. 'In fact, she's more than that.' He sniffed and looked as if he was deciding to tell them the next bit. 'She's Z1's sister,' he said.

Danny felt a surge of anger. 'Why haven't you mentioned her before?'

'Because before, boy, she was a dead end,' Kleinman snapped back. He gathered his thoughts for a moment while sparking his lighter. 'Ana Rodriquez is a doctor. She works at the local hospital in Nuevo Laredo. My reading of her is that she's conflicted. She's always been split between loyalty to her brother and contempt for the path he's chosen. For the past few years, she's taken advantage of the fact Z1 has instructed his Zetas not to harm her. She offers medical help to anyone – Zeta or non-Zeta – caught in the crossfire of the cartel conflict. A way of salving her conscience, I suppose. She also has a son, Miguel. I made contact with her three years ago. Told her I could get her and her son into witness protection, if she gave me information about Z1. She showed me the door. Blood thicker than water, I guess.'

'What the hell has this got to do with Spud?' Danny demanded.

'She called me this morning,' Kleinman said quite calmly. 'To talk.'

'We don't have time to chinwag with your fucking narks,' Danny said. 'We need to focus on Spud.'

'You haven't been listening to me, Black,' Kleinman countered mildly. 'I told you, she offers medical help to Zetas and non-Zetas alike. Well, not any more. Z1 issued a threat. Unless she supports

190

only Zeta personnel, people will die. The cartel members know who she is. She could approach that compound and gain access on the pretext of offering to treat their wounded men.'

'But you said she'd been showing you the door.'

'Up until today. Something's changed. She's scared, for herself and her son. I think that gives us some leverage.'

'We haven't got time to play games,' Danny snapped.

'You haven't got time for anything else.' He pointed at Tyson. 'He's right. There's only one way into that location, and it's through the front. You need a Trojan horse. Ana Rodriguez can give it you. One of you can enter through the gate. The other two can take up positions in the buildings overlooking the square to provide fire support. Do it once the sun goes down and you'll at least have the cover of darkness.' He shrugged. 'I'm not going to try to persuade you. That woman could be very helpful to me in other ways. I believe she knows the location of Z1's safe house, for a start. I'm offering you *my* best asset. Take it or leave it.'

Danny felt all eyes on him. He tried to get his head straight. Was this the right call? Was Kleinman's offer really the best way of helping Spud? He didn't understand the CIA man. Before, he'd seemed unwilling to have a British team on this job. Borderline unhelpful. Now he was giving up his best asset? 'How would she know the Zetas have wounded personnel?' he said.

'Are you kidding me, boy?' Kleinman said. 'Those kids will be on their cell phones non-stop. Half of Nuevo Laredo will know there's been a shoot-out by now. It'll be on the blogs, Twitter . . .'

Danny gave it a moment more thought.

'It adds up,' Tyson said. 'It's our best chance of getting to him.'

'Do we call the headshed?' Spike asked.

'No,' Danny said. 'There's no point. They don't have time to deploy and we don't want them telling us to stand down.' He turned to the CIA man. 'What game are you playing, Kleinman?'

They exchanged a long look. 'I'm playing hunt the Zetas,' Kleinman said. 'What game are *you* playing?'

'No game,' Danny said. 'I just want my friend back.' And Kleinman's contact, he realised, was the best way of making that happen. The *only* way. 'Where do we meet this woman?' he said.

Ana Rodriguez woke with a start. She instinctively checked if Miguel, who was lying in the bed next to her, was asleep. When she saw he was, she turned her attention to the vibrating cell phone on her bedside table.

The caller's number was withheld. Ana answered anyway. '*Si?*'

Silence.

'Who is this please?'

A monotone, almost robotic American voice spoke to her in English. '*Expect visitors. Do what they say. When it's done, we will make arrangements. Make sure you're ready to leave.*'

A click, and the line died.

Ana realised she was sweating. She quietly climbed out of bed and started padding around the bedroom, her hands trembling as she silently started to gather together some clothes for Miguel and pack them into a small rucksack. She did the same for herself, then got dressed and went out into the main room. She retrieved her handgun from the back of the cutlery drawer, then took a seat, nursing the weapon and facing the main door of her little house.

It was hot, but she couldn't stop shivering. She checked her watch. It was one o'clock in the morning.

0200 hours.

Danny was preparing himself thoroughly. He felt the sickness of urgency. The longer he took, the more time there was for the Zetas to slot Spud – if they hadn't done it already. But if he went into a manoeuvre like this unprepared, he was asking for trouble.

His ops vest lay on the bed. Next to it, his rifle and handgun. He'd replenished the magazines and replaced all the grenades and other gear in his vest, in case the water in the tunnel had damaged them. He was now quickly putting on fresh, dry clothes. His head was spinning. Spud's safety relied on Kleinman's contact, but that contact was an unknown quantity. What if she wasn't up to the job? What if she messed things up? Too many things had already gone wrong on this operation. Something wasn't right. He felt a deep sense of unease.

He moved into the bathroom. The shaving gear Kleinman had supplied was sitting untouched in the cabinet above the sink. He grabbed the unopened packet of razors. Took them back into the bedroom. Removed a med kit from a new, dry North Face rucksack and took a roll of sticking plaster. He tore off a three-inch length and used it to stick two razor blades to his skin on the inside of his thigh. Experience had taught him your average tough guy didn't linger around the groin area if he was patting you down. And it wouldn't hurt, he told himself, to have a couple of weapons nobody knew about.

He pulled on his trousers, then carried his ops vest and Bergen out of his bedroom. Tyson and Spike were already by the Tahoe, loading their gear into the trunk. Kleinman was watching them quietly. He limped up to Danny. 'You know what you're doing?'

'Sure,' Danny said.

Kleinman handed him three American passports. They were not only completely authentic, they were also well-thumbed and contained stamps from all over the world. The completely unsuspicious passports of well-travelled men. Danny shoved his into the pocket of his dry clothes, then walked over to hand the other two to his unit mates.

He looked over at Kleinman. 'You want me to deal with Jesús?'

'It's already done,' said Kleinman.

'Where's the body?' Danny said.

'Off-site,' Kleinman said. He sounded slightly evasive. 'You'd better go. The border crossing gets busier close to dawn.'

Danny loaded his stuff into the back of the Tahoe. The unit's weapons were stowed in a heavy flight case. They'd packed more than they needed. Several rifles and shotguns from Kleinman's armoury. Plenty of ammunition of different flavours. Night-vision gear. The works. Danny shut it, covered the case with a blanket and slammed the Tahoe shut. He turned back to Kleinman.

'Who took the body?'

'It's dealt with.'

They locked gazes.

'Who else knows the details of our operation, Kleinman?'

'Nobody. You think this would get approval from Langley, Black? I'm sticking my neck out for you. You know what to tell Ana Rodriguez?'

Danny nodded. 'You've booked the room?'

'Holiday Inn, room 735,' Kleinman said. 'It's booked in the name of Sofia Ortiz. You better get moving. The border crossing opens at 0800 hours, but the line starts long before that. First thing in the morning is the busiest time, so you'll have the best chance of getting through without anyone checking your vehicle.'

Kleinman limped back toward the ops room. Danny watched him go. He felt very uncertain. But the clock was ticking. They needed to get across the border.

He climbed behind the wheel, knocked the vehicle into gear and hit the gas.

Spud's world was spinning. Not that he could see it, because he was hooded. But he had a sensation of dizziness. Nausea. Every time he tried to stand, he fell.

His right arm and left leg throbbed with pain. It was here that the pit bulls had sunk their teeth into him. He'd felt teeth scrape against the bone in his forearm, and both limbs were still bleeding, which probably accounted for the dizziness. His wrists and ankles were cable-tied, and there was also a cable tie around his neck. Tight enough to restrict his breathing slightly, not quite tight enough to throttle him. But his captors only had to tug at one end of the cable tie for him to be a dead man. What did he know? They'd driven quickly at first, but then slowed down. Lots of left and right turns in quick succession. Noise – car horns, sirens. So he was in an urban environment. That was good. More people around. If the opportunity arose to alert someone that he was being held, he would grab it.

But until then . . .

He'd been in this situation before. More than once. He knew how to deal with the fear. Accept it. Compartmentalise it. Put it in a little box in his brain. Draw strength from it if he needed to.

Easier said than done.

Spud knew why he'd been taken alive. He knew what the Zetas liked to do to their enemies. He'd seen the pictures of guys with their heads and bollocks cut off. Innards spilling out. Multiple knives sticking into them.

He also knew this: if Danny and the guys suspected he was still alive, they'd be doing everything they could to get to him. Spud's job was to stay alive long enough to give them that chance.

No man left behind. The Regiment's unofficial, unspoken mantra.

Which meant keeping quiet. Feigning suppliance. Not giving them any reason to finish him sooner than they intended.

Cold comfort.

He lay on the ground, breathing deeply. Preserving his strength for the moment when he may need it.

Sunrise.

It hit just as they passed a green overhead sign that read *International Bridges to Mexico*. Now, as they sat in a slow-moving line of traffic on the bridge over the Rio Grande that led across the border checkpoint, the rising sun reflected violently off the line of vehicles ahead. Danny put on his shades and continued to scan the area from the passenger seat of the Tahoe.

They were halfway across the bridge. Up ahead was a wide line of checkpoints, like a toll booth on a busy motorway. They crawled forward at a maximum of ten metres every minute. Danny regularly cursed under his breath. Every minute they wasted here was a minute lost to their main objective: finding Spud. It was all he could do to stop himself from grabbing his handgun, storming up to the checkpoint and shooting his way through.

The air stank of exhaust fumes from the trailing cars. Already the vehicle was like an oven, causing them to sweat heavily.

Because the line was so slow, people were getting out of their cars. Leaving their driver doors open to ventilate the vehicles. A mixture of Americans and Mexicans, but although people were chatting to each other and walking up and down the line, the two nationalities didn't mingle. Occasionally they didn't get back to their vehicle in time to move on, and there was a flurry of car horns and much waving of arms.

Time check: 0810 hours. Danny looked in the rear-view mirror. Spike was in the back. Anxiety was written all over his face. Which figured. Spud was his cousin, after all. Danny himself had a nasty, gnawing sensation in his stomach. He blamed himself. He'd agreed to enter the warehouse when he knew something was wrong. He'd left Spike there. It was his fault . . .

'Your two o'clock, my ten o'clock,' Tyson said suddenly. Danny snapped his attention back to his surroundings. He could see two Mexican guys, each of them about ten metres away in the direction Tyson had indicated. They seemed to be looking directly at the Tahoe.

Danny calmly leaned forward. Removed his handgun from the glove compartment. Kept his gaze on the two guys while unlocking the weapon by touch alone. Tyson was doing the same thing.

'You telling me the cartel knows we're here?' Tyson breathed.

Danny had no answer. He felt sweat dripping down the nape of his neck.

Danny raised his weapon slightly, so it could be seen through the windscreen. At the same time, several car horns sounded. The two Mexican men looked over their shoulders. Turned. Walked back to their vehicles.

'This is fucked up,' Tyson said.

'It was probably nothing,' Spike said from the back. 'Not every Mexican that looks at us is a Zeta, right?'

Danny didn't reply. He didn't know if he was being paranoid or careful.

The car edged forward.

'You don't trust Kleinman, do you?' Spike said.

Danny sniffed. He didn't know who he trusted or what he thought. Earlier that morning he'd even suspected Tyson.

Paranoid or careful?

Maybe they were the same thing.

It took twenty minutes to reach the border checkpoint. Up ahead, on the far side of the checkpoints, Danny counted four separate open-top Hilux vehicles, each with the words *Policía Federales* marked in white lettering on the side. Each vehicle had between two and four guys in the open-top section: Kevlar helmets, body armour, M16s across their fronts. Serious kit. Danny and Tyson stowed their weapons back in the glove compartment.

'This is fucked up,' Tyson repeated. 'The *Federales* are good men and well equipped. We should be using them, not hiding from them.'

But they all knew they didn't have a choice. Kleinman had vetoed that idea, and they didn't have time to argue. They pulled up to a border-control agent. Tyson handed over the three fake passports, along with their vehicle documents. A stony-faced customs woman examined them carefully. Checked the photos. Peered into the vehicle to check they matched. Hyper-aware of the hardware in the trunk, Danny clocked three CCTV cameras pointing in their direction from various angles. He kept his shades on, knowing it would make any facial recognition software less reliable.

What was the problem? The woman was still flicking through the passports. Looking at Tyson, then back at his photograph. Her brow was furrowed. Tyson simply maintained an easy smile.

What the fuck was the problem?

The customs woman handed back the passports. Waved them through. Tyson drove carefully across the border. He kept the speed low. Twenty metres to their ten o'clock, one of the parked-up *Federales* vehicles was pointing toward them. Sunlight glinted off its windscreen, but one of the armed guys in the back was definitely following them with his gaze.

197

Danny snapped his gaze away and looked straight ahead. He was aware of Tyson glancing in the direction of the *Federales* vehicle as he passed.

'Welcome to Mexico,' he muttered.

Ana Rodriguez hadn't moved from the seat facing the front door of her house. She still clutched the handgun. She shivered occasionally, but not because she was cold.

The sun rose. She'd been sitting in darkness, but now a grey light seeped in through her windows. She kept the shutters open so she could tell if anyone was approaching. Nobody had.

At seven o'clock, Miguel woke up. She heard him padding out of the bedroom they shared. Sensed him standing at her shoulder. She made no attempt to hide the gun she was holding.

'Go back to the bedroom, sweetheart,' she said. 'Get dressed. Stay there. Keep the door shut. You're not going to school today.'

'Where am I going? Are you coming with me?'

'Go to your bedroom, sweetheart.'

'Is it because of Uncle Augusto?'

Ana took a deep breath. 'Go to your bedroom,' she repeated.

Miguel stood there for a moment longer. Then he turned and walked back into the bedroom. From the corner of her eye, she could tell he was clutching Buzz Lightyear by its good arm.

Ana could hear the clock on the wall ticking. Her heart beat heavily in counterpoint. The voice at the other end of the phone had told her to expect visitors after dawn. But who *were* these visitors? How would she know they were friendly? Her head was muddled. Confused. She continued to breathe deeply, trying to keep the panic at bay.

The clock ticked. She thought that, maybe, she could hear Miguel gently sobbing in the other room. She resisted the temptation to go and engulf him in her arms. She had to stay alert, for his sake more than for . . .

It happened suddenly. Unexpectedly. A hand clamped itself round her mouth from behind. A second hand covered her eyes. She was ripped from the chair, which clattered as she was hauled to the ground. She struggled and kicked, but a second set of hands ripped the handgun from her grasp and held her legs. She tried to cry out, but her voice was muffled. She fell silent and still when she felt cold steel against her forehead.

The hand covering her eyes moved. She saw a tall man with black hair holding Miguel by his forearm, a pistol in his free hand. He was unshaven and had black, mirthless eyes. The person holding her legs and pressing a gun to her forehead was younger. He had piercing blue eyes and the remnants of acne on his cheek. She could not see the person covering her mouth from behind.

Ana went limp. But something kept her from the cliff edge of overwhelming dread. These men were not Mexican. They were not Augusto's men.

'You want your son to be safe?' said the man with the black hair and the mirthless eyes. 'Then you keep quiet. Nod if you understand.'

She nodded.

The hand moved tentatively from her mouth. The man with acne removed his weapon from her forehead.

'Are . . . are you Kleinman's people?' she asked.

'Rule one,' the man with the dark hair said. 'You don't mention Kleinman to a single soul.' He let go of Miguel, who scampered into the corner of the room, looking frightened. 'Get to your feet,' the man said.

'What . . . what's your name?' she said.

The man didn't answer for a moment. Ana had the impression this was not information he wanted to share. But after a moment he spoke.

'My name's Danny Black,' he said. 'Rule two: you do exactly what I tell you.'

SIXTEEN

'Tyson, guard the back entrance. Spike, watch the front.'

Danny turned to the woman Ana. 'Kleinman says you're Z1's sister. That you have immunity from his Zetas.'

Ana flinched slightly, but she nodded.

'He says you're under pressure to give medical aid to cartel members.'

Ana nodded again.

'You need to answer me a question, and answer truthfully. Your life depends on it. More than that: your son's life depends on it. Does anyone – *anyone* – know you're in touch with the CIA?'

She shook her head vigorously. Danny believed her.

'Your brother's men have something I want, a friend of mine, so this is what's going to happen. There's a Zeta enclosure on the southwestern edge of Nuevo Laredo. We're going to wait until nightfall. Then I'm going to secrete myself into the back of your vehicle. You're going to drive to the gate on the southern edge of the enclosure. We expect there to be two cartel guards at the gate. You'll tell them you've heard they have wounded men. When they let you in, you'll open the back of the vehicle. I'll deal with the guards and you'll be free to leave the enclosure.'

She stared at him. Then, in heavily accented English, she said: 'You're completely insane.'

Danny ignored that. 'Before we leave, we're going to move your son into a room at the Nuevo Laredo Holiday Inn. The only people who'll know where he is will be us and Kleinman. He'll be safe. When we've left the Zeta enclosure we'll take you straight to him. Kleinman will have a man at the hotel waiting to get you into the US. You'll both have a new identity in twenty-four hours. Where is the boy now?'

'Miguel?' Ana called uncertainly. A boy appeared from the adjoining room. He was holding a Buzz Lightyear toy, which had one arm missing. Ana ran over to hug her son. For the briefest moment, she reminded Danny of himself. He understood the fear she was feeling about the safety of her child. He stepped toward her. 'Does the boy speak English?' he said.

She shook her head.

'Listen to me,' he said. 'The Americans can hide you. Completely. After today, you don't need to worry about your brother ever again.'

'What if something happens to me?' Ana said. 'What will happen to Miguel then?'

'Nothing will happen to you. You'll be in and out of that place in less than a minute. You have my word.'

'But who are you? What is your word worth?'

Danny glanced toward the boy. 'I'm a father,' he said quietly. 'Nothing will happen to you. By tomorrow, you'll be in the US. Safe. Both of you.'

Ana stared at her feet. Danny could tell a riot of emotion was surging through her mind.

She looked up. 'I can't do it,' she whispered. 'It's too dangerous. If something happens to me . . .' She looked toward her son.

Silence.

Danny took a step back. 'Fine,' he said. He walked toward the front door, but stopped halfway there and looked back over his shoulder. 'He won't last forever, you know. Your brother. One day, maybe soon, some rival cartel guy will kill him. And you know how these people work. They don't just kill off the head of the family. They kill the *whole* family.' He looked meaningfully at Miguel. 'Your decision, Ana,' he said. He walked to the door again.

'Wait,' Ana said.

Danny stopped.

'How do you know there will only be two guards at the door?'

'My friends are going to put in surveillance on the enclosure. If anything changes, we'll know and we'll react accordingly.'

'What do we do between now and nightfall?'

'We get Miguel into his room at the Holiday Inn. Then we put ourselves in position near the enclosure. We don't think they'll try to move my friend before it gets dark, but if they do I'll be in a position to hit them. As soon as that happens, we'll go pick up Miguel. Meet with Kleinman's guy.'

She stared at him. Then she nodded. 'When do we have to leave?' she said.

'Now. We need to put in surveillance as soon as possible.'

Ana licked her dry lips. She hurried over to Miguel and started talking to him in fast, nervous Spanish. The kid listened carefully. He looked confused. She put one hand on his cheek, then hurried over to the window and started closing the shutters.

'There's no time for that,' Danny said. 'Leave everything behind. Let's go.'

Spike and Tyson were waiting for them. There were two cars here: a beaten-up, dented old brown saloon, and an old van. Ana led them to the van and opened up the back. It had a strange smell – a mixture of old paint and medical disinfectant, as if the vehicle was used for many different purposes. There were boxes of medical gear piled up and strapped to the right-hand side of the van. A solid metal panel separated the back of the van from the cab, and there were more boxes piled up against it.

Danny turned to the others. 'Let's get the gear,' he said.

Spike and Tyson opened the flight case full of weaponry in the back of the Tahoe. Ana's and Miguel's eyes widened as they started removing the hardware. Tyson and Spike took their respective rifles and started stripping them down into constituent parts. That way, they would fit inside their North Face rucksacks. They could sling them over their shoulders as they made their way from their vehicle into the buildings that overlooked the square where Spud was being held. They stashed their helmets and NV goggles into the rucksack, along with fistfuls of cable ties and rolls of duct tape for suppressing prisoners. They double-checked their handguns, holstered beneath their jackets. Checked over their personal comms – covert earpiece and a tiny microphone clipped to their jacket. Once they were done, aside from not looking Mexican, they appeared pretty unremarkable. A couple of guys with rucksacks. Nothing more. As he was doing this, Tyson eyed Ana up and down quite overtly. 'Live here by yourself, darling?'

'With my son,' Ana said curtly.

'You should call some time, when you need someone to keep the bed warm, eh?'

'Drop it, Tyson,' Danny said. He kept his own rifle in one piece. He stashed it in the back of Ana's van, along with the ops vest he'd replaced back at the motel, and his helmet and NV goggles. Like the others, he kept his handgun on his person. He sorted his comms, then turned to Tyson and Spike. 'Alpha One,' he said, pointing to himself. 'Alpha Two.' He pointed at Tyson. 'Alpha Three.' Spike. 'Estimated time to the target location, twenty minutes. It's 1040 hours now. Kleinman will have booked the hotel room. We'll check Miguel in, then get in contact with you. Let's get moving.'

Tyson and Spike closed up the trunk of the Tahoe, loaded themselves into the front and drove away.

Danny turned to Ana. 'Ignore Tyson,' Danny said.

'I've dealt with worse than him,' Ana said. Danny didn't doubt it was true.

'He and Spud are going ahead. There are buildings surrounding the square that we need to enter. They're going to set up surveillance and firing positions from the roof. They'll have the advantage of height. If there's any kind of trouble, they'll be able to supply fire support. If you hear gunfire once we're inside the enclosure, hit the ground and don't move. Is there anything you don't understand about that?'

'You promised nothing would happen to me.'

'It won't. If there are only two guards by the gate, which is what we expect, I can easily deal with them. But we always plan for contingencies. So if you hear gunfire, you hit the ground, okay?'

She nodded mutely. Danny removed a map of Nuevo Laredo and pointed out the target area. 'Avenida Hidalgo. You know how to get there?' he said.

'Of course.'

'Then let's go. We'll get Miguel to the hotel first. Then we can park up near the Avenida Hidalgo when it's time for me to get into the back of the van.'

Danny climbed into the passenger side of the van. There was a single long bench. Ana took the wheel. There was room between the two of them for Miguel. The kid was obviously nervous of Danny. He shuffled up toward his mum, clutching his Buzz Lightyear. Ana held the wheel tightly for a moment, breathing deeply before she started the engine. She looked back toward the house that she obviously knew she would never see again. Danny felt a moment of great respect for this woman. He knew she had very little choice but to follow his instructions, but this took guts and most people would have crumbled.

'It'll be fine,' Danny said quietly. 'You'll be over the border by midday tomorrow.'

Ana didn't reply. She knocked the van into first and hit the gas.

The morning rush-hour traffic was constricting the roads of Nuevo Laredo. Ana knew them well. She drove down side streets and took innumerable short cuts as she wound her way north. Miguel asked a few questions in Spanish as they went. Ana answered him with a pretence of calmness. Danny kept quiet. She was the kid's mum. She knew how to handle him.

The sky was a fierce blue, the morning sun bright. It gleamed dazzlingly off the traffic. Shades were essential. Ana wore a fashionable pair of Jackie O sunglasses that hid her tired eyes. She was a good-looking woman, but Danny's mind couldn't really be further from such thoughts. He felt like he was on a knife's edge. He didn't know how much time he had to get to Spud. Maybe they'd moved him already. If so, he had no leads . . .

It took ten minutes to reach the Holiday Inn – a squat tower of glass and brown brick surrounded by scraggly palm trees. It overlooked a main road and, beyond it, the Rio Grande, glittering in the sun. A *Federales* vehicle was parked up alongside the river. It wasn't the first Danny had seen in the journeys to and from Ana's house. Several of these vehicles had been parked in various locations. His instinct was that they were there as a deterrent more than for any real tactical reason. Ana caught him looking at the vehicle. 'They have their places where they always park,' she said. 'It's stupid, really. The cartel always knows where they are.'

'Decoy vehicles,' Danny said. 'That's all.'

As they climbed out of the car, Danny saw Ana look across the parking lot over the river toward the US, half longingly, half apprehensively. Then she put her arms around Miguel and drew him closer to her.

'The room's booked and paid for. It's in the name of Sofia Ortiz. Go and check in.'

Ana entered the hotel hand in hand with Miguel. Danny kept a ten-metre distance and watched from the bland lobby as she checked in and took her key cards. The receptionist pointed her toward the elevator. Danny met her by the elevator doors. They were silent as they ascended to the seventh floor. Miguel kept close to his mum. As the doors slid open, Danny stepped into the corridor first and looked left and right to check it was empty. It was, so he nodded at them to exit the lift and led them down the corridor to room 735. Ana used one of her two key cards to open it. They entered.

It was a very ordinary hotel room. A double bed. A desk with mahogany-effect veneer. A TV with a welcome message in Spanish for Sofia Ortiz. A small shower room. The room had a faint smell of stale cigarettes, but was otherwise neat and clean. Danny stood by the door while Ana installed Miguel on the bed. She put Nickelodeon on the TV, then hugged him desperately and issued a series of instructions to him in Spanish. Miguel said nothing. He was obviously frightened and confused, but he seemed to be taking on board what his mother was telling him.

'We have to go,' Danny said after a couple of minutes.

Ana nodded. She hugged her son again, then kissed the top of his head and left one of the key cards on his bedside table. Now, however, his attention was on the TV. Ana kissed him again, then moved over to where Danny was standing by the door. Miguel was staring at the TV.

'He knows not to leave the room, or answer the door to anyone?'

Ana nodded. 'He's a sensible boy,' she said. 'Sometimes I leave him alone at home.' She sounded like she was trying to persuade herself it was true.

Danny grabbed the *No Molestar* sign from the door handle, then opened the door. The adults stepped outside. He closed the door and put the sign on the exterior. He could see Ana was trying not to cry. 'We really need to go,' he told her.

They were back in the car two minutes later. Ana drove, but she kept looking in the rear-view mirror for as long as she could still see the Holiday Inn. Only when it was out of sight did Danny feel her concentration was truly on the road.

They were heading west around the southern perimeter of Nuevo Laredo. Once, Danny supposed, this would have looked like a regular, slightly down-at-heel border town. Now, everywhere he looked, there were signs that Nuevo Laredo was a place that knew violence. The shell of a car. A burned-out, dilapidated house. Occasionally they would pass under a concrete pedestrian bridge. Without exception, these bridges were plastered in cartel grafitti. The same graffiti became more prevalent as they headed toward the southwestern side of the town. It covered whole buildings. Danny didn't understand the Spanish, but he could pick out the words *Los Zetas* with ease.

Their surroundings became more and more run-down. The tarmac on the roads was split and broken. The buildings on either side were a mish-mash. Some were constructed from bare breeze blocks, their pointing rough and eaten away. Others had once been painted in bright colours, though the paint was now fading and peeling. Other, older buildings were made of timber. Some of the exterior walls were pockmarked with bullet holes. And although, in places, there were a few old men sitting together on rickety chairs on the pavements, Danny had a general sense that this area was less busy than the other parts of Nuevo Laredo he'd seen. A sense that people were avoiding being on the streets, even in the daytime.

Danny felt his mind shifting into the cold, analytical mode that preceded such an operation. Stripping away anything that wasn't necessary. Now was not the time to worry about the hit on the plane. About the disaster in the tunnel. About the fuck-ups that had preceded this moment. There was no point dwelling on mistakes. They had a situation that needed fixing, and Danny was going to fix it. End of story.

'Who is he?' Ana said. The first words she had spoken in five minutes.

Danny snapped out of his mental preparations.

'I told you. A friend of mine.'

'He must be a good friend. For you to do this.'

Danny saw her glancing at him from behind her sunglasses. He stared straight ahead.

'We go way back,' Danny said. It was impossible to explain, so he changed the subject. 'Was he always like this? Your brother, I mean.'

Ana made a disdainful noise. 'Did he burn villages? Cut people's heads off? As a child? No. Of course not.'

'So what happened to him?'

She didn't answer immediately. When she did, her voice was emotionless. 'You want me to tell you some story of a terrible childhood? A great trauma?' She shook her head. 'There is none. We were poor, but our parents looked after us. Made sure we went to school. Made sure we had food and clothes. They were very proud when Augusto joined the military. Do you have a brother, Señor Black?'

Danny kept his voice level. 'Yes.'

'And do you understand him?'

Danny didn't reply.

'I guess not,' said Ana. 'I do not understand my brother either. He is just a bad man. An evil man.'

Danny felt a pang of guilt, thinking about his own brother. How he'd dumped him in that police station. Truth was, he was just another victim of people like Ana's brother. Z1's influence was far-reaching.

'I have to get away from him,' Ana said quietly. 'He wants to bring Miguel under his wing. I can't allow him to have that influence over my son.'

'Where does he live, Ana? Your brother. Where's his safe house?'

Another brief silence.

'You were right, what you said back at my house,' Ana said. 'One day, someone will kill him. It will be someone like you or someone like him. But I will not be the person who gives them that information. He is a monster. But he is still my brother. Family means everything to him. I suppose it means something to me too.'

There was a finality in her voice that brought that line of conversation to an end.

'Are you clear what you have to do?' Danny said. 'Tonight. When we enter the enclosure.'

Ana nodded. Danny noticed she was gripping the steering wheel unusually hard. There was a tear on her cheek. He hoped she was up to this.

'We're two blocks away,' Ana said.

'Pull over here. I'm going to take the wheel. This is where we sit it out until it gets dark. If I get word that they're moving my friend, I'm going to floor it to the entrance of the enclosure. You'll need to get out.'

She nodded mutely and pulled up into a deserted side street. Even when the car came to a standstill, however, she kept her hands, knuckle-white, on the wheel and stared ahead.

'You'll be safe,' Danny told her. 'You'll be back with him tonight. Just do what we said, okay?'

She nodded again. Said nothing. Danny exited, slipped round to the driver's side and helped her out. She seemed very frail. He wondered if she was up to this.

Time would tell. Danny settled in behind the wheel and prepared himself to sit it out until it got dark.

★　　★　　★

1115 hours.

'Alpha One, this is Alpha Two and Alpha Three, check.'

'*Check. We're in position. What's your status?*'

'Preparing to enter the target building. Over.'

Tyson had parked the Tahoe one block north of the target, in a regular parking place outside a shabby mini-mart. Fifty metres along the road was an open-topped *Federales* vehicle. Tyson had noticed a few of these artfully positioned vehicles around the city. Here, he could make out the shadow of two federal police officers in the front, but he didn't allow himself to stare too closely and attract their interest. Not with an M4 rifle in his rucksack and a Sig 9mm about his person.

Instead, he and Spike quickly headed south. They were now standing in front of a fast-food joint. It was closed at this hour, a metal shutter pulled down over its frontage. The shutter was covered with cartel graffiti. The sidewalk was littered with polystyrene burger boxes. The two men stared at the building in front of them, their heavy rucksacks slung over their shoulders.

'Do you think the building is occupied by cartel members?' Spike asked.

'Doubt it, Snowflake,' Tyson said. 'It's a dump. My money's on poor locals. They're probably terrorised by the cartel, so if the Zetas use their premises, they can be sure no-one's going to grass them up. It makes sense for them to have places they can hole up dotted around the town.'

Tyson continued his examination of the building. It was four storeys high. Concrete render. Securely shuttered windows. No visible entrance. This was the northern edge of the square where Spud was being held. The gate where Danny Black would attempt to gain entry was on the southern edge. To provide decent surveillance and effective fire support, he and Spike needed to be up high – preferably on the roof of the building, with one of them on the western side and one on the eastern side.

Which was why they were about to split up.

A homeless guy staggered past. Tyson waited for him to be out of earshot before speaking. 'There's no external staircase to the roof,' he said. 'We'll have to try and gain access from inside the building. You go west, I'll go east.'

Spike nodded and instantly headed east along the road. Tyson strode west. Took a right after twenty metres. He was now walking along the eastern edge of the building. It looked similar to the northern side. Ageing concrete, metal shutters. But also, twenty-five metres along, there was a door. Made from solid, varnished wood, with dull brass fittings, it looked oddly out of place against the concrete. It was locked, of course. On the right-hand side was a wide panel of intercom buttons. Forty: ten buttons for each of the four floors. Tyson pressed one of the fourth-floor buttons: 43. There was a pause of twenty seconds before a voice answered. '*Si?*'

'*Entrega,*' he said in good Spanish. 'Delivery. For number 42, no answer.'

There was a mumbled response that Tyson couldn't hear. A buzz from the door. Tyson kicked it open and slipped inside.

It was dark in here, and considerably colder. Stone floors and concrete walls sucked the warmth from the air. As Tyson's eyes adjusted to the darkness, he saw a rack of pigeon holes for mail on his left, and a wide flight of stairs to his right. He removed his handgun, unlocked it and started to move upstairs.

Spike's voice in his ear. '*Alpha Three check.*'

Danny Black: '*Alpha One check.*'

'Alpha Two check.'

He encountered nobody until he hit the second-floor landing. Here, he heard footsteps coming from above. He swiftly moved on to the second floor and waited by an open door until he heard the same footsteps descending to the ground floor. When all was silent, he moved up again.

He wanted to get to the roof. When he reached the fourth floor, he found it was not going to be possible. There was no emergency exit, no fire door. He cursed silently. His backup plan was considerably more risky. He would need to gain access to one of the apartments overlooking the square. He quickly adapted his thinking. A third-floor apartment would be best.

Probably a quarter of the way along from the south edge. That would give him enough height to stay hidden, but a close enough angle to provide effective covering fire if it was required. He hurried down the stairwell, hit the third-floor landing and turned left. There was a very pronounced stench of greasy cooking along here. Tyson fully expected to find a poor, run-down apartment behind the door of number 33 – which was where he was headed. Impossible to know, however, how many people would be living there.

He positioned himself outside the door. Listened in. He could hear a TV blaring. Nothing else. He rapped twice on the door.

No answer.

He rapped again.

Footsteps approaching.

The door opened a couple of inches. Tyson shoulder-barged, putting all the force of his considerable bulk into the action. The door slammed open and Tyson was immediately aware of a middle-aged man falling back into the room. He had a bit of a belly, and wore baggy trousers and a string vest. Kicking the door shut with his heel, Tyson raised his weapon, holding it steady with both hands and aiming it directly at the Mexican, who stared down the barrel in utter terror.

'*Quién más vive acqui?*' he demanded in perfect Spanish. *Who else lives here?*

The man shook his head. '*Nadie . . .*'

Tyson quickly took in his surroundings. It was a bedsit. Unmade bed against the left-hand wall. TV in the corner. Small kitchen area with piles of unwashed crockery. Several full ashtrays. An open window overlooking the central square where Spud was being held.

'Get on the floor,' Tyson said. 'Face down. Now.'

The man did as he was told. Tyson lowered his weapon and opened up his rucksack. He pulled out cable ties and duct tape. He bent down and cable-tied the struggling man's wrists and ankles. Then he wrapped duct tape around his mouth and head. He put his handgun to his skull. 'Make a sound,' he said, 'I'll kill you.' The man went rigid with fear. Tyson turned the TV up slightly, just in case his threat failed to work.

'*Alpha Two, check.*'

'Alpha One, check. State your location, Alpha Three.'

'*On the roof. I've got eyes on. You?*'

'Third floor. Do you copy, Alpha One?'

No reply.

'Do you copy, Alpha One?'

'*This is Alpha One, check.*' The comms was scratchy and unclear. Tyson guessed Black was a couple of blocks away, so the short-range radio connection was flaky. He quickly pieced his weapon together and moved over to the window. The square was instantly recognisable from the drone footage they'd watched earlier. The northern half of it was covered with thick trees – a strange miniature jungle in the middle of the city. He could make out the roofs of the two small shacks in the northwestern and northeastern corners. Spud was being held in the former. The wounded Zetas were in the latter. He cast his eyes over the solid metal gates on the southern edge. It was covered in cartel graffiti. There was a tiny hut to one side of the gate – Tyson had missed that on the drone imagery. That was where the guards would be sheltering from the sun. He looked up toward the opposite rooftop and could just make out the form of Spike, lying on his front, his weapon covering the gates.

'All quiet on the western front,' he said into his comms, ignoring the muffled complaints of the Mexican man on the floor.

'*Roger that,*' came the reply.

SEVENTEEN

London.
1400 hours GMT.
'Status?' Tam spoke into his comms.

'*We've seen nine guys enter the gym. Two guys leave.*'

It had been a slow morning. Nobody had entered the Paradise Gym until midday. Only now did Tam feel he could risk entering without seeming suspicious.

He stood up, stepped away from the edge of the rooftop and removed his raincoat. The clothes underneath didn't look too bad, but he brushed them down with his hands anyway. Then he ran back along the rooftop to the metal staircase that led down to street level. He walked back past the rear entrance to the gym, past Webb who was covering the rear at ground level, and hooked a left toward the main street.

It was busy. The early afternoon traffic was queuing both ways. Somewhere in the distance, Tam heard a police siren. He loitered on the corner of the road until it faded, the warning from their faceless handler ringing in his ears: '*Under the radar . . . we don't want the UK authorities to know you're involved . . .*'

Tam clocked Brooks and Dixon in the skate park on the opposite side of the road. He strode along the sidewalk until he reached the front entrance. The words *Paradise Gym* above the shop front looked even seedier by daylight than they did by night. Tam tried the door. It was locked, but there was an intercom to one side. He pressed the button.

There was a twenty-second pause. Then a voice came over the intercom. 'Yeah?'

'Hi,' Tam said, making no attempt to hide his American accent. 'I'm in town for a few days. Friend of mine told me this was a good place to relax.' There was no reply. Just a crackly silence that told Tam the intercom was still active. 'So whaddya say?' he added.

There was a buzzing sound. The door latch clicked. Tam pushed it open and walked inside.

He found himself in a dimly lit hallway. There was a sweet, pungent smell in the air. Tam neither knew, nor wanted to know, what it was. Thin carpet. Yellow walls. There was another closed door at the end of the hallway. Tam moved forward and opened it.

He found himself in a reception area. There was a desk, a threadbare sofa and a vending machine. Several pictures hung on the wall. Each one depicted a bronzed, muscle-bound topless guy. Tam immediately noticed the security camera in one corner of the room. Red light glowing. A young man sat at the desk. He had chiselled features and intricate, expensive tattoos on his right arm. He looked Tam up and down with a faintly lascivious expression. Tam smiled back. 'Hi,' he said.

'Well, hi,' the young man replied. 'We love an American accent. Welcome to the Paradise Gym. We haven't seen you here before?'

'Like I said ...' – Tam jabbed one thumb over his shoulder to indicate the intercom –'I'm new to town.'

'Nothing like fresh blood,' the young man said.

'I was thinking I could maybe use the gym,' Tam said. 'Then, you know, hang out?'

'Yeah, hang out,' the guy replied. 'I know. So ... you don't seem to have any gym gear.'

'Hoping you could sell me some,' Tam said. He fished a wad of notes from his back pocket. 'Happy to pay.'

'Most people are,' the young man said. 'I'm afraid we don't sell gear, but I'm sure I can find something for you to borrow, although it may be a little tight.' He looked Tam up and down appreciatively. 'Why don't you have a seat? You'll need to fill in a temporary membership application.'

The application form was a joke. A slip of paper, shabbily xeroxed from the original, on to which Tam inscribed a fake name and fake address, before signing something that said he knew how to use the gym equipment. He handed it back to the young man, who didn't even look at it. 'This way,' he said.

Tam followed him through a door at the back of the reception room. It led to another corridor. A door to the locker room was on the left. A staircase at the end on the right. A fire door at the very end. Tam deduced this was the rear entrance he'd been watching all night. 'Just wait in there,' said the young man, indicating the locker room. 'I'll see what I can find for you.'

Tam entered the locker room. It was grim. Open urinals along one wall. An open shower along the opposite one. Lockers along the third, and a bench with pegs along the centre of the room. It stank of sweat and piss, and maybe something else. Seven sets of men's clothes were hanging on the pegs. They corresponded to the nine minus two punters Brooks had seen entering.

The door opened. The young man entered, carrying a pair of shorts and a T-shirt. He handed them over to Tam with a wordless smile. 'I'll leave you to get changed?' he said, without showing any sign of leaving.

'That would be swell,' Tam said.

Another smile. The young man turned his back on Tam. 'Shout if you need anything,' he said as he left the locker room.

Alone again, Tam hung the gym gear on one of the pegs. Felt under his jacket for his side arm. Cocked and locked it, then left it loose in his holster. He waited another minute before exiting the locker room.

The corridor was empty. He quickly hung a left, toward the staircase at the end of the corridor. Hurried up it. The staircase wound back on itself at a half landing. Tam noticed a security camera here, too. A lot of security cameras, he thought, for a simple gym. But by the time anyone looked through this footage, he hoped to be long gone.

'Heading up the stairs,' he spoke into his comms. It was important the guys knew his rough location, in case anything happened.

'*Roger that.*'

He stopped at the first floor, even though the staircase continued up to a second. A glass door set into a glass wall looked on to a very ordinary gym. Rowing machines, cross-trainers, free weights, the works. Seven guys were working out. Tam looked straight past them toward three doors on the far side of the gym. All closed, and no indication what was behind them.

He hesitated for a moment. Then he made the call to continue up the stairs. If he didn't find what he was looking for up there, only then would he risk trying to gain access to the doors across the gym.

Half landing. Security camera. Red light. Tam carried on up. 'Second floor,' he said into the comms.

The second floor was quieter, and for a good reason: there was a no entry sign on the door that led off the staircase. Tam went through it. He found himself on another corridor that led to the front of the building. It contained three doors, evenly spaced along the right-hand side. Tam's sense of the geography of the building told him these doors led to rooms above the gym. He tried each of them in turn. They were all locked.

He was about to remove his tension wrenches from his wallet when the door leading to the staircase opened. A thickset man with several days' stubble and a face like a bulldog appeared behind him at the end of the corridor. 'Can't you fucking read?' he said.

Tam gave him his most winning smile. 'I was looking for the gym,' he said.

'Fucking fag,' the bulldog muttered under his breath. 'Gym's downstairs.'

'Right,' Tam said. 'Okay. Downstairs.' He turned and sauntered easily back up the corridor to where the bulldog was holding open the door to the staircase. He fixed him with an easy stare, making sure the bulldog had absolutely no idea that Tam was going to attack the moment he was in reach.

The two men were a metre apart when Tam performed a sudden, textbook palm strike. He thrust the heel of his hand upwards against the bulldog's nose. It was Tam's go-to manoeuvre. A nose broken in that way was much more painful than a nose broken from the side. It would put pretty much anyone out of play. The bulldog let out a deflated groan and moved his hands up to protect his bleeding nose. Tam was already preparing his second hit: a strike to the carotid artery. The bulldog was a tough, sinewy guy, but nobody was invulnerable to violent strikes to vital soft body parts like that. As soon as Tam's hammer fist hit the artery, the bulldog crumpled to the floor with a solid thump.

Tam worked quickly. He rifled through the guy's pockets and immediately found keys. He checked the stairwell to ensure nobody was coming, then moved quickly toward the first of the three doors. He found the correct key after three goes. Opened the door and looked inside.

It was a dark room. The walls were painted matt black. There was an unpleasant, sticky carpet. No furniture, except a table against one wall with a plastic box full of condoms. Against the left-hand wall, three glory holes at dick height. And against the far wall, a further locked door. Tam didn't need much imagination to work out what this room was used for, but he figured these were mostly night-time activities. He grabbed the bulldog by his ankles and dragged him into the room. He could be out for anything between five and fifteen minutes. He shut the door on him and tried the second.

Same deal. The glory holes leading into the first room were on the right-hand wall.

He backed out and found the key for the third room.

Bingo.

It was an office. Desks, computers, in-trays. A Xerox machine. But against the right-hand wall was the flight case Tam was looking for. He tried to move it with his foot. It was very heavy. He wondered what he'd find inside. Weapons? Ammunition? Whatever it was had a good, solid weight to it. He knelt down in front of the case and tried to open the latch. Predictably, it was locked.

Tam was in the process of taking the tension wrenches from his wallet when his earpiece burst into life. '*Okay, buddy, we've got a problem.*' Brooks's voice sounded suddenly very tense.

'Go ahead,' Tam said, as he picked the lock of the case.

'*Aiden Bailey's here. He's got five guys with him. Motherfucker looks like he means business. I think you've been made.*'

'Armed?' Tam demanded as he raised the lid of the case and looked inside.

'*Heavy coats, bulges at the back, each of them. They've got substantial firearms slung over their shoulders.*'

Tam stared at the contents of the case. He cocked his head. This wasn't what he'd expected. There was no military-grade hardware here. This was a trunk full of neatly packaged white-brown powder. Approximately 100 kilos. Street value? Tam didn't know, but surely several millions.

'How long have I got?' he said as he removed his phone, captured an image of the dope and closed the case.

'*They'll be at the main entrance in thirty seconds.*'

It would take at least forty-five seconds for Tam to get out of the building. If Bailey and his men were on a war footing, and it sounded like they were, he'd be confronting them anyway. There was going to be a contact. But Tam still needed the smoking gun that would allow him to nail the crime boss for weapons trading. His handlers would accept nothing less. 'We don't want a firefight in the street,' he said. 'Let them enter, then follow. Wait for my instruction to engage.'

Tam looked around the room. There was a metal storage cupboard in one corner. He moved toward it and opened it up. There was nothing of interest – just reams of blank paper and boxes of pens. He turned his attention to the desks. One was relatively empty, while the other was piled with paper. He moved over to the paper-filled desk and started rummaging through the documents. There was nothing of any particular interest here either. Catalogues for gym equipment. Invoices. Bills.

'The targets have entered the building . . .'

Tam's skin prickled. He glanced toward the door and made his handgun ready. He should get out of here . . .

Something on the desk caught his eye: a manilla folder, with a small sheaf of photographs slightly spilling out. He opened the folder, pulled out the top photograph and examined it carefully.

The photograph showed two men. The first was Aiden Bailey. Tam recognised him from the image their handler had sent them the previous day. He was shaking hands with a Hispanic-looking man, smiling broadly for the camera like he was very pleased to be seen with his companion. Tam recognised this guy too – he was one of the two men who had dropped off the flight case full of dope at the Paradise Gym that morning. But it wasn't his face that interested Tam.

It was his forearm.

It was covered with a very intricate tattoo. Even though this picture was taken from a distance, Tam could make out what it depicted, because he'd seen such a tattoo before. It was a skull, an angel of death, its jaws fixed in a gruesome grin. The skull wore a military red beret and was pointing an assault rifle. Woven behind the skull and through its eye sockets and mouth was an intricate, Gothic letter.

Z.

Tam glanced back toward the flight case full of dope. Then back to the picture. It looked like Aiden Bailey was getting friendly with the Mexican Zeta cartel.

'We've accessed the building,' Brooks's voice came over the comms. *'Reception area clear. What's your location?'*

'Top floor,' Tam said.

'Fucking hell, buddy, you need to move. This is going noisy.'

Tam continued to flick through the photographs. There were three more, very similar to the first. He wondered why Bailey was keeping a record of this meeting. Probably, he decided, so he could use his contact with the Zetas to impress people. Or to put the shits up them. The guy was clearly a class-one scumb—

He took a sharp intake of breath. He had reached the fifth photograph in the pile.

Like the other photographs, this one had been taken from a distance, at some kind of party or gathering – there were a lot of people milling around, smartly dressed. On the far side of the room were some large windows looking down on to a floodlit soccer pitch. The photo was taken covertly, Tam deduced from the shakiness of the image. But although it was blurred, Tam could clearly discern several of the faces.

There was Aiden Bailey. He was wearing a black suit with an open-neck white shirt, and had a gaudy medallion on show. He was shaking hands with a man Tam knew. A man he had seen just three days previously at Brize Norton RAF base.

'Tyson,' Tam breathed.

What the hell was the SAS man doing pressing flesh with a low-life like Bailey? But then, he thought of Tyson's reputation. All those rumours that he'd been on the take in Afghanistan.

Tam flicked through to the next picture. Bailey again, and Tyson. But this time there were three other men in their little group. Tam recognised them all. The black-haired one with dark eyes and a scowl. The short, squat one, slightly balding. The kid with piercing blue eyes and acne on his cheek.

It was the unit Tyson had been travelling out with. All of them in conversation with Bailey.

Tam looked over again at the flight case full of dope.

Bailey had links to the Zeta cartel. Tyson and his unit had links to Bailey. Tyson had spent time in Mexico and his unit was heading back across the Atlantic just three days ago.

Alarm bells were ringing.

He turned back to the photographs. Took out his phone again and snapped some more images. What the hell was a British SAS unit, operating in the US, doing with a known criminal involved with illegal arms shipments who apparently had links with the Mexican Zetas?

'Get Bailey,' he instructed over the comms. 'Alive. Nail anyone else if you have to. Webb, keep eyes on the back. If Bailey tries to escape, grab him. Brooks, Dixon, *go!*'

Tam pocketed his phone. Headed to the door. Stepped out into the corridor, weapon at the ready. There was nobody there. He moved swiftly along the corridor, opening the door to the glory-hole room where he'd left the bulldog. The man was groggily pushing himself to his feet. Tam raised his weapon and delivered a single headshot. He was heading to the stairs before the bulldog hit the floor again. He stopped to listen. He could hear shouting further down the stairwell. Male voices, London accents. 'Status?' he demanded into the comms.

'*Ground floor clear. We have two targets down in the changing rooms.*'
'Shooters?'
'*Negative. We think Bailey and his guys are heading upstairs.*'
'I'm coming down from the second floor.'

He descended, pointing his weapon down the stairwell, ready to fire at the slightest threat. The shouting had fallen silent, but he could hear footsteps coming up. At the half landing between the first and second floors, he pointed his weapon at the security camera and released a single round. The camera exploded in a shower of sparks as Tam continued down until he almost reached the first-floor landing, where the glass door set into the glass wall looked on to the gym area. Seven guys were still working out.

He stopped. Listened hard.

Silence.

And then, suddenly, gunfire.

It was a single shot, and it echoed heavily up and down the stairwell. Tam knew instantly it came from a shotgun – not from the sound of the report, but from the nature of the ammunition: a heavy, single cartridge that spewed pellets over the entirety of the first floor landing. The glass wall and door shattered and noisily collapsed. At the same time Tam heard the sound of a shotgun's pump action, and he knew a second cartridge was about to be discharged. He was momentarily shocked at the heavyweight nature of the attack: these men were viciously armed and had come to kill. He threw himself back just as a second report blistered around the stairwell. There was shouting from inside the gym as the pellets scattered indiscriminately across the landing and past the shattered wall. Tam heard a third round go off, more distant: it sounded like it was at the bottom of the stairs, and he knew there was a chance the others were being pinned down.

Tam had two choices. Retreat upstairs, or get into the gym where he could take cover and hold his position while Brooks and Dixon found the opportunity to attack from the ground floor. Upstairs was no good: he'd be cornered. He had to go for the gym. The seven guys in there had hit the ground. Distance to the nearest weights machine: fifteen metres. It was situated in the middle of the gym, and was both broad and high enough to provide cover. Tam pointed down the stairwell and blindly fired two covering shots, a three-second gap between them, before hurling himself across the shattered glass toward the gym.

'Stay down!' he barked at the gym users, not out of concern for their safety but because if they stood they could draw fire, or get in his way. He sprinted to the weights machine where he took cover, just able to see through the weights stack what was going on in the fifteen metres between himself and the stairwell.

Two figures appeared. Older guys, mid-sixties maybe, broad-shouldered and squat. Each of them carried a pump-action shotgun, sawn off at the barrel and at the butt, a string hanging from the barrel that they had clearly used to sling the weapons over their shoulders when they were outside. Tam knew those shotguns could have been doctored to hold up to five cartridges, and he knew why the men favoured them. There was no need to aim a sawn-off with a regular cartridge. The pellets would spread around the room and badly wound everyone in it, if it didn't kill them. A blunt, unsophisticated weapon, but effective.

Tam heard a voice. Pure cockney. 'Screw the fuckin' Oyster Bays!' it shouted. 'Plug the black septic with the gun!'

It took a moment for Tam to work out what was being said. Oyster bays: gays. Septic tank: Yank. He crouched down behind the weights stack just in time. One of the guys stepped forward. He had a craggy, weathered face, and he held his sawn-off with one hand as he aimed it into the centre of the room and fired.

The shrapnel from the cartridge ricocheted off the weights machine, but he could tell from the sudden screaming it had also hit at least four of the gym guys. At the same time, he heard distant gunfire from the ground floor. His earpiece burst into life. *'Two targets down,'* Brooks said. *'Bailey's on his way up now.'*

A second, ferocious blast from the shotgun peppered the gym with pellets. The screaming from the gym guys became more intense. Tam moved quickly, before the shooter had time to pump his weapon again. Holding his handgun in both hands, he twisted out from behind the weights machine and, in a split second, took aim and fired a single round at the broad target of the craggy shooter's chest. He hit the ground with a solid thump. Tam was aware the seven gym guys were all in a shit state, bleeding out on the ground, writhing in agony. But his attention was firmly focused on what was on the stairwell landing.

He saw two figures. One of them was the second shooter. He was raising his sawn-off, preparing to take another shot into the gym. The second was Aiden Bailey, well tanned, grey hair slicked back, also holding a sawn-off but showing no sign of planning to use it. He was clearly rattled, looking behind him in panic, then toward the carnage of the gym. Tam just had time to see him run toward the staircase heading back up to the second floor before he took cover behind the weights machine again. There was another heavy shotgun blast, an immediate clunk of the pump action, then yet another blast. The walls were pockmarked with indentations from the pellets. The gym guys were moaning quietly now.

Tam prepared to take aim at this second shooter. An instant later, he knew he wouldn't have to. He heard the dull thud of a suppressed handgun from the direction of the stairwell: a characteristic double tap that he knew came from one of the members of his team. Brooks's voice came over his earpiece, but Tam could also hear it in real time from about twenty metres. *'Target down. It's just Bailey left.'*

Tam swung out from behind the weights machine. He could tell that five of the gym guys were dead. The remaining two were in a shit state. But they'd seen him, and that wasn't acceptable. He casually released a round into each man's chest as he stormed past them, toward the stairwell. He arrived at the landing at the same time as Brooks and Dixon. He pointed upstairs and, weapon engaged, led the way. Despite his tiredness, his senses were acute. Bailey was armed, and he was going to be cornered. Nothing more dangerous. As he hit the second floor, he paused by the door that led from the stairwell. Listened. There was silence.

He held up three fingers toward Brooks and Dixon.

Two.

One.

He kicked the door open. Brooks and Dixon fired several covering rounds through the opening. Tam swung round into the now-familiar corridor, ready to fire a wounding shot the second he saw Bailey.

But there was no sign of him.

There were two open doors: the one leading into the office at the far end, and the one leading into the first glory-hole room where the bulldog lay dead. The second glory-hole room was closed.

Silence.

Tam advanced carefully, his weapon raised in two hands. The first glory-hole room came into view. He sensed Brooks and Dixon moving behind him to check the other rooms.

'Mother*fucker*!'

The bulldog's body was still there, lying in a pool of his own blood, but the door at the far end of the room was open. Tam advanced toward it. It led to a second room with a bank of surveillance screens. And beyond that, a further room with a locked door on the far side. Tam could tell the line of rooms connected this building to the adjoining one.

Brooks: '*Clear.*'

Dixon: '*Clear.*'

Which meant Bailey wasn't on the second floor. He'd slipped the net. He was moving along the terrace of houses to escape.

Tam got on the comms. 'Webb, Bailey's going to be leaving from one of the other buildings in this street. Fucking *find him*!'

He turned to the surveillance screens. A digital tape was recording everything on a machine below one of the screens. Tam removed it to excise any evidence of their presence, then he sprinted back toward the stairwell along with Brooks and Dixon. They thundered down the stairs, past the carnage in the gym, past more dead bodies on the ground floor – Tam recognised the reception guy, who had a catastrophic wound to his chest – and out on to the street, where it was raining heavily.

Tam saw it immediately, and swore: forty metres down the road, Bailey was getting into the back of a white VW, which immediately pulled out into the traffic and sped off. They had no chance of getting to him.

At the same time, he heard the sound of sirens again. They were getting louder this time. Approaching.

'Get out of here,' he told his team urgently. '*Now!*'

He powered through the rain, shoulders hunched, head down, weapon secreted. As he walked, he pulled out his encrypted phone. Dialled. The featureless male voice answered immediately. '*State your identity.*'

'Yankee Bravo Nine,' Tam said.

'*What the hell's going on? There's been a report of gunfire at your location. British police are on their way now. Do you have what we need?*'

'No,' Tam stated. 'I've got something else. Listen carefully. You have a British SAS team operating somewhere out of the UK. Guy called Jack Fletcher is involved. Goes by the name Tyson. If my guess is right and they're operating in Mexico, you've got a big fucking problem. They're compromised. They're affiliated with Bailey in some way and I think they're working with the Zeta cartel. I can send you photographic evidence.'

And Tam Garrick proceeded to tell his handler exactly what he'd found.

Tyson looked down on to the enclosure. The Mexican whose room he'd commandeered was still lying zip-tied and taped up on the floor, but had fallen silent hours ago. It was getting dark outside and even darker in the room. He scanned the layout he'd already memorised from the drone imagery back at the motel. The rectangular enclosure, forty metres wide, eighty metres deep. The small urban forest that covered the northern half of the square, thick and verdant, like a patch of jungle growing up among the concrete, and hiding two low buildings on either corner. The wide metal gate leading to the Avenida Hidalgo on the southern side of the enclosure. He'd seen the two guards emerge from the little guard house on the far side of the gates three times during the day. Twice to smoke a cigarette, once to piss up against the cracked concrete wall. Apart from them, however, there was no movement of armed personnel. Nothing to suggest Spud wasn't still incarcerated in the enclosure, most likely in the building on the northwestern corner, among the trees.

Time check: 1700 hours. He spoke into his comms. 'Alpha Two, check.'

'*Alpha Three, check.*'

'*Alpha One, check.*' Danny Black's voice was clipped and stressed. '*Any sign of Spud?*'

'Negative.'

'*We have three more hours of daylight. Hold your positions.*'

'Roger that,' said Tyson.

'*Roger that,*' said Spike.

Kleinman, Rav and Hernandez sat in the darkening motel ops room. They each had a fresh cup of coffee, but none of them was drinking it. There was a tense silence. A fresh drone was hovering high above the square on Avenida Hidalgo. They saw no movement of personnel. Everything was as it had been when the SAS team surveyed the scene.

'You ever get the feeling,' Rav said quietly, 'something ain't right?' He stared at Kleinman, obviously waiting for a response. He received none.

Kleinman's sat phone was lying on the desk in front of him. It rang. Kleinman answered it quickly. 'Yeah?'

A voice at the other end said, '*This is Zero Alpha.*'

'Go ahead.'

'*What is the current location of the Hereford team?*'

Kleinman knew this voice well, although he had never met its owner. It sounded slightly different this morning. There was an edge of panic. 'Cross border,' Kleinman said evasively. For very good reasons, he did not want to tell his handlers the details of the situation.

'*Your orders are to close down your operation immediately.*'

A pause.

'I'm not sure I understand.'

'*Lock down your centre of operations. Now. Remove yourselves from the area. We'll send people to clean up after you. Cease all communications with the Hereford unit. Your sat phones will be disabled within a minute.*'

Rav and Hernandez were staring at him. They could tell something was wrong.

'Can I ask,' Kleinman said, trying to keep his voice mild, 'why?'

'*Negative.*'

'I think,' Kleinman said, a hint of steel in his voice, 'that I insist.'

Another pause. Kleinman knew the owner of the robotic voice was judging which was more important – secrecy, or Kleinman's compliance.

'*We have credible evidence,*' said the voice, '*that the Hereford unit is compromised.*'

'In what way?'

'*Affiliation with the Zeta cartel.*'

Kleinman's eyes met Rav's.

'That sounds unlikely,' Kleinman said.

'*I repeat,*' said the robotic voice, '*you're to remove yourselves from the area, lock down your centre of operations and cease all communications with the Hereford unit. Return to Langley by covert means.*'

The line went dead.

Kleinman kept his phone to his ear for a few seconds longer than he needed to. Then he looked at the screen. No service.

He turned to Rav and Hernandez. 'Disable the drone,' he said. 'They're closing us down.'

EIGHTEEN

Time check: 2000 hours.

'It's time,' Danny said. It was fully dark outside. They needed to make the assault before the Zetas had chance to move Spud.

Ana looked straight ahead as she nodded. Again, Danny wondered if she was up to this. Not that they had any choice. Not now.

'I'm going to get into the back of the van. You know what to do?'

She nodded once more. Said nothing.

'You just need to tell them . . .'

'I know what to tell them. Let's get it over with.'

They alighted. Danny opened up the back of the vehicle and climbed in. He briefly saw Ana's worried face as she closed the doors. Then there was nothing but darkness. He felt for his NV goggles, which he fitted to his head and switched on. The interior of the van became visible under the familiar spooky green haze. He found his ops vest and strapped it on. He found his assault rifle. By the time he picked it up, the engine had started and the van pulled away.

Danny put himself down in the firing position, facing the rear of the van but fully aware of his surroundings to 180 degrees from the peripheral vision tubes. He felt the vehicle swing left, then right, then continue straight ahead for 45 seconds. He knew that meant they were in the Avenida Hidalgo. He didn't move from the firing position as he spoke into his comms. 'Alpha One, approaching target.'

'*Alpha Two, check.*'

'*Alpha Three, check.*'

The vehicle swung right and came to a halt.

Danny heard the driver's door open. Three echoing bangs on the metal gate of the square. Ana's voice. '*Olá!*'

Silence.

'*This is Alpha Two, we have movement on the inside of the gates. Two tangos as expected, repeat, two tangos only.*'

Danny found himself holding his breath. He could just hear Ana's voice, talking in rushed Spanish.

'*This is Alpha Two. I don't think they're buying it. They've stepped away from the gate. They're talking to each other. Shaking heads.*'

'Shit,' Danny breathed.

Abort? Or continue?

'*Scrap that. They're nodding. One of them's approaching the gate. The other guy's holding back.*'

Danny could hear a high-pitched creak as the gate swung open. He exhaled slowly. Breathed deeply. Kept his pulse down. His brain calm.

'*We have eyes on your vehicle, Alpha One.*'

He heard Ana getting back behind the wheel. Closing the door.

The car moved forward.

It came to a halt.

Since Danny was facing toward the back of the van, the sound of the gate banging shut was now in front of him. He pressed the butt of his weapon a little harder into his shoulder. Raised his NV goggles to protect his vision against the sudden influx of light he would experience when the rear doors opened.

It never came.

Instead, there was a scream.

Ana.

'*Mother*fuckers!' came Tyson's voice.

'What the hell's happening?'

'*They've got Ana on the ground . . . Shit . . . We've got Zetas swarming into the square from the fucking trees.*'

'How many?' Danny hissed.

There was a moment's pause.

'*Fifteen, including the two guards at the gate. They're heading for the vehicle.*'

'Take them out!' Danny instructed. '*Take them out now!*'

Suddenly the air outside the vehicle exploded with the sound of gunfire. Danny could tell from the timbre of the shots that every weapon was suppressed. But there were at least ten people firing. He heard the unmistakable scattershot sound of rounds against concrete, and he knew, even before Tyson spoke into the comms, that the enemy targets inside the square were aiming not at the vehicle but at the buildings surrounding the square.

At Tyson and Spike.

'*Motherfuckers!*' Tyson repeated. '*Jesus, they know we're here. They're opening up on the building . . .*'

But before Danny could reply, the back doors of the van swung violently open. Danny instinctively laid down two rounds. They pinged ineffectively off the graffitied metal of the sliding gate.

The van shook. There was someone on the roof. Danny immediately raised his weapon to a forty-five-degree upward angle, ready to blast some rounds blindly through the top of the van. He hesitated for a moment as he tried to predict the likely effect of any ricochet. In that split second, the person on the roof chucked something into the back of the van. Danny had less than a second to clock that it was a flashbang grenade before it exploded.

Danny had detonated enough flashbangs to know what was coming. A deafening bang slammed through his body. It made his ears ring and the whole vehicle shake. At the same time, a blinding white light robbed him of his vision. He felt a sudden, horrible sense of deja vu – the effect of the flashbang was identical to the effect of the spotlights at the Zeta warehouse where Spud had been taken. He staggered back, knowing that his only option was to fire blindly. He released a burst of rounds. The sound told him the opening round had clipped the roof of the vehicle. As he swung his rifle down he was able to fire through the open doors.

But by then it was too late.

Two figures had burst into the van. They hurled themselves on either side of Danny and his rifle, knocking him heavily on both

231

shoulders. Danny lost his grip on the weapon. The burst stopped as Danny fell back. He felt a crushing blow from a hammer fist to the side of his face. Another to the pit of his stomach. He roared in pain and threw every ounce of strength he had into pushing himself up from his prone position. Through his dazzled vision, however, he saw that a third person had entered the back of the van. A moment later he received a sharp, heavy kick to the groin. More hammer fists to the face and stomach. His strength left him.

He felt his weapon being ripped from his hands, his NV goggles from his head. Someone was dragging him from the van. As he crossed the threshold, his body fell heavily to the ground outside and his head cracked against the metal floor of the van on its way down. He heard the sound of dogs somewhere close by.

Everything spun. Half of him wanted to vomit. The other half struggled desperately to stay conscious. He opened his eyes, and immediately saw that he was fucked.

Six armed men, with full body armour and Kevlar helmets, encircled him in the darkness. Each one was aiming his assault rifle directly at Danny's body. Beyond, Danny was just aware of a further guy holding two snarling dogs, each one straining on a chain about two metres long. He caught a glimpse of their titanium-tipped teeth and knew they were the same beasts that had attacked Spud.

There was more gunfire from elsewhere in the square. Danny's earpiece burst into life. Tyson's hoarse, desperate voice. *'I'm under fire! They know my position! Reply, over.'*

Spike: *'I'm pinned down! I can't take a fucking shot!'*

Tyson: *'Alpha One, reply, over!'*

But Danny couldn't reply. At that moment, a seventh man appeared. He was tall, thin, and wore a sleeveless flak jacket. Both arms were covered with tattoos, and he had a medallion with an ornate letter *Z*. It glinted in the sunlight. He bent over so his face was close to Danny, then slowly blinked. He had fake eyes tattooed on his eyelids.

And a knife in his hand.

'You move one muscle,' he said in serviceable English, 'I cut your throat, then feed you to the dogs. You come with me without struggling, you live.'

Rule one: never agree to being moved. If he didn't have firearms pointing at him, Danny would already have attacked, with all the aggression and violence he had in him. Tried to disarm this guy.

But he couldn't. Not at the mercy of an entire firing squad.

The tattooed man lowered his knife to the right-hand side of Danny's abdomen. Now pure, violent survival instinct kicked in. Danny grabbed the man's wrist with one hand, then slammed it on the ground – once, twice, three times until the knife fell from his grasp. With his free hand, Danny grabbed his opponent's neck. Squeezed hard, so the tips of his strong fingers were embedded deep into the vulnerable exposed flesh.

The reaction from the gunmen was immediate. Two of them, one either side of Danny, knelt down and pressed the barrels of their assault rifles against his skull.

'*Alpha One, what's happening?*'

'They will kill you on my command,' said the tattooed man, his voice constrained by Danny's hand on his throat, by his fingers pressing into the carotid artery.

Silence. Instinct was replaced by logic. Danny realised he had no option. He slowly released his grip.

'Good decision,' said the man, rubbing his neck. 'Now *I* can kill you when I want to. Trust me, it's going to hurt. But not yet.'

The man took hold of his knife again. Moved it closer to Danny's abdomen.

Sliced.

Danny felt his ops vest loosen. The man had cut the side straps. Ten seconds later, the entire vest was removed. The guy with the tattoos rummaged around and quickly disabled his comms unit. Danny's earpiece went dead, his contact with the rest of the unit gone.

'Get up,' said the man. 'You have three seconds.'

233

Danny obeyed. He felt blood trickle from his nose and was still breathless from the beating he'd received. The gunmen didn't waver in their aim. The guy with the dogs seemed to be struggling to restrain them. When Danny was on his feet, the tattooed guy patted him down. Satisfied himself there were no hidden firearms. Pulled his handgun from his own shoulder holster and pointed it at Danny's head. 'Walk,' he said.

He forced Danny to turn and walk to the front of the van. As the whole square came into view – it was lit up only by the van's headlamps – the brutal reality of his situation hit him. Ana was face down over the front of the van. Her face was bleeding. She was shaking heavily, and crying. The mixture of tears and blood made a grotesque mess of her face. She screamed when she saw Danny was at gunpoint. A Zeta guard whacked the back of her head with his handgun to silence her. Elsewhere in the square were the remaining eight heavily armed gunmen. They were dressed in weird combinations of military clothing. Most wore camouflage gear. Some had camo hats and sunglasses, others wore black bandanas over their faces, or even full balaclavas. Five of the guys wore heavy bandoliers of ammo across their shoulders. They carried a vast variety of weapons – AK-47s, M16s, MP5s. One of them even held a rocket-propelled grenade launcher. They were better equipped than a regular army platoon.

And they looked like they knew what they were doing. They had positioned themselves in two flanks: one pointing up toward the eastern wall of the square, one pointing up toward the west. Every five seconds or so, one of the gunmen on each side fired a suppressed round. Sound, experienced military tactics, Danny realised, and enough to keep Tyson and Spike down. The sound of children crying drifted over the square from the open windows of the bullet-marked buildings. In the distance he heard the wail of an emergency siren. But it was just that. Distant.

Danny was being forced toward the northwestern corner of the square. The tattooed guy had his pistol pointed at the back of Danny's head. In his peripheral vision Danny could tell he was being flanked by at least two of the original six gunmen. He was finding it difficult to walk after his beating. Even more difficult to think straight.

What was his next move?

He was unarmed. He was at gunpoint. Fifteen enemy targets. But at least he was alive. There had to be a reason for that. The same reason they'd kept Spud alive? So the Zetas could make a grisly example of them both? The thought was like a further punch in the stomach.

They were among the trees now. This little urban forest was unusually thick, with a heavy canopy. Night-time visibility was only five or six metres. He was forced onward until he could see, through the trees, the rough shack where he believed Spud was imprisoned. They were heading for that building. A single armed guard was at the door. He looked younger than the other Zetas, and reminded Danny a little of Jesús. He also looked anxious. Danny added him to the head count of fifteen Zetas. It meant he had at least sixteen of the fuckers to deal with.

Unarmed.

Distance: five metres. The guy with the tattoos barked an instruction at him in Spanish. The young guard nodded. He unlocked the door and entered the shack. Danny felt himself being grabbed from behind. One of his guards placed a coarse hessian hood over his head, pushed him further toward the building, then bound his wrists together with thick, sticky duct tape. Danny counted the number of wraps. Three. Once they were secure, he did the same to Danny's ankles. Five wraps. Another push. Danny stumbled into the shack and fell heavily on to his front. He heard the door being shut behind him. Locked.

His breathing was hot and heavy under his hood. He felt the blood from his nose sticking to the hessian. His body bristled with pain. Outside, he heard a woman scream. Ana. There was more gunfire. Men shouting.

'Spud?' he said.

NINETEEN

Tyson stood with his back to the wall next to the open window. On the ceiling, two metres in front of him, was a bullet hole. Plaster had fallen into the room, and over its other occupant – the fat Mexican guy whose wrists, ankles and mouth Tyson had cabled up.

'Alpha Three,' Tyson said tersely into the comms. 'What's your status?'

There was a definite edge of panic in Spike's voice. '*I'm still under fire . . .*'

'They'll be coming for you, kid,' Tyson said. 'Get off the roof. Back down into the street if you can. We can't help them from up here. Do it now.'

'*Roger that.*'

Tyson knew the Zetas wouldn't only be coming for Spike. They'd be coming for him too. Somehow, they had known there would be covering fire. 'Standard operating procedure,' he told himself. The Zetas had proper military training. It figured that they would guess where he was.

It was fully dark in the room. Tyson peered at the Mexican guy on the floor. 'Sorry mate,' he muttered. 'It's you or me.' He pulled his NV goggles from his rucksack and fitted them to his head. Everything became visible. He strode over to where the guy was lying. Bent down and hauled him up to his feet. The guy's eyes were wild. He tried to say something but was only able to grunt because of the tape over his mouth. Tyson forced him back on to his bed. Made him kneel up. Put his weapon to his head and told him not to move. He was hit with the stench of urine – the

Mexican guy had pissed himself through fear. That was completely normal, and it meant he would stay compliant. For the time he had left, at least.

Tyson moved over to the main door. Stood to one side, back to the wall, hidden in the darkness. Just in time. He could hear voices in the corridor outside. Harsh, barking voices, speaking Spanish. He heard the sound of a door being battered down. A woman screaming. More male voices shouting. The guy on the bed slumped a little in fear, but he remained in position. That was the most important thing. Because when the Zetas came knocking, as they would any second, Tyson needed something – someone – to distract them.

There was a sudden, violent thump against the door. The Mexican guy slumped some more. A second thump. Tyson could tell it was somebody forcing their body weight against the door. They'd have it open within five seconds.

He engaged his handgun. Pointed it into the room.

The door crashed open.

Three men burst in. Their attention was immediately drawn to the Mexican man on the bed, taped up and terrified. The three men were all armed. Each of them raised a handgun. In less than two seconds they had each released a round, peppering the Mexican's body with lead.

But that two seconds' grace was all Tyson needed.

He released a single round into the back of each man's head. They went down in quick succession. Tyson, however, had turned his attention from them even before they hit the floor. With his weapon still engaged, he moved out into the corner of the door frame. Listened carefully. There was total silence. He wasn't fooled. On the opposite side of the corridor was the door to apartment 302. The brass plaque with the number was tarnished, but in the green haze of his NV vision Tyson could just make out the reflection of one more guy. He estimated he was three metres to his left along the corridor.

And moving.

Tyson held his weapon steadily with two hands. Breathed deeply to slow his pulse.

He saw the barrel of his target's AK-47 before he saw the man himself. It was being held at shoulder height, which gave Tyson a good indication of the level of his target's neck. Tyson raised the trajectory of his pistol by an inch. A second later, the target himself came into view, between one and two metres away. Body armour. Helmet. But his neck, as Tyson expected, was unprotected. Tyson clinically released a single round. It slammed into the soft flesh with a sudden torrent of blood. The target fell against the far wall.

Silence. No sign of anyone else in the brass plaque. That didn't mean the corridor was empty, but at some point Tyson was going to have to step outside the apartment.

That moment had come.

He holstered his pistol. Flicked his rifle to automatic and made it ready. Stepped outside, his finger brushing the trigger.

There was no need to fire. Aside from the dead Zeta, the corridor was deserted.

Tyson advanced. The peripheral tubes of his NV illuminated the walls and doors directly to his right and left, as well as the corridor up ahead. The stench of cheap cooking was now masked by the familiar odour of cordite. The next door along to his left was open. As he reached it he swung round, his rifle now an integral part of his body. Huddled in the darkness in the far corner of this apartment was a woman clutching two young children, tear-stained mascara dripping down her face. Tyson moved on. He reached the stairwell in fifteen seconds. Stopped and listened again on the third-floor landing. Heard nothing. Aimed his weapon up, then down. Then he stepped carefully and silently down the stairwell.

His deep breathing wasn't working. As he descended the stairs he felt his heart pumping heavily and quickly. What was his next move? He needed a strategy. He tried to estimate the chances that Danny Black and Spud Glover were still alive. Pretty good, he thought. He had caught a glimpse of them manoeuvring Black to the same shack that was holding Spud. They clearly didn't want him dead just yet.

What chance did he and Spike have of storming the square, just the two of them?

Zero. The Zetas had a minimum of fifteen men, well armed and well trained.

He reached the exit of the building. The main door was swinging open. The latch was bullet-wrecked. In the distance – somewhere to the northeast, he estimated – he heard a siren. It was getting closer.

He raised his NV goggles, then spoke quietly into the comms. 'Alpha Three, this is Alpha Two, do you copy?'

Silence.

'Alpha Three, this is Alpha Two, do you copy?'

The line was dead.

Shit. What was happening? Had Spike been taken out? What was Tyson's next move?

Save himself? Leave his unit mates to their fate?

Storm the square by himself? Risk a firefight with at least fifteen Zetas?

Try to locate Spike? Hope that between the two of them they could mount some sort of attack on the square?

None of these was an option.

His earpiece burst into life. He heard Spike's voice say a single word – '*Alpha* . . .' – before it died again. That was something, he told himself. Comms were down, but Spike was alive. He could concentrate on Black and Spud.

He needed support. Extra personnel. Extra firepower. It was the only chance he had of getting close to the guys.

And he had only one way of getting it.

Kleinman.

He grabbed his sat phone. Speed-dialled their handler.

The line was dead.

Tyson suddenly felt as if the buildings around him were toppling. As if *everything* was toppling. *Why* was the line dead?

Pieces of a jigsaw started to slot together. Someone had been tipping the Zetas off. That was beyond question. Kleinman's face, his small, watery eyes, entered Tyson's mind. Was *he* behind the failure of their previous operations? Was *he* tipping the Zetas off? Was that why he was so insistent they shouldn't receive any help from the US military, or even the Mexican *Federales*?

He narrowed his eyes and, under his breath, repeated that single word.

'*Federales*.'

His mind flashed back to Kleinman's briefing in the ops room of the motel across the border. What had he said about the Mexican Federal Police? *They wouldn't chance a confrontation with the Zetas unless there was definitely a high-value target on-site.*

Whatever Kleinman's motives, he was right about that. Tyson knew those *Federales* guys. If there was a chance to catch a big fish, they'd go in all guns blazing. Literally.

Which meant that suddenly, Tyson had a strategy.

His plan was clear in his mind. He kept his weapon engaged as he stepped out into the street. There was nobody around. Had any pedestrians heard gunfire and hidden? Perhaps. Either way, he wasn't inclined to hide his weapon now, even though he was out in the open. He let it hang from its lanyard as he ran north. At the corner of the street he stopped. Checked left and right for any sign of enemy targets. Nothing. He sprinted across the street, still heading north. In his mind, he had only one picture: the *Federales* vehicle that was parked up the road from where they'd left the Tahoe. He knew how it was with those patrol vehicles. They had their places to lie up, waiting for a call to action. If there was a *Federales* vehicle there this morning, there was a good chance one would be there now.

He passed three pedestrians – two old men and a woman hand in hand with her little boy. When they saw him with his weapon, they all huddled into doorways. Perhaps they'd call him in to the police. Tyson couldn't worry about that now. It took him 45 seconds to reach the street where they'd parked. He pinned himself out of sight against a concrete wall. Quickly disassembled his weapon and shoved it in his rucksack along with his NV. Cocked and locked his pistol and kept it secreted in its holster. Stepped round the corner and into the street.

There was no *Federales* vehicle. Tyson cursed. *Think*, he told himself. The *Federales* officers would have heard gunfire. Of course they wouldn't have stayed in position, like a sitting duck. They'd be doing a circuit, keeping themselves moving, maybe trying to find the source of the gunfight ...

And as that thought crystallised in his mind, a *Federales* vehicle appeared at the far end of the road. It was moving quickly, toward Tyson.

Distance: fifty metres. Was it the same vehicle he'd seen this morning? Tyson didn't know, but he could see there was now only a single occupant. This morning there were two, but this was better for him. Then he checked how many pedestrians there were. Perhaps twenty. He figured they'd make themselves scarce once he carried out what he had in mind.

He was right.

He allowed the vehicle to come within fifteen metres of his position. Then he stepped out into the road. Presented his fire-arm and aimed squarely at the front driver's-side tyre of the vehicle. Released a single round. The rubber burst impressively. The police vehicle swerved, narrowly missing a pedestrian who was already trying to sprint away from the scene. It burst up on to the pavement and crashed into the wall. It was a sturdy vehi-cle, though, and the impact caused more harm to the wall than to the car.

At the moment of impact, Tyson was already alongside the driver's door. He yanked it open and immediately pressed the barrel of his gun against the temple of the *Federales* officer inside. The officer was wearing a dark blue uniform with a sleeveless flak jacket and a peaked cap with the star-shaped *Federales* insignia. The vehicle's two-way radio was hissing and alive with voices. He spoke in perfect, quiet, urgent Spanish.

'If you want to live,' he said, 'you do exactly what I tell you. Understood?'

The officer nodded. His brow was covered in sweat. Tyson looked briefly over his shoulder. The street had emptied. He looked back at the officer.

'You're going to get on to your radio,' he said. 'Then you're going to alert all *Federales* units in the area that Augusto Chavez, Z1, is currently involved in a firefight on Avenida Hidalgo. In the square behind the graffitied metal gates. If you say anything else, I'll kill you. Tell me now if you don't understand anything.'

'I understand,' the officer breathed.

'Do it now.'

The officer reached for the radio handset on the dash of his vehicle. His voice was nervous and shaking as he spoke, but his words were clear enough. He repeated Tyson's message practically verbatim. Once he released the pressel on his handset, the sound from the radio burst into life again. Tyson heard other *Federales* officers shouting instructions at each other. All the signs were that his strategy was working.

Tyson grabbed the handset of the police radio and yanked it hard. The cable came away from the main housing. 'Remove your jacket,' Tyson said. 'Now.'

The officer quickly wriggled out of his dark blue flak jacket. While he was doing it, Tyson took his peaked cap. Once the flak jacket was off and resting on the guy's lap, Tyson quickly changed his grip on his handgun so that he was holding it by the barrel. 'Sorry bud,' he muttered in English. With a sudden, violent strike, he cracked the weapon heavily against the side of the officer's skull. The officer's eyes immediately rolled. He slumped over the steering wheel. Tyson made a quick, cursory check of his pulse. It was strong. The officer would have a bitch of a headache when he woke up, but he'd be okay. That made Tyson feel a bit better. Men were going to be killed in action in the next ten minutes. No reason for this guy to be one of them. And even if he did wake up, his radio was out of action, so he'd have trouble warning the *Federales* they were being deceived.

He grabbed the flak jacket and put it on. Crammed the peaked cap on to his head – it was a little small. Removed his rifle from his rucksack and reassembled it. Now that he was dressed as a member of the *Federales*, he could wear his weapon openly.

Then he ran. South, back toward the Avenida Hidalgo, where fifteen minutes earlier it had gone noisy.

And where, in a few minutes more, it was going to get a hell of a sight noisier than that.

Luis Garcia was twenty-eight years of age. He was born in the village of San Cristobal. Raised there. He was baptised and married in its church where two years later his son, little Alejandro, was baptised.

And his younger sister, Maria had died there three days ago. On Friday evening. Forced inside the four walls of the church by the animals from Los Zetas. Burned to death. She was seventeen years old.

On the Saturday he returned home. Sat numbly with his mother and father in their small house. Visited the smoking remains of the building that was now his sister's funeral pyre. It had a police cordon around it. Nobody was allowed to approach. Nobody wanted to. The village was in shock and mourning, but Luis understood that to be seen on the site of the atrocity was somehow to declare a defiance of the cartel. And nobody had the stomach to do that.

Nobody except him. He stood at the top of the central square, staring at the smouldering remains of the church, a lone figure, his shoulders hunched in grief.

There could be no funeral because there was no body. At some point, Luis promised his parents, there would be a memorial service for Maria. He wasn't even sure they heard him say it. On Saturday night he left them to their tears and returned to Nuevo Laredo. He could think of nothing else to do, other than to throw himself into his job. As a member of the *Federales*, he was one of the few people in this part of Mexico who acted in open defiance of the cartel. Never before had he felt so eager to get to work.

Which was why the call over the radio sent a rush of fire through his veins.

All units. Suspected involvement of Augusto Chavez, Z1, in a fire-fight on Avenida Hidalgo. In the square behind the graffitied metal gates.

Luis's partner, Jorge, had the wheel. His grim, sweaty face was illuminated by the light from the dash. In the back of the open-top Hilux police vehicle were four more guys, all dressed in the standard *Federales* garb: black flak jackets, Kevlar helmets, M16s. They were on their way to the Mexican side of the US border crossing when the call came in. But as soon as he heard those words, Luis turned to his partner.

'Get there,' he said.

'Spud ...'

Danny's voice was muffled under the hood. He didn't dare speak loudly. He knew there was a Zeta guard just on the other side of the door. He wanted to give him no reason to come in and investigate anything.

'*Spud!*'

A long pause. 'Mate?'

Danny could tell from the sound of his voice that Spud was hooded too. His friend's voice was cracked and thin.

'Are you zip-tied?' Danny asked.

'Ankles, wrists, neck,' Spud confirmed. 'You?'

'Duct tape,' Danny said. 'Ankles and wrists.'

'Then get a fucking shift on.'

Danny didn't need to be told twice. Duct tape was the first resort of the kidnapper – inexpensive, easy to buy and seemingly difficult to escape from. But the Zetas had made a mistake using it on Danny, because he'd long ago learned how to defeat it. He manoeuvred himself up to his feet and took a moment to steady himself. He could feel that the duct tape around his ankles stretched from just below the ankles to about three inches above them. He'd counted five wraps. It meant the duct tape was thickly layered, which made what he was about to do much more difficult.

He stood straight and fanned his feet out in a v-shape. He breathed deeply, then suddenly squatted down, letting his entire body weight fall toward the floor, and pointing his knees outward at a sharp angle. The effect on the duct tape was immediate.

Danny felt it ripping in a vertical line down the front and the back. His legs weren't quite separated – he could feel that the duct tape was still joined toward the bottom of the tear – but it was a moment's work now to wriggle his legs out of their restraint. He quickly turned his attention to his wrists. They were still tied behind his back. He crouched down again and slid his right foot backwards over his wrists, then his left. Now his wrists were in front of him. He stood up and stretched his arms straight ahead. With another sharp, sudden movement, he thrust his elbows outwards. The movement drove his wrists in toward his body and caused the duct tape binding them to split. He winced slightly as he tore the sticky duct tape from his skin.

A second later, however, he was removing his hood.

Ana Rodriguez was on her knees.

Spreadeagled over the front of her van, she watched them take the man who called himself Danny Black toward the trees. She fully expected to hear the gunshot that killed him. The gunshot didn't come.

Instead, one of her captors grabbed her by the hair. Ana screamed as she was dragged across the square and through the pitch darkness of the trees that covered its northern half. They took her toward a shack in the northeastern corner of the square. A cartel man was standing guard outside it. Inside, the shack resembled a sickbay. There was a single bare bulb hanging from the ceiling, which illuminated four wounded men lying on the floor. Their shirts were removed to reveal heavily tattooed torsos and catastrophic bullet wounds. Three of them had been hit in the shoulder, one in the stomach. Ana wasn't even sure if the stomach guy was still alive.

Another person entered the room. The sight of him chilled Ana far more than anything she had yet seen. He wore a sleeveless flak jacket. His arms were covered in tattoos. A medallion of the letter *Z* hung from his neck. He carried a handgun, and when he blinked she saw the eyes tattooed on his eyelids. It was him who had forced her to her knees. He turned to the two men who had dragged her into this makeshift sickbay, and nodded. They approached and both held rifles to her head.

The tattooed man removed his smartphone. Tapped the screen. There was a ringing sound, then a voice over the speaker that Ana recognised immediately. '*Si?*'

'We have her.'

'*Let me see.*'

The man handed the phone to Ana, who took it with a trembling hand. Her brother's face filled the screen. He stared at her with those dead eyes. '*I thought I made myself clear,*' he said.

'How did you know?' she whispered. Then she closed her eyes briefly as she answered her own question. 'Kleinman.'

'*My influence extends further than you can imagine, Ana.*' He sniffed. '*My men have been instructed to kill you if you give them any more trouble. If you do as they say, however, they will simply bring you to me. Don't make a stupid mistake, Ana. Miguel is a good kid. Don't make him pay for your mistakes. You don't want him to end up like your British friends.*'

The picture died. The man snatched his phone back, then pointed at the wounded men. 'Treat them,' he said. 'We leave here in thirty minutes. Make sure they're fit to travel.'

He turned and left the shack along with the two armed guards. Ana heard the door locking from the outside. She found she didn't have the strength to get to her feet.

She doubled over, head to the ground, and started to dry-retch out of fear. She could think of only one thing: Miguel.

'*Get there.*'

Luis's driver Jorge didn't need telling twice. He knew about San Cristobal. About Maria. But he knew a hell of a sight more, too. He'd witnessed the horrors of the Zeta cartel up close. He'd lost count of the beheadings and disembowellings he'd seen. He didn't need any encouragement from Luis.

They performed a sudden U-turn across the broad Avenida Guerrero, forcing a line of civilian cars to brake sharply. Jorge hit the gas and accelerated quickly in a southerly direction, before curving off that road to head southwest toward Avenida Hidalgo.

246

The radio was suddenly alive. The control base was barking instructions, trying to organise a coordinated response to this new, unconfirmed intelligence. Luis was vaguely aware of the voice on the radio trying to raise the patrol vehicle that had called in the sighting, without success. It didn't matter to him. He felt his palms sweating. His mouth had gone dry. Every cell in his body seemed to throb with hate. He had the face of Augusto Chavez, Z1, fixed in his mind. They all knew what he looked like, even though they had never seen him. Week by week they would examine pictures of him and his closest associates. Try to work out where he was, how to find him. Z1 was the prize catch. The one man every member of the *Federales* wanted to bring in, dead or alive. Preferably dead.

The vehicle screamed through the southwest suburb of Nuevo Laredo. It took five minutes to reach the western end of Avenida Hidalgo. It was clear the residents of the area knew something was going on. As they sped past the worn block-work houses, there were no pedestrians or passers-by. Vehicles were parked on both sides along the sidewalk. Their drivers were absent.

Luis could see a second vehicle facing them at the far end of the Avenida Hidalgo. Its headlamps were bright, but he could just make out the silhouette of another Hilux, with men in the open-top back. A second *Federales* unit. Good. The two vehicles were speeding toward each other. Distance: one hundred metres.

Fifty metres.

Twenty-five.

'There,' Luis said. He pointed ahead of them and to their left. Set back from the sidewalk was a metal gate, about five metres wide. Their headlamps illuminated the harsh cartel graffiti that covered it. They screeched to a halt. As the four guys in the back of the Hilux jumped out of their vehicle, scattering themselves in a semicircle formation between seven and eight metres from the gates, the other *Federales* vehicle stopped on the far side of the gate, fifteen metres away. The four armed men in the back jumped out and mirrored the position of Luis's guys.

*   *   *

Danny allowed himself a couple of seconds to take in his surroundings. It was almost pitch black, but Danny's night vision was good enough now to tell him he was in a single room, ten metres by five. Apart from Danny and Spud, it seemed empty. The door was slightly ill-fitting. He thought somebody must be holding a torch outside because there was light seeping in through the quarter-inch gap between the door frame and the door. He saw there was a single locked bolt. It would be a moment's work to burst out of the room. Almost in the same instant, however, he saw the shadow of their Zeta guard cross the gap. He would be armed. They were not.

Danny turned to Spud. His mate was slumped, hooded as Danny had suspected, in the corner of the room. Danny strode up to him and removed the hood.

His mate stank. 'Throat,' he whispered. Danny touched Spud's neck and felt it had thickened slightly where the cable tie was constricting it. He moved his hands to Spud's arms and legs where he knew the dog bites were. He could tell they were bad just by touching them. The clothes were torn, shredded and wet. The wounds themselves were suppurating, and it was difficult to feel where torn fabric ended and damaged, open flesh began. Spud hissed with pain at Danny's touch, and there was the buzzing of a fly that Danny suspected had been attracted to the open wounds.

'How did they know?' Spud said weakly. 'The Zetas. How did they know we were in the tunnel?'

'Same way they knew I was coming to find you,' Danny muttered.

'Kleinman?'

'Has to be.' Danny reached into his trousers and peeled the sticking plaster from his inner thigh. The blades he had secreted there had slightly cut into his skin. He felt a little blood as he removed them from their adhesive backing. He approached Spud and quickly slit the zip ties that bound his mate's ankles and wrists. 'Turn,' he told him, before slicing the final zip tie where it was touching the back of his neck. Spud inhaled deeply as the constriction round his neck eased.

'Can you stand?' Danny breathed.

Spud nodded, but winced badly as he pushed himself to his feet. He staggered once he was up.

'Spike and Tyson?'

'Under fire. We can't rely on them.'

'How did you get inside in the first place?'

'Long story. But there's a woman held captive here too. We need to get her out.'

He endured Spud's uncomfortable silence, knowing full well what it meant: their chances of escape were slim enough as it was, without having to deal with a third person.

'Plan?' he said.

'Take this.' Danny carefully handed him one of the two razor blades. 'We need to keep things quiet. There's a minimum of fifteen Zetas out there, all armed. If we can get our guard to come inside, then as soon as the door's open we can deal with him and take his weapon. Then we've got a chance of fighting our way out of this place.'

Spud nodded grimly. Danny could see his silhouette clutching the razor blade between his thumb and forefinger. He noticed his mate's hand was shaking, but didn't mention it.

He approached the door. Spud did the same. Danny stood in front of it, Spud just to the left, back to the wall. Both had their razor blades ready.

Danny lifted his hand to knock on the door and grab the guard's attention.

Tyson was crouched on the sidewalk, his back up against a parked car, twenty-five metres east of the gates. He had concealed himself the moment he saw the two *Federales* vehicles speeding toward each other from either end of the street. Now he could hear their engines turning over.

From inside the square, he heard the frenzied barking of two dogs. They had clearly heard or sensed something. He tried his comms. 'Alpha Three, this is Alpha Two. Do you copy?'

Silence. Tyson cursed under his breath. He had no way of

knowing if Spike was dead or alive. Truth to tell, he didn't like the kid's chances.

It was down to Tyson alone to get Spud and Black out of there.

With a little help from his friends.

The *Federales* Hilux was positioned seven metres from the gate. Its headlamps illuminated the aggressive Zeta graffiti.

'Hinges on the left-hand side,' Luis said. 'Hit the right.'

Jorge nodded curtly. 'Ready?' he said.

Luis pushed his seat hard back and raised his weapon. The barrel was about a foot from the windscreen. He glanced down to check he was properly strapped in. 'Ready.'

Jorge revved the vehicle heavily. The engine screamed as he kept it at biting point. Then, suddenly, he released the clutch and slammed the vehicle hard into the metal gates. A loud, metallic crash echoed through the air. The jolt of the impact was violent, but Luis was expecting it. Although his whole body shook, he managed to keep his weapon poised and his attention straight ahead. The Hilux, heavily armoured underneath its bodywork with a thick skeleton of Kevlar, had absorbed a massive shock. But the damage to the metal gate was clearly far greater. As Jorge slammed the vehicle into reverse, Luis saw a substantial dent in the bottom right-hand corner of the gate, where the vehicle had hit it.

From the other side of the gate there was a sudden blast of automatic fire. A high-pitched, metallic ricochet told Luis the fire was directed at the inside of the gate. Fifteen or twenty convex bullet points appeared on its exterior.

'Again,' Jorge said.

'Go.'

The engine revved. Seconds later the car slammed hard against the gate once more. The jolt was not so shocking this time. Luis knew this meant they'd broken the locking mechanism on the inside. The gate creaked slowly open, just a few inches.

'We're in,' said Jorge.

★ ★ ★

'What the fuck?' Danny whispered to himself, his hand halfway to rapping on the door to grab their guard's attention.

He'd heard the huge, metallic, echoing sound of a collision. It was coming from the direction of the gate.

'The boys?' Spud breathed.

Danny didn't get the chance to answer. The noise of the collision was immediately followed by the deafening racket of automatic fire. The high-frequency ricochets sounded like they were coming off the metal gate.

There was a second collision. At the same time, the door in front of Danny rattled. The guard was entering. Danny moved quickly to the right of the door. Put his back to the wall. Just in time. The door swung open and their guard – a thick-necked Mexican with shaved hair and a flak jacket – entered the room. There was very little light spill coming in, but Danny could tell he was holding his pistol by his side.

Danny's attack was sudden and brutal. With his left hand clawed, he wrapped his arm round the guard's head, sinking one finger hard into his eye socket, pulling the head backward and exposing the soft flesh of his neck. With his right hand, he violently stabbed the corner of the razor blade into the man's carotid artery, then pushed and sliced a deep gash up toward his Adam's apple. There was a sudden volcano of warm blood. The man made a gruesome gurgling sound. He tried to stop the stem of blood with his hands, but sank to his feet almost immediately, then collapsed on to his front.

There was a further burst of automatic fire from the square outside. Danny rolled the bleeding corpse on to its back. In addition to the pistol he was carrying, there was an AK-47 strapped around his neck.

Danny handed Spud the pistol, then started unclipping the Kalashnikov for his own use.

Luis and Jorge wound down their side windows and opened their doors. They climbed out and, using the doors as cover and extra protection on top of their body armour, pointed their weapons through the open windows. Clutching his weapon with his right hand, Luis raised his left, made a hammer fist and jabbed one finger forward. It was a manoeuvre they'd trained for and actioned many times before. The hammer fist represented a fragmentation grenade, the finger the direction in which Luis was instructing them to throw it.

He held up three fingers.

Two.

One.

Four frags arched over the top of the metal gate just as there was a fresh burst of automatic fire against the opposite side. Luis kept his position, rock steady. Counted to three in his head. The frags exploded in quick succession. A split second later there was a thunderstorm of shrapnel hitting the metal gates.

And then there were the screams.

It was hard to tell, but Luis estimated there were seven or eight men screaming. The grenades had been effective. It would be chaos behind that gate.

Luis looked across the interior of the car toward Jorge, who was also behind the protection of his open door. They nodded in unison, then jumped back into the vehicle and slammed the door shut. Jorge revved once more, then forced the vehicle hard up against the gate, pushing it open. Luis kept his weapon engaged up against the interior of the windscreen. The vehicle's wheels spun slightly as it pushed itself into the square beyond the gate. There was a hot stench of burning rubber. Luis could still hear screaming over the high-pitched noise of the engine.

The square came into view, illuminated by the vehicle's head-lamps, which were still intact despite its collision with the gate. There was a smell of explosives from the grenades, and a thin pall of smoke. To their ten o'clock was an old van, its back doors open, parked about ten metres into the square. Luis immediately saw four armed men to the right-hand side of the van – about five metres from where they'd come to a halt – writhing on the floor, one with a terrible shrapnel wound to his face, the others clutching their bleeding bodies. There were two dogs, their bodies horribly butchered, lying on their sides. He knew from the screaming there were other wounded men on the far side of the van. His attention, however, was more focused on the men who were *not* wounded. There were seven or eight of them. They were dressed in a weird selection of gear: camo, bandanas, balaclavas, military hats, bandoliers. But they were in a state of immediate panic, running from the position where the grenades had landed toward the cover of the trees, thirty metres away, that covered the northern half of the square. It took a moment for Luis to assimilate that there was thick vegetation in the northern half of the square. It would afford their enemy targets good cover. Sure, they were panicking, but Luis knew that panic would not last long. They would start returning fire within seconds.

Unless the *Federales* opened up first.

In the side mirror of the vehicle, Luis saw the eight dark-uniformed *Federales* officers swarming into the compound, their M16s at eye level. Seconds later there were several bursts of fire toward the Zetas, who hit the ground to avoid the torrent of bullets. One of them was hit in the back of the head. He collapsed in a mundane heap, spraying blood as he fell.

A second later, however, there was another burst of fire from the opposite end of the square, from behind the cover of the tree line. It sounded like an MP5, and there was a glimpse of muzzle flash in the darkness. Rounds slammed hard into the armoured windscreen of the Hilux. The toughened glass didn't shatter, but Luis knew it probably wouldn't withstand another burst. He opened his side door and, using it as protection, jumped out of the vehicle.

Just in time. A second MP5 burst hit the windscreen. Then a third. The glass didn't so much shatter as collapse in on itself. Jorge hadn't moved in time. Several rounds hit him square in the face. A horrific shower of red spattered over the dashboard as Luis's friend slumped over the wheel.

Luis felt himself burn up inside. The image of Augusto Chavez, Z1, fixed itself more firmly in his mind. With his weapon engaged, the safety switched to semi-automatic, he moved from behind the open door of the Hilux and immediately fixed two of the cowering Zetas in his sights. They were in the process of pushing themselves up to their feet. Luis shot each man in the back. With the release of each round he felt a moment of satisfaction. But only a moment. His desperate hate of the cartel flooded straight back over him as he took cover again behind the open door of the vehicle.

He looked over his shoulder. Ten grim-faced *Federales*, down in the firing position, weapons raised, looked back. Then one of them shouted: '*Get down!*'

In Luis's head, it happened in slow motion. He heard, rather than saw, the rocket-propelled grenade, instantly recognising the distinctive fizzing sound as it flew from the cover of the trees toward the beaten-up old van. It slammed into the vehicle with a brutal, deafening explosion. The van immediately went up in flames, and a shrapnel shower of twisted metal rained down over the immediate area. Luis hunkered down, covering his head, protecting himself from the burning metal as it skewered its way into the ground.

The air was filled with the heat, sound and fierce orange light of flames, and of secondary explosions from the van. There was acrid, billowing black smoke. Luis knew instantly that he'd lost men. It was only when he looked up, however, that the full consequence of the RPG strike became clear.

Seven of his comrades were prone on the floor. One of them was on fire, but clearly already dead because he wasn't moving. The others had gnarled chunks of metal embedded in their bodies, or were simply lying there, bleeding. One guy's ribcage was exposed from the back. The remaining three guys were pushing themselves up from their protective positions, their faces blackened with the smoke pumping from the burning van. They looked around in shocked disbelief at their fellow *Federales*. Then they looked toward Luis, and he could instantly read the determination in their faces. None of them had any desire, or intention, to retreat. They had friends to avenge.

'He's here somewhere!' Luis barked over the noise of the flames. The voice of the *Federales* radio system had stated as much, but Luis could sense it: Z1 was in this square. He jabbed one finger forward. His instructions were clear. Advance.

'For you, Maria,' he whispered as he moved back out from behind the vehicle door. There were three Zetas halfway across the open ground, running to the protection of the tree line. He took them out with another three shots and kept his weapon raised. He fired randomly toward the trees as he advanced, hyper-aware of his fellow *Federales* advancing alongside him, each of them laying down defensive, suppressing fire as they moved toward the trees.

All of them prepared, even eager, to kill every last human being in this square.

Tyson stood up from his crouching position behind the parked vehicle on the other side of the street. There were bursts of gunfire coming from inside the square. In the distance, he could hear sirens.

Then he heard the explosion.

He swore under his breath and sprinted across the street, checking that the *Federales* vehicle was empty. As he approached the gate he moved to its right-hand side and stood with his back to the wall. Gingerly, he peered into the square.

He needed just a second to take stock. Ana's van was a mass of flames. He counted at least six dead *Federales* officers on the ground. The remaining four were advancing in a flat attacking line, each of them at least five metres from the other. They were advancing slowly across open ground toward the trees that covered the northern half of the square. They fired regular cover-ing shots to suppress their enemy targets. More dead bodies littered the ground they were crossing. There were no Zeta personnel between Tyson and the *Federales*. Which meant the enemy were concentrated on the northern side of the square, and Danny and Spud, if they were still alive, had to be in the *Federales*' line of fire.

Tyson's eyes fell on the burning van. He suspected Ana Rodriguez was dead, but her vehicle could still provide him with cover. He ran quickly and silently, covering the ten metres of open ground between himself and the van with barely a sound of footfall. Wincing from the heat, he moved round to the far side, where several more bleeding bodies littered the ground. He tried to count the number of dead Zeta personnel he'd seen. Nine, he reckoned. That meant a minimum of six still alive and armed. He took cover five metres from the inferno, keeping his breathing shallow so he didn't inhale too much smoke. The *Federales* were still firing. They were fifteen metres from the tree line. Tyson could do nothing while they were still in open ground. Maybe, once they'd moved into the trees, he could advance. For now, however, all he could do was hope that Black and Spud had somehow managed to use the distraction to their advantage, and be there to provide fire support if they needed it.

He crouched down in the firing position, sweating heavily, weapon raised.

Danny exited the shack first. Panned left and right in the darkness. Visibility: poor. It was dark, and the trees deadened any ambient light.

Then he heard the explosion.

The roar of flames.

He was trying to work out what the hell was happening. It sounded like somebody else had raided the square and was engaged in a firefight with the Zetas. Could it be Tyson and Spike? Not just them, surely, because he was certain he'd heard gunfire from more than two different weapons.

The smell of burning hit his senses.

He could now hear sporadic gunfire from the front of the square, but there was no sound of voices. If the Zetas were under fire, their special forces training had instilled in them the crucial SOP not to shout to each other and give away their positions. The trees that had sprouted up within this square were surprisingly dense. Their foliage hung low. He couldn't see more than ten metres ahead, let alone out into the square itself.

Spud appeared in the doorway, brandishing the dead Zeta's pistol. Even in his peripheral vision, Danny could tell his mate was unsteady on his feet. He could see the dog-bite wounds a bit better now. They were bad. It was impossible for Spud to fight at a hundred per cent.

A scream split the air. Female. It came from the adjacent corner of the square, where Danny knew there was another building. It had to be Ana.

Simultaneously, a round slammed into the bark of a tree four metres to Danny's three o'clock. The bark splintered with a loud crack. He sensed movement to his one o'clock. Panned round. Immediately caught in his sights a Zeta gunman with a black bandana over his face. Danny couldn't hesitate: the gunman was holding his weapon like a pro, and wouldn't miss a second time. He released a single round with a harsh bark from the AK-47. It hit the left-hand side of the gunman's chest. He crumpled to the floor, but Danny could tell the round hadn't landed quite where he'd expected. The sights of his weapon weren't properly zeroed in: it was firing about an inch to the left over a distance of ten metres. He'd have to adjust his line of fire.

Danny and Spud moved quickly through the trees in the direction of the scream.

Tyson made out the sound of gunfire from the northwestern corner of the square. He knew that was Spud and Black's location. Either somebody was firing at them, or they were laying down rounds themselves.

In a firefight, you have to go with your instinct. Tyson's instinct told him it was the latter.

The *Federales* gunmen had moved beyond the tree line. The southern side of the square was empty now apart from Tyson himself. He quickly scanned the windows of the buildings overlooking the square to check there were no threats, and prepared to move toward what he believed to be Spud and Black's location.

As he was about to move, however, he heard the scream. It was faint over the fierce noise of the burning van. But he knew it was the woman. Alive.

Tyson cursed under his breath. That complicated things, because Spud and Black would have heard the scream too. And Tyson's instinct told him they wouldn't just be leaving her to her fate.

He hesitated for a second. Then he made the call. He emerged from behind the burning vehicle and ran diagonally across the open ground toward the northeastern corner of the square, preparing to engage his NV goggles as he hit the tree line.

More rounds found their way into the trees, mostly slamming into the trunks, though Danny felt the telltale sense of air displacement as a single one flew inches above his head. He heard shouting among the trees. As he surged through the darkness toward the far corner of the square he tried to establish the number of different voices. Three. Maybe four.

Gunfire from behind him.

He glanced back. It was Spud. He'd released a round into the trees. He nodded at Danny to continue.

Ten seconds later, the other building came into view. It was a single-storey shack, three times the size of the one they'd escaped. Distance: fifteen metres. The door was open. There were three Zeta guards with their backs to the entrance, weapons raised and pointing back toward the tree line. They were clearly focused on a threat coming from that direction, so they didn't appear to notice Danny and Spud.

Quietly, Danny aimed his Kalashnikov. He focused on the nearest of the three Zetas, adjusting his aim to compensate for the skew of the rifle. It was crucial that the first round scored a kill, because as soon as he fired, the remaining two Zetas would turn and open up.

Distance, twelve metres.

Danny held his breath.

Fired.

The round slammed straight into the side of his target's head. Immediately, as Danny expected, his two companions turned. Even as the first target was crumpling to the floor, however, Danny was lining up the next one. He released his second round just a moment after the first. It found its mark, drilling into the target's back. The guy fell sideways into the third target. Danny was forced to adjust his aim as the third target staggered toward the building. But he fired in time to take him out before he disappeared behind the open door.

Rounds continued to ping through the trees. One every five to ten seconds. Other than that, there was silence. Danny and Spud moved stealthily toward the open door. They'd closed the distance to five metres when the door swung slightly on its hinges. There was someone on the other side. Danny stopped. Aimed his weapon just ahead of the door's leading edge. Rested his finger on the trigger as he prepared to take down his next target.

But his next target was not what he expected.

The door swung shut. Standing behind it was Ana. And standing behind Ana was another Zeta. He was pulling Ana's head back by the hair, and he had a knife pressed against her throat. Ana was hyperventilating, while clearly trying not to move too much. The Zeta was nervous. Trembling hands. He barked something in Spanish. Danny didn't understand the words, but he understood their meaning. *Drop your weapons.*

Danny had the side of his head in his sights. But he couldn't take the shot. Even adjusting for the weapon's skew, he was as likely to hit Ana as the Zeta. However, he didn't lower the Kalashnikov. Stalemate was better than the alternative. He moved his eyes from the sight to give himself a better field of view.

Only then did he see a figure step out from behind a tree, eight metres beyond the Zeta. Weapon raised. Night vision engaged.

He looked Ana straight in the eye.

Then he looked beyond her, and nodded at the figure.

He waited for the shot.

★　　★　　★

Tyson had a tree trunk immediately to his left, and the northern wall of the square ten metres to his right. The back of the Zeta's head was precisely in the cross-hairs of his sight, but he could also see Black's face, sweating and serious, on the edge of the viewfinder.

Black gave him the nod.

Tyson took the shot.

The Zeta collapsed, the back of his head fully blown away by the entry wound. Ana staggered, gasping, toward Danny Black. But Black had already turned 90 degrees, his back to the northern wall, his weapon pointing into this thick, urban forest. Tyson did the same.

'How many have you put down?' Tyson demanded.

'Five,' Black said, bending down over the dead Zeta to take his weapon – an M16 – which he quickly handed to Spud.

Tyson did a quick calculation. 'There's at least one still alive. We have four *Federales* approaching. They think Z1 is here.'

'Why do they think that?'

'Long story. But they'll shoot anything that moves.'

'Spike?' Spud asked. He sounded like shit.

'Missing,' Tyson said bluntly. 'He had a Zeta unit after him. His comms have gone quiet.' He looked into the trees. 'The *Federales* will have heard those gunshots. They'll be closing in.'

Danny lowered his weapon slightly. He pointed west, back the way they'd come, toward the shack where he and Spud had been imprisoned. 'That way,' he said, before turning toward the door of the nearest shack and laying down a burst of rounds into the swinging door. Tyson understood his strategy: it would attract the *Federales*, who seemed to have an appetite for a fight.

Danny turned to Ana. 'Stick with him,' he said, indicating Spud. Ana nodded, and allowed Spud to grab her by the right arm and usher her back through the trees.

Danny and Tyson followed.

The four *Federales* officers were twenty metres into the forested area when Luis heard the single shot followed by the extended burst of rounds from the northeastern corner of the square. He jabbed his finger in that direction. His three comrades, who were panning round with their weapons, followed his lead.

They moved seven metres through the trees. A ramshackle building, its door swinging open, appeared a little more than ten metres ahead in the northeastern corner. There was no sign of enemy personnel, but Luis sensed the sharp taste of excitement on his lips. Something told him Augusto Chavez was in that shack.

Z1 was close.

Luis was so eager to get to that building that for a moment his situational awareness let him down.

He heard a single round being fired somewhere behind him. He turned just in time to see one of his comrades hit the ground a mere three metres from Luis's own position, while a muzzle flash accompanied another gunshot. A second man went down.

Luis fired in the direction of the muzzle flash, but instinctively knew he hadn't hit his mark.

And a second later, he knew it was all over.

There was an ear-splitting noise and a flash of blinding white light. Luis knew it was a flashbang grenade, but was powerless to withstand its disorientating effects. He staggered back, unable to see, his ears ringing horribly. He heard the harsh bark of a third round being released, and knew he was the last *Federales* officer standing. He let a random burst of automatic fire explode from his weapon, but it was unaimed and unfocused. Less than a second later, a bullet hit him in the arm. His weapon fell to the ground. He staggered back. Still semi-blinded by the grenade, he could only sense a silhouette of a man bearing down on him. He launched himself toward the figure, one hand clawed, the other in a hammer fist, trying to judge where his enemy's most vulnerable points were – the eyes, the neck, the groin. But before he could attack, he felt a second round slam hard into his knee. His legs immediately gave way beneath him. He fell to his knees, just as a booted foot slammed against his chest, knocking him on to his back.

Luis's eyes had started to recover now. As the silhouette bent down over him, he saw a medallion in the intricate shape of a Z hanging from his neck.

And he saw the gun that he knew would kill him.

The man pressed his pistol hard against Luis's mouth. He closed his eyes slowly, and Luis saw a new set of eyes tattooed on the eyelids. '*Buenas noches, Federales escoria*,' the man whispered.

Goodnight, Federales scum.

Luis did not hear the shot that killed him.

Danny heard six shots from the other side of the square in quick succession. Was it Zetas killing *Federales*, or *Federales* killing Zetas? Danny couldn't tell, but he knew his unit would draw fire from whoever was still alive. He, Tyson, Spud and Ana had reached the tree line. Tyson had raised his NV goggles. Looking out from it, they could see the empty square and the van, still burning ferociously. Choking smoke filled the air.

Distance to the exit: forty metres.

Danny turned to Spud. 'Get her to the exit,' he said. 'We'll cover you.'

Spud nodded. He understood. The open bite wound was on his dominant arm. It would compromise his ability to fire effectively. He was incredibly pale. His face was sweating. The effect of the bites was showing, and it made sense for him to be the one to chaperone Ana.

Tyson engaged his weapon. Faced east and moved out beyond the tree line. He crouched down in the firing position and started scanning the trees for movement.

'Go,' Danny said.

Spud took Ana by the arm and brandished his stolen rifle slightly clumsily in his free hand. He had something of a limp as he ran with her toward the cover of the burning van. Danny joined Tyson in scanning the tree line for movement.

Nothing.

Distance to the fire: twenty metres. Spud and Ana reached it in ten seconds, then stopped in its cover. Danny could only just make out their silhouettes behind the flames. He stayed in the firing position while Tyson sprinted across the open ground to join them. Then, while Tyson laid down some covering fire into the tree line, Danny followed. He could feel his face was dripping with sweat and dirt as he approached the blaze.

The *Federales* vehicle was situated ten metres to the east of the burning van. That was their next staging post. They needed to take cover there before getting to the exit gate. Danny barked the instruction. He and Tyson covered Spud and Ana as they ran toward the open-top Hilux. On the edge of his hearing, Danny heard sirens from somewhere beyond the square. He heard Tyson roar: 'More *Federales!*'

Danny glanced toward Spud and Ana. They were halfway between the burning van and the Hilux. He turned his attention back to the tree line, scanning for movement, checking for threats.

He barely heard the bullet over the noise of the flames.

But in his peripheral vision, he saw Ana collapse. She was hit.

Spud's momentum carried him forward to the cover of the Hilux, leaving Ana sprawled in the open ground. She was screaming, and clutching her leg. It looked to Danny like she'd taken a round somewhere above the knee. Danny and Tyson both laid down fire toward the tree line, but Danny couldn't see the shooter, or any sign of movement.

He looked toward Spud. His mate's face was stricken as he stared powerlessly at Ana lying on the ground. Any second now, she could take another bullet. It would finish her off.

Danny met Spud's eyes across the open ground. Something passed between them. An acknowledgement that whatever happened, they couldn't leave a wounded woman to the mercy of this remaining gunman.

Spud nodded grimly. It was clear it had to be him. He was wounded, which meant his covering fire would be less effective than Danny and Tyson's.

Spud's shoulders slumped momentarily. Then he seemed to inhale deeply and bring himself up to full height. He stepped back from the Hilux. Pointed his handgun toward the tree line. Then he opened up as he ran toward the screaming Ana.

At the same time, Danny and Tyson opened fire. Three streams of rounds blistered toward the tree line as Spud hurtled across the five metres that separated him and Ana. As he reached her, Spud stopped firing. He bent down and, with obvious effort, hauled Ana over his good shoulder. He turned and, with Danny and Tyson still covering him, started to run back to the protection of the Hilux.

Everything happened within an instant.

Danny and Tyson's weapons fell silent almost simultaneously, their magazines empty. Danny saw a muzzle flash from behind the tree line as the hidden gunman – no longer pinned down by the Regiment's covering fire – discharged a single round.

The moment froze. The round slammed into the side of Spud's head.

There was a shower of blood and bone and hair. Danny's mate collapsed.

'*NO!*' Danny roared.

Blood rushed to his head. He was only half aware of Tyson loading a new clip from his ops waistcoat. He sprinted from behind the burning van toward the prostrate figures of Ana and Spud. A round pinged inches from his shoulder, but he kept running. As he reached them, he heard Tyson laying down a further burst of automatic fire toward the trees, suppressing the shooter.

Danny crouched. Everything was spinning. Spud was lying on his back, the entrance wound in his head mercifully out of sight, but with a pool of blood spreading around it. Danny went through the motions of checking his mate's pulse at the neck. Nothing. His hand came away covered in sticky blood. He wanted to vomit.

'*Black! Move!*' Tyson shouted, even as he released another burst of suppressing fire.

But Danny felt himself momentarily paralysed. He stared at his mate's lifeless face. The horror of the moment felt like it was crushing him.

'*MOVE!*'

Tyson's roar snapped Danny out of it. He turned to Ana. She'd stopped screaming now, but was shivering badly. With a final look at Spud, Danny grabbed her, put her over his shoulder and sprinted for the cover of the Hilux. Tyson was following, spraying the open ground with rounds.

The approaching sirens were louder. Danny's instinct told him they were advancing along the Avenida Hidalgo. He told himself to focus. Forced himself not to look toward Spud's corpse. They had to get out of there before more *Federales* arrived.

Distance to the exit: ten metres. It meant crossing open ground again. There was a clunking sound from Tyson as he loaded yet another magazine. Ana continued to shiver over his shoulder.

'*Go!*' Tyson shouted. '*Go, go, go!*'

Danny sprinted for the exit. Tyson followed, firing back toward the trees as he ran, successfully suppressing any more fire. Danny burst out into the Avenida Hidalgo, Tyson following just a couple of seconds later. They took cover to the side of the open metal gate. Danny looked east along the Avenida Hidalgo. It was from here that the sirens were coming. Sure enough, a *Federales* vehicle was screaming down the street toward them. Headlamps blazing. Emergency lights flashing. Distance, fifty metres.

Danny looked in the opposite direction. Another vehicle was reversing at speed toward them. Distance, thirty metres. The vehicle was a black Tahoe. Its engine, over-revving in reverse, was screaming.

'Spike,' Danny breathed. Then he yelled to Tyson. 'It's Spike!'

'Where the hell's he been?' Tyson roared. 'I thought they'd nailed him!'

But Danny couldn't think about that now. He was already working out their next move. They needed to get across the open gate. Tyson gave Danny a curt nod, then stepped out into the gateway, his weapon once more raised. Danny followed. Every ounce of his attention was on the Tahoe as it reversed toward them – twenty metres, fifteen metres – but then he heard Tyson shout: 'Mother*fucker!*'

He looked to the right. Standing boldly in the middle of the square, just in front of the trees, was a figure. He had an RPG launcher over his shoulder, and was clearly preparing to fire it. Even from this distance, Danny recognised the silhouette. It was the tall, muscular Zeta commander with the Z medallion and the tattooed eyelids.

Danny knew from the way the firefight had unfolded that there was only one Zeta left. Which meant he was looking directly at the man who had killed Spud.

All Danny wanted to do was kill him. He could taste the hate, feel it burning through him. He even started instinctively to feel for his weapon, forgetting that he was out of ammo. But there was the ferocious screeching of wheels on either side of him. The *Federales* vehicle to his right. The Tahoe to his left. He felt Tyson grabbing him, and was brought back into the moment. They couldn't risk a renewed firefight with this fresh batch of Mexican police. With Ana still slumped over his shoulder, he sprinted toward the Tahoe, which had screamed to a halt ten metres from their position, Spike at the wheel. He opened up the back door, manoeuvred Ana inside and scrambled into the back seat next to her. Tyson took the front passenger seat. '*GO!*' he commanded.

'*What about Spud?*' Spike shouted.

'*JUST FUCKING GET OUT OF HERE, SNOWFLAKE!*'

Spike knocked the vehicle into first and hit the gas even before the doors were shut. They shot like a bullet westward along the Avenida Hidalgo. But still Spike was yelling. '*Where the hell's Spud?*'

Danny twisted himself round to look out the back window. He was just in time to see it all unfold.

The *Federales* Hilux had stopped right in front of the open gate. None of the armed officers had time to jump out of the open-topped back of the vehicle, or to exit from the cab. The rocket-propelled grenade slammed into the broad side of the vehicle with deadly accuracy. The explosion was immense. The Hilux burst into an orange and black fireball, more smoke pumping up into the air. There was zero possibility of any survivors.

Spike put fifty metres between them, and was still accelerating, the souped-up engine of the Tahoe screaming loudly. He and Tyson were shouting at each other, but Danny had zoned out. He saw a figure emerge from the gates and stand in front of the burning fireball that had been the Hilux. Tall, lean, muscular. Danny couldn't make out his face, but he knew who it was: the man with the tattooed eyelids. He felt his eyes narrow, and a hot surge of loathing pulse in his gut.

Then Spike pulled a sharp right and Ana moaned loudly in pain. Danny turned toward her. Their eyes met. She didn't have to say anything. The fear in her expression said it all.

'Get to the Holiday Inn!' Danny barked.

'What?' Tyson protested. 'We need to ...'

'My son!' Ana shrieked. 'Kleinman's a traitor! He knows where my son is! You promised me he'd be alright! Drive there – *now!*'

TWENTY

The town was suddenly alive with *Federales* vehicles. Sirens screamed. Lights flashed. Regular civilian vehicles swerved up on to the sidewalk to let the open-topped Hiluxes through. But Danny and his team – what was left of it – were travelling against the flow.

Ana was whimpering in the seat next to Danny, and not just from the pain of her bullet wound. Tyson was staring through the windscreen at the road ahead, constantly warning Spike of any upcoming obstacles. Spike was driving like shit. The engine was whining from being in too low a gear. The wheels were spinning. Spike's knuckles on the wheel were white. Any Regiment skills he had seemed to have deserted him. His eyes were wild. '*They had me pinned down!*' he kept saying. '*I came as quick as I could! They had me pinned . . .*'

He hit the brakes sharply to stop himself colliding with a car in front. He slammed his fists against the wheel, then clutched his hair with his hands. 'I came as quick as I . . .'

'Fucking drive, Snowflake!' Tyson bellowed.

Danny jumped out of the car, despite it being in the middle of the road, and had to manhandle the distraught Spike out of the driver's seat. 'Spud's dead,' he told him brutally. 'Deal with it.'

Somehow it made the worst part of Danny feel better, laying the bald truth on Spike. The kid seemed to crumple. Danny bundled him into the back of the vehicle next to Ana, then took the wheel. He hit the gas and accelerated past the vehicle in front of them, ignoring the angry horns as he sped furiously up the wrong side of the road. He was glad to have something to focus on. Something to take his mind off Spud. He could hear Spike pounding his fist in fury and frustration against the passenger door of the car, but couldn't bring himself to look at the kid in the rear-view mirror. He needed to keep his mind somewhere else.

The Holiday Inn came into view five minutes later. The squat building glowed up ahead, green and blue in the night. Danny screeched into the parking lot and came to a halt ten metres from the entrance.

'Give me the key card,' he told Ana.

Ana fumbled in the pocket of her jeans, wincing from the pain of having to move. The key card she handed him was smeared with blood.

'Watch her,' Danny told Spike, and for once received no argument. He and Tyson jumped out of the vehicle. Tyson removed his NV and his rifle, but they still looked like men who'd been into battle. Smoke-stained, blood-spattered and drenched in sweat. It didn't matter. They had to get to room 735 immediately. If Z1's people hadn't already got to the kid, they could be there any second.

The two Regiment men drew stares from the hotel guests as they burst into the reception. They didn't bother with the elevator, but simply ran to the far side of the hotel where a door led to the stairs. They ascended three steps at a time, until they reached the seventh floor and sprinted along the corridor toward Miguel's room. Tyson drew his handgun, then nodded at Danny, who placed the key card against the sensor by the door. The LED light flicked from red to green. Tyson raised his weapon, holding it with two hands, and kicked the door open with his foot.

The only light inside the room came from the TV. Tyson led the way. Danny followed. *The Simpsons* were on, dubbed in Spanish. Danny looked toward the bed.

Miguel wasn't there. The sheets were twisted, as if there had been a struggle. Buzz Lightyear, his left arm missing, was lying on the floor, face down.

Tyson kicked in the door to the shower room. Checked it for personnel. Nothing. Room 735 was empty.

'The kid could have gone walkabout,' Tyson said. 'He's only, what, ten? Maybe he got hungry.' He didn't sound as if he believed his own suggestion.

Danny certainly didn't. 'They've got him,' he said. He strode round the bed and picked up the handset of the telephone on the bedside table. He dialled Kleinman's number and put the phone on speaker. The line rang once, then an automated message by a female computer-generated voice clicked in: '*Operation terminated. Return to UK. Operation terminated. Return to UK . . .*'

Danny killed the line. Looked up at Tyson, who was covering the half-open door with his weapon. 'Kleinman was screwing us all the time,' Tyson said.

'We should have seen it,' Danny berated himself. 'The Zetas knew our moves. Kleinman must have been tipping them off – the money on the plane, the tunnel guys, the men in the enclosure just now. They all knew what was happening.' He swore under his breath. 'We should have known when he gave us Ana. Why the hell would he give us his best asset – the one person who knows Z1's probable location? If he really wanted to nail Chavez, he'd have kept her for himself. He was just getting our trust, making us walk into his fucking trap while sacrificing Ana and the kid at the same time. He's been in Z1's pocket since the start.'

'We've got to leave,' Tyson said. His voice was clipped and tense. 'They'll be expecting us to be here.'

Danny nodded. He headed to the door. He almost stopped to pick up Buzz Lightyear, but decided not to. If Ana thought Miguel had his favourite toy, it might make the news they had to give her a little easier to bear.

Two hotel security guys were emerging from the elevator just as Danny and Tyson hit the stairwell. Back down on the ground floor, the receptionist made a call as soon as she saw them reappear, but they were back out in the parking lot before anyone could stop them. They jogged to their vehicle. Even though Ana was still in the back of the car, Danny could hear her screams from ten metres away. '*Where is he? Where's my boy?*'

They jumped back into the Tahoe, Danny behind the wheel. Danny knocked the vehicle into reverse and screeched out of the parking lot, doing what he could to zone out Ana's screams. Tyson was right: they had to get away from this location. He sped on to the main road adjacent to the hotel and headed south.

'Do you think Kleinman can still track our vehicle?' Tyson said.

'*Where's Miguel?*'

'It's possible. We need to strip it down, find the tracking device.'

'*WHERE IS HE?*'

There was a large gas station fifty metres up ahead. Danny pulled into it and parked up beyond the pumps. He killed the engine, then turned round and looked directly at Ana. There was no good way of saying it. 'He's been taken,' he told her.

'*You promised me! YOU PROMISED ME!*'

Her face was sweating, her eyes rolling. 'We need to get your leg fixed,' Danny said.

'Forget about my leg. *Find my son!*'

Danny closed his eyes. Drew a deep breath. Images flashed through his mind like a movie reel. Kleinman, standing in the shadow of the motel, his small, watery, treacherous eyes watching him. Spud, Danny's best mate, dead on the ground. The Zeta fighter with the tattooed eyelids, standing in front of the blazing *Federales* vehicle. Buzz Lightyear on the floor of the hotel room.

The face of Augusto Chavez, Z1, whom Danny had never met, but against whom all his hate was now directed.

He opened his eyes again and scanned the personnel in the gas station. There were four vehicles refuelling. A woman walking out of the payment area. Nothing suspicious. He looked round at the others. Spike looked like shit. His face was drawn, his eyes haunted. Danny wasn't the only one numbed by Spud's death. Ana was weeping, her head in her hands. Only Tyson appeared capable of thinking straight.

'Options?' Tyson said.

'One,' Danny said, 'we make contact with Hereford. They'll tell us to ditch Ana and lie low until they can extract us.' Tyson's blank expression made it perfectly clear this was not an option he favoured. Spike looked like he was somewhere between fury and tears.

'They killed Spud!' he hissed. 'They fucking killed him, Danny. Are you telling me that's the end of it? Are you telling me we're going to let this Z1 twat get away with it?'

Spike grabbed a clump of his own hair in frustration. Danny saw his hand was trembling. 'Option two,' he said quietly, 'we find Augusto Chavez and teach him what happens when one of *his* guys kills one of *our* guys.'

'How can we?' Tyson said. 'Without Kleinman? Without the headshed? We don't know where the fucker is.'

Silence. Tyson was right. Without any intel, they were shooting in the dark. After ten seconds, however, he realised Ana's sobbing had stopped. He turned to her. Her haunted, tearful eyes were wild.

'I know where he is,' she whispered, her voice cracked. She repeated it, a little stronger: 'I know where he'll be.'

The Regiment men stared at her.

'Where?' Danny asked carefully.

Ana drew a deep, shaky breath. Closed her eyes. And spoke.

'The *Hacienda del Colinas*,' she said. 'It's 500 kilometres south of here. Northwest of Ciudad Victoria, where the river meets the hills. We spent holidays there as children and he built a ... a stronghold for himself. That's where he retreats to when he doesn't wish to be found. I've heard it's surrounded by paddocks, and a high wall. And heavily guarded. *Very* heavily. You're just three men. I don't see how you can—'

'We go off the grid,' Spike interrupted. 'Hereford can't know what we're doing. It's just us. It has to be just us, otherwise they'll ...'

Danny turned to Tyson. 'You comfortable with that?'

Tyson nodded.

'I'm coming with you!' Ana said forcefully.

Danny shook his head. 'You can't walk. It's not going to happen.'

'Then how do I know you'll bring Miguel back to me?'

'You don't,' Danny said flatly. 'You don't even know if he's still alive. But we're your only option. If you don't trust us, you've lost him. You've been shot. You need treatment. You know that, right?'

She nodded mutely, reluctantly.

'We have to get you to the hospital. You must know people there. They can register you in a false name so the cartel can't get to you. So *Kleinman* can't get to you. You must have systems in place for this kind of situation.'

'Maybe ... I have friends who ...'

Danny started the engine before she even finished. 'Where's the hospital?' he said, knocking the Tahoe into reverse.

'West,' said Ana, her voice suddenly very weak indeed. Danny looked over at her. Her eyes were rolling. He wasn't sure she was going to make it.

Kleinman was alone.

Hernandez had left forty-five minutes ago. Rav, half an hour. Both of them were nervous and sweating. News of the firefight in Nuevo Laredo had come over the intelligence wires. An estimated fifteen *Federales* dead. An eyewitness reported a woman with a bullet wound fleeing the site with three men. There was no hint that the authorities knew Danny Black's unit had been involved, but that didn't quell their anxiety. They headed off in different directions, taking their notebooks and hard drives with them. Just as instructed. It would take twenty-four hours before Langley realised Kleinman himself wasn't returning for a debrief, and they started looking for their missing agent, ostensibly for his own safety, but in reality because a missing agent meant panic stations that he might have been flipped. Twenty-four hours was enough time for him, however.

He was still there, in the motel that doubled as their ops centre. He'd double-locked the doors to all the rooms except this one. The armoury. Here he stood in silence, shining a flashlight with a red filter over the shelves and boxes of weaponry and other military equipment.

He limped up to a gun rack and selected an M16. Night sights. Surefire torch. Next he chose his favoured suppressed Heckler and Koch HK45C – the same firearm he'd watched Danny Black choose just two days previously. Ammo. He took an NV helmet – the last one – and a flak jacket. He located a baseball cap with the Dallas Cowboys blue-star insignia on the front. He put it on and pulled the peak down over his forehead. He packed the gear into a sturdy carry bag. It was heavy. As a result, his limp was a little more pronounced as he exited the armoury. The ops room was dim and ghostly silent, lit only by a single lamp. Kleinman grabbed his notebook and stuffed it into the carry bag. Then he turned the lamp off and exited the room. He double-locked it from outside. Soon – before dawn, probably – CIA operatives unknown to him would be here to clean up. By morning, it would be an empty motel again.

He limped across the parking lot, occasionally shielding his eyes from the headlamps of the oncoming traffic on the adjacent road. On the far side of the parking lot was an old saloon car. Beige in colour, with rust-spattered panels. It was Kleinman's car, and he had taken care to ensure that it was below the CIA's radar. He opened the trunk, stowed his gear, then took the wheel.

His reflection in the rear-view mirror surprised him. He looked gaunt. His eyes were red. He had a blank, thousand-yard stare. He altered the mirror so he wouldn't have to look at his face, turned the engine over and left the parking lot.

He headed west on to the main road, past the fast-food joints and hotels. After a mile or so he came to a red light at a crossroads. A large green signpost bridged the head of the road. Kleinman felt his eyes scanning it.

To the right, Laredo International Airport. Once there, he could dump his vehicle and be on the next flight to Norfolk International Airport. He could be at Langley by close of business.

To the left, the Mexican border.

He closed his eyes. Faces presented themselves. Danny Black and his team. Ana Rodriguez.

There were too many loose ends. Kleinman didn't like loose ends.

He heard car horns behind him and opened his eyes. The lights had turned green and there was a line of traffic behind him. He looked up again at the signpost. Airport right. Mexico left.

He knocked his vehicle into gear, hit the gas and swung left toward the border.

TUESDAY

TWENTY-ONE

SAS headquarters, RAF Credenhill, Hereford.
1000 hours GMT.
'It makes no sense.'

Lieutenant-Colonel Dominic Hardcastle, commanding officer of 22 SAS, was a big man with a quiet voice. Hardcastle was a veteran of Northern Ireland, Bosnia, Sierra Leone and Afghanistan. He had the full respect of every man in the Regiment – not a group noted for their fondness of the officer class – because he was a soldier who had soldiered more than most.

So anyone who took that quiet voice for weakness would be making a big mistake.

The brash American voice, direct over the secure line from CIA headquarters in Langley, Virginia, was making that mistake right now.

'*It is what it is, Hardcastle. Your guys are dirty. Swallow it.*'

The CO, sitting in his sparse office deep in the Regiment buildings at Hereford, stared at the phone on his desk. He had it on loudspeaker so he could take notes as he spoke, but he wasn't writing at the moment.

'*We have photographic evidence,*' the voice continued. '*Pictures of your team with the head of a UK crime syndicate by the name of Aiden Bailey. He has direct links to the Zeta cartel in Mexico who your boys are supposedly targeting. They're compromised, Hardcastle. In it up to their goddamn necks. My advice to you is get them back on UK soil and deal with it internally. Military tribunal, however the hell you limeys like to play it. Because trust me, if Washington gets a sniff of it, more important heads than theirs will roll.*'

There wasn't a lot that fazed him. But this? This was like ice in his veins. He knew these men. Danny Black and Spud Glover in particular. They were proper guys. It didn't stack up.

'I'm going to ask you to leave this with me,' he said quietly.

'*You're going to need to move quickly on—*'

'Thank you for keeping me informed,' Hardcastle said, and killed the line.

Hardcastle was a measure twice, cut once kind of guy. Not given to knee-jerk reactions. He sat in his chair beneath the black and white picture of himself shaking the hand of General Petraeus at ISAF headquarters in Kabul, his fingers pressed together, staring into the middle distance. Five minutes passed before he picked up the phone again and dialled an internal number. Major Ray Hammond, ops officer of B Squadron, answered immediately.

'*Hammond.*'

'It's me,' Hardcastle said.

'*Yes, sir?*'

'When did we last hear from Danny Black and his team?'

'*Not since they crossed the Atlantic, sir. The Yanks have been i/c that operation, you'll remember.*'

'Yes, I remember,' Hardcastle said. He paused for a moment, then relayed the salient points of the conversation to Hammond.

'*Impossible, sir,*' Hammond said. '*Black's a wildcard on occasion, I'll give you that. We've had to brush a few things under the carpet. But he's not dirty. No way.*'

'The Yanks have cut them loose. So why haven't we heard from them?'

Hammond had no answer to that.

'I want to know their current location,' Hardcastle said. 'Get GCHQ on to it. Just them. No NSA involvement. I want facial recognition scans of every damn CCTV camera in Mexico. I want them to run a voice recognition scan of all mobile communications originating from the Texas–Mexico border. If they find a face or voice match with any member of our unit, I want to know immediately.'

'*Understood, sir.*'

'We have men on jungle training in Belize?'

'*D Squadron, sir.*'

'Where are Air Troop, currently?'

'*Jungle exercises, sir. I can have them on standby within two hours.*'

'Do we have any Navy assets operating close to the Eastern seaboard?'

'*I'll find out, sir.*'

The uncertainty in Hammond's voice was pronounced, but he was professional enough not to question his CO's thinking. Which was a good thing, Hardcastle thought as he put the phone down, because right now he didn't know what kind of operation he might be ordering D Squadron to carry out. A simple pick-up, if Danny Black and his team got in touch. Or something darker, if it turned out the antagonistic American voice from Langley had been telling the truth. One thing was for sure: nobody in the murky hierarchy of government or the military would thank him for bringing the unit back alive if they really *were* dirty.

'Trust,' he muttered to himself. 'But check.'

Words to live by, in this line of work.

He pressed his fingers together again. Then, after a couple of minutes, he took his personal mobile phone from his pocket and dialled a number. It rang twice before a voice answered.

'*Dominic. Long time.*'

'I need a favour, Richard. On the QT.'

You didn't get to a position like Hardcastle's without meeting a few influential people on the way up. Richard Meeks, the Met's chief commissioner, was one of them.

'*Go ahead,*' Meeks said, his voice a little uncertain. He knew that an off-the-record request from the commanding officer of 22 SAS was likely to involve some bending of the rules.

'Aiden Bailey. I need to know where to find him.'

'*You could make an official request for that information, Dominic.*'

'I don't have time for official requests.'

There was a pause.

'*I'll call you back,*' Meeks said.

The line went dead.

Hardcastle laid his phone on his desk. He started reading some documents that required his attention. Two recruits had become dangerously ill on a recent selection course. The usual questions were being asked about whether special forces selection should be made less brutal. That would happen over Hardcastle's dead body. These men were applying for the SAS, not the Boy Scouts. It was an old Regiment joke that if unsuitable recruits ended up on the lower slopes of Pen-y-Fan with a saline drip stuck in their arse cheeks, it was nature's way of telling them they'd failed. But there was truth in it.

The mobile buzzed. Hardcastle answered it immediately. 'Richard?'

'*We have a detective sergeant on Bailey's payroll,*' Meeks said without ceremony. '*With our full knowledge, of course. There's been some sort of shoot-out at one of Bailey's premises. Five are covering it up for some reason, but Bailey's nervous. He's arranged to meet this DS at the bandstand in Battersea Park, nineteen hundred hours. If your guys are there, he's all yours. Just keep him in one piece, Dominic. If he ends up face down in the Thames, I'll have to open an investigation.*'

'I owe you one, Richard.'

'*You do. Don't think I'll forget about it.*'

Dominic Hardcastle wouldn't be making that mistake. He ended the call, then dialled another internal number on his desk phone. A male voice answered. 'Are Vic Marshall and Russell Hunter in camp?' he asked.

'*One moment, sir. I'll double check.*' A fifteen-second pause. '*Yes, sir, they're here.*'

'I want them in my office immediately.'

Hardcastle had to wait less than five minutes for the knock on his door. Marshall and Hunter entered. They both wore civvies. Marshall was a red-head, shaved short. Hunter was almost completely bald. Big, broad-shouldered men, they stood respectfully on the other side of Hardcastle's desk, only speaking when they were spoken to.

It took Hardcastle less than two minutes to explain what he wanted. Marshall and Hunter assimilated the information, nodded curtly and left the office, shutting the door quietly behind them.

As the sun rose over the Mexican–US border, it illuminated a long line of traffic at the border crossing, and a fog of exhaust fumes. Anonymous cars, some waiting patiently, others less so, sounding their horns as if that would make any difference.

Kleinman was one of the patient ones. A career filled with tedious days and weeks of surveillance had taught him that quality. As he approached the checkpoint booths, he put on his sunglasses and double checked in the rear-view mirror that his Dallas Cowboys baseball cap was covering his eyes. It was hardly a perfect way of fooling the facial recognition technology at the border, but it was the best he could do.

His pristine US passport was in a false name, of course. And it was, to the best of his knowledge, undocumented by the CIA. The border control officer barely glanced at it as he waved Kleinman through. It seemed to him the *Federales* presence was heavier than usual, and the lines of traffic waiting to cross over into the US were longer. It made sense. They'd lost men during the firefight in Nuevo Laredo. They'd be thinking some of the Zeta shooters would be trying to slip across the border to lie low for a while. In fact, Kleinman knew they'd be more likely to head further into the Mexican interior, deep into cartel country where nobody could touch them.

He checked the time as he drove away from the border: 0845 hours. Up ahead he saw a sign saying *Restaurante*. He indicated right and pulled up into the small parking lot round the back, where he took the final parking space. He removed a GPS unit from his glove compartment and switched it on. He hadn't really expected the screen to indicate the location of the SAS unit, so he wasn't surprised that it didn't. He put the GPS unit back and then, retrieving his laptop from the carry bag in the trunk of his vehicle, he entered the restaurant. It was a low-rent place, busy exclusively with Mexican men – construction workers, by the look of their clothes. The air was thick with the smell of Mexican food. Kleinman approached the counter, instinctively checking for security cameras. There were none that he could see. He ordered coffee and the wifi code in immaculate Spanish, then found himself a table and got himself online.

Langley would not yet be aware he was disobeying his instructions to return, so his access to the secure section of the CIA intranet was not yet rescinded. It took a couple of minutes to go through the relevant security protocols, but by the time his cup of strong, black coffee arrived at his table, he was in.

Kleinman worked quickly. He knew his way around the system as well as any of the technicians at Langley, so it was the work of less than a minute to search the admissions registers of the local hospital. If Ana Rodriguez had been shot, hospital was the most likely place to find her.

And he *was* going to find her.

The firefight had taken place at approximately 2000 hours. Since then there had been thirty-two hospital admissions, not including those dead on arrival. He assumed they were the *Federales* officers from the firefight. The dead Zetas would be left for the cartel to clear up. Kleinman scanned the names of the admissions. Ana Rodriguez was not among them.

Her absence didn't surprise him. She was smart. She was a doctor. She would know people in the hospital who would register her under an assumed name. Nor did her absence throw him off the scent. Even if she were registered in a false name, it would need to be female. Of the thirty-two admissions, twenty-nine were male, which left only three: Imelda Castel, Helena Gomis and Carmen Satoras. Imelda and Helena were on the maternity ward.

Which meant, if Kleinman's powers of deduction were worth anything, that Carmen Satoras was Ana Rodriguez.

'Got you,' he muttered to himself.

He logged out of the secure section of the intranet, checked the address of the hospital and brought up a Google Maps window to check its location. He estimated it would be a fifteen-minute drive to the hospital. Factor in another fifteen minutes to find a florist and buy a bunch of flowers – an essential prop for anybody wanting to move unquestioned around a hospital – and he would be face to face with Ana Rodriguez by 0930 hours.

He closed his laptop and, leaving his coffee untouched, left the restaurant. He limped back up to his car, opened the trunk and stowed the laptop inside. He looked over his shoulder to check he wasn't being watched, then pulled out the Heckler and Koch handgun, which he slipped into the inside pocket of his jacket. He shut the trunk, slid behind the wheel and pulled back out into the Nuevo Laredo traffic, heading west toward the hospital, looking left and right for a florist as he drove.

Ana was in a morphine-induced haze.

A solitary moment of good luck arrived when Danny Black and his team brought her to the hospital. Her friend, a surgeon called Sebastián Zabala, was arriving for his early-morning shift. When he saw her staggering toward the entrance, supported by the Spanish-speaking man Black called Tyson, Sebastián ran up to her.

'Ana, what on earth—'

Tyson yanked out a flat palm to push him away. 'No,' Ana breathed. 'It's okay, he's a doctor, a friend.'

Sebastián gave Tyson a very unfriendly look as she collapsed, pale-faced, into his arms.

'What's happening, Ana?' Sebastián asked. He looked around nervously. 'The cartel?'

She nodded. 'Don't put my real name on the forms, Sebastián.'

Sebastián looked reluctant. 'They always find people, Ana,' he said. 'In twenty-four hours, they'll know where you are.'

'Twenty-four hours is all we need,' Tyson said in immaculate Spanish.

Sebastián gave him a severe look and nodded, his eyes a little wild. As he held her, Ana looked over his shoulder at Danny Black himself, who was behind the wheel of the black Tahoe, parked where the ambulances ought to be. She gave him a brief nod. Danny, his face glowing slightly in the light of the dash, waited for the silent Tyson to return to the vehicle, before easing the vehicle away from its parking place and driving away from the hospital. Ana couldn't drag her gaze away from the tail lights as they disappeared. Then her knees gave way beneath her. If Sebastián hadn't been holding her, she'd have collapsed.

Minutes later, once Sebastián had given her a brief triage and determined the severity of her wound and the extent of her blood loss, she was on a stretcher bed, a drip stand of bloods and saline hanging above her, being rushed through the shabby corridors of the hospital, Sebastián striding purposefully beside her. 'Where's Miguel?' he asked urgently. 'Who's looking after him, Ana?'

The stricken look she gave him said immediately there was a very big problem. 'Do you need me to call the *Federales*?' he said.

'No,' Ana said, her voice incredibly weak. 'There's nothing they can do.' She grabbed his wrist. 'The forms, Sebastián.'

'I understand.'

Her friend had operated on Ana under local anaesthetic. It was quicker that way, and it took just forty-five minutes for him to retrieve the bullet from her flesh and stitch up the wound. 'You're lucky,' he told her when she was in recovery. 'It missed your bone by a centimetre. It'll take a few weeks, but you will walk again.' Sebastián had found her a private room and taken personal charge of her post-operative meds. As he spoke, he was inserting cannulas in each arm: one for saline, one for morphine. The moment the morphine hit her system, she felt a curious sensation of relief. She knew what was happening. She knew Miguel was in danger. But somehow, she felt disassociated from the events. She closed her eyes and let the drugs do their work.

'I have to go,' Sebastián said. 'I'll check in on you later this morning. You need anything, press this button. I've told the nurses to leave you alone otherwise.' Ana didn't need to open her eyes. She knew he was talking about the button on the beige handheld control panel connected to the wall by a cord. She heard his footsteps move across the room, and opened her eyes just as he reached the door.

'Sebastián,' she said. He turned. 'Thank you.'

He nodded and left, closing the door behind him.

Ana lay very still and shut her eyes again. The regular beep from the blood pressure and pulse monitor by her bed was strangely comforting. Images swam in front of her eyes. Burning vehicles in the Zeta compound. Danny Black and his grim-faced friends. And of course, Miguel, clutching his Buzz Lightyear toy. Even through the effects of the morphine, she felt a throb of panic. Her pulse monitor beeped a little faster. She opened her eyes and tried to push herself up from the hospital bed, but she had no strength and a sharpness from the wound cut through her pain relief. She collapsed back down into the bed with a little whimper.

Time passed. She didn't know how long. She lay with her eyes shut, forcing herself to breathe deeply. The morphine was wearing off. Her anxiety was increasing. She needed another hit, but she didn't want it. It didn't seem right, making the panic go away when she didn't know where her little boy was.

She heard the door open, and knew it would be Sebastián, back to check on her. 'I don't want it,' she said groggily without opening her eyes. 'Just give me something for the pain.'

Sebastián didn't reply. Ana heard the door close. It seemed like such an effort even to open her eyes, so she kept them shut.

'They'll find him,' she said, only vaguely aware she might not be making sense. 'I know they'll find him.'

She heard Sebastián's footsteps across the room.

Only when he had taken three or four paces did she notice there was something different about them.

Sebastián's gait had been even. Regular. These footsteps weren't. They were uneven. Irregular. As if they belonged to someone with a limp.

A bolus of fear rose in Ana's throat. Her eyes flickered open. She saw a slightly scruffy older man with a greying beard and watery eyes. He was carrying a large bunch of oriental lilies. Ana recognised him, of course. He'd presented himself to her three years ago with an offer of witness protection in the US if she informed on her brother. And she'd spoken to him on the phone just yesterday.

'Good morning, Ana,' said Kleinman. 'It's been a long time, hasn't it? I was worried I might not be able to find you.'

He was three metres from the bed. Ana was suddenly paralysed with terror. Kleinman limped another couple of steps toward her, still clutching his flowers. She caught a glimpse of a gun, hidden behind the paper wrapped round the stems.

She broke through her fear and reached out for the handheld control with the alarm button. But her hands were shaking and the sudden movement caused a shock of pain to splinter through her body. She gasped in agony and fumbled the movement, knocking the control from her bedside table so that it swung by its cord out of reach. At the same time, she felt Kleinman's hand – cold and dry – grasp her wrist. She wanted to shout out, but he had dropped the flowers and, with his free hand, was aiming his handgun directly at her face.

'I think it would be best,' he said, 'if we didn't make any kind of noise. Don't you, Ana?'

TWENTY-TWO

Danny, Tyson and Spike had endured a long night waiting for the sun to rise. Tyson had explained what Ana's friend had said – that within twenty-four hours, the cartel would likely find her, even if she was registered in a false name. In any case, going dark from the Regiment after their op had been cancelled was high-risk for them. Twenty-four hours they could explain away. Any more than that, not so much. It meant their hit on Z1's hacienda *had* to be made the following evening.

By mutual agreement, however, they decided not to risk the road while it was still dark. They were heading south, deeper into Zeta territory. The cartel owned those roads – Tyson had assured them of that. During the day, there was a good chance of moving unhindered. At night, it was a different matter. Zeta patrols stopped cars at random. Advice to civilians was to avoid driving outside the city at night, and while the unit had confidence in their ability to deal with any threat they came across, they didn't want to announce their arrival by leaving a trail of dead Zeta patrols on their way south.

So they waited it out. They found a lay-by in the main thoroughfare of Nuevo Laredo. Killed the lights, then examined the chassis of the Tahoe. Top to bottom. Side to side. They scanned the undercarriage and the engine, the glove compartments and the trunk. Danny was on the point of slashing open the seats when Spike located the item they were looking for. The tracking device was about the size of a cigarette packet. It was clipped to the main body of the exhaust. They'd missed it at first because it looked like part of the car, caked in grease and dust. It unclipped easily. A green light flashed on its underside. Danny found a fist-sized rock on the side of the road and destroyed the tracker with three sharp strikes. He crushed it into the ground with his heel.

They made a stag routine, two guys on, one guy off, forty-five-minute shifts. It gave them each a couple of shifts of shut-eye while the other two watched for threats.

They stayed put, even when the sun rose. They only moved at 0800 hours, when the rush hour was at its peak and they were just one vehicle out of thousands. They crawled out of Nuevo Laredo in numb silence and hit the road heading south. Danny was behind the wheel, Tyson in the passenger seat. Spike was in the back. The empty seat next to him seemed to shriek the bitter reality of Spud's absence. It felt like an unreal day.

With every mile of featureless Mexican highway that passed underneath them, Danny felt his anger growing. He did his best to keep a lid on it, knowing anger was no help when you needed to keep a clear, ruthless head. Like Danny, Tyson and Spike wore shades to protect their eyes from the fierce Mexican sun, but he didn't need to see the emotion in their eyes. The air prickled with it.

The sun climbed higher. The parched surrounding terrain shimmered in the heat haze. The horizon, a sharp demarcation between brown sand and deep blue sky, appeared not to move. The tense silence in the vehicle persisted. And each time Danny looked in the rear-view mirror and saw an empty seat where Spud was supposed to be, it was like a knife in the guts.

'We should have known,' Tyson said, after they'd been travelling for a silent hour.

'Know what?' Danny replied.

'About Kleinman. It all fits together. We should have knocked this whole fucking thing on the head after the plane hit went wrong.'

'I dunno,' Danny said. 'He was smart. He didn't *have* to tell us the money wasn't on the flight. He covered his tracks by doing that.' He checked the rear-view mirror. Spike was staring out the side window. He appeared to have nothing to add. 'How long do you reckon Kleinman's been on the Zeta payroll?'

Tyson shrugged. 'Who knows? But he'll have cost Chavez a frickin' fortune. A dirty asset inside the CIA doesn't come cheap. My guess is he's on his way right now to a nice little hidey-hole somewhere we'll never find him, to spend the rest of his life with his money.'

'Yeah,' Danny said. 'Maybe.' He wasn't so sure. He knew, deep down, that they'd left a loose end back in Nuevo Laredo. Even if Ana had registered in the hospital under a false name, she wouldn't be that hard to track down if it was known she'd taken a bullet. Ana knew where they were going, and Kleinman would want those loose ends tied up. No wonder Danny was instinctively keeping track of the vehicles behind him on the highway. No wonder he was occasionally slowing down in order to flush out any potential tails.

No wonder he had an uneasy sensation that they hadn't seen the last of Kleinman yet.

After two hours of travel Danny pulled off the highway again. Time was precious, but they needed food and water. They also needed a plan. Five miles from the highway they came to a small town. It was clear this was a place that had seen the dark side of cartel activity. On the outskirts of the town were tumbledown, half-demolished buildings with corrugated iron roofs, their walls plastered with cartel graffiti. Danny didn't understand it, but he could recognise the words *Los Zetas* almost everywhere. They drove past the shells of a couple of burned-out cars. They were rusted, but also graffitied. The centre of town was grim and obviously poor. Cheap old cars. Empty, rusted oil barrels and litter on the sidewalk. Along the main street, which was pitted and bumpy, there were more shop fronts shuttered up than were open. The black Tahoe drew a stare from every single pedestrian it passed. They looked suspicious, even frightened. Danny supposed they thought it was a cartel vehicle.

He pulled up outside a cafe of sorts. It had a couple of empty metal tables outside, and a Coca-Cola insignia painted on the front window. The three men exited the vehicle, drawing yet more stares from the pedestrians, none of whom kept Danny's gaze when he stared back at them. Danny calculated that if the inhabitants of the town believed this was a cartel vehicle, they wouldn't interfere with it. So he felt confident leaving it in the road and walking into the cafe. 'You know what we need?' he said to Tyson, the only Spanish speaker among them.

Tyson nodded.

The cafe wasn't much to speak of. A few chairs and tables. A couple of old men nursing small cups of coffee. A corpulent Mexican guy in a spattered apron standing behind a counter. He watched them nervously as they entered. Danny saw Tyson giving him a winning, friendly smile. He pulled a wad of American dollars from his pocket and peeled a few of them off, chatting in fluent Spanish, his monologue punctuated by an occasional '*Sí*' from the guy in the apron. After a minute of this, and with three of Tyson's bank notes clutched in his fist, the guy disappeared into a back room. He returned thirty seconds later with a very old, chunky laptop. He set it up on one of the tables. '*Por favor,*' he said, making a 'Take a seat' gesture with one hand. He shuffled off and started preparing coffee and glasses of water for them.

Danny, Tyson and Spike sat at the laptop. Danny opened it up and, using a very slow internet connection, brought up a web browser. He navigated to Google Maps, toggled to satellite view and zoomed in on the town of Ciudad Victoria. He reckoned they were still two hundred miles out. At their current rate, that meant approximately four hours.

'Northwest of Ciudad Victoria,' Spike said quietly. 'That's what she told us. Where the river meets the hills.' He pointed at the screen. To the north of the town there was indeed a river. It ran from west to east. To the west of the town was a substantial mountain range. Spike was tapping the screen exactly where the river met the mountains. Danny zoomed in. It took a moment for the internet connection to catch up and the pixellated screen to become clearer. Danny, who was used to examining terrain on satellite imagery, saw that the general area at the foot of the mountain range was arid desert brush, much like the terrain they'd been driving through that morning. He didn't immediately see any sign of human habitation in the region. Just parched Mexican countryside.

The apron guy brought their coffee and water. Danny scanned the map left and right, up and down. It was Spike who saw it. 'There,' he said, tapping the screen again.

Danny downed his water, then zoomed in again. Spike was right. There was a patch of terrain that looked different. It was to the south of the river, from which a small offshoot ran, leading to a much greener region, about five hundred metres by five hundred.

'That's been irrigated,' Tyson said.

Danny agreed. In the centre of the irrigated area was the outline of a perimeter wall. Rectangular, with only one entrance, on the northern side. There were two buildings within the compound: one almost exactly central, one flush up against the eastern wall. In the southeastern corner was a small blue patch that indicated a swimming pool. A road ran from the entrance on the north side, winding northeast.

'*Hacienda del Colinas?*' Danny said.

'Got to be,' said Spike.

Danny looked at Tyson, who nodded his agreement. 'It's going to be guarded to fuck, you know that? Chavez will have his best men surrounding the place.'

'He'll need them,' Danny said.

'So what do we do?' Spike demanded. There was a raw ferocity in his eyes and voice. 'How do we hit them? *When* do we hit them?'

'Easy, Snowflake,' Tyson growled.

Danny stared at the screen. It was a start, but it wasn't enough. In order to formulate an offensive strategy, he needed to get eyes on. He needed to know how many men were guarding the hacienda, what their movements were and their rotas. He needed to know how they were armed, and to have a more detailed understanding of the terrain than they could determine from a satellite

293

image. 'We need to get there first. Make an OP, put in some surveillance.'

'But we hit them tonight, right? Just the three of us?'

'We don't have any choice,' Danny said sharply. 'I think we've established that.'

Spike flushed. 'I need a slash,' he said. He stood up and walked over to a door with a stick drawing of a man on it. Once he'd disappeared into the can, Tyson looked directly at Danny. 'This is a tall fucking order, Black,' he said. 'We don't need any sulking teenagers losing their heads.'

'He's angry, that's all.'

'We're all angry. That's why we're here. But if he can't control it . . .'

'He'll be fine,' Danny said. Truth was, he saw a bit of himself in Spike. Danny knew what it was like to feel the red mist come down. If he'd learned to keep a handle on it, so could Spike. And anyway, he felt he owed it to Spud to look out for his younger cousin. Not that Tyson would understand.

The arrival of the food Tyson had ordered put an end to the conversation. The apron guy put big plates of bread, beans and spice in front of them, and one in front of Spike's empty seat. Suddenly ravenous, Danny started to wolf his food down. 'What the hell's Spike doing?' Tyson said when their meals were half gone. 'Giving birth?' At that moment, Spike reappeared. He was still red-faced, but kept silent as he sat down to his food. Danny kept his gaze on the satellite map of the hacienda as he ate. In the light of his conversation with Tyson, he found himself coming to terms with the obvious: that under normal circumstances, the Regiment would likely deploy an entire troop to ensure a successful assault on a target like this. That they weren't only undermanned, but also underpowered in terms of firearms and military equipment. That what he and Tyson made up for in experience was counterbalanced by Spike's inexperience.

That against a fighting force of highly trained former SF Zetas, their odds were lousy.

And what of Kleinman? Would he guess what they were doing? Would he find out by other means? If so, he would surely tip the Zetas off, which meant they wouldn't only be undermanned and underpowered, they'd be expected.

Had they made a tactical error, leaving Ana alive and with full knowledge of their destination?

'We need to get moving,' he said as he finished his last mouthful of food. He checked the map again, zooming out and taking a mental snapshot of their route. They left another bank note on the table. Then they headed out again into the burning heat of the Mexican noon, and hit the road.

It had taken Vic Marshall and Russell Hunter three hours to make the journey from Hereford to London. The rain, which they'd been expecting, had hit just as they crossed the M25 at 1730 hours GMT. Now it was coming down so heavily that their visibility was reduced to ten metres. They crawled along Prince of Wales Drive and came to a halt on a double yellow right in front of an entrance to Battersea Park. They placed a disabled driver permit behind the windscreen, then reached into the back seat for their foul-weather gear: heavy black waterproof coats with hoods that could be pulled far enough over their heads to obscure their faces. They checked over their firearms – Sig 9mm, standard special forces issue – and secreted them, cocked and locked, in the pockets of their raincoats. Their personal comms were already set up, the radio packs strapped to their hips.

It was almost fully dark. Cars passed in both directions, their headlamps and tail lights shimmering in the rain. There were hardly any pedestrians, which would make Marshall and Hunter's life a whole lot easier. Time check: 1842 hours. The RV was at 1900, which meant it was time for Hunter to put himself into position. He grabbed a carry bag from the back seat, exited the vehicle and disappeared into the rain.

Marshall sat in the car until 1855 hours. There was no let-up in the rain. He left the vehicle and the lower part of his body was soaked by the time he'd walked the ten metres to the park entrance.

The park itself, so far as he could tell, was deserted. Heading toward the old bandstand, which was a hundred metres away in a north-westerly direction, he counted three indistinct figures taking shelter from the elements. As he grew closer, he saw two of them were female, one of whom had a pushchair. That was good. If things went noisy, the first instinct of the women would be to protect the kid, which would keep them out of Marshall's hair. The fourth figure was clearly male. He was standing at the edge of the band-stand, looking out. Marshall could tell the guy was watching him and made the working assumption that this was their target, Aiden Bailey. He was alone, which made sense. Hardcastle had briefed them that Bailey was expecting to meet a Met officer whom he mistakenly thought was his guy. A one-on-one sort of meeting. Marshall scanned the surrounding area, looking for potential threats. He saw nobody. Not even Hunter, who he knew was standing behind the tree line of a little copse of trees fifty metres east of the stand. Nobody else was out in this weather.

Which of course made Marshall more obvious. He pulled the hood of his raincoat a little further over his brow so Bailey wouldn't see his features until he was close enough to make contact.

A crack of thunder echoed overhead as he reached the steps leading up to the bandstand. He kept his head down, his hands plunged into his raincoat, his right fist clutching his weapon. Distance to Bailey, ten metres. The two women were at the far side of the bandstand, backs to him, the pushchair between them, looking out into the rain. Marshall adjusted his trajectory so that he wasn't heading straight for the target. He made a positive ID of Bailey – he was wearing an expensive waterproof overcoat and an affected-looking trilby – and sensed his target's attention moving back out to the open ground beyond the bandstand. Marshall headed to the centre of the covered area, then approached Bailey from behind, covertly pressing the barrel of his weapon against the inside of his coat so it was pointing, through the material, directly at Aiden Bailey. The strong smell of aftershave caught the back of his nose.

The rain made a tremendous clattering sound as it hit the roof of the bandstand. It meant Marshall could speak quite clearly without running the risk that the two women would hear him.

'Can you imagine,' he said, 'the kind of mess a nine–millimetre would make of your guts, if I shoot you from this range?'

Marshall sensed his target tensing up, but Aiden Bailey didn't turn. 'And who the fuck,' he said, his voice dripping with contempt despite his precarious position, 'would *you* be?'

'I'm an old mate of Danny Black's,' said Marshall. 'Name mean anything to you?'

A beat.

'I meet a lot of people.' There was a slight crack in his voice.

'Yeah? Well you're about to meet another one. See those trees to your eleven o'clock? There's a bloke standing out of sight behind them. I'll give you two guesses what he's holding.'

'His knob?'

'Not his knob, pal. Something even bigger. Look at your chest.'

Marshall watched from behind as Bailey looked down. He knew what his target would be looking at, even though he couldn't see it himself: the tiny red dot of a laser sight dancing on his overcoat.

'Now then,' Marshall continued. 'You and me, we're going to walk toward him. If you make a run for it, *he'll* shoot you in the front, *I'll* shoot you in the back. We're very good shots. Chances are our rounds will meet somewhere behind your rib cage. Have a little party while you're bleeding out.'

'Have you got any fucking idea,' Bailey breathed, 'who you're talking to?'

'Sure,' Marshall replied, keeping his voice light. 'You're the cunt I'm going to nail in the back if you don't start walking in the next five seconds.'

Marshall could almost hear the response on his target's lips. But it didn't come. Bailey was scared. Marshall could sense it on him. From the moment he'd mentioned Danny Black's name, the vibe had changed. The situation was volatile. There was a good chance of Bailey doing something stupid.

'Make that three seconds,' he said.

Bailey stepped forward. Stumbled slightly down the steps. Marshall kept a distance of three metres behind him. He saw Bailey's head turn toward the entrance to the park. He was clearly contemplating running.

'Don't do something stupid, Bailey,' Marshall shouted over the heavy rain. 'I'd actually quite like to put one in your spine.'

Bailey kept walking. 'You've made a mistake!' he shouted. 'I've never met no Danny Black . . .'

'Keep walking, dickhead.'

It took them forty-five seconds to reach the trees. Hunter was waiting for them just a couple of metres behind the tree line, his weapon pressed into his shoulder and the sights still aiming directly at Bailey's chest. Even when he was standing just a metre away, he kept it raised.

'Get to your knees,' Marshall said.

'Go to . . .'

Bailey didn't finish his sentence. A sharp heel-jab on the back of his right knee made him collapse. Now they were in the camouflage of the trees, Marshall pulled his weapon from his pocket and pressed it against the back of Bailey's head. Bailey's shoulders started to shake, just as Marshall knew they would. There was something about being in this position that especially frightened people. He supposed it was because they'd seen the image so many times, of victims kneeling with a gun to their head, pre-execution.

Hunter lowered his weapon and let it hang from his neck. Gave Bailey a look of absolute disdain. Then he knelt down in front of him and grabbed Bailey's little finger in one hand, the remainder in another. He smiled. Then, with a sudden yank, he twisted the little finger away from the others. There was a splintering crack. Bailey tried to shout out in pain, but Hunter had quickly pressed his hand against their target's mouth, so the shout was muffled. Bailey bent over in pain, but Hunter pushed him up by the neck and held him there.

'Maths was never my strong point,' Marshall said when Bailey's muffled shouts subsided, 'but I think that means we've got nine fingers left. It's the thumbs that are the real fuckers, Bailey. Ever tried taking a piss with two broken thumbs? Messy business, my friend. Very messy business.'

'What do you want?' Bailey hissed.

'I want you to tell me everything there is to know about your dealings with Danny Black and his team.'

'I'm a good mate of Tyson's. If he knew you were . . .'

Hunter moved like lightning. He grabbed the index finger of Bailey's right hand and, as easily as if he was ripping a leg from a roast chicken, tore it to a ninety-degree angle. Bailey inhaled sharply. He tried to bend over again, but once more Hunter's hand was at his neck, holding him up.

'You were saying?'

Bailey's whole body was shaking now. Marshall couldn't be sure, since he was standing behind him, but he almost had the sense that the big bad crime lord was crying.

'Course, if we run out of fingers and thumbs,' Marshall said, 'we'll only have your dick left. And after that we'll need to start getting creative.'

A look from Hunter silenced him. A look that said: leave it, he's about to talk.

And he was.

'They'll kill me,' Bailey breathed.

Marshall smiled. Paused. Then he bent over and whispered near Bailey's ear: 'You know what I'm about to say, don't you, sunshine?'

Bailey was definitely sobbing.

'Do another finger,' Marshall said.

'*No!*' Bailey spat. 'Don't. I'll . . . I'll talk.'

'We're all fucking ears, Bailey. Except don't take all fucking night about it. If we have to give you one behind the ear, we'll need a bit of time to disappear you.'

'The Zetas,' Bailey breathed. 'The fucking Zeta cartel. They forced me into it.'

'Into what?'

It always happened this way, Marshall had noticed. They resist and resist, but as soon as they start talking, you can't shut them up. Bailey was no different.

'I done a bit of business with them, that's all. Moving some of their drugs, smack mostly, a few guns and whatnot. We had a good little thing going – the Mexicans provide the gear, I pay them on the nose, everyone's a winner. Then last week I ...'

He faltered.

'Last week you what?' Marshall said as Hunter lifted Bailey's neck a bit higher off the ground.

'Tyson,' Bailey gasped. 'I know him from way back, don't I? I know he's one of your lot. Well, no harm in having friends in high places. Tyson likes a bit of the old hospitality, so I invited him to a little gathering I was having. Private box, at the footy. Arsenal. He asked if he could bring a few mates. From work, like. So I said, of course, more the merrier. Just needed their names for the guest list, didn't I ...'

Marshall narrowed his eyes. He didn't like the way this was leading.

'Go on,' he said.

'They didn't stay long. Left all in a huff. But while they was there, I heard them talking, didn't I? About the Zetas. So I phoned my contact. Never met the bloke, don't even know what country he's in, so don't ask me. Told him what I'd heard. Told him the bleedin' SAS was sniffing around. Just what you do, isn't it? Thought they might repay the favour one of these days.'

'Let me guess, they took another view.'

'I got a visit, didn't I. A couple of hours later. Never seen the geezer before in my life, but he had pictures of my daughter, my mum and my sister. Cunts must have had their details up their sleeves for ages, in case they ever needed them. Told me I had two choices: do what I was told and carrying on trading with the Zetas, or don't do what I'm told and watch them kill my family. Well that's not a fucking choice, is it?'

'What did they want you to do, Bailey?'

'Pick Tyson or one of his mates, didn't matter which. Find out where they was vulnerable. Like, a brother, or a sister, or a parent living by themselves. Get them kidnapped, roughed up a bit, you know. Get it all on video, sent over to the Zetas so they can use it.'

'Why ask you? Why not do it themselves?'

'They don't like their hands dirty if someone else can do it for them. Who does? Any case, I know people. Got a private investigator up west, no questions asked, cash up front. Didn't take him more than a few hours to find out Danny Black had a brother, but he was no good. Had his collar felt the day before. He was in police custody, couldn't get at him. His old man lives by himself, but he's a cripple. Couple of sharp words would have seen him off, and the Zetas wanted their hostage roughed up but alive. There was a girlfriend and a kid, too, but . . .'

'But what?'

'I know a thing or two about blackmail. Danny Black didn't seem like the type to give in to it. You get a nose for it, after a while.'

Marshall was sickened. He felt like squeezing the trigger right now. One look at Hunter's face told him his mate felt the same way.

'So who did you choose?' Marshall breathed.

'Fucking chose himself, didn't he?' Bailey said, and there was a viciousness in his voice that hadn't been there until now. 'His old man lived by himself, easiest thing in the world to nab him. Had to deal with some fucking do-gooder social worker, but he was basically one of those old geezers who nobody notices till they croak.'

'Whose old man are you talking about, Bailey?' Marshall whispered. 'Which member of Danny Black's team are the Zetas blackmailing?'

Bailey's shoulders slumped. 'I can tell you where he is,' he said. 'The old man. If you kill me now, you'll never find him.'

'Oh, you'll tell me where he is alright, you piece of shit. But right now, you're going to answer my question. *Which member of Danny Black's team are the Zetas blackmailing?*'

A pause. Bailey drew a deep breath. 'I told you already. The vulnerable one. The kid. Ramsay. Simon Ramsay. But he's got that fucking stupid nickname.'

Marshall and Hunter looked at each other. For the first time, Hunter spoke.

'Spike,' he said.

'Yeah,' Bailey said. 'Yeah, that's him. Spike.'

The heat of the Mexican afternoon had grown more intense. Danny, still behind the wheel, felt like he was sitting in a pool of his own sweat. There was a mountain range on the horizon to the southeast, but the terrain on either side of the road was as arid as it had been all day. The further south they travelled, the less traffic there was, but the going was still painfully slow. He estimated they had fifty klicks to go.

Tyson was sleeping in the passenger seat. Danny knew it made sense but couldn't help being irritated. With Spud dead, Danny was coldly certain he'd be unable to sleep in Tyson's position. His mind was turning over with thoughts of the ways he wanted to avenge his friend's life, none of them pleasant.

He looked in the rear-view mirror. Spike was awake. Had been for the whole journey. He happened to return Danny's glance at the same time. And for a moment there was something in the young SAS trooper's face that shocked him. His expression was like a flick-knife in the dark. It was sharp, and it was sudden, and it was dangerous. The kid's youthful features had left him, and in that instant Danny saw the expression of a much older, much more troubled man.

Then Spike lowered his eyes and turned to look out the window again. The expression had gone. Spike was just as he had been before. Stony-faced. Detached.

Danny snapped his attention back to the road ahead. The kid was knocked sideways by the death of his cousin. Danny understood. Losing someone on ops always hit the survivors hard. And when the dead guy was a member of your family? Perhaps he was blaming Danny for letting Spud die. Danny wouldn't be surprised – somewhere deep down, he blamed himself too. A horrible guilt gnawed at him. He couldn't process the idea of Spud being gone.

'We good?' Danny asked over the noise of the engine.

'Sure,' said Spike. His voice sounded dry and cracked. Probably just the heat.

'Spud was my best friend,' Danny said. 'Lot of water under the bridge. I know what you're going through.'

Spike didn't reply. Just kept staring out the window.

The miles receded behind them. Danny regularly checked his rear-view mirror. Something troubled him. He tried to identify it. Just a nagging doubt, he decided, that Spike wasn't up to the task ahead.

A task for which Danny knew he needed all the help he could get.

TWENTY-THREE

The figure Marshall and Hunter marched across the rain-soaked grassland of Battersea Park was a shadow of the man they'd first made contact with. Anyone watching them from a distance would have seen the stumbling silhouette of a broken man, limping through the rain, hunched in pain, cradling one arm and occasionally forced onward by his two broad-shouldered guards. But the only people who might have seen them were still sheltering under the bandstand and looking in the opposite direction. Marshall had checked.

Soaked through, they bundled Bailey into their waiting vehicle. Hunter took his place with him in the back seat, a pistol in his guts to dissuade him from trying anything stupid, while Marshall took the wheel. 'The next words that come out of your mouth will be the address where Spike's old man is being held. Talk.'

Bailey gabbled an address in south London, which Marshall committed instantly to memory. He took a moment to sync his wireless earpiece with the secure comms into Hereford, and to swipe the disabled parking permit from the dashboard, before pulling out into the traffic and getting on the line to base.

'It's Marshall,' he said when the call was answered. 'Put me through to God. It's urgent.'

It took a matter of seconds to get Hardcastle on the line. 'Go ahead,' he said, his voice characteristically clipped.

Marshall gave him the highlights. Not much editing required. The CO remained quiet as he spoke. And once Marshall had given him the full clip of bad news, he remained silent for a good while longer. So long, in fact, that Marshall spoke again to check he was on the line. 'Did you copy all that, boss? Spike's compromised, the Zetas have got to him. He must have been tipping them off. If the others are still alive, they're in deep.'

'Copy that,' said Hardcastle, his voice almost infuriatingly calm. 'I've got GCHQ on the other line. We'll send a team to extract the old man.'

'We can do that, boss,' Marshall said fiercely.

'No. Your orders are to bring Bailey back to base. What state is he in?'

'A bit sore, boss, since you ask.'

'Good. Make him a bit sorer, will you?'

The line went dead.

The CO of 22 SAS was still sitting in his office. The display on his desk phone bore a message from his PA: 'GCHQ, urgent.' He quickly pressed the flashing button to switch the line. Danny Black's team out in Mexico were under his command. They were, ultimately, his responsibility. Years of experience had taught him that a coordinated military response to a situation shouldn't be rushed. But he'd also learned the value of quick, decisive thinking. He had men on the ground in more danger than they knew. If Spike was compromised, Black, Spud and Tyson had a human IED in their midst. Which meant he didn't have the luxury of time.

'Hardcastle,' he said.

'We've got something,' said a voice at the other end of the phone. Hardcastle recognised the clipped, old Etonian tones of Tim Thoroughgood, Director of GCHQ.

'Go ahead.'

'We've been running a filter on all communications within a three-hundred-mile radius of Nuevo Laredo. All the usual trigger terms. Also, we have recordings of all four members of your team which our voice recognition systems try to match in real time. There's a bit of a lag, I'm afraid – it can take a few hours for our systems to spew up a positive match. This call was made 90 minutes ago from an unencrypted sat phone in a Mexican village about 150 miles south of Nuevo Laredo.' There was a pause. 'It's not good, Dominic.'

'Just play the damn tape,' Hardcastle said.

'Okay. You're hearing your man Simon Ramsay, commonly known as Spike. The identity of the Mexican voice is unknown.'

There was a click and a hiss. Voices.

— *Where are the others?*

— *We're in a cafe. I left to go to the toilet.*

— *If you're lying, you know what'll happen . . .*

— *Is he safe?*

— *For now.*

— *I want to hear him.*

— *You don't make demands,* pendejo. *You just do what you're told.*

— *Not unless I hear him.*

There was a pause. Then — it sounded very distant to Hardcastle — a recording of an old man begging. *No . . . Don't . . . Please don't do it again . . .* It only lasted a few seconds, but it was enough to sicken Hardcastle to the core.

— *What news do you have?*

— *We're coming.*

— *What do you mean, coming?*

— *To the hacienda. Ana Rodriguez gave us the location.*

— *And where is Ana Rodriguez now?*

A beat.

— *I don't know. In hiding. She thinks you have her son.*

— *She's right. How far away are you?*

— *A couple of hundred miles.*

— *We killed one of your men back in Nuevo Laredo.*

— *I know.*

— *We should have killed the others. Z1 is not happy.*

— *He should be. I've done everything he told me. He should let my father go. We had a deal.*

— *Come to the hacienda and present yourself. But just you. Z1 is tired of your friends now. Get rid of them before you arrive.*

Silence.

– Are you still there, pendejo?

– You can't make me . . .

– He's a very old man, isn't he? Hardly a man at all, if you saw him now. I wonder how much more he can endure. Did you have any more questions, pendejo?

– No . . . I . . .

– Good. Don't mess up. Z1's not in a very forgiving mood at the moment.

The tape ended. Hardcastle said nothing.

'I told you it wasn't good, Dominic. You realise I have to send this upwards. I just wanted to give you the heads-up.'

Hardcastle barely heard him. He was staring into the middle distance, assimilating this new information. At least one of his men was dead. He didn't know who, how or why. Two more were on a hit list. He didn't know if the hits had been carried out yet. If not, they could happen at any second.

'Can you locate the sat phone that made the call?'

'It's offline. Until he uses it again, we're in the dark.'

'Do we have any idea where this hacienda is?'

'Negative.'

'Tim, sit on it.'

'What?'

'A favour to me. Let me get my ducks in a row before we take this any higher.'

'Dominic, you can't fly solo on this . . .'

'Men are going to die, Tim. Shit, one of them already has. If I can't present the FO with an actionable strategy, the suits will pass the buck till the problem goes away. These are my guys. Let me deal with it.'

There was a pause. 'How long do you need?' Thoroughgood asked.

'Just sit on it, Tim. Sit on it till I give you the green light. Can you do that for me?'

An uncomfortable silence.

'Be quick,' Thoroughgood said, and hung up.

Hardcastle replaced the handset. Considered for a moment. Picked up the phone and dialled through to Ray Hammond. 'Get the Belize team on standby to perform a hard drop in Mexican airspace,' he said.

It was secondary jungle. The canopy was very low – fifty feet max. All the primary jungle trees in this region had been cut down during Mayan times, allowing secondary growth in their place.

It was rolling jungle, without any big hills, but plenty of gullies, and particularly thick vegetation when you approached the river beds.

It was dirty jungle: full of ticks, lice and worms because of that impenetrable canopy that let little sunlight through to the forest floor. Ideal conditions for insects to thrive.

It was Regiment jungle.

Ben Brooker, Air Troop, D Squadron, was one of the few mixed-race guys in the Regiment. His father was Nepalese, his mother, whose name he'd taken, a Scouser. In the jungle, however, under beard and sweat and dirt, everyone looked the same. They were seven days into a ten-day training exercise in the jungles of Belize. A Belizean Puma had dropped Brooker and his nine D-Squadron mates, along with a local guide, two grizzled members of training wing and their troop stores, at the LZ approximately a mile to the southwest of his current location. For a week, his uniform had remained constantly wet through humidity and sweat. Only at night was he able to wash off as best he could in the nearby river, then change into his one other set of dry gear before sheltering under the A-frame shelter he'd constructed from the trunks of felled jungle trees, in time for night to fall at 1900 hours. Nowhere is darker than the jungle at night. Like his troop buddies, he would read by the light of a head torch and try to ignore the bites and welts that covered his jungle-sore body. There was no radio or TV, of course, to while away the time. No alcohol. He and the guys understood the need for jungle exercises like this – to blow away the cobwebs, keep your skills sharp. Practically every tactic the Regiment had developed derived from the jungle, so sometimes it was necessary to return there and get back to basics. But it was a drag. An uncomfortable way to spend the time. They were dirty, they stank and they were tired. Their beards were full – Brooker's was the only one flecked with grey – and their skin was itchy. To a man, they just wanted to get their heads down and get through it. Once they were through with this part of the training, it would be back to base for a couple of squadron exercises, and then freefall training for the Air Troop lads, while Mountain Troop went on climbing exercises, Boat Troop did some river navigation and offshore diving, and Mobility Troop performed vehicle contact drills and motorbike training. Then home.

It was now early afternoon, and the lads were preparing to head to the jungle range, specially constructed by the training wing guys. They'd picked out a suitable piece of real estate about a klick to the east, backed by a slight incline in the terrain so any loose rounds didn't go flying off for miles into the distance. They'd cut a jungle lane that wound down two or three hundred metres, and placed targets at random intervals. The exercises involved moving down the range in patrol formation, carrying out their drills and engaging any targets. It was useful practice for getting your eye back in and looking through the different layers of jungle, and for honing your fire and manoeuvre skills in environments where it wasn't always easy to see your team-mates. Basic skills, but ones that could soon rust up if you didn't spend regular time in jungle terrain.

It was Brooker's job to get on to the comms back to base to warn them the troop was about to embark on a range exercise with live ammo, and ensure the squadron chopper was on standby, in case any of the lads got wounded during the drill. Which was why he was now hunched over the comms gear in the patrol store tent – also constructed from felled jungle trees – making contact.

'Zero Alpha, this is Tango Two Delta, do you copy, over?'

A three-second hiss. Then: 'Tango Two Delta, this is Zero Alpha. Stand down your exercise, effective immediately. Something's come in. You're getting extracted to base, further briefings to take place at the airport. RV at the landing zone in one hour. Over.'

The base in question was the British Army Training and Support unit, near Belize International Airport. Brooker blinked. It looked like this afternoon was *not* going to be spent shooting static targets on a twisting jungle range.

'Do you copy, over?' Impatience in the voice.

'Copy that,' Brooker said. 'LZ in sixty minutes. Over and out.'

Brooker hurried out of the patrol store tent. The troop's A-frames were situated in a circle. The lads were all sitting by their shelters, rehydrating in preparation for the afternoon's exercise. 'We're being exfilled,' he announced. 'LZ in sixty minutes.'

He didn't need to give any other instruction. The camp immediately buzzed with activity as the guys squared away their personal kit into their packs – one Bergen each. It took Brooker less than two minutes to sort his gear out. When it was packed, he returned to the patrol store tent and started to move the patrol kit – storage containers of ammo, MREs and medical stores – into a small pile at the mouth of the tent. Five minutes after he'd given the instruction to break camp, all ten members of the troop, plus the two training wing guys, had their Bergens mounted on their backs and divvied out the patrol kit, ready to carry them back to the LZ. A minute after that, they were ready.

They moved silently and alertly through the jungle. The training wing guys, who knew this terrain better than anybody, took the lead and the rear. Brooker was second, his guys behind him in single file. The heat and humidity were oppressive, but they were well acclimatised by now and shrugged it off as they surged up an incline toward the landing zone.

The LZ itself was on a ridge. Even before Brooker's troop arrived, the training wing guys flew in on helicopters and abseiled down to the ridge. There, they used explosives to blast apart the trees on the top of the ridge, then cut the trunks back to make an easy approach to the LZ even for a large chopper. The guys were sweating and dirty as they reached the edge of the LZ. Brooker checked the time. 1424 hours. The chopper should be arriving in six minutes.

It was three minutes early. It had clearly been flying low over the canopy, because the lads heard it before they saw it rise slowly above the ridge line. It was the same Belizean Puma that had dropped them off a week ago. Its nose slightly dipped, it positioned itself over the blasted LZ and lowered down to the ground. Brooker and his troop were already moving their containers of gear toward the chopper by the time it touched down, their backs arched against the fierce downdraught that blew swirling clouds of loose jungle vegetation up into the air. The flight crews opened up the chopper doors and started shouting at the men to load up quickly. It wasn't necessary. The Regiment boys knew they would only be extracted like this if it was urgent. Within a minute all their gear was on board, and so were they.

The doors were shut. Brooker was holding on to the webbing that covered the inside of the Puma, looking out of one window. As the chopper rose, the thick canopy that had been his home for the past week became a sea of vivid green against the azure sky. The chopper banked and headed north, its rotors roaring in Brooker's ears, accelerating fast.

Lieutenant-Colonel Dominic Hardcastle transferred himself from his office to the ops room. It was buzzing with activity. Ten guys in uniform sat at laptops, headsets on, foreheads creased, speaking urgently in low voices to unseen contacts. On a large screen on the far wall was a blown-up map of Central America. A red dot glowed at the location of Belize airport, well known to everyone in the Regiment. A further dot glowed over the jungle to its south. On another screen was a map of Mexico.

Ops officer Ray Hammond was by Hardcastle's side. 'Air troop are en route, sir,' he said. 'Mobility troop are already on the pad prepping the vehicles for the Herc.'

'How long till they're ready for the green light?' Hardcastle said.

'The lads will be on the ground in forty-five minutes. But it'll take another ninety to finish prepping the gear for a hard drop.'

'Do we have any int updates from our sources in the Mexican military?'

'Negative, sir. So far as we can tell, the Mexicans have no idea we're in-country.'

Hardcastle nodded. 'Any word from Black or his team?'

'Negative, sir. They're completely off the grid. If you'd allow us to contact the Americans—'

'No,' Hardcastle said, a bit more sharply than he'd intended. 'We'd be doing our boys no favours. This whole op is an embarrassment to the Yanks. It wouldn't surprise me if they were trying to disappear Black and his team right now.' He turned to the map of Mexico. 'What remains of them, anyway,' he muttered.

'We don't know where they are, sir,' Hammond reminded him, the frustration evident in his voice. 'This hacienda could be in literally any part of Mexico.'

'No,' Hardcastle said sharply. 'It will be in a remote, rural part of Mexico. Easily defended. Away from the authorities' eyes. They're heading south. The mountain range to the west forms a natural barrier. But I grant you, that doesn't narrow it down enough.' He looked from the Belize map to Mexico. From Mexico to Belize. Flight time in a C-130 Hercules from Belize airport to the compromised unit's last known location, approximately one hour. But to launch an op like this without approval from above? To make a military breach of Mexican airspace without authority? He shook his head to himself. Couldn't be done.

He turned to Hammond. 'Get me the Foreign Office,' he said.

The Belizean Puma touched down at the military section of Belize airport at 1515 hours local time. Brooker and the guys spilled out quickly, their Bergens and weapons slung over their shoulders. A Regiment int officer was waiting on the tarmac, distinct from the guys because he was the only clean-shaven one: Brooker's guys all had full, grizzled beards that made some of them look older than they were. The int officer pointed them toward a hangar two hundred metres away. The lads headed immediately toward it. A hundred metres to Brooker's right he saw an RAF C-130 Hercules, its tailgate open, engineers and flight crew swarming about it. Right in front of the aircraft, he recognised the guys from D Squadron Mobility Troop. They were prepping three sand-coloured Jackal vehicles for a hard drop. Each vehicle was being fixed to a metallic platform, with cushioning slabs of three-inch-thick paper honeycomb positioned beneath the wheels and the undercarriage. Main chutes and drogue chutes were being packed to the top of the vehicles. A general-purpose machine gun was being stripped down and packed up. It looked to Brooker like they were nearly ready to move the Jackals up into the belly of the Hercules.

Inside the hangar there were no creature comforts. Just more military personnel and vehicles dotted about. The int officer led them to a quiet corner, partitioned off. 'Okay lads, listen up,' he said. 'We're preparing for a potential hard drop into Mexico. The op is an extraction of military personnel. That's all I can give you at the moment. The situation's fluid, but you need to be ready to go as soon as we get the green light.'

'Uniform or civvies?' Brooker asked. At exactly the same time, one of his troop colleagues said, 'What weapons are we carrying?'

The int officer held up one hand. 'Like I say, the situation's fluid. I'm in constant comms with Hereford, and I'm waiting for an update from the Foreign Office regarding whether we'll be approaching the Mexican government for approval, or going in dark. When *I* know more, *you'll* know more. My advice is to get some food and fluids inside you. The Jackals will be loaded up in approximately forty-five minutes. We could get the green light any time after that.'

The int officer started to walk away. 'These military personnel,' Brooker called while he was still in earshot. 'Are they Regiment?'

The officer stopped. Looked round. His face was unusually severe. 'Roger that,' he said, before leaving the partitioned area and moving out of sight.

Silence among the lads. If they'd been focused before, they were doubly so now. The discomfort of the jungle was forgotten. They had a job to do, and they wanted to do it.

TWENTY-FOUR

The Google map they'd studied in the café was a photographic slide inside Danny Black's memory. He could recall not only the position of the roads and habitations, but also the topographical features. They had crossed a major waterway running west to east about three klicks back, a little before 1700 hours. Now they were driving along the plains to the east of a long, craggy mountain range, whose slopes started approximately three miles to their right as they travelled south.

The terrain on either side of the road was subtly changing. The ground was still hard-baked and arid, but plentiful gnarled trees were sprouting up from the earth. And here, in the foothills of the mountain range, the terrain itself was becoming increasingly undulating, even hilly.

The area they were driving through had grown poorer the further south they travelled. Here and there on the very edge of the road were houses that hardly deserved the name: run-down wooden shacks that looked as if one stiff wind would destroy them. Many of them had trees growing directly in front of them, presumably so that the foliage would shield the houses from the sun. Almost all had rusty, dirty pick-up trucks parked outside. Occasionally, hopeful traders had set up stalls in the litter-strewn sidings of the road from the back of their pick-ups, though who would stop to buy their tawdry collection of garish chinaware and cheap souvenirs wasn't fully clear.

They stopped at a garishly coloured convenience store-cum-gas station at 1730 hours to fill up. Danny attracted unfriendly, suspicious stares from the shopkeeper, but he was more concerned about checking for security cameras. There were none. Not in a run-down joint like that.

Tyson and Spike were awake and alert. Spike in particular. His eyes were sharp. His head was constantly twitching left and right. Occasionally their eyes met in the rear-view mirror. Spike didn't seem to want to hold Danny's gaze, and kept looking away.

They passed what looked like an immense rubbish tip on the right-hand side of the road. There were no fences, cordons or signs to suggest it was an official dump. It just looked like people had chucked their household waste there over a period of years. Flocks of scavenging birds had congregated over it, pecking the litter for scraps.

'Ana said they used to come here on holiday,' Tyson said. 'Give me fucking Margate any day.' He pointed toward a junction a hundred metres up ahead that peeled off to the right. 'There,' he said.

Danny nodded his agreement. He indicated right, slowed down and pulled off the main road. They found themselves on what was little more than a track – dusty, rubbly terrain with no markings – which they followed for two hundred metres over a couple of hillocks until they were out of sight of the main road, in a dip. Danny pulled over. Killed the engine. Turned to the others. 'I reckon we're three klicks from the hacienda,' he said. 'If we stick to the road, there's a chance we'll encounter Zeta patrols. Agreed?'

The others nodded. 'We need to ditch the vehicle then,' Tyson said. 'Make our approach on foot.' He pointed at the terrain to the south. 'It's undulating,' he said. 'We can stay hidden.'

'Agreed,' Danny said. 'Let's find somewhere to hide the car.'

They were alone on this road, so there was nobody to see Danny take the Tahoe off-track. He negotiated the bumpy, undulating terrain expertly, keeping his gear low and utilising the engine braking to stop the vehicle sliding down any loose, stony inclines. After five minutes they found themselves in a gulley about two hundred metres from the track, deep enough to hide the vehicle from general sight, and with a tree sprouting out of it to act as a landmark if they needed to find the Tahoe again in a hurry. The guys exited the vehicle, opened up the trunk and started getting their gear together.

It wasn't much of an arsenal. Danny had been stripped of his gear when the Zetas had taken him in the compound. He had the AK-47 he'd stolen from Spud's guard, but it was out of ammo and they had no spare 7.62s, so he left it in the trunk of the vehicle. Tyson and Spike each had their M16s and Sig P266s, sights, scopes and NV helmets, so Danny took Tyson's rifle, leaving his unit mate with just a handgun. There were a couple of boxes of ammo for the M16s and Sigs – 5.56s and 9mms – but the battery packs in their comms systems were dead.

They adopted a patrol formation: a straight line, each man five metres apart, Danny at the lead, then Spike, then Tyson. They moved with the utmost care, bent low, super-alert to any movement under the hot, late afternoon sun. Whenever they reached the brow of an incline they stopped, put themselves on to all fours and crawled over, their eyes panning the terrain all around. It was slow going. Ninety minutes of dirty, uncomfortable work, the sun beating the backs of their heads like an iron bar. At 1930 hours, however, their target came into view.

The Hacienda del Colinas, if this was indeed it, was a patch of surprising greenery in the midst of the arid, baked ground. It was surrounded on three sides by a circle of hilly terrain, rather like an enormous natural crater. They were viewing it from the vantage point of a very slight incline about 300 metres north of its perimeter wall. Nestled in the foothills of the mountain range, a stream from the mountain snaked about 500 metres beyond the hacienda itself, off into the distance. It was clear to Danny that the stream was used to irrigate the terrain in some way, because the hacienda was surrounded by acres of verdant paddocks with lush grass that wouldn't have looked out of place in the damp English countryside. The paddocks were fenced off into neat squares, and there were three chestnut horses taking shelter under a tree in the middle of one of them. The green area corresponded exactly with the satellite image they'd seen on Google Maps, Danny noted with satisfaction.

The part of the perimeter wall of the hacienda that they could see from this aspect was about seventy metres wide and a good five metres in height. It was covered with shining white render. The unit was facing its northern end. Here, a road led up to a solid metal entrance gate. Fifty metres in front of this, by the side of the road, was a simple gatehouse: a single-storey block, about ten metres by ten, an off-road vehicle parked to one side of it.

Two guys stood stag outside the gatehouse. They were armed with assault rifles, slung across their chests. As Danny, Tyson and Spike lay in watch, two more armed guys appeared from either end of the perimeter wall. They passed each other by the gate, then continued their circuit of the hacienda.

This was the residence of someone expecting trouble.

Potential attacking strategies started to form in Danny's mind. Approaching the gatehouse unseen would only be possible under the cover of nightfall. In an ideal situation, they would take out both sets of guys simultaneously, but that wouldn't be possible with just three men, two rifles and no sniper gear. They would have to wait until the perimeter guards were out of sight, then deal with them afterwards. Even if they managed this, however, the walls were too high to scale without grappling hooks, and the gate looked too sturdy to ram with the Tahoe.

'We need to see if there's another entrance,' Danny said.

'Roger that,' Tyson growled.

Their elevation was not high enough for them to get a full view of the far side of the perimeter wall, nor of the buildings inside it. If they were to do a full recce, at least one of them would have to make a circuit of the hacienda.

'I'll do it,' Danny said. 'You to wait here, keep eyes on.' He looked skywards. 'But I'll wait till after dark.'

They had an hour till nightfall. They used it wisely. They had no entrenching tools to dig in. No camouflage blankets. But the guards were focused only on their immediate surroundings. They did not notice three men in the hills 300 metres to their north, lying very still, observing their every movement. Watching them through their high-powered spotting scopes – the guys had two between the three of them, which they used in rotation – Danny and the guys could practically see the sweat on their faces. They made accurate timings of the perimeter guards' circuit of the outer wall. It was an average of 17 minutes between the time they disappeared from sight around the corner of the perimeter wall and the time they reappeared again, each at the opposite corner. At 2000 hours exactly, there was a stag change. The gates opened. Five fresh guards appeared. The gates shut quickly behind them. Two of the new guys relieved the perimeter guards. The other three hurried up to the gatehouse and swapped with the existing guards – a third had emerged from the guard house – who strode back to the gates. They spoke into their personal radios and the gate opened, letting them in, but closing again within five seconds.

'So we know we've got at least ten guards to deal with,' Tyson said quietly.

'There'll be more,' Danny said. 'Chavez will have personal bodyguards too. I'll bet there's at least fifteen.'

A silence. Nobody said the obvious: that three against fifteen meant the numbers were not in their favour.

'We definitely need another entrance.'

2030 hours. The sun was sinking behind the horizon. Danny prepared to make his move. 'Keep eyes on,' he told the others. 'We need to know if their night-time routine is the same as their daytime one.'

'Just get out and do your fucking recce,' Tyson said, his eye to his scope. Spike glanced across at him. The younger man's eyes flashed in the twilight. For a moment, Danny saw the same expression he'd noticed in the car. Sharp. Dangerous. It fell away.

'For Spud,' he told his unit mate quietly.

Spike looked back toward the hacienda. 'Yeah,' he said. 'For Spud.'

Danny rolled away from the brow of the hill. Got to his feet and started jogging down the incline. His strategy was to move out of sight, then circle below the ridge line that surrounded the hacienda. He could then get eyes on from the southern side, to see if there was any possible entry point from that direction. He was currently facing north. There was an incline up to a second ridge line thirty metres ahead. He decided to clear that before starting to circle. A wider perimeter would help keep him out of sight of the hacienda.

There were no landmarks. The terrain was the same in every direction: featureless, undulating scrubland, dotted with rocks. Unhealthy-looking cacti here and there. He looked up. The stars were out, and very bright. A crescent moon was low in the sky and Danny quickly picked out the constellation of Orion – the three stars of his belt and the lesser stars of his sword. It was rising, as it always did, in the east. As long as Orion was to his left, he knew he was heading roughly south. He set off first in a southeasterly direction to clear the edge of the ridge line.

The moon cast his shadow long against the terrain, but gave him enough light to see unaided. Every thirty paces or so he stopped, went to ground and checked for movement or any other sign of personnel in the vicinity. There was none, and he proceeded quickly. After twenty minutes, he checked the position of Orion, altered his trajectory and headed southwest. Another twenty minutes' careful movement and he moved up the incline. At the brow, he found he was exactly where he needed to be: on the southeastern side of the hacienda, about 500 metres distant from the perimeter wall. A warm glow emanated from inside the perimeter.

A single glance at the perimeter wall, however, told him he was out of luck. The whitewash glowed faintly in the moonlight. From his vantage point Danny could see both its southern and eastern edges. He zoomed in with his spotting scope to confirm what his naked eye had already told him: there were no other gates or entry points visible. Even making an approach across the open ground would be difficult. The paddock areas that surrounded the hacienda were divided into neat squares, delineated by high wire fences. The paddocks clearly served a dual purpose: to be easy on the eye, and to reinforce the perimeter of this Zeta stronghold. Danny reminded himself that Chavez was special-forces trained. He and his guys knew what they were doing.

Danny cursed as a wave of exhaustion suddenly overwhelmed him. He felt Spud's absence more keenly than at any point since they'd lost him. More importantly, he felt a twinge of doubt. They'd made this reckless decision to go after Z1 in the heat of the moment, their decision-making compromised by anger, grief and thoughts of violent revenge. Here, alone under the clear moon of the Mexican sky, the brutal truth started to settle on Danny's tired mind. They'd made the wrong call. They'd left Ana in a potentially dangerous, even life-threatening situation. They'd persuaded themselves too easily that going dark from the Regiment and going after her kid was the right thing to do, whereas deep down, Danny knew they were really here to avenge Spud, and that an assault on this hacienda might, if anything, put the kid's life at risk.

He briefly closed his eyes. Get real, he told himself. They were under-manned, under-equipped. The op was a non-starter.

Danny felt anger rising in his gut. Anger at himself. Anger at Augusto Chavez. Anger at Z1's henchman with the tattooed eyes who'd killed Spud. And most of all, anger at Ethan Kleinman. The CIA man's features swam before Danny's face. The extent of his treachery suddenly seemed all the greater.

Kleinman. The cartel mole who'd been informing on them to the Zetas from the beginning. He saw the old CIA man's greying beard and watery eyes, and heard his quiet voice. He remembered the conversation he'd overheard with Rav, who had raised his concerns about Tyson. Kleinman shut that down immediately. *You're over-thinking things, Rav. The Pentagon have had direct contact with SAS headquarters in Hereford. Each member of that team has been thoroughly vetted.*

Danny opened his eyes again.

In the light of everything he now knew, that conversation didn't make sense. Rav had handed Kleinman the perfect moment to seed some disinformation. If Kleinman was a Zeta mole, he would surely have grabbed that opportunity. *Yes, Rav. You might*

have a point, Rav. You're really cut for this kind of work, Rav. We'll monitor the situation. Yes, there could be more to Tyson than meets the eye . . .
If any questions were asked up in Langley about why the operation was going to shit, Rav could quietly lead them down the garden path. *I raised my concerns about that Tyson character early on. Kleinman agreed with me. We said we'd keep an eye on him . . .*

Things weren't stacking up. And Danny realised his uncertainty had already been germinating in his head. What was it Tyson had said in the car on the way down? That they should have known about Kleinman. That they should have knocked the whole thing on the head when they'd first learned the money wasn't on the plane. Danny's response was instinctive. *He was smart. He didn't have to tell us the money wasn't on the flight. He covered his tracks by doing that.*

Danny swore. With a sudden burst of clarity, he realised he'd been making an elementary intelligence error: inventing a theory to fit what he already assumed to be true. What if Kleinman *hadn't* been covering his tracks? What if he gave them the intel about the money in good faith? What if he wasn't the mole they thought he was?

What then?

But the Zetas had still anticipated their every move. So who had been informing on them? Was it one of Kleinman's lads? Rav? Hernandez? Danny didn't think so. They were too low down the food chain. Why would the Zetas even bother with them? Or know about them?

But if the CIA boys hadn't been informing on them, that left only one option.

Danny felt his blood turning to ice.

He quickly put his scope to his eye. Panned across from the hacienda to the point at which he knew Tyson and Spike were conducting their surveillance. There was no sign of them. Were they too well hidden? Or was something else going down?

As he searched, a jigsaw puzzle was completing itself in his mind. He relived the hit on the meat-packing factory and heard Spike's voice as clearly as if he were standing next to him. *I'm on stag, I know.*

With that one sentence he'd distanced himself from the clusterfuck that was about to come.

He saw the young SAS trooper reversing the black Tahoe down the Avenida Hidalgo, having been entirely absent from the firefight that had preceded his arrival. *They had me pinned down*, he kept repeating. *I came as quick as I could.* Danny and Tyson took him at his word. But if he'd been pinned down by the Zetas, how the hell had he got out of that one? They hadn't thought to debrief him. They were too messed up after seeing Spud killed.

'You little fucker,' Danny breathed. He felt like the whole world was collapsing around him. He rolled quickly back from the ridge line, sprinted down the incline and started retracing his steps at full pelt. It was suddenly completely clear to him what had been going on.

Something else was also clear: Tyson was in danger, not from the Zeta guards whom they were planning to assault, but from the guy lying in the dirt right next to him.

The guy they all thought was on their side.

TWENTY-FIVE

The night was warm, but Spike felt cold. His limbs were heavy. His mouth was dry. He knew this was his best chance, but now the moment had come he didn't know if he could go through with it.

He and Tyson were lying on their fronts, keeping eyes on the hacienda. Tyson was using the scope, but even with his naked eye Spike could see the two guards circling the perimeter wall had just reappeared at the front. 'Regular as clockwork,' Tyson muttered. 'If Chavez knew they weren't breaking up their routines, he'd have their bollocks for breakfast. Fucking elementary.'

'Right,' Spike said.

He checked his watch. 2045 hours. Danny Black had left fifteen minutes ago. He'd be approaching the far side of the hacienda by now. Spike didn't bother trying to look for him. Black was too skilled an operator to be seen, even with a scope. But he was out of the way, which was what Spike needed. He knew he had no chance of making his move against two of them at the same time. But one on one? He could manage that.

He felt for his handgun but realised his hand was shaking. This was a shock to him and he inhaled sharply, clenching his fist to stop the tremor.

'What the fuck's the matter with you?' Tyson said, without removing his eye from the scope.

'Nothing,' Spike said quietly. 'I just . . . Nothing.'

He unclenched his fist. The tremor had stopped. His fingers curled around the handle of his Sig.

He couldn't use the weapon, of course. Even the report of a suppressed round could travel and alert Danny that something was going down.

No. Spike had to do this silently. And quickly. The handgun would be a weapon of last resort.

He was sweating badly. His skin prickled. He couldn't do it.

He closed his eyes, his face screwed up. An image rose in his mind. An old man sitting on a threadbare sofa. Tape wrapped several times around his mouth and head. More tape binding his wrists. A knife pressed up against the loose skin of his neck. His eyes darting wildly around the room, utterly terrified, completely helpless.

Nausea overwhelmed Spike. He opened his eyes again, his face fixed into a grimace. He was a trapped animal. Cornered.

He stared at Tyson again. Spike's attack on his unit mate would need to be fast, silent and unerringly brutal. But this was his speciality. Unarmed combat. He could attack a man with his bare hands as well as anyone in the Regiment. He just never thought he'd have to use it against one of them.

It would help, Spike told himself, to hate him. Aggression was ninety-nine per cent in the mind. He thought of all the moments over the past week that Tyson had patronised him or put him down. He forced them to echo round his head. *Easy, Snowflake. Leave the big jobs to the big boys, Snowflake.*

Spike knew he was working himself up, but it helped, somehow. From now on he wouldn't think of Tyson by name. He would think of him as a target. *The* target. Because that's what he was.

How to do it? The target was a good fighter. Strong upper body. He would counter-attack violently if Spike gave him the opportunity. Spike's best strategy was to use his own body weight. Force himself on to the target's back. The target's own handgun was lying thirty centimetres from his right shoulder. Spike would have to knock that out of the way, then thrust his dominant right arm under his neck. The target's arms would be free, but it would be difficult for him to reach back and make any effective

325

counterstrike while Spike applied a rear naked choke. It would have the added advantage that he wouldn't have to look at his victim's eyes as the light faded from them.

He inhaled deeply again, but quietly this time. Allowed the silence of the Mexican night to settle over them.

Counted down in his head.

Three.

Two.

One.

Go.

Danny was running on pure instinct. He had no time to check the alignment of the stars or to stop and listen for the telltale sights or sounds of enemy targets. He had time to do nothing but run, trusting to his innate sense of direction and doing his best to suppress the panic rising in his chest. The moon, rising in the north, was bright enough to force him to squint as he ran toward it. Ordinarily, he would be hyper-aware of the position of his moon shadow, but he had no leisure now for tradecraft. He needed to get to Tyson before Spike could make his next move.

His lungs burned and his muscles ached. He ignored them and pushed himself to run even faster.

Spike moved quickly, as he knew he would have to against an adversary like this. Clutching his weapon in his right hand, he pushed himself up on his fists and prepared to throw himself heavily on to the target's spine.

But the target was faster than Spike had given him credit for. Instinctively aware of the sudden movement to his side, he dropped the scope and rolled a quarter turn to his left so he had his back to Spike as he felt for the weapon lying on the ground next to him.

Spike altered his strategy in a fraction of a second. He knew if the target got his hands on the weapon, it was all over. He reached out and grabbed his upper right arm with two hands, yanking him violently on to his back. With a sudden, heavy movement, he launched himself so his upper body fell heavily on the target's chest. He felt the ribcage crack as he made contact. The target knew what was coming. He pressed his chin against his chest to prevent access to the throat area. But Spike had the downward momentum and easily forced his forearm under the target's chin, pressing with all his strength against his Adam's apple.

It was a textbook bar choke. Spike's right knee was bent, resting on the ground on the right-hand side of the target, his left leg fully extended. The target's right arm was wrapped around his torso, but Spike's left arm was clamped down over it, effectively neutralising the limb. The target's left arm was stretching for his weapon, but it was a good five centimetres out of reach. His legs were kicking hard, trying to dislodge Spike from his locked-in position. If the target had been struggling against a weaker, less experienced man, maybe it would have worked. It didn't. So long as Spike kept his man pinned down, there was really nothing the target could do.

He kept the pressure of the bar choke hard on the target's throat. A noise – harsh and strangled, but quiet – escaped the target's lips. Spike avoided his gaze, focusing instead on a patch of earth to the left of his head. *Don't look him in the eye*, he told himself. *Don't look the bastard in the eye . . .*

'*Spike . . .*'

The target's hoarse, strangled voice had managed to form a single, desperate word. It caught Spike unawares, and he instinctively looked Tyson in the face.

Bad move.

Tyson's eyes were bulging. Their expression was a mixture of fear and astonishment. He shook his head the very little he was able considering the downward pressure on his throat. *Don't do this*, he seemed to be saying. *We can work this out . . .*

Spike felt himself weakening. His body started to shake. His breathing was heavy. His eyes brimmed. He wanted to drag his gaze away from Tyson's face, but somehow he couldn't.

'I'm sorry,' he whispered.

Tyson shook his head again. Tried to speak but couldn't. Spike blinked and felt tears on his dirty, grizzled cheeks. The thought crossed his mind that he could stop this now. Let Tyson go. Explain to him what was happening.

What would his father tell him to do?

Gradually, almost involuntarily, he felt himself reducing the pressure on Tyson's throat. His shaking forearm relieved the impact on the Adam's apple. He was no longer forcing his full body weight on to Tyson's torso . . .

Gasping in huge lungfuls of air as he ran, Danny tried to estimate his position and ETA. He figured he was three minutes away if he kept this pace. Could he? Damn right he could. The thought ricocheted in his head of Spike compromising this operation from minute one. Of Spud being dead on account of his treacherous cousin.

Why? Had the Zetas been offering him money? Somehow that didn't seem likely. How would they even *know* about Spike? How would they get to him?

It suddenly hit him like a blow to the stomach. *Aiden Bailey.* Tyson's loose tongue at the football a week ago. Danny knew better than most there was a reason Regiment guys kept a low profile. That loose tongues could compromise operations.

The Zetas had a hold on Spike. And there was no way Danny was going to let that continue.

No way he was going to lose another guy in his team.

Teeth gritted, he kept the pace up.

Spike's forearm was still pressed against Tyson's throat, but with only half the pressure. 'Take it easy,' he breathed, and he noticed his voice was shaking as much as his body.

Maybe they *could* work this out. Maybe there *was* a way . . .

When Tyson's counterattack came, it was like an electric shock. His whole body arched upwards in a sudden, violent movement. He had shifted several centimetres to the right.

Almost in reach of the handgun on the ground. His fingertips were a scant two centimetres from the handle. And Spike knew, in that instant, that only one of them was going to end this struggle alive.

He doesn't have a name. He's just a target.

He thrust his forearm even harder against the target's throat. Their eyes met, and Spike felt his face morph into an expression of naked aggression. The target was trying to writhe and struggle, but Spike suppressed it with his weight. The target's eyes bulged even wider. In the light of the moon Spike could see his face was scarlet. And as he kept the pressure on, he could feel the target's struggles were growing weaker.

His eyes were rolling. His fingertips had stopped grasping for the gun. He was going limp.

Danny estimated he was two hundred metres away. He recognised the gnarled trunk of a tree growing out the ground in the pit of a small ravine. He needed to get up to the ridge line. Once he was there, he'd be fifty metres from the OP where he'd left Tyson and Spike. He had to go quietly. If he made any unnecessary noise, he'd alert Spike to his arrival, maybe force him into doing something stupid.

He headed up the hill, sweat pouring down him, lactic acid burning through his veins.

He'd only gone thirty metres when a noise made him hit the ground. It was a vehicle engine. Danny crouched, breathing deeply, as he tried to ascertain its position and direction. It was north. The engine over-revving. Distance: between fifty and a hundred metres. It had to be on the road that led to the hacienda. He couldn't risk exposing himself to someone approaching the Zeta stronghold, and he risked doing that if he hit the ridge line while the vehicle was in earshot.

He forced himself to stay still. Panic rising. Lungs burning.

Spike wasn't a fool. He knew that a lack of consciousness would precede death, and a lack of consciousness could easily be feigned.

So when the target's body was still, and the struggling had stopped, he kept the pressure on. The shaking had returned to his limbs. The tears were coursing down his dirty face. But he held fast for thirty seconds, then a minute.

Somewhere in the distance he heard a car engine. It had to be someone approaching the hacienda. He did not dare make himself known to the Zetas. Not yet. Another reason to keep very still.

Gingerly, his forearm still pressed against the target's throat, he felt with his left hand for a pulse at the carotid artery. There was none.

Only then did Spike move away.

Tyson's face was fixed into a rictus grin. It was swollen. His eyes, still open, were bloodshot in the moonlight. Spike stared at the corpse, numb. There was no turning back now, he realised. He'd gone too far. He grabbed the scope with trembling hands and looked back toward the hacienda. All was quiet. There was no sign of the perimeter guards, and the other guys were still in their guard house.

There was silence. A bleak, sinister silence, broken only by the sound of Spike rolling Tyson's body over on to its front. Tyson was a big man. It took Spike a few more seconds than he expected to roll him over. Viewed from a distance, however, he might now still look like he was conducting surveillance. Spike grabbed his handgun and rifle and scampered quickly away from the OP, from the gruesome evidence of his crime. He realised there was still water in his eyes.

But Danny Black could return any moment. Spike had to think fast, if he was going to nail him.

The distant sound of the car engine had faded. Danny realised he had seen no glow of headlamps. Had it been driving blind, or had the car beams simply been blocked by the undulating terrain? He didn't know.

But he knew he had to move. He forced himself up the incline toward the ridge line. From here, there would be a dip in the terrain leading up to the second parallel ridge line where they'd put in the OP on the hacienda. The distance between the ridge lines was a scant thirty metres. He'd be able to see what was happening from there.

Five metres from the ridge line he threw himself on to all fours and crawled the remaining distance. The moon, high in the sky behind him, illuminated the dip and the upward incline almost as brightly as daylight. His eyes zoomed in on the OP.

There was a figure. Just one. Lying on his front.

Time seemed to pass in slow motion. Danny used the sight on his M16 to zone in. He sharpened the focus, with the sight's crosshair squarely on the head of the prostrate figure.

He wasn't fooled. He recognised Tyson's clothes. And he saw that his head was face down in the earth.

His skin prickled. His instinct was to sprint to Tyson. Administer CPR. There was a chance he was still alive. But he didn't know where Spike was. He panned left and right, searching for him. It was one-on-one now. But there was no sign.

Danny swore under his breath. Evaluated his options. Spike didn't know Danny had worked out what was going on. If he approached the OP from here, he'd be crossing open ground. Spike, if he was still in the vicinity, could have a direct line of sight toward him.

Not an option.

He panned left and right, trying to establish if there was a location where Spike might be hiding. A covert firing point. Camouflage. Cover.

Nothing.

Where the hell . . .

Danny froze. He lowered his rifle. The moon was casting a long shadow from directly behind him. It extended several metres from Danny's position, down the incline from the ridge line. The shadow of a standing man, shoulders hunched, one elbow slightly protruding, as though carrying a rifle in the firing position.

He knew it was Spike.

Nobody moved.

'Put the weapon down, mucker,' Danny breathed. 'We can sort this. We can make it okay.' He had to try very hard to keep his voice level.

Silence.

A strange calm settled over Danny. Spike hadn't fired. It meant there was a chance of talking him down.

'I'm going to turn round now, buddy,' he said. 'No games. I just want to talk to—'

'If you move,' Spike interrupted, 'I shoot.' His voice was cracked. Broken. The voice of a desperate man. And as Danny well knew, desperate men were the most dangerous. He tried to estimate how far behind him Spike was. Ten metres, no more.

'We can get to Tyson,' Danny breathed. 'Give him CPR. He might be . . .'

'He's dead,' Spike said flatly. 'Trust me. You might as well give CPR to Spud. Now throw your weapon.'

Danny felt sick, but he had no option. He placed it to his right.

Danny breathed deeply. 'You don't want to shoot me, Spike. We're going to find a way to—'

'That's what *he* tried to tell me,' Spike snapped. 'But then he tried to fight back.'

'Who do they have, Spike?' Danny said quietly. 'Who are the Zetas threatening?'

'It's more than a damn threat! He's fucked up. I don't even know if he's alive.'

'Who is it?' For some reason, Danny thought of his brother Kyle. 'Your brother? Sister?'

'I don't have a fucking brother or sister.'

'Mother? Father?'

Silence.

'Is it your old man, Spike? Is that who they have?'

No reply. Danny knew he'd hit the mark.

'I get it, Spike. I understand.'

'You don't understand *anything*,' Spike hissed. 'You haven't seen what they've *done* to him.'

'It happened to me, mucker. Bad guys got to my daughter. Spud helped me find them. You want to know how many rounds they took to the head? Regiment swept it all under the carpet. I swear to God, Spike, you lower that weapon, I'll help you hunt down the bastards who have your dad.'

Was Danny telling the truth? Would he restrain himself from nailing Spike if he got the chance? *Could* he restrain himself? He didn't even know. All he knew was he was hyper-aware of his rifle lying on the ground no more than forty centimetres from his right shoulder.

'We'll start with the ones in that hacienda, mucker. You and me.'

'Don't be so *fucking* stupid. They've been a step ahead of you ever since we got in-country.'

Danny saw Spike's shadow twitch, as if he was repositioning himself.

As if he was getting ready to fire.

Danny felt his heart rate increase. He breathed deeply again, trying to lower it. To stay calm. To think straight.

'Spud was proud of you, mucker. If he was here now, he'd tell you that. He wouldn't blame you for trying to help your dad.'

'I didn't tell them where Ana was,' Spike said. 'I kept that from them. She'll be safe . . .'

'You did well, buddy. You probably saved her life. Now all you need to do is lower the weapon and we can put an end to this.'

'They'll kill him,' Spike breathed. 'If I don't do what they tell me, they'll fucking kill him.'

'They'll kill him anyway, Spike. You know that, right? No matter what happens, if we don't get to him first, they'll kill him.'

Silence. Danny could hear Spike's breath trembling.

'I'm going to turn over,' Danny said. 'I'm going to do it very slowly. No games.'

Spike made no objection.

He raised his hands to show no weapon, but gradually rolled toward his M16. He felt it brush his left shoulder. He looked toward Spike.

His unit mate was standing tall, but seemed strangely broken. It was the shoulders. They were hunched, as though he was trying to disappear in on himself. His own rifle was raised and pointing directly at Danny, but there was no way Spike could hide the trembling of his hands.

'Put it down, mucker,' Danny said. 'Lower the weapon, then we can talk.'

Spike started to do it. Danny could see his face. Even in the shadow, he could tell it was a mess. Grimy. Tear-streaked. But the eyes were the worst. Raw and haunted.

'I didn't have a choice,' Spike whispered. His weapon was pointing thirty degrees from the horizontal.

'I know,' Danny said carefully.

'They were . . . they were going to kill him.'

'I get it.' Danny forced himself not to look sideways at his M16, but he felt it pressing against his flesh. Barrel facing north, toward Spike. Locked. It would take Danny approximately two seconds, he estimated, to grab the weapon, unlock it and fire. Spike could take a shot in a quarter of that time, and would if Danny gave him cause to. He examined Spike's body language carefully, looking for the minute, telltale signs that he could be about to fire. The position of the trigger finger. The tightening of the skin around his dominant eye. The tensing of his right shoulder as he prepared for the report of the rifle. There was no indication that a round was imminent, but Spike was still holding the weapon at a thirty-degree angle. Danny was still in his line of fire. 'Put it down, mucker,' he said. 'We can only talk when you've put it down.'

It happened in a split second. Danny saw the change of expression in Spike's eyes before any of the other warning signals. The sudden, flick-knife stare he'd seen earlier in the rear-view mirror of the car. He knew, with the raw instinct of a man accustomed to combat situations, that his unit mate was about to fire.

He was right. Spike raised his weapon. Tightened his eyes. Jutted the butt of the rifle hard into his shoulder. Danny moved at exactly the same time. He knew he only had one chance. He grabbed his rifle with his right hand and, in one movement, rolled a full turn to his left while disengaging the safety. By the time he was on his back again, he was raising the rifle one-handed to point directly at Spike's chest: the broadest part of his body and the easiest, safest target.

But too late. Spike's weapon was fully engaged and his aim had followed Danny's position precisely.

There was the dull, muffled thump of a single suppressed round.

TWENTY-SIX

Time stood still.

Danny had already braced himself for the impact of Spike's round. He felt like his whole body had juddered with the dull report of the weapon, a shock so thorough he couldn't tell if or where he'd been hit. Torso? Lower body? Shoulder?

But as Danny's mind was making these precise, fast enquiries, he saw Spike fall.

Danny's thoughts changed gear. He hadn't been hit. It was Spike who'd taken a round. There was an explosion of blood from the right-hand side of his neck and he was falling to his left. There was no dignity to it. No chance for the kid to fade away in slow motion. He hit the earth with a solid, heavy thump, and an accompanying crack of a bone breaking from the impact.

Danny acted on instinct. Autopilot. He kept his weapon pointing out and up, his breathing heavy, sweat pouring. The round had come from the northwest. He panned his weapon so it was pointing in that direction. He squinted through the sight. There was a squat tree with a thick trunk about seventy-five metres down the incline to his ten o'clock, its moon-shadow stretching out toward him. Branches, many of them, spread at different angles. That was the only covert firing point he could see. Was it a Zeta guard hiding there? The image of the guy with the tattooed eyes entered his mind, and he felt another surge of anger. He lowered his weapon, momentarily pushing himself up into the firing position, one knee on the ground. He had to resist the urge to fire blindly toward the tree.

Then he saw it.

336

The red dot of a laser sight danced first on his face, before settling just to the left of his chest, between his heart and his shoulder. It sat there, unmoving. Desperate for cover, Danny wanted to roll out the way, but he knew the laser sight would simply follow him. He was out in the open and targeted.

So why hadn't he been shot?

A male voice rang out across the night from the northwest. It spoke English, but with an American accent. 'Throw the weapon!'

Danny narrowed his eyes. He recognised the voice.

'*Do it now!*'

Danny lowered his rifle. Engaged the safety. Threw it on to the ground a couple of metres in front of him. It slid a further half metre down the incline.

'*Raise your hands!*'

Danny did as he was told. The laser dot moved to a more central position on his chest. 'Show yourself!' he shouted. Even as he said it, however, he saw a figure emerging from the darkness next to the tree. His moon-shadow stretched several metres in front of him, and he was carrying the weapon that was still aimed directly at Danny's chest.

He walked with a limp.

Slowly, the figure approached. When he was thirty metres away, Danny saw he was wearing an NV headset. He dismissed any thoughts of diving for his rifle. The man continued to approach. Twenty metres. Ten. Five. He stood, immobile, directly in front of Danny. Then he lowered his weapon. Danny saw his greying beard and, as the man raised his NV goggles, his small, watery eyes.

'You're a tough guy to track down, boy,' said Ethan Kleinman. 'If you hadn't trashed the tracker on your vehicle, I'd have found you quicker.'

Danny's eyes flickered between Spike's dead body and the CIA man standing in front of him. Kleinman was the last guy in the world he expected to see here. 'So how the hell did you . . .' But as the question formed on his lips, the answer popped into his head. 'Ana,' he said.

'She took some convincing to give up your destination, boy,' Kleinman said. 'Never seen a person so scared as she was. Hope I never do again. She seemed to think I was working with her brother. Seemed to think I was there to kill her.' He limped over to where Danny's weapon was lying on the ground, bent down to pick it up and handed it over to Danny. 'Lucky for me you didn't hide her so well, boy. When she realised I wasn't the guy she needed to worry about, she gave up your destination pretty quick. Told me you were launching an assault on the Chavez hacienda to get her son back.' He sniffed. 'How's that going, by the way?'

'Do you have backup?' Danny demanded.

Kleinman smiled. 'Backup? I'm afraid I'm here on my own time, boy. The Company cut the cord on our little operation. They think you're dirty.' He glanced at Spike. 'Turns out they were right.'

'Only him,' Danny said. 'The Zetas got to his father. They were blackmailing him.'

If Kleinman was surprised, he didn't show it. 'Family, huh?' he said bitterly. 'That's a bitch.'

'He's been compromising the operation from the beginning.'

Kleinman nodded slowly. 'I figured somebody was. When I saw him holding you at gunpoint . . . guess I arrived just in time.' His eyes narrowed. 'Augusto Chavez has a lot of cheques to settle.' He limped over to Spike and started patting down his clothes. He straightened up, holding something: an old mobile phone, its battery removed so it couldn't be traced. 'And I guess this is what he was using to communicate with Z1's people . . . *Really*, boy?'

Danny had raised his weapon and was pointing it at Kleinman.

'I've got three guys dead, Kleinman. I don't intend to be number four. If the CIA have closed down the op, what the hell are *you* doing here?'

Kleinman fixed him with a stare. 'I'm here to help you kill Z1,' he said simply. 'The CIA have called me back to Langley, but I'm damned if I'm going to throw away an opportunity like this. Even if I told them I know Chavez's location, they'd pull me in. Spike's actions makes the whole thing too hot for them. Give it a few hours, they'll have every agent south of the border looking for me. One thing they hate, it's one of their guys going rogue. So stick a bullet in me if you like, but seems to me you could use all the help you can get.'

The two men stood there. Danny found himself inclined to believe the CIA man, but he said nothing for the moment. Sometimes, he knew, silence was the best tool for forcing somebody to speak. Kleinman smiled ruefully, as if he knew this was Danny's strategy. 'Don't blame you for being cynical, boy,' he said. 'If I was in your shoes . . .' He glanced in the direction of the hacienda, though it was out of sight. 'Augusto Chavez and I have a little history,' he said. His voice cracked slightly. 'I had a son. Mikey. Took a road trip through this part of the world, seven years back.' Kleinman took a deep breath and Danny realised he was suppressing a wave of intense emotion. 'I warned him not to go off the beaten path, but what can I say? He was his own guy. He ran into Chavez and his Zeta entourage. Early days for them. They were making a name for themselves. They . . .' Another deep breath. 'Have you heard of *El puerco espín*? The porcupine? They call it a symbol of the cartels' violence. A dead body, with twenty knives sticking out of it. *El puerco espín* is my boy. So go ahead, son. Put a bullet in my chest. Be a relief anyway. But if you're not going to, put your gun down and let me go. I'm going to kill Augusto Chavez with or without your help. Or I'll die trying, so help me God.'

Five seconds passed.

Danny lowered his weapon.

'Was it your vehicle I heard arriving fifteen minutes ago?'

Kleinman nodded.

'Where is it?'

Kleinman pointed in the direction of the tree he'd used as a firing point. 'Two hundred metres.'

'What equipment do you have?'

'Only what I could take from the motel. This rifle. A handgun. Sights and ammo.'

'Grenades?'

He shook his head.

'Sat phone?'

'Yes.'

'Encrypted?'

'Yes.'

'Can the CIA access it?'

'No.'

'You said you had a GPS unit?'

Kleinman nodded.

Danny gave himself a moment to think. The assault on the hacienda had always been a long shot. Now, with two men down, it was a non-starter, no matter how bloodthirsty Kleinman was feeling.

So he had a big call to make. Twenty-four hours ago, Danny and his team had gone dark from the Regiment. Under ordinary circumstances, they'd be neck-deep in the shit for a move like that. But these circumstances were far from ordinary. Three SAS men had been killed. In the briefing rooms, squadron hangars and rifle ranges of Hereford, that meant something. Spud, Tyson and Spike were dead on account of one man. Augusto Chavez. Z1. Whatever the hell he wanted to call himself, that man was now top of Danny Black's hit list. And if the anger and hatred that flowed through Danny's veins was bad news for the Zeta leader, it would be nothing, he calculated, to the collected fury of 22 SAS, when they learned that their guys had been manipulated, blackmailed and murdered.

Would the SAS's top brass sanction Danny for going dark? Or would they pull the strings required to punish the cartel for their offensive against Regiment personnel, the way only the SAS knew how?

Danny didn't know.

'So what do we do, boy? What's the goddamn plan?' A pause. 'I don't have your military expertise in the field, Black. You're calling the shots now. But you'd better call them quickly, because if Chavez finds out his boy Spike is dead, he'll know something's coming.'

The dynamic had changed between Danny and Kleinman. Back in the US, the CIA man had been giving the orders. Now he was waiting on Danny's decision.

Danny looked in the direction of the hacienda, then back at Kleinman. 'We're going to contact the Regiment,' he said.

WEDNESDAY

TWENTY-SEVEN

'It's Black. He's made contact.'

It was unheard of for ops officer Ray Hammond to burst into the CO's office without knocking first, but that's what he'd just done, kicking the door closed behind him. It was 0330 hours GMT. Both men looked exhausted. Neither was contemplating sleep. Hammond was brandishing a mobile phone. He placed the handset on Hardcastle's desk. The hissing sound from the speaker told the CO it was on hands-off.

'Can you hear me?' he demanded.

'*Roger that.*' Black's voice was very distant, the line scratchy.

'Spike's compromised,' Hardcastle said.

'*Spike's dead. And Spud. And Tyson.*'

Hardcastle felt the familiar sickness that always came with news of the loss of military personnel. You never got used to it. 'Explain,' he instructed.

Danny Black did just that. A curt, no-nonsense debrief, his unemotional voice betraying none of the riot of unpleasant emotions Hardcastle knew he was experiencing. He and Hammond listened with increasing shock. When he'd finished, there was a moment of deathly silence in the room.

'*Do you copy, sir?*' Black's voice came over the speaker.

'We copy,' Hardcastle said. 'We have Air Troop D Squadron on standby in Belize. They'll have wheels up in the next five minutes. Prepare for a hard drop in approximately one hour from now. You have approximately seven hours until dawn. You know what to do.'

'*Roger that, sir.*' A pause. '*We have the go-ahead to launch a full assault on the Zeta hacienda?*'

'Damn right you have the go-ahead,' Hardcastle said. 'We heard Spike's conversation with his contact. They're expecting him to have nailed you and Tyson before approaching, so you have the element of surprise. Teach those criminals what happens when they interfere with our lads. And Black?'

'*Yes sir.*'

'This kid is not priority. You have unit command. Make sure all my men come back in one piece.'

A pause.

'*Understood, sir.*'

Hardcastle looked up at the ops officer. 'Green light,' he said.

The worst thing about waiting for an op, Ben Brooker knew from several years' experience, was just that: waiting. They'd been in the hangar for a little over six hours now. Fair play to the int officer, though. He'd been keeping them in the loop just like he said he would. Every twenty minutes there was a fresh update: 'The Herc's loaded and ready to fly.' 'We've had the green light from the Foreign Office to breach Mexican airspace.' 'When, if, the call comes, we'll be going in covertly. Full battle gear but no identifying documents or markers, you know the drill.'

And now: 'We've had contact from our guy on the ground: it's a go for a hard drop. Operational requirement has changed: you're to RV with our point man and prepare for an immediate assault and hostage extraction. *Move!*'

The team was fully prepped. Digital camouflage gear, plate hangars, Kevlar helmets, boom mikes and full comms systems operational. Packs and personal weapons had already been loaded on to the Hercules. Brooker and his guys were running out on to the airfield within seconds of the go. 'Who is it?' Brooker asked the int officer as he jogged past him. 'The guy on the ground.'

'Danny Black,' the int officer said.

Brooker nodded. Black was well known in the Regiment. His reputation truly preceded him, which had the advantage that Brooker would be able to make a visual ID of him when they were on the ground.

The tailgate of the C-130 was still down and the turboprops were powering up, the whine of the engines increasing in intensity as they neared the aircraft. As Brooker sprinted up the tailgate and into the cargo compartment, he saw the three sand-coloured Jackal vehicles were loaded and fastened along the centre of the Herc. The Mobility Troop guys had finished strapping them to their cushioning platforms. The main chutes and drogue chutes were fitted. The vehicle at the front had a container lashed to it that Brooker knew held general-purpose machine guns. All three vehicles were resting on roller rails that would allow them to slide smoothly out of the aircraft when the fastenings were detached. Further up the centre of the aircraft, a heavy flight case of gear was sitting, chuted up and ready for the drop. A loadie wearing heavy cans and a boom mike was ushering them urgently up to the bench along the starboard side of the aircraft. The guys' chutes, packs and personal weapons were already loaded and waiting for them there. They took their seats against the padded side of the aircraft, five on either side of the vehicles, next to the sheets of orange webbing that covered the sides and beneath the static line wires that ran overhead. They strapped themselves in and each fitted a set of headphones hooked to the side of the Herc. The cushioned cans deadened some of the noise of the aircraft as the tailgate closed, entombing them within the Herc's belly. It was hot, noisy, cramped and smelly. The Jackal vehicles took up most of the space inside the aircraft. Once the team was sitting, there was very little space to move.

There was a crackle over the cans. The patrician tones characteristic of every SF flight crew captain Brooker had ever met came over the comms. 'Okay, gentlemen, wheels up in two minutes. Flight time to the drop zone approximately one hour. We'll be doing a heavy drop at 2300 hours local time from approximately 600 feet. We'll be coming in blind, so expect a full blackout fifteen minutes before insertion. The flight crew have prepared static lines for the drop. I'll be back on with you when we're twenty minutes out with any updates from London. For now I'm patching you through to Hereford.'

There was another crackle, then a second voice came over the line.

'Air Troop, this is Hereford. We have three SAS personnel KIA and a child hostage situation. We have two men on the ground lighting up the LZ and coordinating the assault. One is Regiment, one is CIA, but this is *not* a US-sanctioned operation, repeat, this is *not* a US-sanctioned operation . . .'

The guys gave each other sidelong glances, but nobody said anything. Brooker closed his eyes. Took a moment to put his head in the right place. He felt the aircraft judder into movement. A minute later the G-force kicked in. The Herc was screaming down the runway and taking to the air.

Kleinman's vehicle was by the roadside, two hundred metres from the position where he and Danny had made contact. Danny made the journey twice: once with Spike's body over his shoulder, once with Tyson's. Kleinman made it very clear he didn't approve of the delay, but there were sound operational reasons for doing it. There was a chance of Zeta patrols in the area. If they found the corpses, they would be on heightened alert.

It was a grim, difficult job forcing the two bodies, already stiff-ening with rigor mortis, into the back seat of Kleinman's beige, rust-spotted Lexus, which in his hurry he had left artlessly by the side of the road that wound up to the hacienda. By the time Danny had finished, he was sweating heavily and smeared with blood from the bullet wound in Spike's neck. He took the wheel. He would have preferred to take the vehicle off-road, but he didn't feel it was up to the job and time was short. Instead, he killed the headlamps, took charge of Kleinman's NV goggles and drove the three klicks blind, to the point where they'd taken the Tahoe off-road. Here, he risked leaving the road. The saloon bumped and juddered over the rough terrain, but Danny was a skilled enough driver to keep it on track. Two minutes later they came to the Tahoe in its hiding place. They left the bodies in the car, switched vehicles and transferred all their gear, including the GPS unit Kleinman had been keeping in the glove compartment of his vehicle. Within a minute, the Tahoe was speeding back up to the road.

Time check: 2200 hours. 'We only have 53 minutes,' Kleinman said tersely as they sped up to the main highway, their headlamps burning now they were further from the hacienda.

'Thanks for the update,' Danny growled.

'How will they know where to make the drop?' Kleinman said.

'They'll know,' Danny told him. He wasn't in the mood to talk. He had to concentrate on action. On getting everything prepared. But a voice in his head reminded him Kleinman had just saved his life, and Danny was relying on his cooperation. 'We passed a refuse tip on the way here,' he said. 'We need to stop off there first.'

Kleinman gave him a perplexed look, but didn't question him any further.

It took them five minutes to reach the tip. It was on the left-hand side as they headed north along the highway. During the day it was covered with scavenging birds. As Danny ran toward it, leaving Kleinman in the Tahoe, he saw the birds had left for the night. Rummaging through the refuse at the edge of the tip, however, he heard other movements nearby. There were clearly nocturnal animals foraging here, attracted by the appalling stench of rotten food. From the corner of his eye he thought he saw the outline of a coyote. Whatever it was, it kept its distance from Danny, who scavenged like the best of them. By the light of the moon he saw all manner of rubbish had been discarded here. Plastic bags of food waste. Old electrical items. Loose fast-food wrappers. Old white kitchen goods. The works. It didn't take more than a minute for him to find four empty cans that once held different types of beans, and two empty paint tins. Elsewhere, he located a dirty old piece of material. Maybe it had once been a sheet, or a tablecloth. Now it was stained and dirty, but dry, which was essential. Danny bundled the tins up into the material and starting running with his package back to the Tahoe, but something else caught his eye at the last moment: an old washing machine, the front panel missing so the rusty drum was exposed, but with the rubber water inlet pipe still fitted to the back. The pipe was about three feet long. Danny yanked it from the back of the machine and ran with his stash to the Tahoe. 'Give me the sat phone,' he told Kleinman once he'd dumped the gear in the back seat. 'And the GPS.'

Kleinman handed it over and Danny dialled in to Hereford. 'Go ahead,' a voice said at the other end.

'Requesting coordinates for the Central American package,' Danny said.

'Roger that, we've identified a potential drop zone. Stand by to receive coordinates.' There was a five-second pause on the line before the voice returned with two eight-digit strings of lat and long coordinates. Danny punched them into the GPS unit. The screen lit up a location approximately fifteen klicks directly south of the hacienda. Time check: 2218 hours. 'Coordinates received, out,' Danny said, before killing the line and knocking the Tahoe into gear. He pulled a U-turn across the highway and accelerated south.

The Herc was at its cruising altitude. Brooker and the guys had fitted their chutes and checked over their packs and weapons. Now they were plugged into the cans again, each man holding the carabiner at the end of the bright yellow static lines leading from their chutes, the drone of the aircraft's engines a constant backdrop in their minds.

Suddenly Brooker felt the Herc lose altitude. Almost simultaneously, the captain's voice came over the cans. 'That's twenty minutes out,' he said. 'Repeat, twenty minutes out.'

Brooker looked toward the centre of the Herc. The loadie and a couple of other members of the flight crew were busying themselves around the Jackals. There was movement on either side of the vehicles as the two lines of men started to ready themselves for the jump. Brooker did the same.

The highway was practically deserted as Danny and Kleinman stormed south: five miles, ten miles, fifteen. Far from the Zetas' hacienda, so they would have no idea the drop was happening.

Their grim faces were illuminated by the light of the dashboard. The occasional lorry passed in the opposite direction, but nothing more. Kleinman was holding the GPS unit. Danny noticed he was gripping it very hard.

'When the guys arrive,' Danny said, 'you take a back seat. Got it?'

Kleinman stared straight ahead. 'You're the boss,' he said quietly. 'But when the moment comes, Z1 is mine. Promise me that.'

Danny didn't reply. Truth was, he couldn't make such a promise. The team had to work as a unit, not a collection of individuals.

'Here,' Kleinman said. He pointed to a turning fifty metres ahead on the right, and tapped the GPS screen to indicate they were approaching the coordinates Danny had keyed in. Danny indicated and turned on to the side road. At Kleinman's instruction he followed the road for five klicks to the west. The area was completely deserted. No houses, no vehicles, no nothing. 'We're there,' Kleinman said finally. 'This is it.'

Danny pulled over, killed the engine and the lights. He jumped out the vehicle and, using his spotting scope, scanned the area to the south. This was the terrain that Hereford had identified for the drop, presumably from satellite imagery. Satellite imagery could be deceptive, however. There were frequently topological features that didn't show up, and no sat photograph could tell you about the presence of hostiles or unexpected environmental conditions. As he examined the terrain, however, Danny saw Hereford had got it spot-on. It was a perfectly flat area, about the size of two football pitches. Hard-baked arid terrain, no pits or bumps and no indication of habitation or the presence of any locals to hear or witness the drop.

Danny lowered the scope, then grabbed the cans and material from the vehicle. He ripped the material into six lengths, then stuffed one length into each of the tins. Now all he needed was fuel. He opened up the fuel tank of the Tahoe and inserted the washing-machine inlet pipe. Kneeling at the wheel arch, he sucked the other end until the foul taste of the petrol hit his mouth. He stoppered the end of the pipe with his thumb, then reached for one of the cans before siphoning a quantity of fuel over the torn material stuffed inside. A minute later he had drained the tank and the material inside each can was saturated. He turned to Kleinman. 'We need to light up the drop zone,' he said.

'Using these?' Kleinman sounded dubious.

'The flight crew will be wearing NV. They'll see our torches from a distance. We'll light them up between two and five minutes before the drop.'

On Danny's instruction, they took three cans each. They marked out the corners of a rectangle, 200 metres by 100, Danny running to the far southern corners and leaving a can at each, while Kleinman limped to the two northern corners nearer the Tahoe. They reconvened at the centre of the square, where they placed the final two cans, ten metres apart in a north–south alignment, before returning to the vehicle. Danny grabbed Kleinman's sat phone and dialled into Hereford for a third time. '*Go ahead.*'

'Drop zone is marked out for the package,' Danny said. 'Waiting your instruction to light it up.'

'*Keep the line open and wait out.*' There was a twenty-second pause, then the voice came again. '*We're patching you through to the flight crew now.*'

There was a crackle on the line, then a new voice. '*This is flight Delta Three Bravo, do you copy, over?*'

'Roger that, over.'

'*We are five minutes from the target, repeat, five minutes from the target. Light her up at will.*'

It was all Danny needed to hear. He turned to Kleinman and pointed to the west. 'Get as far that way as you can,' he told him. 'At least two hundred metres from the drop zone. We've got some big wagons coming down.'

Kleinman nodded and started limping away from the Tahoe.

'Kleinman,' Danny called. The CIA man turned. 'Your lighter,' he said.

Kleinman dug into his pocket and removed the Zippo he perpetually tinkered with. 'Don't lose it,' he said. He threw it to

Danny, who caught it with one hand and immediately sprinted toward the nearest, northeastern, corner of the drop zone. He put the lighter to the petrol-soaked rag in the can. A fierce flame erupted, but Danny had already turned to sprint to the next corner. He had less than five minutes to light up the drop zone and get the hell out the way. The Regiment was coming in heavy.

Brooker and the guys were on their feet. Each man had clipped the carabiner of their yellow static lines to the overhead steel wire. They stood in a line, the loadie at its head. Their packs and rifles were positioned in front of their legs, hooked to the straps of their parachutes and fitted to a fifteen-foot lanyard. Their helmets and NV were fitted. The cargo bay was in complete darkness, except for the red light that would turn to green the moment it was time to jump. The aircraft was still losing height, and the whine of the engines drowned out any other sound. The men, the Jackal vehicles, the whole plane was vibrating heavily.

The aircraft banked. Brooker's internal compass told him they were changing from a northwesterly to a northern trajectory. The drop would come any moment now. Brooker felt the tension ramping up. Hard drops were dangerous. When the moment came, the vehicles would shoot out at immense speed. If any of the guys got caught up with them, there'd be loss of life. No question – Brooker had seen it happen on a previous training operation in Belize. Young kid, fresh from selection. The boy was a mess when they scraped him off the ground.

The tailgate started to lower. Brooker saw a crack of night sky appear, the opening increasing in size until the ramp was fully lowered. The persistent whine of the engines was joined by the rushing sound of air displacement. The temperature dropped slightly and the air, previously thick with the usual greasy stench of all military transports, cleared a little. The night sky was inky, but dotted with stars. At the bottom of the opening, he caught a momentary glimpse of the ground. He estimated their height as 600 feet. They would lose no more than 100 feet before jumping.

Both side doors opened. The two lines shuffled forward, quickly but awkwardly because of their packs hanging in front of their legs, clipped to their chute harnesses.

The loadie raised one arm. Three fingers. Two. One. Lowered his arm.

The three pallets containing the Jackals slid fast along the roller belt, smoothly and silently and with astonishing speed. They were followed by the crate containing the gear. A small drogue chute trailed behind each one, but it only took a couple of seconds for the whole cargo load to slip out. Immediately the red light turned green. Brooker felt the loadie slapping him on the back to encourage him out, but he was already shuffling fast toward the side door, the carabiner of his static line sliding along the steel rail as he moved. He raised his arms, stiffened his body to ensure he'd fall steady and threw himself from the aircraft.

Estimated height: 500 feet. He felt a rush of air hit his body as he hurtled toward the earth. With a low-altitude jump like this, it was essential that the chutes deployed immediately. Brooker's did. The static line had done its work. There was a sudden jarring sensation as the chute filled with air and his velocity reduced. The rest of the guys had jumped quickly. He could see all nine chutes deploying and floating to the ground, and he could both see and hear the Herc as it banked sharply to the east and immediately started gaining height. It was out of sight and earshot, however, within ten seconds.

On the ground, he could see four flames marking out the drop zone – two in the centre, two at the northern corners. Danny Black, it seemed, had marked it out skilfully. Brooker was falling accurately in the southern half of the drop zone. He could see a couple of the guys adjusting their direction of fall to ensure they hit it.

In a matter of seconds, his altitude decreased to sixty feet. He unclipped the lanyard that attached his pack to his body. It swung beneath him, hanging like a pendulum as he fell to the ground.

Five seconds later, the pack hit the earth. And five seconds after that, Brooker did the same.

★   ★   ★

Danny was lying on the ground, Kleinman prostrate next to him, watching the hard drop occur through the CIA man's NV goggles. The deafening roar of the Herc vibrating through him. He saw the three vehicles and one hardware case spill out under canopy from the black shadow of the aircraft flying with no lights. The hard drop was immediately followed by the ten guys in quick succession, their chutes deploying immediately as they fell to earth. The drop had taken a matter of seconds, and now the Herc had banked and was gaining height, disappearing back into the Mexican sky toward the coast.

The petrol torches were flickering into nothingness and the Regiment guys were immediately putting themselves down on one knee in the firing position as their billowing chutes settled behind them. Danny directed his laser sight toward the first of the guys to have jumped. He signalled three short bursts with the IR beam and watched it slice through the night in his NV. Seconds later, he received an identical response to his signal: three short beams cutting through the blackness toward him.

'Keep your position,' Danny told Kleinman as he jumped to his feet. He didn't wait for a reply before sprinting out on to the drop zone, directly toward the guy with whom he'd exchanged the signal. He raised his NV goggles as he ran, allowing his natural eyesight to grow accustomed to the darkness. His point guy was still in the firing position, weapon engaged. It was impossible to make out his features. He was wearing full battle gear: digital camo, Kevlar helmet, NV goggles, boom mike. Only when Danny was standing five metres from him did he appear to make a positive ID. He lowered his weapons and raised his goggles. 'Black,' he said.

'Brooker, right?' Danny knew him by reputation. Half Nepalese, half Brit. He was well respected at Hereford.

Brooker nodded.

Danny looked around. The drop zone was dotted with nine other men collecting up their chutes. To the south, he could clearly see by the light of the moon that the three vehicles had made a safe landing. Their silhouettes were black and rugged in the moonlight.

'You've been fully briefed?' Danny asked.

'They said you'd lost three guys. Sorry to hear it, buddy.'

'There's a cartel hacienda twenty klicks to the north of here. They have a ten-year-old boy we need to extract. The main guy is head of the Zeta cartel, codename Z1. He's responsible for our guys KIA. Whatever happens, we nail him.'

Brooker gave him a flinty stare.

'Our brief was not to compromise the op on account of the hostage.' You could tell he had Gurkha blood. Vicious as hell.

'Your brief was also that I have unit command. We're getting the kid out. Do you have a problem with that?'

Brooker shook his head. 'They said you had another guy with you.'

'He's a rogue CIA agent.'

'Do we really want him along? We don't need any dead weights.'

Danny looked over his shoulder. No sign of Kleinman. He was clearly still on the ground, like Danny had instructed. Danny hesitated for a moment. 'We take him with us. He can enter the hacienda once we've secured it.' He looked around the airfield again. The team had collected their chutes and appeared to be waiting for instructions.

'Get them moving,' Danny said. 'I want the vehicles unloaded and ready in five minutes. We make the assault before dawn.'

TWENTY-EIGHT

The drop zone was a sudden flurry of activity. Danny accompanied Brooker and his men as they ran to the Jackals, unfastened them from their landing pallets and drove them down on to the hard-baked Mexican ground. They were fearsome-looking machines: heavily armoured; enormous sturdy wheels; heavy blast shields under the driver and navigator cockpit; sturdy, rugged bars covering the headlamps at the front; more metal bars covering the open top. Each one had a compact but sturdy shovel attached to it, in case the vehicle needed digging out, but Danny didn't foresee that happening. Super-mobile, super-strong, they were designed for extreme mobility, fire support and rapid assault. Danny saw the silhouettes of two guys unloading a box from one of them. Within ten minutes he realised this was a general-purpose machine gun: the guys fitted it together and attached it to the firing post on the Jackal.

Two guys opened up the equipment case. Brooker handed Danny everything he needed, and which he'd been missing since the firefight in the Nuevo Laredo compound. Camouflage gear, body armour, a Kevlar helmet, a boom mike and radio equipment already patched in to the unit's comms. A Diemaco C8 SFW carbine. Sights and Surefire torch. An ops waistcoat, fully loaded with a complement of fragmentation grenades and flashbangs, and enough space to stash extra ammunition for the Diemaco. Danny suited up in his heavy battle dress as Brooker gave him a run-down of the equipment they'd airlifted into the drop zone.

'We've got two G3SG1 sniper rifles, a Javelin ...' He pointed toward one of the Jackals. 'Only one Gimpy.'

'Drones?' Danny asked.

'Four black hornet nanos. They've got a range of about a mile so we can dig in at a safe distance and get eyes on.' He spoke with terse, brisk military efficiency. Danny felt his confidence grow.

'Body armour for the spook?' Danny said, clipping his Diemaco to a lanyard round his neck. Brooker nodded, and Danny found an extra set of plate hangers among the rest of the gear. He closed the equipment case. 'Load it up, guys,' he said to two of the Regiment men who were checking over the nearest Jackal vehicle.

Three minutes later, the Jackals were manned: five guys in one, four in another, Danny and Brooker in the third – the one with the machine gun – with Brooker behind the wheel. Brooker took the convoy lead and, on Danny's instruction, drove the couple of hundred metres to where Kleinman was still lying on the earth. Brooker made no comment as the ageing CIA man limped up to the Jackal and took a seat, but he didn't need to. His slightly frosty silence said it all. Danny handed Kleinman his body armour, which the CIA man donned with the efficiency of someone who had worn it before.

They travelled in a single line, twenty metres apart, Brooker leading. No headlamps. Danny had taken the top gunner's position behind the Gimpy. He was glad to take a role that occupied his mind. The events of the evening were haunting him. Spike's treachery, and Danny's self-loathing at not having seen it coming, was like a weight pressing down on him. Tyson dead. And Spud . . . Danny set his jaw at the thought, clenched his teeth. Focused on the one thing keeping him together: attacking Z1, and making the bastard pay.

He scanned the surrounding countryside carefully as they drove. They were well back from the main highway, and travelling over rough, bumpy terrain that no civilian vehicle would be able to manage, but that was no reason not to be on high alert. Both vehicles behind him had three guys scanning for threats with their rifles. If they were to encounter any Zeta patrols, the Regiment unit would clock them immediately.

358

But they didn't. The SAS convoy moved unchallenged toward their target. Expertly driven, the Jackals made a minimum of noise at the relatively low speeds at which they moved – no more than 20 mph. The moon rose higher in the sky as midnight approached. The terrain became bumpier and more treacherous, but the Jackals and their drivers were up to the task of closing the miles between them and the hacienda without problems or delays. They'd trained for situations like this until they were second nature.

They'd been going for an hour and were in the valley between two inclines when Kleinman, who'd been following their location on his GPS unit, covering its faintly glowing fascia with his hands, called: 'We're about a mile out.'

Brooker came to a halt and turned round to Danny. 'You know the terrain,' he said. 'How close can we get?'

Danny considered that for a moment. They were heading to the south side of the hacienda: the position from which he'd viewed the target by himself. He'd been able to get eyes on from a distance of 500 metres, but it would be risky for a mechanised convoy to approach that close too early, especially when they had the advantage of drones for surveillance purposes. 'We'll dig in here,' he said. 'Get those nano-drones up, make a strategy.'

Brooker gave instructions over the comms, before making a three-point turn so the Jackal was pointing south in the event that they needed to extract quickly. The driver of one of the other vehicles did the same. The third positioned his Jackal facing east. Together, the vehicles formed three sides of a protective square, the open side facing south. Danny told six of the guys to surround their lying-up point in defensive surveillance positions at a perimeter of fifty metres. They melted silently into the night. After a minute, even Danny was unable to tell they were in the vicinity. A heavy quiet descended on the convoy as the remainder of them – Danny, Kleinman, Brooker and the two remaining Regiment guys – positioned themselves in the protective square of the three Jackals. None of them spoke unnecessarily. They used no torches. Comms were totally quiet. Even Danny's breathing sounded too loud to him. He found himself taking shallower breaths as he crouched down inside the protective ring of the Jackals.

One of the guys, on Brooker's quiet command, took up a firing position facing south. While they did this, the other unit member retrieved a nano-drone base station – it looked like a chunky, beige iPad – and charging unit from the equipment case. He fitted the base station to his chest in a tactical pouch system. He clipped a robust external antenna to the base station, then opened up a compartment on the right-hand side. It contained two drones. He removed one and held it at head height.

The Black Hornet nano-drone was tiny – only about 10 centimetres long. It resembled a miniature helicopter, with both top and tail rotors. That minuscule package contained a lot of tech, however. Each drone had three cameras: forward-facing, downward-pointing and one tilted at a forty-five degree angle. Each camera had night-vision capability. 'Hundred and fifty grand's worth of kit right there,' Brooker commented to nobody in particular, as the drone operator powered up the base station. 'Buy half of Nepal with that.' The rotors of the drone started to spin, and the device made a buzzing sound, like an angry wasp. The operator released it into the air and started piloting it using the base station. The buzzing sound disappeared almost immediately. After ten seconds, Danny couldn't even see the device itself. At its cruising altitude of 500 feet it would be invisible even during the day – especially in a sunny climate like this, where people rarely looked up. At night, there was no chance of it being spotted.

'Tell me when you get eyes on,' Danny told the operator. He turned to Kleinman, who was staring up the incline in the direction of the hacienda. 'When we hit them,' he said, 'it's going to be hard and fast. You'll need to hold back. We'll call you in when the threats are neutralised.'

Kleinman looked at him, his head slightly inclined, as if Danny didn't quite understand something. 'Have you any idea,' he said, 'how long I've been waiting to get this close to Augusto Chavez? If you think I'm going to take a back seat now ...'

'I can't guarantee your safety—'

'*Safety?* You think I give a shit about my safety, boy? You think I care if I die tonight? He killed my boy, Danny Black. Do you know what that means? If you were this close to the man who killed your child, what would *you* do?'

Danny narrowed his eyes. The truth was, he *had* been in such a situation, or one very like it. And the men who'd threatened his daughter? They wouldn't be threatening anyone ever again. Not after what he and Spud had done to them.

Spud. The thought of Danny's mate pierced him again.

'We have a visual,' said the drone operator.

'In any case,' Kleinman said as Danny turned away from him. 'I know how to fire a weapon. Ask your friend Spike.'

They exchanged a long glance. Danny broke away and approached the drone operator. Brooker joined him. The drone operator unclipped the display from its tactical sling so they could see it properly. The men stared at it in silence for a couple of minutes as they assimilated everything the drone's camera was telling them.

The drone cameras were on night-vision mode. Despite their tiny size, the image they gave was sharp, affording Danny and the others a distinct view of the compound and its surrounding area. It was clear Danny had been right that there was only one entrance: the gate he, Tyson and Spike had surveyed on the northern side of the rectangular perimeter wall. He could clearly see the road that headed north from the gate and past the guard house fifty metres from it. There was no sign of any targets outside the guard house, though Danny was certain there would be at least three guys inside. He could, however, see the two perimeter-wall guards. They were at the point of crossing over at the middle of the southern wall, before continuing their circuit.

The hacienda itself, which Danny had not been able to view from his OPs, was situated exactly in the centre of the compound, its shape precisely congruent with the rectangle of the perimeter wall. There was a terrace along the eastern side, and an illumin-ated swimming pool. There was movement in the pool: a single person taking a midnight swim. Danny watched the person carefully. He or she emerged from one end of the pool just as a second person exited the hacienda and wrapped the swimmer in a towel. 'One male, one female,' Danny said.

'Roger that,' Brooker replied as they continued to watch the screen.

Three vehicles were parked neatly in the northeastern corner. It looked like two pick-ups and a large Transit. There was only one other structure inside the compound. This was a rectangular building, half the size of the hacienda itself. It was positioned against the southeastern corner of the perimeter, and the perimeter wall itself formed its two external walls. Danny tapped that area of the screen. 'We need to establish what this building is,' he said.

Brooker nodded his agreement. 'When do we need to get another nano-drone up?' he asked the drone operator.

'We've got another fifteen minutes left on this one. I'll send a second one up in ten.'

Danny and Brooker kept eyes on the screen. The swimmer and her companion had retreated into the hacienda. Danny's attention was drawn to a region beyond the pool, against the western length of the perimeter, where there was an area of foliage. 'Can you switch the camera to thermal?' he asked the operator.

The drone operator nodded and made an adjustment on the display. The picture changed to a vibrant heat map of the compound. The two buildings glowed yellow. The swimming pool was orange, as were the three cars, although there was no distinct heat spot near the engine, which suggested the chassis were simply radiating the heat they had absorbed during the day. However, at either end of the area of foliage by the pool were two distinct heat spots. 'Concealed shooters,' Danny said.

Brooker nodded. 'Get the impression our guy's on the paranoid side?'

'So he fucking should be,' Danny said, glancing over at Kleinman, who had his back to them and was staring out across the silent Mexican night.

The drone operator pointed out a particular hot spot at the northern end of the main house. 'I can't be sure,' he said, 'but I think this is an electrical generator.'

Danny stored that information.

'How did they keep this place a secret for so long?' Brooker said.

Danny shrugged. 'By threatening to kill the families of anyone who grassed them up. And nailing a few of them for good measure, just to show they're serious.' He turned back to the screen. Everything was still, apart from the two guards making their circuit of the perimeter wall. 'I already timed them,' Danny said. 'Seventeen minutes, give or take.'

The two guards had almost completed a full circuit when the drone operator engaged a second nano-drone, which flew wasp-like from their location five minutes before the original was brought in. The operator plugged it into the charging station. Danny left Brooker keeping eyes on the screen for a moment and stepped to the edge of the protective ring of Jackal vehicles. It was utterly quiet. Unnervingly so. Danny reminded himself he was surrounded by a cordon of Regiment shooters, each of them invisibly watching the surrounding area for suspicious movement. Nevertheless, he found himself wondering how accurate Hereford's intel was. Could Z1 be expecting an assault? Was he relying on Spike to have dealt with Danny and Tyson? Was he expecting to hear from Spike? Any offensive strategy they formed needed to take these possibilities into account.

'We've got something,' Brooker said, his voice quiet but urgent.

Danny quickly returned to where Brooker was crouched with the drone operator. He looked at the screen. Five figures had just emerged from the small building in the southeastern corner of the compound. They stayed close as they headed north toward the exit gate. When they reached it they paused, evidently waiting for the two perimeter guards to meet on the other side.

Danny checked his watch. 0100 hours. 'They did a stag change at 2000 hours,' Danny breathed. 'Five hours ago. That means the next changeover is likely to be 0600. We'll hit them halfway through the stag, at 0330.'

'Good,' Brooker said. He didn't need to explain himself. The small hours of the morning were an efficient time to launch an assault like this. People were more likely to be asleep, especially halfway through a stag. Off their guard. Even if they were expecting a night-time attack, by 0330 their assumption would be that it wasn't happening.

But Danny was disinclined to be too blasé. 'Remember these guys are SF-trained,' he said. 'If they're like the Zetas I've seen before, they fight well. We need to put the fuckers down very quickly.'

As he spoke, there was more movement. The gates had opened. The two perimeter guards entered the compound, replaced by two of the newcomers. The three remaining guards walked to the guard house. Only when these fresh guys were in position did the existing three guards walk back to the entrance and through the gate, closing it behind them. Danny, Brooker and the drone operator watched the five guys who'd been relieved walk back to the corner building, while the two new perimeter guards started their circuit. At the same time, another two guards emerged from the smaller building and headed over to relieve the shooters hidden in the bushes.

It was Brooker's turn to tap the screen. 'That's the fucking staff house,' he said. 'We hit that, they're neutered.'

Danny nodded, but he was already a couple of steps ahead. 'We should plan for three sets of seven guards,' he said. 'That means there could be a minimum of fourteen guys in the staff house, plus the two in the bushes and the five guarding the exterior.' He glanced toward the equipment case and went through his mental check list of the equipment Brooker had listed. Sniper rifles, Javelin missile, GPMG. Three armoured vehicles. Ten guys, plus Danny and Kleinman. He turned his attention back to the screen and, as he watched the changeover guys enter the staff house, another part of his brain was observing the hacienda from the two OPs at the north and south. Tactical possibilities started presenting themselves. Even with the arrival of Brooker and his men, the Zetas likely outnumbered the Regiment. But that was okay. It just meant Danny and the others had to fight harder, and smarter. They had to stack the deck in their favour and make sure that when they made their strike, it was so brutal and so swift that the Zetas would, quite literally, not know what had hit them. If Danny and his men played it right, Z1's entourage would be dead before they'd figured out what was going on.

'Keep eyes on,' he told the drone operator. 'I want to know if you see any movement of personnel.'

The drone operator nodded. Danny turned to Brooker. 'You got pencil and paper?'

Brooker fetched a pad and pencil from his pack. He handed them to Danny, who spent thirty seconds drawing a quick sketch of the hacienda and its surroundings. When it was completed, he drew sets of arrows pointing toward the perimeter, from the east and the north. Then he showed it to Brooker. 'This is the assault plan,' he said. 'We divide into three teams. A two-man Javelin team, a two-man sniper team and a seven-man assault team.'

'Seven plus one,' Brooker said, glancing at Kleinman.

'Roger that,' Danny said flatly. 'Seven plus one.'

'Does he have combat experience? He can't get in the fucking way.'

'He knows to hang back until we've secured the hacienda.'

Brooker clearly didn't like it, but there was no argument. The line of command was clear. 'When we get in there,' he said, 'we can't leave any survivors. Women, kids. We're under the radar. No witnesses. Orders from the headshed.'

'Just the boy,' Danny said. 'The hostage. We get him out.' Because Danny had made a promise to Ana, and he was damned if the Zetas were going to stop him keeping it.

'It's your call,' Brooker said.

Danny nodded. 'Let's get moving. We've got two hours to set this thing up.'

Two hours, he thought to himself, to show Augusto Chavez and his Zetas *exactly* what happens when you pick a fight with the Regiment.

TWENTY-NINE

0200 hours. The Regiment was moving again.

The Jackal vehicles were crucial to their assault plan. Danny and Brooker led a convoy of two – Brooker driving, Kleinman sitting next to him, Danny top-gunning at the Gimpy.

They'd left two guys back at the southern side of the hacienda, along with the third vehicle and, crucially, the Javelin missile and its command launch unit. Their job: to position themselves over-looking the eastern edge of the perimeter, in line of sight of that section that formed the outer wall of the staff house, then use the CLU to light the target. That Javelin could take out a lot of wall, and a lot of guys. When Danny gave the word over the unit comms, it would do exactly that.

In the meantime the convoy headed east, moving very slowly so that the engine noise was kept to a minimum, driving with the benefit of night-vision goggles. The nano-drone operator surveyed the route carefully to ensure the convoy didn't have any unexpected surprises, but the terrain was deserted. When they were a klick to the east of the hacienda they turned north and, after twenty minutes, the road that curved down toward the haci-enda's entrance came into view 500 metres away. They stopped in a protective dip in the ground.

Now it was time to set up the principal flank of their attack at the northern end of the hacienda.

Two guys dismounted from the second unit of the two-vehicle convoy. They were each carrying a G3SG1 sniper rifle, telescopic sights attached, bipods folded up underneath the body of the weapons. Accompanied by Danny and Brooker, they prepared to advance to their firing position, while the remaining five guys silently put in a defensive ring around the Jackals, disappearing into the darkness just as they had on the southern side of the hacienda. Led by Danny, the sniper team started moving into position. A thick silence had settled over the area, broken only by the faint crunch of their footfall as they moved stealthily, in patrol formation, toward and up the same incline where Kleinman had taken out Spike. Danny tried to keep that moment from his mind as they headed toward the OP that he, Spike and Tyson had used. At the brow of the incline they crawled into position.

The hacienda came into view. There was the glow of electric light behind the outer wall, though they couldn't quite see which parts of the compound it came from. They saw no personnel guarding it, but that didn't mean anything. The two perimeter guards were simply out of sight, and the guardhouse guys were in their little building fifty metres along the road from the entrance. It had no windows, but Danny could make out a strip of light at the bottom of the door. They were in there, no question.

The two snipers set up their weapons, swiftly, quietly, efficiently. By the time they were in position, their bipods down and their eyes to the sights, the two perimeter guards had reappeared at each corner of the outer wall. Distance: 300 metres. They walked at a steady pace toward the main entrance, blithely unaware they were being precisely tracked by the two snipers, who were ready to take them out in a moment, when that moment came.

But it hadn't come yet. 'The perimeter guards are Tango One and Two,' Danny said. 'The guys in the guardhouse, Tangos Three, Four and Five. When I give you the go, you need to wait until Tangos One and Two have each moved approximately fifteen metres from the corners of the perimeter, toward the main gate. When you confirm their position, we advance to contact. Understood?'

'Roger that,' came the reply from the two snipers, who didn't take their eyes from the sights.

Danny and Brooker left them in position, before returning to the two-vehicle convoy.

Time check: 0245 hours. Forty-five minutes till the go. A lone cloud drifted across the moon as Danny and Brooker reached the others. A night bird called somewhere in the distance. The SAS were still in their defensive positions, silently scanning the surrounding area for threats. In the shadow of the Gimpy, Danny spoke quietly into the comms. 'Javelin Team, what is your status?'

There was a momentary pause, before a crackly voice came back over Danny's earpiece. '*The target is lit, repeat, the target is lit.*'

'Copy that.' He turned his attention to the sniper team. 'Sniper Team, what is your status?'

'*We have eyes on.*'

Danny turned to Kleinman, who was still sitting in the Jackal. His fingers were pressed together. He looked strangely as if he was praying. 'You understand what's going to happen, Kleinman?'

Kleinman nodded calmly. He pointed to the other Jackal. 'When you give the go, that vehicle approaches first. This vehicle will approach once the perimeter guards are dealt with.'

'And what do you do as it approaches?' Danny said.

Kleinman gave him a long look. 'I stay down, boy.'

His reluctance was evident. Danny and Brooker exchanged a look. 'If it was my call,' Brooker said, 'he wouldn't stay down, he'd stay here.'

Brooker was right. In any other situation, Danny would hate having a guy along who didn't know the drill. But Danny hadn't told Brooker about Kleinman's very personal reason for wanting to be in on the assault. He was prepared to cut the guy some slack. 'Just don't get in the fucking way,' he told the CIA man.

'Where do you think the target will be?' Brooker said.

'Best guess, first floor,' Danny said. 'But he might move when he hears the attack. I reckon he'll keep the kid close to him.'

He checked the time again. 0255.

Thirty-five minutes to contact.

Danny engaged his comms and addressed himself to the lead assault team. 'Assault Team, preliminary positions,' he said. 'That's a go.'

There was no comms response, but within thirty seconds the remaining five guys in the assault team emerged from the surrounding darkness. They silently took up their positions in the vehicles. Kleinman remained in the Gimpy Jackal. Danny and Brooker changed vehicles, taking the second Jackal with three other members of the assault team. They engaged their rifles as the vehicles started up again and moved north, very silently, up an incline and across the undulating terrain toward the road. Danny's every sense was on high alert. He felt like a silent predator, skirting round a dangerous animal. Occasionally he looked up, trying to spot the nano-drone he knew was keeping eyes on the area. He couldn't, but he told himself that was a good thing. Their plan of attack relied on suddenness and on the element of surprise. The Javelin team and the sniper team were dug in and covert. But the assault team's vehicles were potentially the weak link. If anyone saw them approaching, there was a chance the Zetas might pre-empt their attack. That was unacceptable. As Danny well knew, the secret of a successful assault was to make damn sure it wasn't a fair fight. To do that, you had to be in complete control.

They stopped out of sight of the road again, fifty metres south of it. Time check: 0312 hours. Eighteen minutes to contact. Danny made some mental calculations. He estimated it would take 45 seconds to get to the road. Once there, approximately a minute to make it to the guardhouse, for thirty seconds of which they would be out of sight of the guards if they happened to have emerged. He made contact with the sniper team: 'Sniper team, what is the position of Tangos One and Two? Repeat, what is the position of Tangos One and Two?'

'*Out of sight for approximately fifteen seconds,*' a voice replied. It took them approximately 17 minutes to do a full circuit. Which meant that next time they appeared in front of the hacienda, the op would be a go.

'Javelin team, is the target still lit?'

'*Roger that.*'

'We'll advance to contact in approximately 14 minutes. Sniper Team, advise when Tangos One and Two reappear.' Time check: 0314 hours. 'Assault Team, we advance to the road at 0326.'

The comms fell silent. Everyone in the assault team was deadly still. A slight breeze blew from the east. Danny knew the snipers would be taking that into account, adjusting the trajectory of their fire in compensation. He felt sweat on the nape of his neck in any case.

0317 hours. Time was ticking slowly. It felt to Danny as though this night had lasted forever. And although it was silent and still, inside Danny's head it was noisy. He heard the gunfire that killed Spud. Ana, screaming for her boy. Spike, justifying his betrayal, his voice trembling. He tried to empty his head. To focus only on the op in hand. Easier said than done.

0319 hours.

In his mind's eye he saw the guy with the tattooed eyelids, the man who'd nailed Spud. He wondered where the bastard was now, and felt his blood run hot as he started to calculate how hard it would be to hunt him down. Do for Spud what he knew Spud would do for him . . .

Focus . . . One thing at a time . . .

0323 hours.

'Assault team, that's three minutes,' he breathed into the comms.

No movement from the guys around him in the Jackal. But somehow, an escalation in the tension. Danny found himself breathing slowly, reducing his heart rate. He looked to his left and saw Kleinman sitting in the Gimpy Jackal. Their eyes met. Kleinman nodded. Danny didn't nod back.

0324 hours.

'Assault Team, positions,' Danny said.

Immediately, the drivers of the two vehicles turned the engines over. They moved slowly across the rugged, arid terrain, keeping the engine noises as low as possible, headlamps off. The road came into view again. Danny's estimate of 45 seconds to reach it was good. Both vehicles turned left on to the road. Danny checked his watch. Ten seconds later . . . 0325 hours.

'Assault Team, approximately one minute to the go. Javelin Team check.'

'*Check.*'

'Sniper team check.'

'*Check.*'

Silence descended again. The same night bird called in the distance. Danny felt his pulse thumping in his neck as he waited for the Sniper team to announce that Tangos One and Two had appeared at the front of the hacienda.

0325 hrs.

No word. Everything was still.

Then . . .

'*This is Sniper Team. We have Tangos One and Two in our sights.*'

'That's a go,' Danny announced.

There was no hesitation. The lead Jackal turned over its engine and illuminated its headlamps. It accelerated to a steady 30 miles per hour as it followed the road that wound down toward the hacienda. Danny's calculation was that the headlamps would obscure the military identity of the vehicle, and that their approach would encourage the three guys in the guardhouse to emerge to investigate, which would put them exactly where the Regiment wanted them: in the line of fire.

'*Sniper team, Javelin team, standby!*' he shouted over the noise of the engine as the road wound south and the hacienda came into view. Distance: 100 metres. Danny focused not on the perimeter guards – he knew the sniper team would have them covered – but on the guardhouse. The driver of the Jackal was using a low gear to ensure that the engine now made as much noise as possible, in order to attract the attention of the guardhouse guys.

With 75 metres to go, it became apparent that the strategy was working.

The door of the guardhouse opened. Light spilled out, and so did one of the three guys. He wore an assault rifle across his chest, but did not have it engaged. He squinted toward the vehicle as a second guy emerged.

'Wait for it,' Danny said, and he could hear the tension in his own voice as the vehicle advanced. He didn't want to give the go until all three guardhouse guys were out in the open.

Distance: 65 metres. No sign of the third guy.

Fifty metres.

A figure appeared in the doorway.

'*Take the shot!*' Danny instructed.

The response to his order was immediate.

The snipers fired in unison, so the sound of their double shot, which came from their firing position approximately 200 metres to Danny's seven o'clock, sounded like a single report. Danny didn't have his eyes on Tangos One or Two: he had complete confidence that the snipers would have put them down. Instead, from his position in the Jackal, and with his assault rifle switched to automatic, he opened up on Tangos Three, Four and Five, his fire accompanied by simultaneous bursts from Brooker. The guards hit the ground with dull, lumpen finality. No screams, no showers of blood. Just instant death. Exactly as Danny had planned it. The driver killed the Jackal's headlamps. They'd served their purpose, and now the unit was driving blind again.

One of the guards had stepped out on to the road. His corpse was lying directly in the path of the Jackal, but the driver didn't swerve as he headed straight for the hacienda. Over the comms, his voice perfectly calm, Danny gave his next instruction.

'Javelin Team, go!'

Moments later, the wheels of the Jackal rumbled over the corpse of the dead Zeta on the ground. There was an unpleasant crunching sound as his bones splintered under the weight. At the same time, a distant fizzing sound filled the air. It came from the southeastern corner of the hacienda, and Danny knew exactly what it was: the thrust of a Javelin missile as it made its way toward the target.

Less than a second later, it hit.

A ferocious explosion resonated across the hot Mexican night. The Jackal was no more than twenty metres from the hacienda, but Danny could still see a brief orange flash light up the sky from the southeast. As the brutal detonation of the Javelin died away, it was replaced by the distant sound of rubble and shrapnel raining down on to the earth. Danny knew the impact of the missile had been considerable. Anyone in the demolished staff house, if they weren't dead, would be seriously fucked up.

The Jackal was accelerating toward the gate. Danny quickly glanced back. He could see, seventy-five metres behind him, the moonlit silhouette of the second Jackal, the outline of its Gimpy harshly visible. It too was accelerating fast toward the hacienda. Danny faced the front again, and braced himself for impact.

Two seconds later, it came. The Jackal smashed hard into the front gate of the hacienda. The jolt was shocking – Danny's whole body juddered hard – but the vehicle itself, well armoured and designed for forceful impact, inflicted more damage with the sturdy bars and bumpers at its front than it received. The heavy gate splintered inward. The Jackal driver reversed hard. Danny braced for another impact, aware of the engine of the second Jackal maybe twenty metres behind. The first Jackal rammed the gates again. They crashed open.

Danny caught a glimpse of the main house, attractively lit from below, vibrant flowers creeping up its side. There was screaming from somewhere inside the perimeter. Male voices, agonised. Danny figured they came from injured guys in the staff house. He blocked them out and tried to focus on any other sounds. For now, nothing. The Jackal reversed hard again and swung to the left, allowing the Gimpy vehicle direct access straight through the broken gates and into the hacienda. Danny and the other guys in the vehicle jumped out, while the Gimpy Jackal positioned itself at the entrance. The gunner swung the Gimpy round to his two o'clock. Danny knew he was aiming across the swimming pool directly toward the bushes where the nano-drone had picked up the heat signals of two hidden guards. As Danny moved, weapon engaged, toward the entrance, another earsplitting noise ripped the air: the familiar bark of the general-purpose machine gun spewing rounds across the compound toward the bushes. The report lasted for a full ten seconds. By the time it had finished, each member of the assault team, with the exception of the machine gunner and Kleinman, had gained access to the inside of the hacienda. Kleinman was still huddled in the back of the Jackal.

The others had spread out at three-metre intervals, down in the firing position, weapons engaged.

Danny quickly took in his surroundings. The ground was covered in chunky gravel. A simple security measure: it was impossible to walk on without making a sound. The parked vehicles – two off-roaders and a large white Transit van – were in position to his three o'clock. The main house was fifty metres to his one o'clock, underlit on both sides he could see by lamps in the ground. Positioned against the closest wall of the house, exactly where the nano-drone operator had pointed out an intense heat-spot, was a wooden housing, about four metres wide by two metres high. There was a faint hum coming from it. Danny was sure this was an electrical generator, as the hacienda had shown no sign of being attached to any kind of grid.

The house itself somewhat blocked his line of sight toward the swimming pool, of which he could only see the first few metres to his two o'clock. The pool lights were on. To his eleven o'clock, the staff house. A thick pall of smoke hung over it, and the devastation the Javelin had inflicted was evident. The roof had collapsed, and so had substantial sections of the front wall. The air was thick with the choking stench of burning rubble, and there was a faint orange glow of flame from one section. Danny's ears were ringing from his proximity to the Gimpy, but he could still tell that for now the only other sound came from the direction of that staff house. It was the same screaming he'd heard from outside the perimeter wall. It was weaker now, however. He reckoned that whichever injured Zeta was making the noise, he was bleeding out good and fast.

He turned his attention back to the main house. Two storeys. A pitched roof. Rambling plants covering the near end. No movement. Yet.

The screaming faded away. A sinister silence fell over the whole hacienda. The noise of their approach and assault had lasted no more than a minute.

Danny spoke quietly into the comms. 'Hit the generator.'

The machine gunner responded instantly. He fired a burst of rounds into the wooden housing at the end of the building. It exploded noisily into a short-lived fireball, reverting after a couple of seconds to a smoulder. Instantly, all the lights in the compound died, including the uplighting of the building and the pool lights. Somehow, the silence that followed seemed all the deeper.

Danny lowered his night-vision goggles, and was aware of the others doing the same. Immediately, his view of the compound was as good as daylight, though tinged with green. A beam from his IR laser sight cut across the compound, and he saw four more beams from the other guys's sights, all fanning out to cover different parts of the space.

Sudden movement. A figure emerged from the smouldering staff house. He was staggering. But not for long. The soldier to Danny's left didn't even have to alter the trajectory of his IR beam. The figure simply limped in its way. Danny heard the sound of a single suppressed round. The figure went down.

Silence again.

Danny spoke into the comms: 'Assault Team, advance.'

Danny, Brooker and two more guys got to their feet. The machine gunner stayed in position, as did the remaining unit member who was covering the staff house and the vehicles to the left. Danny led the advance, the others fanning out behind him. He kept his footfall light to keep the crunching on the gravel to a minimum. But there was no doubt the occupants of the hacienda knew he was coming. So he was ready to fire at the faintest hint of a threat, the butt of his rifle pressed hard into his shoulder, the weapon ready to move with any turn of his body, his finger lightly on the trigger.

Distance to the external wall of the house, twenty metres. Danny was aware of two of his guys peeling off to the left to move round the back of the house to its far end, so they could have it surrounded. He moved relentlessly forward, Brooker on his right shoulder, another guy on his left.

There was a sudden sound of screaming. A different pitch and timbre from the previous scream. Higher.

Danny stopped and held up one hand. The guys behind him halted immediately. It was either a woman or a child, stressed and tearful. It lasted no more than two seconds. There was the dull thump of a weapon from inside the hacienda. The screaming stopped. Terminally.

Danny felt a knot in his guts. Had that been Miguel? He didn't think so. The voice sounded different. He tried to figure out what just happened. Had one of the women in the house lost their head, only to be silenced by Chavez or one of his guys? He continued his advance. When he was five metres from the wall, he altered his trajectory to advance along it. With the extended field of view of his NV goggles he could see the two Jackals to his right, the gunner carefully covering the swimming pool area. The compound had been plunged into silence again. He could hear nothing but the crunch of his footsteps and the beating of his heart.

He reached the corner of the house. The swimming pool came fully into view. There was no sign of the two bathers, and although there were faint ripples in the water, Danny knew they'd probably been caused by the aftershock of the Javelin strike. There was no sign of enemy personnel. At least, no *live* enemy personnel. Danny picked out two corpses, butchered by the Gimpy, each lying on their front on the far side of the pool.

There was a terrace between the house and the pool. Several heavy wooden tables were dotted around, as well as sun beds and large closed umbrellas. At the front of the house, a raised, covered veranda, with three steps leading up to it. Opposite the steps, the main entrance to the house. The front of the veranda was a raised wall. Danny was about a head taller than it. Distance to the steps: twenty metres. At the far end of the terrace, Danny could see movement, but quickly identified it as one of his guys who had made the circuit of the house. Danny held up one hand and jabbed a forefinger toward the terrace steps. He advanced, Brooker at his shoulder, the wall of the veranda to his left. The guy opposite did the same.

They were ten metres from the steps when the main door opened. Danny instinctively moved his body so that his weapon was pointing up and in the direction of the door. He was in time to see a small oval object tumble out on to the veranda itself.

'Frag,' he hissed into his comms. He threw himself against the veranda wall, keeping his body low. Brooker and the other guy did the same. Two seconds later, the fragmentation grenade exploded with a sharp crack and shower of shrapnel. But it was impotent. The Regiment guys had protected themselves well. Danny stood up to his full height again and saw the main door was still open. He continued advancing toward the steps, reaching them at the same time as his opposite number. 'Covering fire,' he breathed. His unit mate nodded, then turned his weapon up toward the open door and let loose three suppressed rounds. They splintered into the door, which swung a little further open.

Danny advanced, moving up the steps with his weapon aimed directly at the open door, the beam of his IR sight cutting through the opening. He knew Brooker was on his shoulder because there was a second beam parallel to it. Distance, ten metres. Through his night sights, it appeared to open not into a corridor but into an open room. No sign of movement.

Five metres.

Three.

A figure suddenly appeared, framed by the doorway, approximately five metres beyond it. He was carrying a pistol, held two-handed like a pro, raised at shoulder height. He wasn't pro or fast enough, however. Danny's IR beam was already squarely on his chest. Danny fired a single suppressed round, putting the target down before he had a chance to fire. As the figure hit the ground, Danny was immediately aware of movement inside the room beyond the door. Danny jabbed one finger to indicate positions on either side of the door. He and Brooker took those positions, then Danny removed a flashbang grenade from his ops vest, pulled the pin and lobbed it into the room.

Seconds later, an immense crack spliced their hearing, and the flash of the grenade, seeping out from the doorway, illuminated the veranda as light as day. There was the noise of several men shouting in confusion. Danny held up three fingers.

Two.

One.

He and Brooker swung round, aiming their weapons into the room. Danny went left, Brooker right. He saw three targets, all adult, all male. They were armed, but plainly disorientated from the shock of the flashbang, staring blindly across the room, not knowing where to aim or fire. Danny and Brooker had them down in less than five seconds, the single rounds from their assault rifles completely unerring.

Silence again.

In his peripheral vision, Danny saw a fourth body – female – face down on the floor. He remembered the scream and gunshot he'd heard a minute before. The room itself was large. Luxurious. There was an arty marble statue of a naked woman in the middle, taller than Danny. Comfortable chairs and sofas all around. Book cases and ornaments. A door on the left-hand wall, and one on the right. On the far wall, opposite Danny and Brooker, an elaborate staircase was winding up to the first floor.

Danny became aware of four more of his guys entering the room. He couldn't identify them because of their night-vision goggles, but he knew the sniper team and Javelin team would have made their way to the hacienda by now, bolstering their numbers. With another jab of his finger, he indicated that the new arrivals should clear the rooms to the left and right. All Danny's instincts told him, however, that at this hour Z1 would be upstairs in his bedroom. But approximately four minutes had passed since they'd breached the perimeter wall. Plenty of time for Chavez to put himself on a war footing. Danny told himself to expect the unexpected. He and Brooker advanced past the statue, toward the staircase, weapons engaged.

Danny took the lead, his rifle pointing up toward the first floor, the way ahead bright and sharp but tinged with green through his night-vision goggles. Halfway up the stairs, he heard something. He stopped and listened hard. It was a whimpering sound. Faint. Distressed. It sounded like a child crying.

Danny advanced carefully. The staircase wound to the right. As he followed it round, the landing came into view. It was fifteen metres wide. Perhaps twenty metres long. Marble floor.

Art on the walls. Mirrors. Several doors on either side, and one at the end.

And Miguel, Ana's son.

The boy was on his knees in the middle of the landing, ten metres from Danny's position. His hands were behind his back, though Danny couldn't see if they were tied. His face was not only streaming with tears, but also bruised and beaten. His lip was cut. He was wearing his pyjamas, which seemed to hang off his thin frame. His face was etched with terror.

Approximately five metres behind him were two open doors, one on either side of the landing. Danny understood the set-up at a single glance. Behind one of these doors, maybe even behind both, was a gunman with Miguel in his sights. The kid was their collateral. Come any closer, the situation was telling Danny, and the kid gets it. The little boy was staring blindly into the pitch black of the landing, but everything about his demeanour suggested that Miguel fully understood his predicament.

Except Miguel didn't have the situational awareness of Danny Black, who had trained for these moments until they were second nature. Like a chess player, he found himself thinking two moves in advance. If Danny advanced to grab the kid, what then? He knew the Zetas were equipped with frag-mentation grenades. He was certain that these trained soldiers would use one, or more, if Danny put himself in the kill zone, and to hell with the kid's life. And if the Zetas were calculating that he would simply kill their hostage to remove their collat-eral, they would use the same method of attack: throw frags the length of the landing the moment Danny made his pres-ence known.

Danny crouched on one knee at the top of the staircase. He remained very still. The boy didn't seem to have noticed his arrival in the total darkness. He was still staring blankly over Danny's head. With one hand, Danny gestured to Brooker that he should crouch next to him. His unit mate stealthily took that position. Miguel's head suddenly tilted in their direction, as if he'd sensed them. Danny willed him not to say anything, or to give any indication that they were there. The boy's breathing became a little more panicked, but he said nothing and didn't move.

Danny indicated the two open doors, then silently flicked his weapon to automatic. Brooker did the same. Danny put the left-most door in his sights, Brooker took the right.

The kid must have seen something. A shadow in the darkness. A faint movement. His night-blind eyes focused directly on Danny. He screamed.

'*Take the shot*,' Danny instructed.

He and Brooker fired in unison directly at the open doors, aiming approximately halfway up – head height for anyone kneeling in the firing position, abdomen height for anyone standing. The rounds ripped through the solid doors as if they weren't even there. Two figures crumpled forward. Danny and Brooker rose immediately and, weapons still engaged, advanced along the landing. The kid collapsed in terror. As they reached him, Brooker leaned down and, with no concession to gentleness, manhandled him roughly off the ground and bundled him back toward the back end of the landing. 'Hostage acquired,' he said over the comms. 'He's at the top of the staircase.'

Danny, in the meantime, was advancing toward the two targets. Distance, five metres. The guy on the left wasn't moving. Danny's instinct told him the target was dead. The guy on the right, however, was shaking violently, as though he had no control of his limbs. His weapon was hanging round his neck and, sure enough, a fragmentation grenade, the pin still intact, had rolled away from his hand.

Danny felt a prickle of recognition. Almost nonchalantly, he fired a precautionary shot into the body of the dead man to his left. Then he advanced on the live one.

Brooker's rounds had peppered the left-hand side of his target's torso through the door. He was bleeding heavily from several entry wounds. His breath was coming in short, sharp gasps. But it was his face that Danny focused on in the clear, green-tinged aspect of his night vision. It was the same face he had seen leaning over him in the compound at Nuevo Laredo. The same face he had seen beyond the burning vehicle. The face of the man who had killed Spud. His eyes flickered closed momentarily, revealing the fake eyes tattooed on the lids. They opened again and Danny could tell that, despite the darkness, the wounded man knew there was a figure standing over him.

A single shot to the skull would do it. But somehow, for Danny, that wasn't enough. He wanted this bastard to have a bad death. Worse than it already was. And he wanted him to know who had inflicted it.

'Trust me,' he breathed, echoing the tattooed man's own words to Danny. 'It's going to fucking hurt.'

His target's eyes narrowed in contempt. He clearly understood who Danny was. Danny altered his angle of fire so his Diemaco was pointing at the target's knee and, without hesitation, released a single round in the most sensitive of body parts.

The target didn't shout, but his agony was evident from the increased, uncontrollable shaking of his body. Danny moved his weapon back to point at his target's face. Hate was burning from the Zeta's tattooed eyes. Danny aimed at the left one, waited a moment, and released a single round into the eye socket.

The explosion was obscene. A quarter of the man's skull came away as the round slammed into, and cracked, the tile beneath it. Blood and brain matter spattered across a metre radius, and the body fell still.

'Finished playing with your food?' Brooker said. He was two metres to Danny's seven o'clock. Danny didn't have time to answer. A fresh scream emerged from behind the door at the far end of the landing. Distance: five metres. Both men aimed their weapons directly at it.

A voice over the comms. '*Ground floor clear. Moving upstairs.*'

'Watch the kid,' Danny instructed, without taking his eyes from the door. He and Brooker remained immobile for a moment.

'The big guy's bedroom?' Brooker muttered.

'Could be,' Danny said. He was aware of his team members emerging on to the landing behind him. He and Brooker advanced toward the door. Danny stood to its right, where the door knob was. Brooker to the left. Gingerly, Danny tried the door knob.

Locked.

He stepped back. Aimed his rifle at the door. Fired a burst. The area around the door knob splintered and, as Danny stepped aside, the door swung ajar.

There was more screaming from inside. A woman's voice and, maybe, a kid's. Danny prepared a second flashbang grenade. He kicked the door wider open, preparing himself for gunfire from inside. There was none. He threw the grenade into the room. He closed his eyes to protect his own vision. Seconds later the deafening crack rang out, accompanied by the blinding light. Danny opened his eyes and looked into the room.

It was indeed a bedroom. A lavish one, with a large bed directly opposite the door, beneath an ornate mirror on the wall. A sitting-room area to the left. A further open door to the right, presumably leading to a bathroom. On the bed were three people: a woman and two kids. The woman was screaming and pulling the sheets up to hide her nakedness. Danny could see a large diamond ring on her left hand. It had to be Chavez's wife and kids. The children, who were wearing pyjamas, were clinging to their mother, one of them crying, the other one staring into the darkness in perplexed, disorientated, silent terror.

Danny and Brooker entered the room, checking all the corners before advancing any further. There was no sign of Augusto Chavez, but there was a noise of someone moving around in the adjoining room. 'Watch them,' Danny said. He strode across the room toward the open door, his trigger finger ready to fire at the first hint of a threat.

As he approached the open doorway to the bathroom, his target came into view.

Augusto Chavez, Z1, the man they had been hunting since their arrival in the Americas, the man who had outwitted them at every turn, was dressed only in a pair of underpants. He was standing in the darkness on the edge of a roll-top bathtub, trying to reach a high window on the far side of the room. He was overweight, and his fingers were slipping on the ledge just in front of the window as he tried to escape.

Danny didn't shoot him immediately. It wasn't enough. All his hate and anger demanded something else. He moved into the room, grabbed Chavez by the ankle and yanked, so his target collapsed into the bathtub. Chavez cracked the side of his head against the porcelain, and a trickle of blood dribbled down the side of his face. Danny stood over him and aimed his weapon at his chest.

'You made a bad mistake, fat boy. Fucking with us.'

Chavez curled his lip in the darkness. Danny could tell he couldn't see anything, because he was staring just to his left. 'How is your young friend?' he spat, his Spanish accent very strong. 'Little Spike. How many of you did he kill in the end?'

Danny's cheek twitched. 'You can ask him yourself in a minute.'

He prepared to take a shot at Chavez's knees. Before he fired, however, a voice came over the comms. Unimpressed. *'We've got your CIA boy demanding entrance.'*

Danny hesitated. 'Are the house and grounds secure?'

'Roger that.'

He looked at Chavez again and remembered just why Kleinman hated this guy so much. He owed Kleinman one, no doubt about that.

'Send him up,' he said. He raised his NV goggles and switched on the Surefire torch on his rifle, directing the beam straight at Chavez, who winced in the bright light. 'Get out of the bath,' he said.

Chavez scrambled out of the bath tub without taking his eyes off Danny, who kept his rifle firmly directed at Chavez's chest. When the semi-naked man was standing, Danny ordered him into the bedroom. The woman and the two kids were still whimpering here. Brooker and one other guy were still covering them. They too had turned their torches on, so Chavez's family were now illuminated, their tearful eyes blinking in the bright light. Danny ordered Chavez himself to his knees on the ground, two metres to the right of his bed. The drug lord looked up defiantly, jutting out his chin, seemingly unaware of how ridiculous he looked, or not caring. Danny felt his intense hatred of the man double.

Movement at the door. Kleinman arrived. He was brandishing a Heckler and Koch handgun. Danny caught a glimpse of his face in the torchlight as he limped past. The face was hungry. He stood directly in front of Danny, whose torch lit up Kleinman's back, which cast a long shadow over the kneeling drug lord and the wall beyond.

The threat of extreme violence hung over the room. Danny turned to the two Regiment men at the door. 'Leave us,' he said.

There was a pause. With a definite reluctance, Brooker and the other SAS guy left the bedroom and closed the door.

'Do you know who I am?' Kleinman asked.

There was no answer from Chavez. Just the sound of him spitting.

'I am the father of *El puerco espín*,' Kleinman said. 'I am the father of the porcupine.'

There was a heavy silence, broken only by a sob from one of the kids on the bed.

'I'm going to kill you,' Kleinman breathed. 'Whether it's a good death or a bad one is up to you.'

'Whatever you do,' Chavez said defiantly, 'it won't be as bad as what we did to your idiot boy.' Chavez spat again.

Silence.

Kleinman took the shot suddenly. It made Danny start. Chavez wasn't his target. The woman in the bed slammed violently back on the headboard. The sheet she was holding up to preserve her modesty was splashed with red. The two kids screamed.

A voice in Danny's head asked if he should stop Kleinman. Another voice reminded Danny what he himself had once done, when his own child had been threatened.

'His name is Mikey,' Kleinman said, 'and you are going to tell me where my boy is buried.'

'What does it matter now?' Chavez said. He was trying to remain defiant, but there was a definite quaver in his voice now.

'It matters,' Kleinman said.

'In a hole,' Chavez said. 'Where you'll never find him.'

Danny hardened himself for what he knew was about to happen. Kleinman's second shot was as accurate as his first. The little girl in the bed crumpled. Danny heard Chavez exhale heavily. The boy started crying.

'So,' Kleinman said. 'Just your boy left. Your son and heir, Chavez. Are you going to let him live, or shall we send him off to see his mom and his sister?'

No answer.

'You got my lighter, boy?' Kleinman asked Danny.

Danny still had it. He pulled it from his pocket and handed it to Kleinman, who lowered his weapon to take it. Danny covered Chavez with his rifle.

'Funny how simple things become precious,' Kleinman said. 'Mikey gave me this the last time I saw him.' Kleinman sparked the lighter. For the first time since Danny had met him, he allowed the flame to catch. He stepped forward and held the flaming lighter under Chavez's chin.

The narco was pretty tough. He endured the pain for a good seven or eight seconds. The room filled with the stench of burning skin. Chavez shouted out in pain and pulled his head back, his scorched chin burned and blistered.

'My son,' Kleinman pressed, still holding the lighter. 'Where is he?'

Chavez breathed deeply. When he finally spoke, his voice was broken. 'By the road heading south from the village of Guayalejo,' he whispered. 'Behind the roadside shrine to the Virgin. That's where my men buried him and the others.' He paused. 'Just do it!' he spat.

'Oh, I will,' Kleinman said. He killed the lighter. Put it in his pocket. Then he raised his weapon again. He fired. Not at Chavez, but at the whimpering boy on the bed, whose desperate crying immediately stopped.

Kleinman stepped to one side. Now Danny's torch was illuminating Chavez himself. He was still kneeling, but Danny had the sense that it was taking all his strength to remain upright. His face was contorted. A gruesome mixture of hate and grief as he looked from Kleinman to the bed, then back to Kleinman.

'I've finished with him,' Kleinman said. 'Do what you want.' He turned his back on the kneeling man and started limping toward the door.

Danny, however, still had the target in his sights. Augusto Chavez. Z1. The narco's shoulders were shaking. He knew what was coming. He knew he was about to experience the conse-quences of taking on the Regiment, and losing.

There was nothing to say. Danny released a single round. It drilled into Chavez's forehead. The drug lord crumpled into a semi-naked, blood-spattered heap on the ground. A mundane, ignominious, unpleasant death, and no more than he deserved.

Danny turned his back on the scene of bloodshed and followed Kleinman out of the room.

EPILOGUE

The ops room at Hereford was tense. For the past couple of hours all eyes – including those of CO Dominic Hardcastle and Ops Officer Ray Hammond – had been on an electronic map of a small patch of Mexican terrain. The GPS signals broadcast by D Squadron's comms unit had appeared as dots on the map. They'd watched them appear after the hard drop, divide into three units and move in on the target compound. It looked like everything was going as it should. But you can never be sure, until the communication comes in.

Which it did at 1100 hours GMT.

'Sir, we have contact,' one of the guys, dressed in camo with a headset and boom mike, told the two officers.

'Put them on,' Hardcastle instructed.

The guy nodded and spoke into his boom mike. 'Go ahead,' he instructed.

A familiar voice came over the line. Danny Black. *'All targets down. Hostage acquired. Over.'*

'Survivors?'

'Negative.'

Hammond and Hardcastle exchanged a look of hard relief. It was Hammond who spoke. 'Do you have the means of extracting to a safe pick-up point?'

'Roger that, we have enemy vehicles we can use.'

'We have an RAF Merlin on a boat approaching the Mexican coastline. Stand by to receive coordinates for a pick-up at zero hundred hours tonight.' He nodded at the guy with the headset. 'And Black?'

'*Yes, boss?*'

'Leave no trace.'

'*Roger that, boss,*' said Black.

Miguel was terrified. He was shaking, unable to talk. There was no time to mollycoddle him. The Regiment had done what they came here to do. Now they had to bug out. Fast. One of Brooker's men moved the kid to where the three Zeta vehicles were parked in the corner of the compound and, having located a blanket in the hacienda, wrapped him in it. The grim-faced soldier left him crouching by the wheel arch of the white Transit van and went to help the rest of the team with the housekeeping.

Having made contact with Hereford, the unit silently and efficiently swarmed over the hacienda, checking there was no one still alive, and dealing with anything that might point to the involvement of a British unit in the carnage that surrounded them. The big giveaway was the Jackals. The armoured vehicles had served their purpose. The Regiment couldn't risk sending in choppers to undersling the Jackals and extract them out of country, and the guys could hardly drive them up the Mexican highway without being noticed. They would have to be destroyed. The guys stripped them of all weaponry and accessories, which they loaded into the back of the Transit, then drove the Jackals up alongside the demolished staff house, end to end. Each Jackal carried an anti-tank bar mine – a metre-long strip of high explosive. They put a bar mine in the middle of each Jackal on a timed charge, cleared the area and detonated them. The Jackals went up like a bonfire, filling the air once more with a thick stench of smoke. Anybody arriving here would find nothing but three twisted, burned-out metal frames.

While this was happening, the guys opened up the back of the Transit. There were several pallets of brown powder on wrapped pallets. They pulled out the drugs, then loaded up every last piece of gear and weaponry into the back of the vehicle. There was still just enough room for most of the unit to secrete themselves in the back for an uncomfortable journey to the pick-up point. Within twenty minutes, they were ready to get out of there. As the guys loaded themselves into the back of the vehicle, Danny looked around for Kleinman and the kid. He saw them standing at the entrance to the hacienda. The kid was still wrapped in his blanket. Kleinman was down on one knee, talking to the boy at his own height. As Danny approached, the CIA man looked up.

'I was telling him his mom's okay,' Kleinman said. 'That you guys will look after him until he can see her again.' He sniffed. 'You will look after him, right?'

Danny stared at Kleinman for a moment. He'd just witnessed him kill Chavez's children in cold blood, yet here he was acting all concerned for his enemy's nephew, his flesh and blood. He tried to understand what was going through Kleinman's head. He thought maybe he did.

'He's coming with us,' Danny confirmed. 'We'll make arrangements.'

'When it's safe,' Kleinman said, 'I'll contact Ana. Tell her to be in touch with the British embassy. They'll take it from there.'

Danny nodded. 'And you?' he said.

Kleinman looked out from the open gate of the hacienda. 'I'm going to need my car,' he said. 'I've got a journey to make.'

Brooker strode up to them. 'We're ready to go,' he said.

Danny led the kid to the Transit and entrusted him to the care of his unit colleagues, who'd climbed into the back among all the hardware. The kid mumbled something in Spanish and pointed at Danny. 'He wants to stay with you,' Kleinman translated.

Danny shook his head. They had a long journey to the pick-up point, and he wanted the kid out of sight. Danny, Brooker and Kleinman climbed into the cab of the Transit. Danny took the wheel and drove out of the compound, past the dead perimeter guards and along the road that snaked away from the hacienda. He didn't look back.

It took them five minutes to reach the point where Danny had taken Kleinman's old saloon car off-road. Danny turned off the road and on to the rugged, hard-baked terrain. A couple of minutes later, Kleinman's Lexus came into view. Danny parked the Transit alongside it and the three men climbed out of their vehicle.

Removing the bodies of Tyson and Spike from the Lexus was rough work. Somehow, Danny felt the need to do it himself. Liquid had begun to seep from their noses, mouths and eye sockets, and their limbs were rigid. While Danny manhandled them out of the saloon, Brooker prepared two body bags. There was no question of leaving their guys behind. Not even Spike. It was hard-wired in the Regiment guys for them to bring their dead back with dignity. No man left behind.

When the corpses were zipped up in their body bags, Danny and Brooker carried them, one end each, into the back of the vehicle, where the guys received them. The vehicle would be high by midnight. Only when he'd dealt with the corpses did Danny turn to Kleinman, who was staring toward the west as the sun rose behind the mountains in the east.

'You can come with us,' Danny said. 'We're heading to a deserted area near the coast. A Merlin's picking us up at midnight. We can get you out of country.'

Kleinman shook his head. 'Out of the country?' he said. 'I don't think so, son. I'm heading south. I have a grave to visit.'

'What then?' Danny asked.

Kleinman shrugged. 'Then,' he said, 'it doesn't really matter any more.'

Danny stared at him. Then he turned to the Transit again, opened up the rear doors and removed one of the sturdy compact shovels that had been fitted to one of the Jackals. He closed up the van, then handed the shovel to Kleinman, who took it with a curt nod. Neither man needed to explain what it was for.

'The CIA will start looking for you if you don't get to Langley in the next few hours,' Danny said.

'They can look,' Kleinman said. 'Finding me, different matter. I'm not going back.' His eyes narrowed. 'I thought it would feel different,' he said.

'What?'

'Revenge. I've been hunting Augusto Chavez for years. Now he's dead . . . it's not as sweet as they say.'

Danny thought about that for a moment. He relived nailing the tattooed Zeta who'd killed Spud. Plugging Z1. Did it make him feel any better? Not really. 'We don't do it because it's sweet,' he said.

'No. No, we don't.' Kleinman nodded grimly, then held out one hand. 'Good to know you, Danny Black,' he said. 'I guess we'll never see each other again.'

'I guess not.' Danny shook his hand. 'I hope you find what you're looking for.'

Kleinman walked toward his saloon, but stopped halfway there. 'I'm sorry about your friend Spud,' he said. He pointed toward the van. 'Sorry about them too, of course. But Spud . . . I've lost friends before. I get it.' He pulled his lighter from his pocket, looked at it for a moment, then threw it to Danny. Danny caught it one-handed. Kleinman nodded at him, then limped back to his vehicle, climbed in and turned over the engine. Danny pocketed the lighter, then he and Brooker returned to their van.

They led the way over the bumpy terrain back to the road, Kleinman following in his Lexus. Danny was twitchy. He wanted to get the hell away from the area as quickly as possible. They had a long journey to the pick-up point, and early morning was the best time to make it, because there would be fewer authorities on the road, and morning was when the bad guys slept in.

Nobody was in a greater hurry than Kleinman, however. As soon as they hit the road, he accelerated past the Transit and his battered old saloon disappeared in a cloud of dust, illuminated gold by the rising sun. Danny watched him go. An image entered his mind of a battered, bearded older man, standing at the side of a mass grave marked by a gaudy shrine to the Virgin Mary, his head bowed.

'Black,' Brooker said. 'You with us?'

Danny nodded. He could no longer see Kleinman's vehicle. He fished his sunglasses, which had miraculously survived the assault, from his pocket. 'Let's go,' he said, putting them on. 'We've got a chopper to catch.'

A new non-fiction book by the bestselling author of *The One That Got Away*

Published in hardback and ebook on 19th October 2017

CHRIS RYAN

HOW TO STAY SAFE IN A DANGEROUS WORLD

SAFE

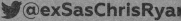